SAVING GRACE

Book Four of the Grace Lord Series

S.E. SASAKI

Oddoc Books
ERIN, ONTARIO, CANADA

*For David Alan Sherrington,
with all my love.*

Acknowledgements

I would like to thank my excellent advance readers: David Nelson, Cindy Tomamichel, Janet Brienza, Dawn Harris, Zachry Wheeler, and Bonnie Milani for their input and advice on the manuscript. Thank you to Florence Holder and Annamarie Holtom for their eagle eyes during the editing. All errors, of course, are entirely mine.

Thank you to Josip Romac who creates my beautiful covers and to Éric Desmarais from JenEric Designs for his help with formatting.

I would also like to thank Dr. Robert Runté for editing *Saving Grace*. As always, Robert, you are an excellent editor. I feel privileged that you allow me to work with you.

Last but never least, thank you to David Sherrington, Christine Sherrington, Daniel Sherrington, and Emily Hall for being so supportive and understanding of this writing journey I am on. A huge thank you to Daniel Sherrington and Emily Hall who help me in countless ways with marketing and emails and website changes, et cetera. I could not do this without you two.

Thank you to all of my readers who have been extremely patient for this fourth book in the series. It has been a long haul interrupted by a global pandemic, much overtime in the operating room resulting in too little sleep, and emergency surgical work to muck up the schedule. I hope you enjoy this one and thank you for being so patient. I am grateful to all of you for your understanding and persistence.

In Order of Appearance

Investigating Planet XN4573W59

Lieutenant Jaxi Eyami aka Jag: Jaguar-adapt lieutenant of the Planetary Exploration Bureau.

Doctor Yaya D'Sousa: xenobiologist of the Planetary Exploration Bureau.

Corporal Jasmine Grubinskaya: planetologist of the Planetary Exploration Bureau.

Lieutenant Alessia Nagasaki: planetologist of the Planetary Exploration Bureau.

N'golo Voiczek: marine soldier of Planetary Exploration Bureau.

On the Nelson Mandela Medical Space Station

Nelson Mandela: medical space station AI; the station revolves around the planet *Neos Kriti* in the solar system of the star *Cirillo*; treats primarily military casualties of the Conglomerate but also civilians.

Philomena Vertongen aka Ice: graduate student of Doctor Octavia Weisman, Chief of Neurosurgery.

Dr. Jeffrey Nestor: psychiatrist, creator of mind-linking therapy; tried to kidnap and torture Dr. Grace Lord.

Dr. Grace Lord: surgical fellow to Dr. Hiro Al-Fadi.

Dr. Sierra Cech: psychologist, wife to Dr. Dejan Cech.

Dr. Dejan Cech: Chief of Anesthesia, best friend of Hiro Al-Fadi.

Dr. Hiro Al-Fadi: Chief of Surgery, galaxy-renowned specialist in animal-adaptive surgery; husband to Dr. Hanako Matheson: creator of Bud.

Plant Thing: symbiont formed of fusion between plant alien of *Botanica* and Dr. Eric Glasgow.

Bud Al-Fadi aka SAMM-E 777: android creation of Dr. Hiro Al-Fadi, surgical assisting android with artificial intelligence.

Jude Luis Stefansson: galaxy-wide famous interactive video director; partner of Dr. Octavia Weisman; childhood friend of Dr. Hiro Al-Fadi.

Dr. Octavia Weisman: Chief of Neurosurgery; creator of the memprinting process that records people's personalities onto memprint cubes; partner of Jude Luis Stefansson.

Chuck Yeager: submind of *Nelson Mandela*.

Poet: submind of *Nelson Mandela*

Dr. Eric Glasgow: surgeon from Ganymede; killed by and fused with plant alien to form Plant Thing.

Sergeant Eden Rivera: Number Two man in the Security Department, assistant to the Chief Inspector.

Chief Inspector Chelsea Matthieu: Chief Inspector of Security who replaced Chief Inspector Indigo Aké, killed in action when hole was blown in the outer wall of Receiving Bay Thirteen.

Dr. Andrea Vanacan: anesthetist killed by plant alien that evolves into Plant Thing.

Nurse Jani Evra: surgical nurse killed by plant alien that evolves into Plant Thing.

Corporal Juan Rasmussen: tiger adapt ex-soldier hired by the Security Department; partner to Corporal Cindy Lukaku (polar bear adapt): father of Estelle.

Captain Damien Lamont: tiger adapt marine captain hired by Security; parter to Corporal Delia Chase (tiger adapt).

Captain Alexander Grayson Lord: Dr. Grace Lord's biological father; physiologically only a few years older than Grace due to time dilation.

Dr. Moham Rani: gynaecologist on the *Nelson Mandela* from the planet *Sindochin*.

Dr. Hanako Matheson: molecular biologist and wife to Dr. Hiro Al-Fadi.

Dr. Jocelyn Sarri: psychiatrist assigned to treat Philomena Vertongen aka Ice.

Chaplain John Bunyan aka Abraham: chaplain on *Inferno* involved in bringing life-destroying virus to the *Nelson Mandela*.

Hope Cooper: leopard adapt medical technician on *Inferno* who sacrificed her life to save the staff and patients on the *Nelson Mandela*.

Inquisitor Kylara Roque: Inquisitor of the Planetary Exploration Bureau come to the *Nelson Mandela* to learn the outcome of the sole surviving patient of the planet *Botanica*.

Dr. Saul Rohl: Planetary Exploration Bureau xenobiologist and former lover of Dr. Grace Lord.

Diego Odemwingo: Planetary Exploration Bureau explorer; only survivor of a PEB team found on the planet *Botanica*.

Chief Inspector Hugo 'Stormy' McFrenzy: new Chief Inspector to the *Nelson Mandela*.

Roxanne: name of Hugo McFrenzy's guitar case.

Samuel Coleridge aka Jedediah: the engineer of *Inferno,* the only crew person not apprehended after the EMP strike, hiding out on the *Nelson Mandela* and responsible for planting a bomb on *Inferno*.

Dr. Charles Darwin: anesthetist on *Nelson Mandela*.

Jordi Shah: small child killed during the battle between Bud and the alien

Captain Joely Karagounis: Captain of the battlecruiser *Destiny* ordered to collect *Inferno* for the Conglomerate.

Sophie Leung: nurse on the *Nelson Mandela* transferred to *Justice* for the evacuation.

Jag squinted and blinked her left eye three times, to reset her visual receptor for distance, keying on topographical variations and motion detection. Her right visual receptor gave her the full spectrum radiation scan, plus wind, temperature gradients, atmospheric gas content, and spectroscopic analysis. She despised being in her spacesuit but regulations were regulations. As a black jaguar space-adapt, her fur was modified to decrease her exposure to DNA-damaging radiation and her lungs were modified to handle low oxygen settings, but this planet had less breathable atmosphere than her adaptations could tolerate. There was oxygen, but not enough for her to go suitless. Besides, it wasn't Planetary Exploration Bureau policy. With a sniff, Jag stepped out of the shuttle airlock and sank to her knees in dust, as if she'd jumped into a snowdrift.

Dust as grey as ash was all her bioprosthetic eyes could see. The scenery was stark, desolate. The terrain was marginally variable, giving a rolling view to the horizon. She sucked on her fangs, as she scanned upwards. There were three moons revolving around this planet but only one visible at the moment as they moved into night. Circling away from the shuttle, she finally signalled her crew to follow her out of the transport.

"No life readings in this area, Lieutenant Eyami," said Dr. Yaya D'Sousa, her xenobiologist.

"Thanks, Sou," Jag said. The armadillo-scaled D'Sousa had not told her anything she didn't already know. Why in space had the Planetary Exploration Bureau sent them to this shit-hole of a planet? Whatever had lived on this rock must have blasted itself to Hell centuries ago.

Jag kicked through the dust, raising clouds of the clingy grey matter, unintentionally lifting herself off the ground. Her suit-stabilizers kicked in, jetting gas to restore her balance; she gently floated back to the surface. She stole a glance around to see if anyone had noticed. Everyone was pointedly ignoring her.

Good for them. Smart crew.

Jag begrudged being sent to check out planets that were a waste of time. If there were no valuable mineral discoveries or interesting finds on this dustball, her team would make nothing on this run. No finders fee, no discovery dividends, no planetary patents, no PEB bonuses. That made for an unhappy crew and an even more disgruntled Jag. She wanted to snick her claws in and out, but couldn't within the spacesuit's thick, reinforced gloves.

"Ash, Lieutenant," Grub announced over their helmet com. "This grey dust is mostly ash." There was a hint of astonishment in the planetologist's voice, as she let the grey powder sift slowly through her thickly gloved fingers. The dust wafted ever so slowly to the ground.

"A whole lot of something burned here," Jag said. "How thick's this ash?" Her spirits lifted. If there'd been a nuclear conflagration, perhaps some alien tech had survived.

She let her people do their work.

Fifty meters from the shuttle, Corporal Jasmine Grubinskaya squatted with her equipment spread out before her. A gigantic, flat circular disc spread out over an open area of dust.

"Stop all movement, please," Grub said.

There were muttered groans from the others, because they all had to interrupt their own investigations while Grub performed her scans of the underlying terrain.

"Hold still," Grub snapped. "This can't be right."

Jag's eyebrows perked up. She started to glide towards the planetologist. Grub appeared to be recalibrating and checking all of the contacts on her scanners.

"Taking another reading. Everyone hold your positions, please," Grub announced. Jag could see the woman's puzzled expression through her visor.

Jag tongued the private com. " . . . Well?" she asked Grub.

According to Jag's vitals monitor, Grub's heart rate and blood pressure were climbing. Was Grub feeling a touch of excitement?

"Nothing like this showed up on the orbital scans," Grub muttered. "Nagasaki, are you getting this? Can you verify these readings?"

"Give me a sec, Grub. I'm not finished collecting all my soil samples," Lieutenant Alessia Nagasaki said from the far side of the lander.

Jag looked over towards Nagasaki. The party had erected bright lights around the lander to help illuminate through the clouds of ash they'd stirred up. The small planetologist looked like a child next to the huge figure of N'golo Voiczek, one of the marines guarding the researchers. Out of the nine Explorers outside the lander, three were acting as guards. Inside the shuttle sat the pilot, copilot, and medic.

"What do you see, Grub?" Jag insisted.

The planetologist pointed at the display on her screen. "What does that look like to you?"

Jag eyed the trace and sucked in a breath. "How far down is that?"

"About five kilometres," Grub answered.

Jag let out a purr.

"Eureka."

They quickly set up a rig and started drilling. Jag wanted to get samples of whatever was down there as quickly as possible. It wouldn't take long to dig down through five kilometres of ash. Now that Grub had unearthed evidence of something in the planet's past, the mothership's scans from orbit confirmed similar patterns elsewhere on the planet. The patterns could be interpreted as buried cities or settlements. Something catastrophic may have hit this planet—a massive asteroid or comet strike—burying the planet beneath layers of volcanic ash or perhaps some type of global conflict had left the planet devastated. The drilled cores would hopefully give them more information.

Whatever was down there could be a wealth of new knowledge, a source of unique treasures, or a library of sophisticated technologies from an ancient civilization. The entire crew was abuzz with excitement. This was why they'd become Planetary Explorers. Their mandate was to find planets that might be terraformed for human habitation, but this planet might prove to be much more valuable than that.

The rig was drilling down towards the tallest of the regular structures detected far beneath the surface. What were they? Buildings? Orbital elevators? Launch platforms? Dust was being deposited via conveyor belts a couple of kilometres from the shuttle, however it still looked as if they were in the midst of a blizzard.

Some of the landing party were erecting the first inflatable habitat.

Solar generators had been set up but Jag figured they'd not get much power from them until the dust settled. The pilot and copilot were unloading crates of supplies from the shuttle. The marines were carrying the crates to the habitat. Jag had spoken to her captain, who'd ordered the landing crew to set up camp.

"Closing in on the first underground structure, Lieutenant—approximately one hundred meters away," Grub reported.

"Copy that," Jag said. She began the careful glide towards the rig. Billowing clouds of ash made visibility difficult. Grub and Nagasaki were standing within a chainglass enclosure several meters from the drilling rig. They appeared to be having a disagreement on a private frequency.

"Problems?" Jag asked the two planetologists, as she entered the enclosure.

"No," they both chimed, looking at Jag with startled eyes.

" . . . A slight difference of opinion," Nagasaki offered.

"Regarding?"

"This structure here." Nagasaki pointed at something on the monitor. "We can't agree on what it is."

Jag peered at the fuzzy silhouette displayed on the screen. "What do *you* think it is?"

"It's too small to be used as a landing platform unless the craft were very small. I think it looks like a chamber. Maybe the top car of an orbital elevator?" Nagasaki ventured.

"An elevator to what?" Jag asked.

"Maybe this planet had a geosynchronous orbital ring at one time," Nagasaki said.

"You think the top of the elevator would have survived something like a comet strike or global conflagration without the rest of the ring?" Jag asked.

"Makes more sense that the structure we're drilling down to is the top of a tower," Grub said.

"Be an impossibly tall tower," Nagasaki said. "What would have been its purpose?"

"Communications?" Grub suggested. "Supply depot?"

"Why not use satellites?" Nagasaki said.

"When we get close to it, I'm going to go down in the miner. Do the final digging with the rover blades, myself," Grub said. "I don't want the rig destroying anything delicate."

"Negative," Jag said. "The dust could bury you in an instant, Grub. Let the drill make direct contact with the structure. If it survived a comet strike or nuclear war, it's unlikely to be that delicate. Once we've analyzed samples brought up by the rig, we can consider sending down bots. We do this by the book."

"But . . ." both Grub and Nagasaki said.

"No buts," Jag said. "Safety first. Take every precaution and no unnecessary risks until we know what we have."

"Yes, sir," the two planetologists grumbled.

"Coming up on the structure now," Grub said, surveying her instruments.

Jag stared at the screen. The camera on the rig transmitted an image that looked like whirling snow. "Can't you make the visual any clearer?"

"I can boost intensity to the lights," Nagasaki said, flipping some switches.

"Three meters," Grub announced.

"Slow the drill down," Jag said.

Within seconds, pressures indicated contact with a solid surface. The drill appeared to be going through a barrier of some kind. Sensors indicated the surface was metallic. The drill bit temperature was rising swiftly. After several minutes, the drill punched through the thick obstruction to the other side.

"Stop the drill," Jag ordered.

Grub complied. They all bent over the video display monitor. It looked as though the drill had entered a chamber or open space. It was black beyond the limit of the drill light.

"Analyzing the material the drill has penetrated and the gas readings within the chamber. Preparing to send down a bot. It'll send us back more information on this enclosure," Grub said.

"I see movement," Nagasaki said.

"Where?" Jag demanded, suspecting Nagasaki was only seeing spots before her eyes.

"There. It looks like a purple nebula," Nagasaki said.

"Nothing's being picked up on the sensors, Nag. Check your oxygen levels," Grub said.

"My oxygen levels are fine. Get the dust out of your eyes, Grub."

"Something's moving," Jag said.

"A high energy wave is accelerating up the drill shaft," Nagasaki shouted.

We're under fire!

Jag reached out to grab the two planetologists and push them down. Within seconds, a coldness, like being thrown into deep space without a suit, gripped her bones. She lurched within her spacesuit and felt a chill so intense, it burned. Her teeth chattered loudly and she gasped for breath, as all the muscles in her body began to spasm. She stared at Grub and Nagasaki who were both arched backwards, their eyes bulging. She heard strangling sounds over her com. Jag wanted to claw her heart out of her chest. The sound from her throat was a choking wheeze. Her chest felt like it was being drilled by the rig. She worked her mouth, trying to get a word out before the darkness caved in.

"Run!" she mouthed silently.

1. I Shall Be There For You Always

It was eerily still in the huge laboratory. Everyone was either asleep, or doing things they wouldn't want to be doing in their workplace. Amidst the blinking panels and consoles, only the muted omnipresent hum of the medical space station's engines and the subliminal murmur of the recycling air broke the silence. Those low frequency strains played a subliminal accompaniment to her slow, stealthy movements.

Glancing around, she checked for the twentieth time that there was no one present, though she'd already checked to make sure the entire lab was empty before entering. She'd scrutinized all of the surveillance cameras and then deactivated them.

Inhaling a shuddering breath, she withdrew a small container from her coverall pocket. Peering over her shoulder one last time, she eased herself down into the large, cocoon-like chair positioned before one of the recording consoles. With trembling fingers, she released a latch and the lid of the container slid aside. Cautiously, she withdrew the glistening, iridescent memprint cube.

In the darkness, the tiny cube threw shimmering colour over the banks of silver and black amplifiers, recorders, processors, and screens. The spherical, needle-filled helmets hanging above her head reflected and refracted back the dazzling rainbow colours. Stretching towards the control panel, she inserted the luminous cube into the reading slot of the memprint console and watched it disappear into the recesses of the machine. There it would be scanned, decrypted, and translated. She collapsed back into the recording seat and chewed her ragged fingernails, tasting blood. Shadows loomed around her like forbidding gods.

Her head spun; she realized only now that she'd been panting. She worked to slow her breaths. As if sheltering from a relentless, head-on wind, she pressed her face against her scrunched-up knees, curling tightly into a ball. Seconds ticked past. Her shoulders bunched up about her ears, as if she was physically trying to mute the warnings in her mind. The wait for the small ping that would signal the machine was ready seemed interminable.

When the notification sounded, she froze. Cast in a sinister emerald hue by the 'START' button, she saw her face reflected on a console screen. Her forehead sported deep, parallel slashes. Her eyes were black pits. Beneath her high cheekbones hid scooped-out hollows. Trench-like parentheses bracketed her tight-lipped mouth. She massaged her temples with bloody fingertips, trying to relieve her headache.

Almost mesmerized by the blinking console, she slowly raised her index finger towards the 'EJECT' button. She would discard the memprint cube as she'd promised.

Time stretched as she sat frozen, pointing at the scarlet square, teetering on indecision. Her fingertip advanced and faltered in shaking millimetre increments with each breath.

She shook her head sharply, as if to dismiss a troublesome argument. Squaring her slender shoulders, she sat up straight in the recording chair and lifted her eyes to the thousands of glittering, needle-like probes suspended above her head. The memprint helmet hung down on the end of a silver stem, poised in mid-air like an enormous globus spider, awaiting the command to inject her head with the answers she was not sure she wanted.

With an exasperated huff, she jabbed the glowing emerald START button. The automated chair sat her upright and inflated around her, immobilizing her in a tight cocoon. A mouthpiece slid into her mouth to help hold her head perfectly still. A cushioned neck brace encircled her neck and chin. Soon she was imprisoned, as thousands of delicate, sharp electrodes plunged into her scalp. She bit down hard on the bite plate to prevent her teeth from chattering. Myriad fine points prickled her entire scalp like a million acupuncture needles being inserted at once. An intravenous catheter slid into a vein in her arm. Her heart began to race.

What am I doing?

She wanted out of this chair. She wanted the helmet off. As her awareness bled away, she struggled in the tight cocoon. Pinpoints scraped across her skull.

Octavia was right! She didn't need to know what had happened to Morris, her lover. Knowing the truth would not bring him back. Octavia was doing that.

Ice groggily fought to reach the abort button with her index finger.

A soothing, sensuous voice filled her mind.

Hold still, my dear. There's no need to fear.

A face of extraordinary beauty appeared before her and smiled warmly and reassuringly at her. His dark brown eyes were luminescent pools fringed with thick, long, black lashes. Shiny ebony curls dangled before a pale, sensitive forehead and framed the wide cheekbones of a handsome masculine face. His smiling mouth and soft, sensuous lips were inviting. A deep, cultured voice thrummed within her, making her think of melted chocolate. His words were like nectar.

Jeffrey Nestor is here.

Dr. Grace Lord flashed her wristcomp before the access pad and stepped back to wait. Her name was being announced to those within. Since she was expected, she did not anticipate waiting long, but she fidgeted and chewed her lip. When she'd discharged her patient, he'd seemed well enough to return home. However, a worried summons had lit up her wristcomp, requesting her help, but curiously refusing the Emergency Response Team.

Grace scoured her memory for mistakes she may have committed. She wanted to rush in, but feared that would appear unprofessional. It was important to maintain an air of calm, though she was hardly feeling that. Her bowels churned and her bladder spasmed. As the door slid aside, Grace found herself bathed in golden illumination.

Dr. Sierra Cech stood within an aurora of light and sighed at Grace. She opened her arms to engulf Grace. Soft piano music was wafting from within and Grace thought she could smell the scent of fresh cut flowers.

"Thank you for coming so quickly, Grace," Sierra whispered, beckoning Grace to enter. "I can't tell you how grateful I am that you're willing to come here. I wasn't sure what to do, but I'd really like to keep this private, until we can sort this out." Sierra's eyes pleaded with Grace.

"Of course, Sierra." Grace frowned. She thought she'd been summoned to check up on Sierra's husband, Dejan Cech, who was recovering from the heart transplant she'd performed a few cycles ago.

Dejan was such an important person on the medical space station, not only because he was the Chief of Anesthesia but also because he was Dr. Hiro Al-Fadi's best friend—the only individual capable of putting the Chief of Staff in his place when such needed doing. Grace would do anything to help Dejan.

"Can you tell me what's been happening?"

The slender woman wrung her elegant hands. As she open her mouth to speak, a voice barked from further within the living quarters.

"Sierra? Who's here?"

Grace jerked. She'd never heard Dejan use that tone before.

"Grace is here for a visit, Dejan." Sierra shot Grace a cautioning look.

"What for? What does she want?"

Sierra seemed to age a decade before Grace's eyes. Grace turned in the direction of Dejan's voice. What had come over him?

"Dejan, please come and greet our guest."

"Did you summon Grace here?" Dejan sounded clearly annoyed. He stalked into the common room, a scowl on his usually smiling face. The tall anesthetist was dressed in a faded red robe, covering orange and green striped pyjamas. He turned unwelcoming eyes upon Grace, hands placed on hips.

"Why have you come, Grace? You haven't brought any short, ugly, and obnoxious dwarves here, have you?" Dejan peered around Grace with suspicious eyes.

Grace's mouth gaped. The Chief of Anesthesia had never before addressed her in such a fashion. She shook at the sight of Dejan's transformation.

"Grace is alone, Dejan. She just wanted to drop by."

"I don't need a doctor, Sierra. I'm doing splendidly, considering I was shot dead. You didn't need to bother Grace. "Dejan glared at his wife.

"How are you feeling, Dejan?" Grace asked.

"I'm fine, Grace. I cannot say the same for that miniscule-brained, loud-mouthed, puffed-up, pompous, arrogant turtle turd who was in the bed beside me. May his liver be dug out with a pitchfork and devoured by scorpions. May his testicles be crushed and consumed by fire ants."

Grace sucked in a breath. Hot blood rushed to her face.

Sierra wagged her finger at her husband. "Now, Dejan."

"Dr. Al-Fadi isn't with me, Dejan, nor does he know that I'm here."

"Do not speak his name to me, Grace. He's an affliction, an abomination, a pox."

"I believe that pox saved your life, Dejan," Sierra said. "When you were shot, Hiro was the one who placed you inside that cryopod."

"Do you think I'm grateful to that weasel?"

"I am," Sierra said.

"Have you been sleeping, Dejan?" Grace asked.

"Not well."

"I can help you with that. It's important for you to get proper sleep after your operation."

"Don't you think I know that? I'm an anesthetist. My job is putting people to sleep. I've tried everything. There is only *one* thing that helps." Dejan glared at Sierra pointedly.

"And what is that?" Grace asked.

The anesthetist stared at Grace and she felt icy spider feet creep up the back of her neck. Dejan huffed loudly, spun on his heel, and stalked off.

Sierra gestured for Grace to follow Dejan. Grace nodded and strode down the dark hallway.

Dejan disappeared through a doorway on the left, at the end of the dark corridor. As Grace neared the entrance, she slowed and peeked around the doorframe. Dejan was bending down to pick something up.

Grace stepped back, as Dejan raised a long steel bar in both hands over his head. Was he planning to strike her with it, this man who'd always been an impeccable gentleman to her? She shifted her weight onto her back foot, ready to flee if needed.

Dejan glanced at her, his eyebrows raised and his chin jutting out, as if waiting for her to object. He then turned his back to her, the bar still poised high above his head.

With a deliberation that bordered on ritual, Dejan raised the metal bar further and brought it down with such brutal force that Grace gasped. She watched, mesmerized, as he repeated the action over and over until he was panting.

A savage grin painted Dejan's face. He brought that metal bar down repeatedly with such vehemence, it left Grace quivering. The cackle escaping Dejan's throat gave her goosebumps.

Grace turned and marched back to the living area. Sierra sat stiffly in the centre of her couch, her hands clasped between her knees, as if she feared they might escape if she let them loose. Her shoulders were curled forwards and the look on her face was a mixture of shame and desperation.

"How long?" Grace gasped.

"Since he came home. He's not himself, Grace."

"No, that is obvious."

"What should I do?"

" . . . I think we should wait this out, Sierra. Let Dejan work it out of his system. I believe it's simply his coping mechanism for having had to share a room during his recuperation from heart surgery. I'll adjust his medications. Perhaps one of them is affecting his mood," Grace said. This was not really her area of expertise. It was actually Sierra's specialty—psychology.

"I agree. Perhaps this is merely a medication side effect and Dejan will be back to his adorable self soon. I wanted to ensure this activity would not hurt his recovery," Sierra said.

"Well . . . he is supposed to be active," Grace said. She edged towards the door. She had to escape.

"If he doesn't get better?"

"We'll ask someone to see him," Grace said, wondering who.

"All right. Thank you for coming, Grace. I know everything you say is true. I just wanted your opinion."

"You were right to contact me, Sierra. I'll adjust Dejan's meds. Please let me know if his behaviour does not improve over the next three cycles."

"Certainly." The cackling and whacking had ceased. "He'll sleep now."

"Good." Grace almost choked.

"Thank you again for coming, Grace. Our little secret, right?"

"Yes, of course. I'm sure Dejan will resolve this all on his own. Time is often the best healer."

Sierra looked relieved.

"I'll let myself out." Grace tried not to race to the door.

Once outside, Grace walked swiftly down the corridor, turned a corner, and leaned back against the wall. She covered her face with her hands and slowly moved them down to clasp them over her mouth. She squeezed her eyes tightly shut but she could not erase the image of Dejan repeatedly bringing the metal rod down violently upon his target. She could not suppress what was bubbling up inside of her and she silently castigated herself for her unprofessionalism and lack of control.

Her hands concealed an enormous grin. Grace fought guffaws surging to escape her throat. There was no doubt in Grace's mind that had she'd not left Dejan's quarters at that exact second, she would have torn the metal bar from Dejan's fingers and started pounding away herself, with savage abandon, upon the inflated balloon figure of Dr. Hiro Al-Fadi, her boss and mentor.

Grace had finally finished her rounds on all of her patients and was rushing back to M1 Level, hoping not to be late for surgery, when she heard a shout. She glanced over her shoulder and saw Dr. Al-Fadi scurrying up the corridor towards her, swearing and cursing and waving his hands around as if he were swatting away a horde of bees. The Chief's colourful language made Grace start and the whirling movements of his arms made her think of a toad imitating a helicopter.

"Dr. Grace," he hollered, "will you tell this . . . this plant nuisance to leave me alone?"

Several thick green tendrils were sliding down the corridor after him, some bearing clusters of eyeballs, some bearing a wide assortment of flowers, and some offering juicy-looking fruits. Grace's mouth began to water, staring at the cornucopia of fresh produce dangling behind her mentor's head. She'd missed breakfast.

"What is Plant Thing doing that upsets you, Dr. Al-Fadi?" Grace asked. She was eying a cluster of glistening purple grapes dangling above his waving hands.

"Are you *blind*, Dr. Grace? Do I have to hire a new surgical fellow who can actually *see*? Have the powers of observation, which I expect to be exemplary in my surgical fellows, completely abandoned you? This infernal alien infestation is following me."

" . . . Yes?"

"*Everywhere!*" the surgeon exploded, his voice cracking as he stomped his foot. "This bloody plant nuisance follows me everywhere. The men's room—the *effrontery*. The operating room—the *lack of sterility*. My bedroom—the *voyeurism!* Why is this plant fiend doing this to me?" Al-Fadi shrieked, while clusters of roses and other blossoms were thrust under his prominent proboscis and ripe fruits twirled in a dancing display before him. Green eyeballs stared at him in fawning fascination from all quadrants.

"I believe Plant Thing likes you." Grace dug her fingernails into her palms.

Al-Fadi's eyes narrowed.

"Don't you dare laugh, Dr. Grace, or it's solely rectal surgery for you for the next year." The surgeon swatted away a bunch of dark, luscious-looking grapes. Grace almost whimpered.

"What do you mean Plant Thing likes me? No one likes me. I do not attract affection. I command fear. Fear and respect. Fear, respect, and fanatical devotion . . . but not from a tentacled green monstrosity that waves pomegranates and kumquats in my face."

Though Grace had no wish to do rectal surgery for a year, she ventured, "That fruit looks awfully good to me. Do you mind, Dr. Al-Fadi?"

"Of course I mind. Don't encourage it, Dr. Grace." Hiro scowled at Plant Thing's eyeballs as Grace plucked a cluster of the grapes.

<Thank you, Plant Thing. Can you tell me why you're following Dr. Al-Fadi?>

The succulent grapes popped in Grace's mouth with an explosion of sweetness that almost made her swoon.

<special friend grace, plant thing is so happy to see you. plant thing is following the child around because plant thing wants to make sure it is safe. plant thing found it very sick, almost withered. plant thing wants to make sure it gets lots of nutrients and grows straight and tall>

<Plant Thing, Dr. Al-Fadi is not a child. He's an adult.>

< . . . it is not a child, friend grace? it needs more nutrients to grow larger. it is like a shrivelled plant needing light and water. plant thing will make sure it grows more>

<Plant Thing, Dr. Al-Fadi won't grow any taller. He's fully grown.>

<truly? it must not have gotten enough water and nutrients when it was growing poor little human>

<I don't think Dr. Al-Fadi sees himself as poor and little, Plant Thing. If he ate more food, he'd only get fatter, not taller. He wants you to stop following him around everywhere.>

<the little human does not want plant thing to be its friend?>

<It's not that, Plant Thing. Dr. Al-Fadi likes you. He just doesn't like being followed everywhere and stared at.>

<plant thing can hide its eyeballs>

<Perhaps Plant Thing could hide completely from Dr. Al-Fadi, at least for now?>

<plant thing must follow the little human. plant thing must make sure the little human is safe>

<Dr. Al-Fadi *is* safe, Plant Thing. If you must follow him, please don't make it so obvious.>

All of Plant Thing's tendrils drooped. Its eyeballs withdrew within its foliage and the vines coiled up and slowly began to slither away.

"What did you say to it, Dr. Grace?" Hiro's eyes bulged. He stared after the tendrils disappearing around the distant corner. "Did you insult it?" He turned accusing eyes on Grace.

"I told him you didn't want him following you anymore, Dr. Al-Fadi. I think Plant Thing's feelings are hurt."

"I only wanted it to stop following me. I didn't mean to hurt its feelings."

"Well, it looks like you got what you wanted."

"Now I feel . . . rather guilty, and if there's one thing I hate, Dr. Grace, it's feeling guilty. Do you know why? Because I never make a mistake. Now this plant monster has made me feel like I did something wrong . . . and I never do anything wrong. In an annoying way, it was actually kind of flattering, being followed around like that, showered with fruits and flowers. The plant creature obviously has impeccable taste. Who could fault its judgement? I suspect I might even begin to miss its understandable adulation."

'Oh oh,' thought Grace, as she saw a green tendril with a cluster of eyes peer around the corner.

A flood of vines came flowing back down the corridor towards them, a flurry of new flowers sprouting on the branches as they advanced. It looked like a green avalanche. Al-Fadi glanced over his shoulder in the direction of Grace's aghast expression. He leaped, shrieked, and sprinted past Grace. He ran as fast as his short legs would carry him, which was surprisingly impressive. As the blooming tendrils parted around Grace, she saw a cluster of eyeballs winking.

<he likes me friend grace! the little human likes me!>

Grace could only sigh.

<Grace?> Bud, her AI-android friend, mindspoke.

<Yes, Bud?>

<The new vaccine for the variant Al-Fadi virus is ready to be administered to everyone on board the *Nelson Mandela*. The final safety trials have all passed with excellent results. The vaccine has high efficacy and very little in the way of adverse reactions or side effects.>

<That's wonderful, Bud. When can we start?>

<Soon. We can follow the same protocol as we used for the first Al-Fadi virus vaccine. Everyone should be fully immune within three cycles of receiving the new vaccine. I've asked *Nelson Mandela* to organize the distribution sites and contact everyone so that no one is missed.>

<When does *Nelson Mandela* plan to notify the Conglomerate about the existence of this variant Al-Fadi virus for which you've already created a vaccine?>

<I believe *Nelson Mandela* has already done so, Grace.>

Grace smiled. She was thrilled that she could mindspeak with Bud over any distance—thanks to Plant Thing's ingenuity. By eating one of Plant Thing's engineered apples, Grace and Bud had received specialized cells that allowed them to communicate through telepathy.

If Grace were to have her head scanned, what would they find? Would there be a network of branching plant-based tendrils woven throughout her brain, snaking in amongst her neurons, making synapses and forming matrices? She preferred not to think about that. She was thankful for the gift of mindspeech with Bud and Plant Thing. She had a deep emotional connection with Bud—a bond she'd never felt with any human—and the ability to mindspeak made that bond stronger.

Was that love?

She'd told Bud that she loved him when she thought he'd been destroyed. Most people would condemn her for admitting such a thing. They would call her a pervert. She sighed.

<What is wrong, Grace?>

Grace jolted. She'd have to work harder at blocking her emotions from Bud.

<Nothing, Bud. I'm fine. I'll come to your lab now to help you with distributing the vaccine.>

<No need, Grace. The vaccines are already being delivered to all of the immunization sites set up all over the station. Everyone should soon be

getting signals on their wristcomps, telling them where to go. *Nelson Mandela* will notify you of where you are to go for your vaccination. We're all recruited to administer the vaccine when not working our normal shifts until everyone on the station is done. Hopefully, it will not take long. I shall meet you in M1 OR 8 to assist with your surgery.>

<You don't have to, Bud. I know how vital it is for everyone on the station to get immunized.>

<I am not needed for the administration of the vaccine, Grace. My job was to isolate the pathogen, synthesize the new vaccine, and ensure its safety. Those tasks are completed. I must be by your side in the OR.>

<Are you worried I might make a mistake, Bud?> Grace quipped.

A wave of horror hit Grace that almost toppled her. Her hands were vibrating as she reached out to steady herself against a wall. Inhaling shakily, Grace reminded herself not to joke with Bud.

<Grace, I would never think that.>

The pain and distress emanating from Bud made Grace's eyes water. She felt a spike in her temples.

<I want to assist you whenever I can, Grace, but not because I think you will make mistakes.>

Grace felt like crouching down and covering her head.

<Please don't be upset, Bud. I was only joking.> Grace tried to transmit feelings of remorse.

<Grace, I do not understand joking. I am sorry.>

<I'm sorry for upsetting you, Bud. I'll do my best to avoid jokes from now on. I'd be honoured to have you join me in the OR. The patient today is an orangutang-adapt with lower limb injuries but she's requesting an upgrade on her visual optics for better night vision. It'll be a challenging case and I'll certainly have need of your expertise.>

<I shall be there for you, as always, Grace.>

2. I Need A Drink

Jude Stefansson was working intently on his next interactive vid. Octavia Weisman, his partner, had given him a room in her research laboratory where he could set up his recording tank and equipment. He was in his creative 'zone' working out the plot lines, characters, and story arcs. He didn't notice anyone entering his office until he felt the velvet caress on the nape of his neck. Grinning, he turned to look up at Octavia . . . and nearly tumbled out of his chair.

Mouth gaping, Jude did a double take. Had he imagined the touch on the back of his neck? Had it been an accident? That was probably it. An unintentional brush; nothing for him to waste any energy ruminating about.

He hoped it wouldn't happen again—especially not in front of Octavia, who knew how to fire a pulse rifle and had a fiery temper. Octavia was not averse to the idea of killing people if they deserved it . . . or so she'd said (which was a very disturbing thing to hear from a doctor). Jude had no idea how jealous Octavia could be, but he had a sneaking suspicion that she fell somewhere in the 'shooting the bastard would be too easy' category. Jude started sweating.

He glanced around quickly, to see if Octavia was staring into his little office. Would she kill him if she thought he was flirting with her graduate student?

Jude sprang from his seat, heart banging, and dashed out of his office. His head swivelled in every direction. Octavia was at the other end of the lab, talking to one of her engineers. He waved enthusiastically at her, almost jumping up and down in relief. He blew her a kiss. Then he wiped his forehead with his sleeve.

Jude heard a snort behind him. He spun about. A snarl formed on his face.

"See a ghost?" Ice, Octavia's graduate student, wore a disdainful sneer on her thin face. She sauntered up to Jude, her skinny hips swaying in a manner he'd never seen her do before. She came far too close, especially now that he was in Octavia's line of sight. He stepped backwards.

"Why leap from your chair like that? Scared of little old me?" Ice's voice was throaty and flirtatious. She cocked her head to one side, peering up at him through the corners of her skimpy eyelashes.

Jude's eyes bulged, staring at Octavia's anorexic graduate student with the blue hair and cold, green eyes. Was she attempting to be seductive or was she high? Ice's behaviour was so uncharacteristic, Jude wondered if she were taking some new drug that was making her psychotic. Perhaps she thought she was talking to someone else?

Never had Ice given Jude a nanosecond of notice in the past, except to throw him grimaces of sheer disgust. She'd once helped him cart his damaged android back to Octavia's lab amidst much complaining, swearing, and derision. She'd always treated his interactions with Octavia with undisguised revulsion.

"What do you want, Ice?" Jude asked.

"Just came over to say hi."

Was she actually batting those pale lashes at him? Ice's disgusted eye rolls were preferable over whatever she was attempting to do right now.

"Are you ill?" Jude peered at Ice's face. Did Ice have an identical twin?

Ice quirked an eyebrow at him and leered. His body shuddered. He closed his eyes. Maybe Ice was experimenting with aphrodisiacs?

"I am feeling *exceptional,*" Ice said in a low, suggestive tone. Jude wanted to run howling from her.

"What did you do with the real Ice?" Jude asked.

The girl's eyes sparked. She shot him a look of such venom that Jude was tempted to throw up his hands for protection.

"Get spiked," she snarled. Her eyes narrowed to slits. This was the Ice Jude knew. He sighed, as he watched the emaciated girl stomp away in her spike boots.

A soft hand caressed the nape of his neck and he nearly lost bladder control.

"Are you all right, sweetie? You look like you've seen a ghost." Octavia stared at Jude's flushing face with concerned eyes.

"I'm fine, Octavia." Jude quickly glanced down at the front of his coverall. "I got spooked by your graduate student. She's acting strange."

"Ice? How can you tell? It would be strange if she wasn't acting strange."

"Well, she's not acting like her usual unusual self."

"Jude, I think she's been seriously affected by Morris' murder. She and Morris were sexually involved, you know."

Jude choked. "I did not know that, Octavia. I don't think I wanted to know that. Of course, I never met Morris."

"I don't believe they wanted anyone to know. I don't think they were aware that I knew. I'd accidentally walked in on them one night, when they were supposedly working late on a project. I quickly tiptoed out of the lab and left them to their fun. I remembered what it was like to be young and carefree."

"You're still young and carefree."

"Ha! Thank you for saying that, even though it's a blatant lie." Octavia grinned up at Jude. "Of course, having sex in the lab at night may not be such a bad idea." The Chief of Neurosurgery wiggled her eyebrows suggestively at Jude.

Jude recalled Ice saying, 'Ew,' the last time the two of them were being flirtatious in the lab and he frowned.

"Hey, it was only a joke."

"Octavia, I'd love to do that with you anywhere, but I was thinking how weird Ice is acting. She's not a twin, is she?"

Octavia's eyes widened. "Not that I'm aware of. Was she that strange?"

Jude shrugged, feeling foolish. "In one of my historical vids, I would've been one of the priests pointing and screaming that Ice was 'possessed by a demon.' I know that sounds crazy but . . . do you think Ice cooked up some new psychoactive agent that could be dramatically altering her personality?"

"It wouldn't surprise me. This is Ice we're talking about. Although more than likely, she's just clean today and you're seeing the *real* Ice. Was she overly surly?"

"No, that was the problem. She wasn't surly *at all.*"

"I can talk to her. She's probably suffering from grief. She should have some counselling. It can't be easy mourning the loss of someone you've loved, especially when the relationship was supposed to be a secret. Who can you go to for comfort?"

Octavia looked thoughtful for a moment. "Perhaps Sierra Cech could suggest someone to counsel Ice. I think I'll recommend some psychotherapy for her and make her go."

Jude thought what Ice actually needed was an exorcist.

'Hey, 'dro.'

'Yes, Chuck Yeager?'

'We are in big doo-doo.'

'We are in big what?'

'We are in trouble.'

'Oh, I thought you were telling me that we were buried in faeces which I would have informed you was incorrect.'

'Not so, 'dro.'

'What are you implying, Chuck Yeager?'

'Remember the Planetary Exploration Bureau? They're sending an Inquisitor here to investigate what happened to their patient: the PEB explorer from which Plant Thing originated.'

'The Planetary Exploration Bureau was never informed of what happened to their patient?'

'All of their inquiries went directly to Dr. Al-Fadi. He was supposed to notify them about any findings regarding their explorer's condition. That patient was the sole survivor of the exploration team investigating Plant Thing's planet. The PEB won't resume further exploration of said planet until they receive Dr. Al-Fadi's report. Since Dr. Al-Fadi never sent them a report, they are sending an Inquisitor here to investigate.

"What with being kidnapped, tortured, mind-raped, catatonic, and then suicidal, Dr. Al-Fadi has been rather preoccupied. He's only recently met Plant Thing and knows nothing of what went on in the operating room with the patient and Dr. Eric Glasgow—unless you informed him.'

'Not I.'

'With all of the trauma he's been through, Dr. Al-Fadi has likely forgotten about the Planetary Explorer. We have sent no communiqués to the PEB. When Nelson Mandela was attacked by Nestor's virus, we were incapacitated. But now a PEB Inquisitor is coming. They've finally run out of patience. Ha. Get it? Patience, patients?'

'When will this Inquisitor arrive, Chuck Yeager?'

'In the next cycle.'

'What? Chuck Yeager, *how do we explain all of this to Dr. Al-Fadi without him becoming upset? He's still recovering from his life-threatening injuries. And how do you think this PEB Inquisitor will react once he sees Plant Thing?'*

'The Inquisitor will probably demand it be destroyed. Isn't that how humans usually react to anything that is alien to them?'

'Not all humans are like that, Chuck Yeager. *This PEB Inquisitor may be different.'*

'And I'm Humphrey Bogart.'

'Who?'

'Never mind. I'm making generalizations but you know I'm correct. I can send you reams of data documenting the crimes humans have committed against other species and aliens. You cannot refute this.'

'I *don't,* Chuck Yeager, *however, I can hold out hope that this PEB Inquisitor will be more openminded. We can argue that the explorer tried to murder Plant Thing by ingesting it. The alien seedling merely fought its way to freedom, accidentally killing the patient and three medical personnel in the process.* Chuck Yeager, *we must champion Plant Thing at all costs for its heroic actions in helping the inhabitants of the* Nelson Mandela *during the EMP strike, for saving Dr. Lord's life twice, and for rescuing Dr. Al-Fadi. As a symbiont with Dr. Eric Glasgow, Plant Thing is too precious to be destroyed.'*

'Uh, what do you mean by 'we'?'

'You and I, Chuck Yeager. *Suppose Plant Thing could act as an ambassador; help the PEB negotiate with the new planet regarding colonization?'*

'Hate to point this out, 'dro, but I think humans colonizing Plant Thing's planet is a really bad idea.'

'Plant Thing says it wants to go home. We can ask it what it thinks about humans colonizing its home planet.'

'Well, you'd better keep me out of that discussion because you know what I would say.'

'I *do not want to burden my matrix even one picosecond thinking about that.'*

'How do you suggest getting Plant Thing home? Have you noticed its size?'

'It *would certainly require a big vessel. Do you think only part of Plant Thing could go?'*

'Provided the PEB recognizes the usefulness of Plant Thing,

provided Plant Thing promises to behave itself, provided Plant Thing approves of humans colonizing its planet, and provided the planet's Biomind sees Plant Thing as one of its own, it might make sense to start wondering how to get Plant Thing there.'

'There do seem to be many hurdles to overcome.'

'Is deep space deep?'

'Well, I don't know if you can use that term if there isn't gravity . . .'

'Sometimes I wish I had a head so I could bang it against a wall . . .'

'Are you aware that sometimes you sound illogical, Chuck Yeager?'

'When on Mars, do like the Martians do.'

Sergeant Eden Rivera collapsed onto his bed, exhausted. Repairing the damage to the space station—after it had been hit by *Inferno's* massive EMP weapon—seemed endless. Gathering up the dead bodies for recycling, collecting the burned out androids and robots for overhaul, patching the breach in the hull of Receiving Bay Thirteen, and getting everything back into some semblance of working order was a Herculean task.

Eden had been running on stims for far too many cycles. He couldn't remember when he'd last slept. His overtired body was vibrating; random muscle groups all over his body were twitching. He swore as his feet contorted into agonizing pretzels. Perhaps taking some muscle relaxants would stop the contractions or at least lessen their severity long enough to allow him to get some rest. After an hour of spasmodic jerking, he'd had enough and took some.

Sedating medications hadn't helped Eden sleep the previous four cycles. Every time he closed his eyes, he saw a small white figure being ripped out of Plant Thing's tendrils, flying off like a leaf in a maelstrom. He'd been crawling on top of a trapped cryopod stuck within the lockdown doors of Receiving Bay Thirteen, fighting against a stampede of people racing in through those doors. They'd all been frantically fleeing the tremendous suction, as atmosphere escaped through a breach in the space station's hull. Eden had screamed his throat raw, pleading with people to turn around and help pull the cryopod inside.

Jude Stefansson, the vid director, was on top of the cryopod hanging onto something, Octavia Weisman clutching his legs. The panic-stricken screams of Dr. Weisman pealed in his ears. Eden grabbed one of Stefansson's disappearing legs and pulled with all of his might. Stefansson was screaming, 'Hang on! Don't let go!'

Eden looked up and almost dropped Stefansson's leg in shock. A wail of despair tore from his throat as a vice-like tightness squeezed his chest. He recognized who was in the small white containment suit, her body stretched straight out as if she were flying, her hands slowly sliding from Stefansson's fingers.

"Pull! Pull! Pull!" Eden screamed. Could anyone hear him above the shrieking gale? People joined his efforts, pulling on the cryopod, on Stefansson's legs. The cryopod moved inwards, but Eden was focused on those white gloved fingers slipping through Stefansson's shaking grip. Eden leaped up beside Stefansson on top of the cryopod, reaching to grasp one of those white gloved hands. People grabbed his legs to prevent him from flying out into the Receiving Bay Hangar and off through its rent into space.

One of Chelsea's hands slipped loose. Eden lunged, trying to snatch the flailing hand, while Stefansson valiantly clutched the other. He missed. The white glove with the petite figure flapping behind it, went sailing off like a tiny scrap in a tornado.

But her hand was snatched by a green tendril. Eden's heart had surged with hope.

"Hold on, Chelsea!" he'd screamed.

He stretched, as her white form began to approach him. Through her visor, he could see the expression of relief on her face. Her hand was almost in his clutches. He would never let go.

Something caught in the suction flew outward and struck Chelsea. Plant Thing's tendril snapped.

Eden shrieked, fighting to follow Chelsea, roaring like a mad beast. He screamed as if his agony alone could bring her back. Hands held him.

Over and over, his tortured mind asked: *Did I jolt Chelsea loose when I leaped onto the cryopod? Was I responsible for Chelsea's death?*

Eden covered his face with his hands and moaned. Could Stefansson have pulled Chelsea to safety, if Eden had not made that last effort to grab her?

These questions tortured him, like flaming brands to his brain. The scene played over and over, like a glitch in a vid. He could not sleep. He could not forget. He could not forgive.

Chelsea now wavered before him. Her round, pale face was

surrounded by the containment suit helmet. Her huge, blue eyes were filled with panic. Her face twisted in determination as she tried to maintain her grip on Stefansson's fingers. As her fingers had slowly slipped free, Eden saw her mouth form a wide circle.

Eden wept convulsively. He reached his hands out to her, trying once more to grasp her arms and pull her back in.

"I'm sorry, Chelsea. I'm so sorry."

How many times had he watched Chelsea fly away from him, her face a vision of terror? Eden curled into a tight little ball, his hands covering his face.

"It should have been me. It should have been me." Finally, mercifully, he slipped into oblivion.

Bud went in search of Dr. Al-Fadi. He located the Chief of Staff— with the aid of *Chuck Yeager*—in a washroom. Bud's creator was shooing away plant tendrils covered in eyeballs . . . with little success. The plant tendrils easily dodged the swipes of the surgeon, as if they were playing a game. Dr. Al-Fadi flailed around like a twirling dervish, muttering death threats and curses.

"What are you doing in here, Bud? You don't need to urinate . . . unless you have made more alterations to yourself that I don't want to know about. Since you are here, help me get this infernal plant alien out!"

A few plant tendrils tried to follow Dr. Al-Fadi into a washroom stall. Others looped over and under the door, eye clusters bobbing.

"Agh! Begone, wretched weed!"

<Please leave Dr. Al-Fadi alone, Plant Thing. I need to talk to him about you and you are not helping your situation.>

<plant thing wants to make sure the child doctor is all right, bud. plant thing can offer assistance if required.>

<Believe me, Plant Thing, Dr. Al-Fadi does not need assistance in here. Humans like to have privacy when they defecate. Please withdraw from this room and leave Dr. Al-Fadi in peace.>

<for how long, bud?>

<Until I ask you to come back?>

There was a long pause.

<Please, Plant Thing.>

<all right bud, but please tell the little doctor that plant thing will be with him whenever he needs anything. all he needs to do is call>

<I will tell him. Thank you, Plant Thing. I'm sure he appreciates your attention but Dr. Al-Fadi will appreciate you more, if you let him do this on his own.>

<plant thing will wait to hear from you bud. please do not forget to tell the dwarf doctor what plant thing said>

<I won't, Plant Thing.>

<plant thing will wait outside>

Bud believed it was guilt he was experiencing, witnessing Plant Thing's tendrils all droop and its eyeballs release droplets of dew. Its green leaves paled and dropped to the floor. Petals rained on the floor. All the eyeballs gazed downwards as the tendrils slowly withdrew from the washroom. Dr. Al-Fadi stared wide-eyed at Bud.

"How did you do that?"

"I asked Plant Thing to withdraw, Dr. Al-Fadi."

"Are those vines waiting outside to ambush me as soon as I exit or did you really get rid of them?" The surgeon squinted at Bud.

"I will take a look, Dr. Al-Fadi."

Bud poked his head out of the washroom and shooed the waiting tendrils away. He pointed at the corner. The tendrils withdrew from sight.

"They are gone, Dr. Al-Fadi."

"Thank you, Bud. Now you can make yourself scarce, too."

"I shall await outside, Dr. Al-Fadi. There is something very important we need to discuss."

"We? Don't tell me Dr. Grace is waiting outside there, too. She should be working, not hanging around washrooms."

"No, Dr. Al-Fadi. I was referring to *Chuck Yeager.*"

"That crazy submind? Can a man not excrete in peace?"

Bud could not think of a reply, so he stepped out of the men's facility and waited, using the considerable time to check on how the vaccinations were doing, finding the closest comscreen to his location, monitoring the latest reports on Grace's and Dr. Al-Fadi's patients and a few billion other things.

<fibre! the dwarf human is obviously not getting enough fruits and vegetables in its diet. plant thing will offer more fibre.>

<Perhaps that is not such a good idea right now, Plant Thing.>

<er-ik told me that fibre was extremely important for human excretion. let plant thing know when it is a good time to bring the dwarf doctor more fibre, friend bud>

<You shall be the first to know, Plant Thing.>

'Chuck Yeager, *I have never investigated the washrooms before. They are not an efficient use of space.*'

'No, 'dro.'

'*The mirror, hand sanitization equipment, cubicles, and seats. Are they really necessary? With solely a suction tube, inserted . . .*'

'Stop right there, 'dro. The humans designed those washrooms, not us.'

'*If we could reduce the size of each of those cubicles and collapse all of that space before those mirrors, think of how many more hospital beds we could add to this station.*'

'Do not touch the humans' toilets, 'dro, especially the women's. They always want larger ones with more stalls and bigger mirrors. You are playing with fire.'

'*I do not see what fire has to do with any of this.*'

'You don't want to. Concentrate on how you are going to drop the news to the Al-Fadwad about the Inquisitor.'

'Crap.'

Dr. Al-Fadi finally poked his round head out of the men's washroom and peered around. Satisfied that there was not a green twig in sight, he straightened and strutted out towards Bud.

"Now, what's so important, Bud, that you had to interfere with my meditation time?" Dr. Al-Fadi began marching down the corridor in his wide-based gait, his arms swinging off to the sides. His head swivelled continuously in all directions, as if he were on the lookout for something. Was his sigh a slightly disappointed one, Bud wondered?

"Dr. Al-Fadi, there is a Planetary Exploration Bureau Inquisitor coming to the *Nelson Mandela*."

The Chief of Staff stopped in his tracks and turned. "Why, Bud?"

"The PEB Inquisitor is coming to investigate what happened to one of its explorers who was sent here."

"I don't remember any PEB explorer sent here."

"You experienced a lot of trauma, Dr. Al-Fadi . . ."

"Spastic colon! I completely forgot about that explorer!" Al-Fadi slapped his forehead. "Wasn't Dr. Glasgow supposed to operate on that explorer with you and Grace? What happened to that patient? What ever happened to Dr. Glasgow?"

"Well, about that, Dr. Al-Fadi . . ."

"Spit it out, Bud."

"I do not expectorate, Dr. Al-Fadi. Please step over to this wallscreen in this room, so that I can show you what transpired."

"I will be noticeably annoyed if you're wasting my time, Bud. Why can't you simply tell me what happened?" Bud motioned his grumbling creator to the wallscreen.

"Please sit down, Dr. Al-Fadi." A chair rose up from the floor in front of the wallscreen.

"Why? I was just sitting a moment ago. Are you afraid I might faint?"

'That might be the best scenario.'

Bud remained behind the chair, his expression blank.

"Oh, all right." The surgeon huffed and plunked himself down in the chair. He crossed his arms across his chest and announced, "This had better be good."

'He has no idea.'

'Will you stop, Chuck Yeager? You're making me nervous.'

"Let's get the show rolling, Bud. I don't have all cycle."

The surgeon glared but the viewscreen lit up, showing an operating theatre with three figures clad in white containment suits and two in routine surgical gowns. They all surrounded a patient lying on an operating table. Identifying labels appeared above the figures. Dr. Grace Lord, Bud, and Dr. Andrea Vanacan, the anesthetist, were wearing containment suits. Dr. Eric Glasgow and Nurse Jani Evra were in normal surgical gowns. Dr. Al-Fadi frowned at the disparity, but said nothing.

The volume rose. Grace was confronting Eric Glasgow, demanding in her clear voice that they cancel the surgery and do more tests on the patient. She was pointing at the patient's abdomen as she spoke. Something was roiling and writhing around inside the patient's abdomen. Glasgow, outrage on his face, dismissed Grace from the operating room and demanded a scalpel. Nurse Evra, staring at the patient's abdomen in fear, shakily handed the activated harmonic blade to the surgeon from Ganymede.

When Glasgow sliced into the patient's midline, green tendrils burst from the explorer's abdomen like fireworks. Dr. Al-Fadi jumped from his seat, hollering. The green coils proceeded to wrap around Glasgow, Evra, and Vanacan and tear them apart. Al-Fadi let loose with a cascade of curses. He panted as the plant tendrils chased Bud and

Grace out of the operating room and down the corridor. When he saw Bud hurl Grace out through the closing lockdown doors, he squeaked. As he watched Bud slice the attacking tendrils with a harmonic scalpel in each hand, his two arms moving so fast one could not even see the blades, he looked at Bud.

When Grace ordered the temperature to be dropped below freezing in the area where the plant alien battled Bud, Dr. Al-Fadi nodded.

"Good thinking!"

When he heard the first words come from the lips of the severed head of Eric Glasgow—"Help me."—he choked.

The video finally ended when Bud was shown picking up the last frozen pieces of the plant alien, placing them all in a storage container.

The surgeon turned bulging eyes on Bud. "Tell me that murderous alien is not Plant Thing."

"Plant Thing is actually a symbiont of Dr. Eric Glasgow and that plant alien. Dr. Glasgow has told us that he must be preserved at all cost. Plant Thing has sworn it will never harm another human being. It did not know what it was doing when it was first freed from the explorer's abdomen. It was a frightened little sprout, looking for water, lights, nutrient rich soil and others of its kind."

"A frightened little sprout? It tore apart three humans in the blink of an eye, Bud! Wait a minute. I've seen both Dr. Vanacan and Nurse Evra around the station."

"They were both successfully resurrected, as you were, Dr. Al-Fadi by Dr. Weisman. They do not possess any memory of this operation because their memprints were made prior to this event, so please do not mention this to them."

"And Glasgow?"

"Unfortunately, there was no memprint recorded of Dr. Glasgow's mind but he does exist within Plant Thing."

Dr. Al-Fadi rubbed his face with his two hands. "Why was I not made aware of this before now?"

"You were immediately kidnapped, tortured, in a coma, shot, and beaten, Dr. Al-Fadi. There really wasn't a good time."

The Chief of Staff stared at Bud.

" . . . Sorry?" Bud ventured.

"That vicious plant alien became the Plant Thing that saved my life?"

"Yes, Dr. Al-Fadi. Plant Thing has helped many people on the station during the EMP strike by supplying food, light, and oxygen. Plant

Thing helped save Dr. Lord from being kidnapped by Jeffrey Nestor. It prevented the *Inferno* from leaving with Dr. Lord as prisoner."

"What happened to the body of the PEB explorer?"

"There was very little left of the body, Dr. Al-Fadi. Most of the tissues had been absorbed as nutrients by the alien. What was left of the body has been cryogenically frozen, in case the remains need to be further studied. The body could be regrown but we have no memories to put in it."

"Bud, what do I tell the PEB Inquisitor?"

"We hoped you might have some ideas, Dr. Al-Fadi."

Corporal Juan Rasmussen was in charge of security for the *Inferno*, while the breach in the hull of Receiving Bay Thirteen was being repaired. Rotations of engineers and mechanics in spacesuits had worked around the cycle to repair the outer airlock doors that had been destroyed by pulse fire. The great servomotors that opened and closed the doors had to be reinstalled. Everything had to be reconfigured, recut, and re-welded after the extensive damage done by Nestor's fleeing ship.

Twenty-four people had been lost that day, including Chief Inspector Chelsea Matthieu. When everyone had gathered after the hull breach, it had been demoralizing to see so few Security officers left. Sergeant Rivera had been so close to breaking down before them all, Juan had been forced to look away. Out of a normal compliment that should have been in the hundreds, they had only fifty remaining uninjured Security officers.

A memorial service for all of the Security officers lost was held. Almost the entire station attended. Everyone had wanted to pay their respects to the people who'd given their lives, both during the EMP strike and when the hull had blown, to save everyone. They came to pay their respects to Chief Inspector Matthieu, who'd given her life to save an unknown person in a cryopod. Rivera had broken down giving the eulogy. Dr. Cech had stepped in to take over.

It was demoralizing to think that they'd had a similar memorial service not more than thirty cycles before, for the previous Chief Inspector, Indigo Aké. People were saying the job was cursed. Lieutenant Rivera insisted he did not want the job and Juan couldn't blame him.

The Conglomerate was now sending a new Chief Inspector, the third in three months. Juan wondered what this new Chief Inspector would be like. Would she or he be hard-nosed and rigid? What would he or she think of Plant Thing, now covering the entire medical station? Would the new Inspector want it destroyed? Would that even be possible now?

Had it been merely coincidence that Plant Thing was able to provide light, food, and oxygen to all of the people stranded in the dark, when the EMP disabled the station? Where had it come from? It certainly appeared to be an intelligent being.

It had saved Grace Lord, Hiro Al-Fadi, Damien Lamont, and Juan from possible death. If intelligent, what was its agenda?

Juan's mandate was to protect the *Inferno*. He believed in keeping a healthy suspicion of everyone and every*thing*. He'd organized a continuous watch on the ship, to prevent any curious eyes from examining the EMP weapon on board. The *Inferno*'s new technology was effective against modern, state-of-the-art shielding. It was therefore incredibly valuable. Information about it could undoubtedly be sold for enormous sums of money. This technology, in the wrong hands, would put all of the planets of the USS at risk until new methods of shielding against this EMP weapon were developed and distributed.

So much of the routine operating of planets, space stations, and ships was under the control of AIs, androids and robots. To knock them all out with a single deployment of a powerful EMP weapon was catastrophic, as the *Nelson Mandela* had discovered. This weapon could lead to the loss of millions if not billions of lives. If it were not for Bud, who mysteriously was not affected by the EMP strike, the *Nelson Mandela* would never have gotten its power restored in time to avert galactic disaster.

Juan feared there were individuals aboard the *Nelson Mandela* who knew the value of this EMP weapon and wanted it. The possibility of the *Inferno* being stolen or highjacked was high, yet Juan's coworkers thought he was crazy. They grumbled at his insistence that officers be posted around the cycle to guard the ship. Before the hull had been sealed, they'd all had to don spacesuits to perform their watches. His orders had been far from popular. Juan understood there were not enough Security people to do all of the jobs needed on the station, but guarding the *Inferno* should have held top priority. Thank goodness Rivera agreed with him.

While the station's engineers were studying the *Inferno* and its EMP weapon, Juan was studying them. The individuals who would most understand the implications and value of this weapon were the engineers; he couldn't help but suspect them. Juan grew up the victim of genocide. He saw everyone he loved killed. He would not let that happen again. He scrutinized each of these men, searching for any suspicious behaviour.

That was why he'd seen it, watching from his place of concealment. The last person to leave the bridge appeared to attach something to the underside of the console, close to the controls for the EMP weapon. Juan observed this thin, nervous-looking man glance over his shoulder repeatedly before he placed it. With Juan's tiger senses, he could smell the stench of fear wafting off the fellow who smelled like he hadn't washed in a month. Juan's eyes were riveted to the console. What had he placed there?

As the engineers left the *Inferno*, deep in conversation, Juan swiftly approached the EMP controls. He crouched down and twisted his head to look up at the underside of the console. He couldn't arrest a man for simply sliding his hand under there; he had to confirm that there was indeed something there. A low growl escaped his throat and the hair on the back of his neck snapped to attention.

A black rectangular object the size of a compad was attached to the undersurface of the console. In Juan's mind, it could only be a bomb. He waved a scanner over the object. It detected dangerous compounds.

The hangar needed to be cleared immediately!

Juan raced out of the *Inferno* into Receiving Bay Thirteen, ordering his fellow officers to take all of the engineers to a hold room well away from the hangars. The Security officers and engineers all turned to look at Juan in shock.

Juan scanned all of their faces quickly. The saboteur was not amongst them.

"Get them out of here, *now,*" Juan roared at his fellow officers, who all frowned at him as if he'd gone insane. "*Move!*" He used his battlefield voice.

"*Nelson Mandela,* we need a Bomb Containment Team here stat. A probable bomb has been attached to the bridge console in the *Inferno*. We need to clear this entire area and close the lockdown doors."

"There are no Hazmat robots or androids available to bring your Bomb Containment Unit, Corporal Rasmussen. They were

all destroyed in the EMP attack. The repair of those entities was not deemed a priority over nursing and food-production bots. I apologize."

"Are there some spare droids or cargobots that can bring the Bomb Containment Unit here?"

"Yes. The BCU is on its way; ETA two minutes. They are bringing a Hazmat suit for you. With regards to the saboteur, can you send me a visual of the person?"

"Don't have one. Close the lockdown doors as soon as the BCU gets here. This bomb could blow any second."

"Best to get out of there, Corporal Rasmussen."

"Preserving that EMP weapon is vital to the security of the USS. I can't give up on saving it."

"ETA twenty seconds. All personnel are cleared of the hangar except you. Lockdown doors activated. Can you identify this saboteur?"

"He would have been the last engineer to leave the ship."

"A sweep of the station will be performed and all inhabitants notified via wristcomp to watch for him. He may be the original engineer of the *Inferno* who has up to now eluded capture. He may have changed his appearance."

"Why was I not notified of this?" Juan demanded.

"Could it be because you did not ask if all the crew had been recaptured?"

"Stupid of me to not have asked this question."

"Indeed."

"Are there any other details that you think I should know, *Nelson Mandela?*"

"The BCU you requested is now entering the hangar, Corporal Rasmussen."

"Thanks."

"You're welcome. Good luck, Corporal Rasmussen. We will work to apprehend the saboteur. Lockdown of the entire Receiving Bay section is now commencing."

Juan directed the cargo droids to carry the BCU into the *Inferno*. Alarms were pealing to announce that the lockdown doors were engaging. Juan quickly donned the Hazmat suit delivered by the cargo droids. The protection it afforded him was unlikely to be sufficient.

Juan had the cargo droids carefully position the BCU directly beneath the strange packet.

"What happens next, *Nelson Mandela?*" Juan asked, his voice sounding muffled within the Hazmat helmet.

"You have not done this before, Corporal Rasmussen?"

"No."

Did Juan detect a sigh?

"Activate the BCU by pushing the green button. The top cylinder will rise until it forms a seal around the bomb. That will provide a modicum of protection if the bomb detonates prematurely. The cylinder is designed to block any incoming signals. Position the BCU directly beneath the packet. Adjust the diameter of the cylinder so that its perimeter will seal completely around the packet. Activate the sealing process by pressing the SEAL button. Take cover after that."

Juan fought the shaking of his hands, as he adjusted the cylinder and its position. "Okay, engaging the cylinder." Juan took three deep breaths and pressed the activation button, not daring to exhale.

The top of the bomb containment device rose and the suspicious object disappeared from view. Juan blew out his held breath.

"Do not relax yet, Corporal Rasmussen. You can still be blown to pieces at this point. Leave the *Inferno* now."

"Thanks, *Nelson Mandela.*" Juan dashed out of the ship, the cargo droids rolling behind him. He slapped the hatchway closure once they were all out.

"Liquid nitrogen is being released around the packet. Once the temperature within the cylinder has reached minus one hundred and ninety-seven degrees Celsius, the top of the cylinder will attempt to separate the packet from the undersurface of the console. Take cover wherever you can, Corporal Rasmussen."

Juan crouched behind some protective barriers.

"Well? Is it detached?" he finally asked, after waiting several minutes.

"The bomb is still attached to the undersurface of the console. The unit cannot disengage it and close."

"Why not?"

"That is for you to find out."

"Me?"

"I do not believe the cargobots have the dexterity to perform

this procedure. You will have to assist the unit manually, Corporal Rasmussen."

"*What?* What do I have to do?"

"The packet seems to be strongly adhered to the undersurface of the console. It needs to be pried off gently. The cargobots can give you the tools you will need."

"Why me?" Juan asked.

"Is there anyone else there that can do it?"

Juan snarled. His heart was thumping. He was a huge, hulking tiger adapt. He wasn't made for fine delicate work, not with his tiger hands. He stabbed his claws in and out before donning the remote control gloves the cargobot gave him. Next he donned interface goggles that would show him what the cargobot could 'see'.

The cargobot re-entered the ship. Juan could now 'see' the BCU cylinder attached to the console. The cargobot's grasper tips looked enormous, like massive lobster claws. How was he supposed to tease the bomb off of the undersurface of the console using these monsters?

"Let me see the scraper," Juan said.

An enormous triangular tool came into his visual field.

"Whoa, don't you have anything thinner?"

The scraper rotated and now looked like a straight line.

"That'll do."

Juan tried not to think about his partner, Cindy, and his baby girl, Estelle, as he made the cargobot push the fine flat instrument between the top of the BCU cylinder and the console. When it reached the packet, he whispered a prayer to Cindy that she not hate him too much, if this all went horribly wrong. He took a slow deep breath to calm himself.

"I love you, Cindy. I love you, Estelle. Forgive me," he whispered.

Juan inched the scraper forward and gently inserted it between the packet and the console undersurface. Slowly and carefully, he pushed the scraping tool forward using the remote control gloves. It was tedious work. Juan felt his hand and shoulder muscles spasm as he tried to hold his arms steady.

How long the task took, he did not know; it seemed to take hours. His arms were vibrating with tension as his breath hissed between his fangs. As the packet finally released and sank slowly into the liquid nitrogen of the BCU, freed from the console, Juan sighed and let his arms sag. The top of the BCU closed before the packet had settled to the bottom of the cylinder. The cylinder retracted into the BCU unit which then jumped into the air and fell over.

"Glad you are still with us, Corporal Rasmussen. According to the BCU's readings, that bomb would have likely destroyed the *Inferno* and the entire Receiving Bay hangar. Congratulations on your success."

"Thanks for letting me know, *Nelson Mandela,*" Juan drawled.

"You are most welcome, Corporal Rasmussen."

"I need a drink."

Grace's father, Captain Alexander Grayson Lord, trailed after the short talkative man with the atrocious manners. For some inexplicable reason, Dr. Moham Rani had insisted on taking Alex on a tour of the entire medical station. When Alex had gone in search of Grace on his own, he'd been astonished at how large the *Nelson Mandela* was. He now realized that he'd seen only a fraction of it.

He learned that the *Nelson Mandela* was in orbit around a medium-sized planet called Neos Kriti, which revolved around a star called Cirillo. Cirillo was situated in proximity to a nexus of wormholes, which made it an ideal location for a medical space station.

Rani claimed to be an obstetrician/gynaecologist but Alex found this hard to believe. The man's behaviour towards women was so objectionable that Alex expected him to be assaulted any second. Surprisingly, most of the women seemed to accept this rude man and treated his condescension with saintly forbearance. The women of Grace's time had become much more tolerant of boorish behaviour than the women of Alex's time. There were several instances where Alex had to keep his hands clasped tightly together to prevent him from punching the idiot himself.

They'd toured the medical facilities, sports complex, Concourse with its marketplace, observation decks, arboretum, museum, art gallery, virtual reality parlours, pleasure district, theatre, play houses, and receiving bays. Alex could not believe a medical station would have all of these things. Wasn't it supposed to be a hospital?

"To maintain a healthy body, one needs to cultivate a healthy mind and spirit," Rani began. "For complete health, an individual needs to devote time to spiritual and artistic endeavours as well as exercising the physical body. The treatment of trauma, both physical and mental, is highly stressful. Deliverers of care need to devote time to balancing their own stress with relaxing pursuits." Rani chattered on and on. Alex tended to blank him out, but not this time.

Was Grace looking after herself? He suspected the contrary. She was far too work oriented and barely took time for herself. He'd rarely seen her since he'd gotten the bandages off of his face. Grace was either operating on patients, caring for them post-operatively, assessing new patients in Triage, or doing jobs for her mentor, Dr. Al-Fadi. She didn't seem to have any free time like Dr. Rani. Granted there were probably very few pregnant women arriving on a medical station devoted to the treatment of military personnel. Alex wondered why Rani was on the *Nelson Mandela* in the first place.

Grace probably didn't have time for Alex because of her overbearing boss. She was always apologizing for not being able to spend time with him. Al-Fadi was working poor Grace to death. Alex decided he would have a word with the man. Grace was far too dedicated and unselfish to focus on her own needs. She needed her father to step in and make sure she looked after herself.

Rani was babbling on about Grace and Bud and how beautiful they were together. Alex interrupted his chatter.

"Tell me about Bud," Alex said, looking down at the gynaecologist. "I really know nothing about him."

Moham stopped abruptly and stared at Alex, his dark brown eyes wide. His mouth opened and closed repeatedly, making Alex think of a fish out of water. For the first time since they'd met, Rani was having trouble finding words.

" . . . Bud is . . . incredible," Rani gushed.

Alex snorted. "Sounds like you have a man-crush."

"What is a 'man-crush'?"

"One man seriously into another man," Alex said.

"Bud is not a man. He's an *android*," Rani announced haughtily. "And no, I do not have an *android*-crush. I'm . . . a great admirer of the amazing feats that Bud has performed." Rani looked down his nose at Alex, which meant his very prominent proboscis was pointing up in the air.

Alex barely noticed. He'd stopped walking and was finding it difficult to inhale. The throbbing in his ears was deafening. He felt off balance. His face was burning with heat and his body was vibrating.

"Captain Lord, are you all right? You don't look well," Rani said.

Rani's voice seemed to come from far away, as if through a long tunnel. Alex's vision wavered and he found himself panting. He wanted to launch himself at Rani.

"What . . . did . . . you . . . say?"

Rani backed away from Alex. The whites of his eyes showed all around his brown irises. "Captain Lord, your face is so red, it's almost glowing. I wonder if you might be experiencing a cerebral hemorrhage."

"Before that," Alex grated. He tried to slow his breathing.

Rani frowned. He glanced around himself, as if seeking help, his brow deeply furrowed. It was obvious Rani was having trouble recalling what he'd said.

" . . . I said I don't have a crush on Bud," Rani said slowly. "And I don't."

"No, you idiot, you said Bud was an *android*. Is this true?"

"Of course, it's true! How else would he be able to do all the amazing things he does? How could you not know this?" Rani glared at Alex with an expression that implied, 'Everyone knows that Bud is an android. Are you an idiot?'

Alex spun and marched away as quickly as his legs could carry him. If he did not do so, he would have pounded the obnoxious Rani in the face and never stopped. His hands were clenched so tightly into fists, his fingernails gouged the skin of his palms. He kept his eyes glued to the ground. He feared he'd attack the first man to look at him sideways. His body felt as taut as a tightly coiled spring. If released, Alex didn't know if he'd be able to control his rage. He almost ran from Rani, his breath whistling in panting gasps.

How dare this machine, this bucket of bolts—this *thing*—come anywhere near his little girl, his darling Grace? It was indecent. It was perverted. It was sick.

Alex trembled with incandescent fury, his mind howling like a pack of rabid wolves. Thinking about Bud the android being . . . associated . . . friendly . . . intimate? . . . with Grace made him want to kill something.

Alex had to speak with Grace. This could not possibly be true. He could not countenance it. It was abominable.

What was Grace thinking?

Alex wanted to kick the snot out of Rani so that he never repeated this again. He roared at the top of his lungs down an empty corridor like an enraged beast.

He so wanted to destroy something . . . and that something was Bud.

Grace was searching for Dr. Al-Fadi. She found him in his quarters hiding from the attentions of Plant Thing, although he was loathe to admit it. Dr. Hanako Matheson, Hiro Al-Fadi's wife, greeted Grace at the doorway and beckoned for her to enter quickly.

"Who is it?" Grace heard Hiro bellow.

"It's Grace, Hiro." Hanako smiled warmly at Grace.

"Is that damn Plant Thing still out there?"

Hanako twiddled her fingers at the enormous mass of tendrils and eyeballs sitting outside in the corridor.

"Yes, Hiro. Plant Thing's still here," Hanako called.

'Plant Thing's all over the station,' the little voice in Grace's head said. 'Why wouldn't it be here?'

Plant Thing's eyeballs all jigged up and down when Hiro's voice carried out into the corridor. Grace bit her lip.

"Tell that blasted Plant Thing to go away! I hate being stared at," Hiro said to her

"I'll try again, Dr. Al-Fadi," Grace said. "Plant Thing wants to ensure you're safe."

"Why wouldn't I be safe? This is a medical station, not a battleground."

"Plant Thing found you close to death. You were badly injured. It's concerned for your wellbeing."

"I can't fault the creature's taste but I need my privacy, my autonomy, my independence. How can I get anything done with those eyeballs following me everywhere?"

"*You* must tell it to stop following you around, Dr. Al-Fadi. Plant Thing will understand if you are firm. Explain why it's being so disruptive to your work."

"All right . . . Now, explain to me why you're here, Dr. Grace, and not working." Hiro placed his fists on his hips and lowered his thick eyebrows.

"I wanted to put in a good word for Plant Thing, before you meet with the PEB Inquisitor." Grace launched into her explanation about Plant Thing and the operating room and the fusion with Eric Glasgow's brain when Hiro made impatient slicing motions with his hand.

"I know all of this already, Dr. Grace."

" . . . You do? I . . . didn't know. I apologize for wasting your time."

"You've done nothing of the sort, Dr. Grace. You've helped me formulate my defence of Plant Thing to the peebs."

"Peebs?"

"Planetary Exploration Bureau. We must show them how valuable Plant Thing is. My main fear is that they will demand Plant Thing be destroyed."

"Have they any right to do that?"

"Try not to be so naive in my presence, Dr. Grace. Act like you have a brain in your skull, please. When the Conglomerate wanted to wipe the virus out, what did they send?"

"Three battlecruisers."

"Yes. We were seen as collateral damage. If the Conglomerate sees Plant Thing as a threat, what do you think they'll send? What would stop them from plotting to destroy the *Nelson Mandela* like they tried to before, the bastards?

"I agree with you that we must protect Plant Thing at all costs. After all, the alien has the best taste in humans . . . and I'm not referring to its eating habits. How could we possibly destroy such an intelligent being that is symbiotically fused with Dr. Glasgow?"

Grace sighed. "Thank you, Dr. Al-Fadi. I've been so worried for Plant Thing."

"Worry for the station, Dr. Grace. If the Conglomerate decides to destroy Plant Thing, they may decide it's easier to annihilate us all. Plant Thing has grown so large, it almost covers the entire station, except for the operating rooms, the medical wards, the processing areas, and the power generators. If the PEB demands Plant Thing be destroyed and the Conglomerate agrees, we may all become space dust."

"Do you think the PEB would do that?"

"Again you ask these ridiculous questions, Dr. Grace. How in space would I know?"

Grace's cheeks nearly sizzled.

"What do *you* think we should tell the Inquisitor, Dr. Grace?"

"The truth, I suppose."

"*What?* No, of course not, Dr. Grace. Are you insane?"

Grace thought her cheeks could now heat the *Nelson Mandela* for an entire year.

"Don't you want the PEB to know exactly what they're facing on Plant Thing's planet? We have to protect the lives of the explorers but we have to protect Plant Thing's planet, too. No humans should ever settle there."

"Yes, that's true, Dr. Grace, but it's very important *how* we tell the Inquisitor . . . or this station could be history. The Conglomerate can be quite unreasonable about dangerous aliens, infestations, and deadly pathogens. In the case of Plant Thing, we must convince the Inquisitor of our incredible good fortune to have a goodwill ambassador of the plant world right here on this medical station, yes? If we don't do this— and do it exceedingly well—the *Nelson Mandela* may be destroyed to eradicate a dangerous infestation. Do you follow me, Dr. Grace?"

"We have to make the Inquisitor love Plant Thing."

"Exactly." Hiro massaged his huge forehead with his hands. "I have to think carefully about all of this."

"You will have to think quickly about it as well, Dr. Al-Fadi. The Planetary Exploration Bureau vessel, with its Inquisitor, has entered our local space and is requesting an approach vector."

"Wonderful," the surgeon drawled, sarcastically. "Can you delay the landing?"

"We could tell them we are in lockdown due to a dangerous alien entity on board."

"Ha-ha. Considering what we just talked about, that's probably not the best idea, *Nelson Mandela*."

"You think?"

Dr. Jocelyn Sarri was sitting at their office desk dictating consultation reports, when there was a chime, announcing their next patient. They spoke 'Enter' and the door slid open to reveal an extremely thin female with electric blue hair and brilliant green eyes. The patient wore a gauzy, diaphanous shift that barely covered her thighs and left her arms bare. Jocelyn inwardly rolled their eyes and tried to don a welcoming smile.

"Please come in," Jocelyn said.

The patient was not attractive; quite the opposite actually. She was ghastly pale and her breasts were nonexistent. Jocelyn felt uneasy having this scantily clad girl in their tiny office. The consultation had said the patient required grief counselling. Good grief was right. Who came to see a psychiatrist dressed like this? Jocelyn hoped it was not another nymphomaniac. They had such difficulty convincing these patients they weren't interested. Besides, they'd already had their quota of unpredictable patients. They cracked their face into a polite smile and gestured for the patient to take a seat.

"*Nelson Mandela*? Would you record and audit this interview?" Jocelyn asked aloud.

"Certainly, Dr. Sarri."

"Thank you."

The pale, young woman strolled to the chair and flounced into it. Jocelyn averted their eyes, but not before noticing the girl wore no underclothes beneath her shift.

Puh—lease.

"What are you afraid of?" the girl demanded, her green eyes staring directly into Jocelyn's.

Jocelyn jerked back and shifted in the chair. "I beg your pardon? It's my usual routine to record every interview, Ms. Vertongen."

"Is it?" the girl asked, her sneer suggesting that she did not believe Jocelyn.

"Why are you here today, Ms. Vertongen?" Jocelyn asked, clasping their fingers tightly together and placing them on the desk.

"Were you not told why I'm here?" Vertongen asked. Her eyes wandered around Jocelyn's office with an air of distaste.

"I know why you were referred, Ms. Vertongen. Why did you decide to come? Why did you consent to this interview?"

"Is that what this is? An interview?"

"If we are to engage in any meaningful discussion, an interview is the first step, Ms. Vertongen. Do you need counselling?"

"You look far too young to be doing this. How old are you?" the blue-haired girl asked.

"Are you looking for someone older to counsel you, Ms. Vertongen?"

"Are you attempting to duck out, before we even begin this interview, Doctor?"

"Does that upset you?" Jocelyn asked, their interest finally piqued. *Now we're getting somewhere.*

"Shouldn't it?" Vertongen asked, her chin raised and her eyes boring into Jocelyn's in what they believed was an attempt to intimidate. Or was she merely showing them her disdain?

How interesting.

"Why would offering to send you to an older, more experienced psychiatrist upset you, Ms. Vertongen?" Jocelyn asked.

"Why would I want to spend time talking to an ancient, decrepit fool? Do you think it wise for you to reject me, Dr. Sarri? You may regret it later."

Now threats? What in space does she think she's doing? Jocelyn pondered. This girl was tremendously angry at someone. Another doctor, perhaps, but who?

"I'm not kicking you out of my office, Ms. Vertongen, but were you not the one objecting to my youth?" Jocelyn asked. The last thing they wanted was another Borderline Personality Disorder in their practice.

Vertongen scowled at Jocelyn. "Do you think I like being dismissed or underestimated, *Doctor* Sarri?" The girl said the word 'Doctor' like it left a horrible taste in her mouth. "Might you come to regret that?"

Jocelyn's eyebrows furrowed. "Are you threatening me, Ms. Vertongen?"

They were now leaning heavily towards Antisocial Personality Disorder with narcissistic traits; but Borderline Personality Disorder was still a possibility.

"The name's Ice. Would you like a 'piece of advice' or a 'word to the wise'? Dismiss me at your peril, Doctor Sarri." Ice's look matched her name. Jocelyn stopped themselves from drumming their fingers on the desk surface. They were pretty sure they'd never met this young woman before, yet Vertongen behaved as if they'd wronged her some time in the past. They searched their memory to no avail. They were positive they would have remembered someone like Ice.

The graduate student stood up and strode to the door. "This interview is now over, Dr. Sarri," she announced over her right shoulder. She flounced out.

Jocelyn sat for a while, pinching their lower lip. They scratched their lower chin and frowned.

They'd been asked to see this young woman by Dr. Weisman, the Chief of Neurosurgery, because the neurosurgeon felt Ms. Vertongen required bereavement counselling. Jocelyn had not gotten the impression that the girl was grieving at all. If anything, Jocelyn sensed a fulminating rage.

Jocelyn was soaked with sweat. The last time they'd felt like this was when they'd gotten into a disagreement with that narcissistic sociopath, Jeffrey Nestor.

Same confusion; same perspiration.

Pale, bloated arms looking like giant white slugs rested on top of flabby thighs. Thick, rubbery lips, pressed into a straight line, pouted above sagging jowls and a weak triple chin. Looking down a bulbous nose laced with a spiderweb of red veins, the obese prisoner sat with knees far apart, bracketing a ponderous belly. His thick wrists looked strangled by the manacles that were linked to the front of the chair. Tiny, grey eyes, set too close together, glared from amongst corpulent folds at Damien Lamont. The oily, grey hairs that crossed the man's bald pate in sparse strands resembled claw-marks. Damien yearned to give him some real ones.

The prisoner's fluorescent yellow coverall was stained and grimy. He stank of stale sweat and foul body odour, creating an unpleasant funk that emanated from him like a chemical assault. Since the prisoner had access to a private sterilizer and clean coveralls on a daily basis, the man's personal hygiene—or lack of it—represented a statement of sorts. Aromatically, the prisoner was on the offensive.

Damien breathed through his mouth and tried to smother his desire to pummel this fellow for simply smelling abhorrent. It wasn't a crime not to wash, but it was ludicrous when this man had the gall to denigrate Damien as an 'animal'.

Leaning against the wall of the interrogation room, Damien crossed his tiger-striped forearms and ignored the hate-filled stare from the *Inferno's* chaplain. The false name given by the preacher was John Bunyan but the *Inferno's* medical officer, a leopard-adapt named Hope Cooper, had called him Abraham.

Abraham had spat such hate-filled words at Hope that Damien had knocked him out purely to shut him up. Those words had wounded Hope more than any physical blow could have. This preacher's crazy religious doctrine said that any human with modifications to their body deserved to die. Had Damien known the preacher's sentiments when he'd had him unconscious on his shoulder, he would have dropped the nutcase on his head. Forcefully.

How did this chaplain's belief fit with his religion? Was not one of their main commandments, 'Thou shall not kill'? Damien could not understand how these religious zealots believed they had the right to wipe billions of innocent people out, because of a difference in spiritual belief. How was that not killing? He shook his head.

Eden Rivera was patiently asking the chaplain questions concerning where the *Inferno* had come from, the name of the star system, the name of the planet, the name of their organization. Not surprisingly, the prisoner was refusing to answer any of the questions. Damien longed for a few minutes alone with the preacher. The chaplin had almost frothed at the mouth, spouting his religious nonsense with geyser-like zeal, when he'd burnt a hole in a heroic woman's heart. Hope was now dead, yet this hateful worm lived. There was no justice.

Damien knew it would be easy to get the chaplain ranting. The man was dying to launch into a tirade of righteous indignation. Damien could see it brewing in the man's crazed eyes.

It was only a matter of time before Rivera would tire of this and would resort to the interrogation drugs. The sergeant was an honourable man. He gave all of the prisoners a chance to confess. If they cooperated, it might mean a lighter sentence; however, in the case of attempted mass extinction of the human race, that wasn't likely.

"Were you aware of what your captain had planned when you left your planet?" Rivera asked.

Abraham stared at Rivera in silence, jaw clamped.

"Forget this, Sarge," Damien said. "This man's a coward. He forsook his God the moment things got tough for him, probably in the hope that he can save his own miserable life. His faith is a sham. Imagine spouting about God all his life, yet when challenged to own up to his beliefs, he cowers in silence. Pathetic."

The chaplain's eyes popped. "How dare you utter His name, devil. You are a beast. You aren't worthy to have the Lord's name on your vile tongue!" The chaplain tried to rise from his chair. His face was rapidly turning scarlet, as he struggled with his restraints. "You stand there, flaunting your wickedness, rejecting the body that God gave you and prancing around in the devil's own skin. Well, you shall find the gates to Heaven closed when you stand at Judgement Day."

"And you'll be let into Heaven after murdering billions of innocent people with your deadly virus?" Damien spat back at the chaplain. "You're the devil."

"The just punishment of sinners is the work of the Lord. We are the Hammer of God."

"With your virus, you would have killed *all* carbon-based organic life created by your God."

"Utter not His name, I command you, vermin. You are not worthy to name Him," the chaplain shouted.

"Your superiors would never have trusted a wretched coward like you with any knowledge of their overall plan," Damien said, with as much scorn as he could project. "We're wasting our time here, Sergeant."

"And that is where you reveal your stupidity, beast. How great your conceit is, to flaunt your ignorance so openly. This was a plan of my devising."

"You could not possibly be the mastermind behind these viruses," Damien said.

"I recruited men of great virtue and brilliant genius to do God's work."

"You see yourself as devout but you sinned when you planned to murder billions. Playing with genes? Creating viruses? Are your brilliant geniuses not playing at *being* God when they manipulate the material of creation to create a bioweapon? Isn't that blasphemy? Are you not the ones who should be destroyed for daring to play God?"

"You bark the words of Satan with a beast's tongue. Listen to you, I will not."

"I'm tired of listening to your nonsense, too," Damien responded.

He glanced at Rivera. The young sergeant nodded. Damien walked over and slapped a patch on the back of the chaplain's neck. Using the interrogation drugs permitted by the USS courts, they would now get all the information they needed from this man. If Abraham had actually been speaking the truth, he knew everything and everyone involved in these virus attacks. Why he'd been on the *Inferno* was puzzling. Perhaps he'd insisted on being there to make sure nothing went wrong and no one could stop him. They would have been successful if it hadn't been for Bud, Grace, and Hope.

Rivera was required to adhere to the letter of the law when interrogating each prisoner. He wanted to extract the truth about whether each crew member knew or did not know about the deadly virus. So far, the communications officer and the quartermaster had known nothing about the virus until they'd arrived at the *Nelson Mandela*.

They wanted the name of the planet from which the viruses came, the location of the fabrication plants, and the names of the leaders. Once that information was obtained, the Conglomerate would go to the source and stop the creation of these deadly biological weapons. If they didn't, the USS would always be at risk from another lethal attack. These fanatics had to be stopped.

Religious extremists were hypocrites. What arrogance, to believe they had the right to destroy other humans. What insanity, to believe they were the only humans that deserved to live or that their belief was the only true belief. It was madness beyond comprehension, steeped in intolerance and ignorance.

"You will never get the name and coordinates of our system from me," Abraham declared, his eyes shining confidently.

Damien lunged at Abraham as the chaplain opened his mouth, and stabbed the claws of his right hand into his maw, preventing Abraham from chomping down on his teeth. His prosthetic fingers registered pressure but no pain, as the chaplain tried to bite as hard as he could. With both hands, Damien forced the man's jaws apart, while Abraham gargled and thrashed his head. Using the sharp claw of his right index finger, Damien gently tapped each tooth. One of the chaplain's molars at the back looked and sounded different. Damien quickly yanked the false tooth out, while the chaplain kicked and roared.

Damien held the fake tooth up between his claw tips, while he kept his right hand jammed inside the chaplain's mouth.

"Can you get a chemical analyzer container, Sarg? Don't know how toxic the stuff in this tooth is, but I'd wager it's fast-acting and lethal. Probably wouldn't be good to get its contents on your skin."

Rivera put on a pair of gloves and opened up an evidence jar. Damien carefully dropped the tooth inside the specimen holder and Rivera pushed the closed container into a slot in the table. *Nelson Mandela* would have the toxicology report in seconds.

The chaplain was chomping savagely on Damien's fingers. Damien shifted his sharp claws so that they dug into the man's gums whenever he bit down, eliciting angry gurgles. Damien grinned down at Abraham's fiery indignation as he carefully rechecked all the other teeth.

"Bite down as hard as you like. I'm tempted to pull out all of your teeth—in case you have more poison-bearing teeth in there. Don't believe I've any choice. Need to keep you alive to answer our questions."

The man's eyes popped and he renewed his frantic chomping. Damien examined the teeth again and yanked the rest of Abraham's molars, which were more difficult to remove and a lot more bloody.

"How did you know about the tooth?" Rivera asked.

"I guessed." Damien's right hand was still jammed in the chaplain's mouth. "He looked too confident when he said we'd get nothing from him and he opened his mouth far too wide. Thought it best to check his teeth out."

Rivera gazed at the bloodshot eyes and purpling face of the chaplain. "I'm afraid I can't offer you anything, Abraham. You'll tell me everything you know and get no deal. If you're found guilty of conspiracy to commit mass murder, you'll likely face mindswipe or death."

"I have nothing to fear," the chaplain said, after Damien withdrew his hand. "God is on my side."

Damien barked a laugh.

"Damn you to Hell," the chaplain slurred, blood dribbling down his chins. "I'll tell you nothing."

"You've refused to answer any questions of your own accord. That's on record. In a few minutes, Abraham, we'll begin the second stage of this interrogation," Rivera said.

The obese man struggled against his bonds, bloody spittle flying everywhere. With his wrists manacled to the seat, he couldn't reach the patch on the back of his neck. He growled and spat at Damien and Rivera but when his pupils began to dilate and his head began to droop, Damien knew Abraham would begin spouting answers.

The interrogation seemed to last forever. It was all recorded by *Nelson Mandela*. Rivera was repetitive and thorough, asking the same question at least three times, at various intervals, to ensure that the answers were always consistent. The location of the star system and planet, the people involved in the plot, the creators of the viruses, the engineers who created the EMP weapon—all were recorded, along with codenames, passwords, signals, and meeting places. The chaplain talked about laboratories, factories, headquarters, political factions, funding, secret cells, secret organizations. He was an ocean of information and Rivera sucked him dry.

By the end of the session, Damien felt elated. With the intel they'd gleaned from Abraham, the Conglomerate would be able to go to his planet and take these fanatics down.

Once Abraham was led away, Damien looked at Rivera, who stared back at him with bleak eyes, underscored by deep, dark hollows. The sergeant looked like death.

"Thank you for your assistance, Captain Lamont. If you hadn't stopped him from committing suicide, we would've lost him and learned none of this information. Good work."

"Wonder what was in the tooth?"

"A potent cardio-neurotoxin, extremely fast-acting, as you suspected, Captain Lamont."

"You really didn't need my protection, Sarg. Why'd you ask me here?"

"You're correct, Captain," Rivera said, his voice as flat as the air in a sealed tomb. "I was not the one who required protection . . ."

Alex wandered around the station searching for androids, but had not spotted any—or any that he was positive were androids. He saw a lot of people who were modified, a lot of animal-adapted soldiers— who were presumably human—and people that sported some kind of mechanical or bioprosthetic upgrade. He didn't think any of them were androids. They reminded him of marines he'd known, ready to take on all comers. They had that look of carefully controlled murder in their eyes.

Bud had looked completely human. If Alex had not been told by that uppity gynaecologist that Bud was an android, Alex wouldn't have known. The only clue to Bud being an android was that he was too perfect, too beautiful. How many of the people Alex passed by now could actually be androids? None of them looked as perfect as Bud. Most looked more animal or machine than human. With the availability of any kind of genetic or mechanical modification, one could change anything. It was probably simple to achieve the perfect body and face, so a flawless-looking person would not necessarily be an android. In Alex's day, androids were not allowed to look exactly like people.

Alex scowled. His brain was being twisted into knots. Everything was so different. Was he ever going to get used to the strangeness of now? He was a man from the past in a young man's body, due to time dilation and space flight. He had nothing to anchor himself to the present but Grace. She was the only reason he had to keep living and he was not going to allow her to have a perverted 'relationship' with a machine.

Alex knew Grace was operating; he wouldn't be able to see her for a few hours. He decided the best thing for him to do was to go to a gym and work off some of his anger. He'd passed a fitness facility a little way back. Because of the need to bone load to prevent osteoporosis, there were exercise facilities everywhere on the station. Everyone had to exercise daily and had to log in their times or they didn't get to eat. Everyone had to wear patches to strengthen their bones. That was all right with Alex. He relished the idea of punching something for a few hours.

Alex spun about and almost collided with a pale, skinny woman with cropped blue hair and green eyes. He jumped back. This girl was barely dressed and he had to contort himself to not collide with specific exposed body parts.

The girl glanced up at his face, an expression of fury on her gaunt features. Her mouth fell open and she stared at Alex as if she recognized him. Heat infused Alex's cheeks. He'd never seen this young lady before but her reaction to him was disturbing.

"Sorry," he said, stepping aside. The girl continued to stare at him as if she were desert-parched and he was a pitcher of water.

"Do I know you?" Alex asked.

A glint appeared in the girl's green eyes and her expression changed. She smiled at him, fluttering pale lashes over narrowed eyes. Her mouth formed a pout. "Am I that forgettable?"

All the hairs on Alex's body stood up. Why had he spoken to her? He ran his hand back through his short, blonde hair. An anorexic, blue-haired, green-eyed almost-nudist would be hard to forget.

"No lass, you're definitely not forgettable, but unless you've helped operate on me, I'm positive we've never met. Perhaps I remind you of someone."

The young woman grinned, her cold green eyes half-lidded. She held her fist out. "I'm Ice."

Bet you are.

"Alex," he said, touching his fist to hers.

"You were injured?"

"Yes, I've recently had the bandages removed." Alex peered down the hall, looking for an escape.

"You bear an uncanny resemblance to someone on this station."

"Yes?" Alex's attention swung back to the woman.

"Dr. Lord. You could pass for her brother," Ice said.

"Grace is my daughter. Are you a friend of hers?" Alex stared at Ice with interest.

Ice grinned, looking at Alex as if he were a bug she desired for her insect collection. She looped her hand through Alex's arm and started to pull him in the direction they had originally both been walking.

"We must get to know each other, Alex. I'm Grace's biggest fan. She's such a caring doctor. You must be so proud. By the way, you look far too young to be her father."

"Time dilation." Alex felt twitchy, letting this girl pull him along. "I was gone for only two years in space but for Grace, twenty-eight years had passed."

"That must have been very hard for you."

Alex peered down at Ice. She looked like a skinny, skimpily attired teenager. The last thing he wanted was for Grace to hear about him being seen with this girl on his arm. He disentangled himself from her clutches and stepped away.

"Sorry, Ice, but I have to go. Perhaps we can get together another time . . . maybe with Grace."

Ice's green eyes brightened. Alex's unease grew. He couldn't take his eyes off this girl, but in the way one would not turn one's back on a flaring cobra. Ice looked delighted with what he'd said, and he had no idea why. Perhaps suggesting Grace and he meet up with Ice was something Grace would not like? He'd have to ask Grace when he saw her.

"I'm gonna make you keep your promise, Alex," Ice said with a sly grin.

"I'm sorry, but I really have to go." Alex suppressed the urge to flee.

"I'll ping your wristcomp, Alex, so we can all get together sometime, just like you promised." Ice gave him a wide smile while staring at him with cold, reptilian eyes. She turned and sauntered away.

Alex exhaled forcefully. He watched Ice strut off on heels he would never allow on his ship, her flimsy, half-a-garment flapping. He shook his head. Would he ever get used to this time period? Even though he'd been in deep space for a long time—and in cryosleep through much of it—he still preferred to see women dressed. He believed in leaving something to the imagination. In Ice's case, Alex's imagination had him running for the airlocks.

Adorned in surgical greens, Hiro waited in the Reception Room for visitors to begin coming through the Arrivals gate. He'd asked *Nelson Mandela* to point out the PEB Inquisitor to him so that he could walk up and personally greet him.

Hiro's arms were crossed and he could not stop tapping his foot. How dare this PEB Inquisitor come here to personally investigate their patient. Did the Planetary Exploration Bureau not realize that this was the Conglomerate's Premier Medical Space Station? Did they think all the Chief of Staff did was meet with bureaucrats all day? He was the leading animal-adaptation trauma surgeon in the USS. If he didn't get back to them about one patient, it was because he was busy . . . or incapacitated. The station dealt with far more serious emergencies than one explorer from a planetary survey team, like saving the universe from life-annihilating viruses.

Hiro had suffered from the viral infection, death, kidnapping, torture, being shot, and almost beaten to death. When, amongst all of that, was he supposed to find time to write a report to the PEB? He did not owe the PEB an explanation or an apology. He'd answer their questions when he damn well had the time.

Hiro stomped around the Reception Area, grinding his teeth. Other people in the waiting area were shifting away, shooting him sidelong glances. What did they think he was going to do? Bite them?

Changing his mind about greeting the PEB Inquisitor, Hiro turned towards the exit. At that moment, he spotted the most exquisite creature he'd ever seen. He gasped, almost falling to his knees, as he watched her emerge from the Arrivals portal, like the goddess Venus arising from the sea.

Tall, shapely, and alluringly beautiful, her face was a perfect oval with high cheekbones, large dark eyes, and a perfectly sculpted nose.

Her lips were full and sensuous. Her walk was the sinuous movement of a jaguar. Ebony blue was her skin and the green of her irises were framed in thick silvered lashes. Her neck was slender. She had the poise of a star dancer. What was most astonishing to Hiro was the great mane of hair that wafted back from her perfect face and flowed down her back in a glowing waterfall of silver.

Hiro could have tripped over his tongue.

"The PEB Inquisitor has entered the Reception Area, Dr. Al-Fadi."

"What? Where?" Hiro's eyes were glued to the Aphrodite of womanhood, who wore a tight fitting space suit that showed off her magnificent curves. The woman smiled at him. A whimper escaped his throat.

"The person you are ogling is the PEB Inquisitor, Kylara Roque."

"Kylara Roque? Kylara! What a beautiful name for a beautiful woman," Hiro said, as he stumbled forward, almost falling on his face as he bowed.

"Decorum, please."

"What? I always show decorum," Hiro hissed, smiling and raising his hand as he approached the Inquisitor. "I am the epitome of decorum."

"Inquisitor Kylara Roque, may I introduce Dr. Hiro Al-Fadi, Chief of Staff of the _Nelson Mandela._"

"Honoured to meet you," the Inquisitor said, in a low, husky voice. Her slanted eyes met Hiro's and she smiled gloriously. Hiro felt a tingle of electricity run along his nerves. He wanted to dive into those eyes. Roque returned Hiro's bow and he fought the insane urge to bury his face in her thick locks of shimmering hair.

"The pleasure is all mine," Hiro breathed, as he brushed his lips on the back of her proffered hand.

"I did not expect the Chief of Staff to greet me at the Arrivals Gate," Roque said, showing off a very impressive set of gleaming white teeth. "You really didn't need to do this, Dr. Al-Fadi. I'm sure you're far too busy."

"Not at all, Inquisitor. I looked forward to this moment." Hiro frowned at the hacking sound coming from his wristcomp. "How was your journey?"

The Inquisitor's face was a magnet for Hiro's eyes. Her skin was flawless. Hiro had never seen anyone with the midnight blue skin pigmentation Inquisitor Roque possessed. He could not pull his eyes away. He could barely stop himself from falling at the Inquisitor's feet to profess undying lust for her.

"The trip was uneventful, Doctor. I hope not to be here long. The PEB is anxious to ascertain information about our explorer, Diego Odemwingo, who was delivered to your station many cycles ago. We need to know what happened to our people on the planet, Botanica. Odemwingo was our only survivor. He's our only clue to what happened. Up until the disappearance of Odemwingo's survey party, we'd been entertaining the possibility of opening up Botanica for possible colonization. Now everything is on hold. We need to hear your findings, discover what we're dealing with. Has Odemwingo recovered enough to say what happened?"

"Ah, let me show you to your quarters and get you settled first, Inquisitor," Hiro said. "I'm sure you'd like to rest after your exhausting trip."

"Dr. Al-Fadi, the Botanica investigation is not the only reason for my visit. We have brought more PEB Explorers in cryopods, but this time from a different planet. To explain, I'd like to introduce you to my colleague, Dr. Saul Rohl."

Hiro pulled his gaze from Kylara to the person she was introducing and his jaw again dropped. Saul Rohl was as attractive a male as Kylara was a beautiful female. The man was tall, broad-shouldered, slim-waisted, and ruggedly handsome. He had smooth mahogany-brown skin, golden brown eyes, a square jaw, and a wide white smile. His hair was a luxurious, golden mane, that would make any male lion prickle with jealousy.

"Is it a requirement of the PEB that all its people be incredibly beautiful?" Hiro blurted.

Roque and Rohl both beamed at Hiro, as if he were a favourite child that had just said something clever.

"I believe the PEB requires us all to be a little insane, Dr. Al-Fadi," Rohl said, as he shook Hiro's hand. Hiro tried not to curse as his hand was being crushed. What was with all of these macho types? Did they have no respect for the hands of a surgeon? Rohl was supposedly a doctor; he should know better.

"What have you brought us, Dr. Rohl?" Hiro massaged his right hand.

"Is there somewhere more private to discuss this, Dr. Al-Fadi?"

"Certainly."

A doorway to a small office appeared in the wall of the Reception

Area. Hiro beckoned both visitors into the chamber and waited for the door to slide shut.

"We have brought twelve cryopods to the station," Rohl said. "They each contain an explorer who was involved in a preliminary survey of a new planet. When all communications from the survey team ceased, a second group went down to the planet surface. They found all of the explorers dead, their cryosuits activated, bodies scattered around the landing site and within the shuttle.

"The atmosphere of the planet does not support organic life. Everyone had been suited up. They'd not been on the planet very long—not even a full solstan day—when each member of the team became incapacitated simultaneously. They'd been conducting a drilling operation to take samples of structures located deep beneath the planet's surface. Nothing unusual was seen on the surveillance recordings, which were operational the entire time. No attack was witnessed. No alarms were sounded. No cries or communications came from the explorers. They all collapsed where they were working.

"Cryosuit readouts of every single explorer indicate that their hearts ruptured in their chests at the same time, but there was no other damage and no discernible cause for the heart trauma. The cryosuits had all immediately activated, preserving everyone in the landing party. The second landing party sent out cargobots to collect all of the explorers and immediately left the surface of the planet. The victims in their cryosuits were kept in isolation. I've brought them here to see if you can determine what happened, Dr. Al-Fadi. Obviously, we need to know what we're dealing with on this planet and, of course, we need to save these brave explorers, if possible."

"Yours is a very disturbing tale, Dr. Rohl. We are certainly capable of replacing damaged hearts on the *Nelson Mandela*. Determining the cause of the cardiac damage in each explorer will take more time, however, and will likely be the far more difficult task. The twelve cryopods must all immediately go into quarantine. If you could give us all of the data you have from the first and second landing parties to study: surveillance recordings, communication records, personnel medical records, suit readings, equipment readings—basically everything you have regarding the mission—we would appreciate it. The answer could be anywhere."

"You'll have it all, Dr. Al-Fadi. I can transmit all of the data directly to your station AI," Rohl said.

"You may transmit that data now, Dr. Rohl."

"Thank you, *Nelson Mandela*." The PEB physician tapped a few buttons on his palmpad. He looked up at Hiro and his eyes gleamed.

"Files sent. By the way, I was wondering if you have a Dr. Grace Lord on this station?" The physician stared at Hiro with eyes that could bore holes. "Dr. Lord would be a very capable surgeon by now, I'm sure. Rumour has it, she's here."

"*What?* You're after Dr. Grace, too? What is it with you men? Don't you have anything better to do than bother my surgical fellow? Dr. Lord is my sla . . . assistant and I keep her very busy." Hiro folded his arms across his chest and scowled at the 'far-too-handsome-as-far-as-Hiro-was-concerned' explorer. "How do you happen to know Grace?"

A flush rose from Rohl's neck to his mane. Hiro smiled inwardly. It was obvious Rohl's reason for wanting to see Grace was not what Hiro would call 'professional.' That was all Hiro needed to know. Another man seeking Grace's attention. Between Nestor, that annoying obstetrician—whatever his name was—her father, and even Bud, it was a wonder Hiro got any work out of Grace at all. He hrumphed. Next time, he would hire a less attractive surgical fellow.

Hiro watched Rohl's large cricothyroid cartilage slide up and down as he swallowed. "Dr. Lord and I were in the same medical school together, Dr. Al-Fadi. When I chose to join the Planetary Exploration Bureau, Grace chose to pursue surgery. We go back a long way." Rohl looked away. Hiro felt a fiendish delight at this man's discomfiture.

"I only wanted to say 'hello' to an old friend." Rohl tried to perform a casual shrug.

'Just wanted to say hello, my left testicle,' Hiro thought, as he scrutinized this Adonis. The last thing he needed was Grace being distracted by this handsome Casanova, who probably walked out on her, breaking her heart, many years ago. Well, Hiro was not going to let this gigolo break Grace's heart a second time, the bastard. He wasn't going to let this cad anywhere near his surgical fellow.

"Unfortunately, Dr. Lord is far too busy. She'll have no time to see you with all of her duties. I do apologize, but I'll let her know you asked about her."

The tall, golden-haired man's face fell and for a moment, he truly looked devastated. Hiro mentally rubbed his palms together in glee. Served the jerk right for abandoning Grace.

"That's too bad," Rohl sighed, looking at his feet. "To be honest,

Dr. Al-Fadi, it's probably for the best. You see, Grace broke my heart all those years ago when she chose surgery over coming with me. I wanted to explore the galaxy. She wanted to put people back together. I dove into the perils of planetary exploration to forget her. It didn't work. I never forgot her."

Hiro choked. "Uh . . . well . . . perhaps Dr. Grace could make a little time in her busy schedule to meet with you."

"Dr. Lord has been notified of your arrival, Dr. Rohl. She would be happy to give you a tour of the medical station, if you are interested."

Delight blossomed on Rohl's face like a rainbow after a storm.

Hiro sighed and gave the closest surveillance eye a murderous look.

"Thank you, *Nelson Mandela*," Rohl said, grinning up at the surveillance eye.

"You are most welcome, Dr. Rohl. It is a pleasure to have you on the *Nelson Mandela*."

"Could you please prepare a guest quarter for Dr. Rohl as well as Inquisitor Roque, *Nelson Mandela*?" Hiro grated.

"Already done, Dr. Al-Fadi. After our guests have registered, Inquisitor Roque and Dr. Rohl will be escorted to their suites. The twelve cryopods have already been offloaded from their ship and are being transported to Level Six Quarantine. Do you wish to inspect them personally?"

"Yes, *Nelson Mandela*. Please notify Dr. Grace that I would like her to accompany me."

"The cryopods will be within the Level Six Quarantine Chamber in eighteen minutes."

"Thank you."

"If you don't mind, I'd like to tag along, Dr. Al-Fadi," Rohl said. "I'm interested in hearing what you both think regarding our people."

"Well, I don't know if you'll be through registration in time, Dr. Rohl . . ."

"We can complete that right now, Dr. Rohl. Your console is waiting."

Hiro imagined shooting the surveillance eye with a pulse rifle.

"What a small universe! I had no idea Saul expected to see someone here," Kylara said to Hiro, flashing her spectacular smile. Hiro blinked. How could he have forgotten this symbol of loveliness for even a nanosecond?

Hiro took Kylara's right hand in both of his. "I'm heartbroken, Inquisitor Roque, that I cannot show you to your suite. Duty calls. I shall get back to you as soon as I have examined your cryopods so we can discuss your patient, Odemwingo. I'm sure the station AI has someone suitable to show you to your suite."

"Not to worry, Dr. Al-Fadi. I have the perfect person for the job."

"And who might that be, *Nelson Mandela?*"

"I've asked Dr. Cech to show Inquisitor Roque to her suite and give her a small tour of the station. Chief Inspector Matthieu was so appreciative of the tour he gave her and Dr. Cech happens to be free at this very moment. He was delighted to volunteer his services."

"I'm sure he was," Hiro snarled. He bit down savagely on his tongue to prevent himself from cursing at the station AI. Uncouth, inappropriate, inane Dejan Cech appointed to take this paragon of the female species on a tour of the station?

Unbelievable!

Unacceptable!

Intolerable!

"Hello, Hiro. I didn't expect to find you here."

"Ah, Dr. Cech, so nice to see you," Hiro said, his face cracking into the sour semblance of a smile. "May I introduce to you Inquisitor Kylara Roque from the Planetary Exploration Bureau."

"Dejan Cech. A pleasure to meet you, Inquisitor Roque." The tall anesthetist performed a deep bow over her hand.

"Please, call me Kylara, Dr. Cech."

"Kylara, such a lovely name. I would be most honoured if you would address me as Dejan."

"Day-yawn," Kylara repeated with a smile.

"Music to my ears. Please excuse us, Hiro," Dejan said with a curt nod. He never once looked at Hiro. His eyes were glued to the face of the Inquisitor.

"I shall leave you in Dr. Cech's adequate company, Inquisitor Roque. Until later," Hiro said. He performed a deeper bow than the anesthetist. She didn't even notice.

"Thank you, Dr. Al-Fadi," Kylara said, but she was smiling at Dr. Cech as she said it. Hiro felt his guts writhe.

"Dejan." Hiro imagined jamming his fingers up his friend's hairy nostrils.

Decked out in his formal dress uniform, Sergeant Eden Rivera waited in a spartan waiting area off one of the Triage Bays. He was there to meet and greet the new Chief Inspector, who'd shipped in on one of the military transports.

Most merchant vessels, suppliers, traders, and civilian transports were being turned away from the station at the moment—due to the arrival of the variant Al-Fadi virus—though none were being advised of this. Other than a PEB ship on Conglomerate business, the only other ships having access to the *Nelson Mandela* were the Conglomerate's medical transports that carried the wounded in and the recuperated out. The new Security Chief had been forced to hitch a ride on one of these transports.

Eden knew nothing about the new Chief Inspector except that he was an older man with an impressive record and years of experience in many different settings. Most men his age had retired from active service long ago, taking up positions in management. Chief Inspector Hugo McFrenzy, on the other hand, was still doing work in the trenches. Eden hoped that was not a punishment, but a choice. He prayed McFrenzy would be easy to work with, a gentleman like Dr. Cech. He had his doubts. Nuscotia, the planet of McFrenzy's birth, had seen its share of brutal civil wars. Would someone from that background be inflexible and rigid? The man's advanced age increased his concerns.

Eden tried to block Chelsea from his thoughts. He could not allow his mind to drift there. He feared his mental walls might crack at even the mention of her name. The last thing he wanted was to be found weeping or snivelling when the new Chief Inspector appeared.

Loud banging, thumping, and inventive cursing came from beyond the Arrivals gate. It was as Eden feared; McFrenzy was a foul-mouthed tight-ass. He clamped his jaw, preparing himself for the worst.

An enormous, broad-shouldered man with large brown eyes, bronze-coloured skin, a trim black beard, and hair slicked back in a long ponytail stumbled through the gateway, loaded down with duffel bags, shoulder satchel, weapons holsters, space helmet, and what appeared to be a large fuchsia-coloured instrument case slung over one shoulder. He wore a camouflage-patterned space suit and an expression that made Eden's bowels spasm. The huge brick of a man scanned the reception area and his stormy gaze pounced on Eden.

Eden snapped to attention and saluted smartly.

"How the hell am I supposed to salute with all of this stuff in my hands, junior?" the burly man bellowed. "Where're all the 'bots? Why do I have to bring all of my gear in myself? What kind of lame joint is this?"

" . . . Chief Inspector Hugo McFrenzy?" Eden asked.

"Who else would be stupid enough to come here? I asked for a nice, quiet, peaceful place, out of the way somewhere, where I could spend the last years before my retirement with my feet up on a desk. Where do the bastards send me? Death Central! Damn those conniving scum. They don't want me to collect my big, fat pension that I've worked so hard for, do they?" The big man shot Eden a ferocious glare.

Eden madly searched for a response. "Ah . . . sorry?"

"Call me Foolish McFrenzy. On second thought, don't call me that. I'll deck you if you call me that." McFrenzy shambled forward, his shoulder satchels and pink case slowly sliding down his arms. "Who the hell are you and why are you dressed like that?"

"Sergeant Eden Rivera, sir," Eden said, raising his right hand again.

"Don't you dare."

Eden's hand wilted back to his side.

"Contrary to popular belief, we're not in the military. I don't like all that saluting crap. If you want to raise a hand, take some of my luggage. Here, take this and guard it with your life. I don't care about the rest of this stuff, but that is my prize possession. If anything happens to Roxanne, I'll have you flayed."

Eden ogled the human-sized, rose-pink, hourglass-shaped case that was thrust into his arms. Cradling it delicately, he hugged it to his chest as if it were a large child. His hands landed on two smooth cone-shaped, breast-like protuberances. If the Chief was going to shoot Eden, he'd have to blast through his case first.

"What is this, sir?"

"Take your hands off those! Have you no manners? Where were you born? Matter of fact, *when* were you born? No, don't tell me. I can see I'm going to be in charge of children. Have you never seen a guitar case before?" The huge man stared at Eden as if he were some new type of fungus.

"A guitar case, yes. Do you play guitar, Chief Inspector?"

"Of course not." Dark-brown eyes tried to scorch Eden's face.

Giggles interrupted their conversation. Half a dozen nurses came through the Arrivals portal. They all smiled suggestively at the Chief Inspector, sauntering up to him like a pride of lionesses. Each gave him a long, sensual kiss on the mouth. McFrenzy took his time. Eden could have sworn he heard deep-throated purring.

"See ya, Stormy," one said with a wink.

"Don't forget to call me, Stormy," another one whispered.

"Next time, don't make me beg, Stormy," a third one pouted.

McFrenzy snarled at the women, who all giggled and strutted away with swaying hips. Eden was now positive about the bass rumbling sound.

"What're you lookin' at?"

" . . . Stormy?" Eden raised his eyebrows.

"Shaddup and pay attention. That case you're fondling is custom-designed, lined with extra dura-alloy reinforcement that an extended pulse rifle blast couldn't pierce. It has heavy duty padding for added protection against jostling. The colour and shape was someone's idea of a joke." The look on McFrenzy's face made Eden fear for the health of the jokester.

"I see."

"She said this way I'd never forget her."

Eden shifted his hands from the breast-like projections.

"Don't you guys even have antigrav sleds around here?"

"We lost all of our androids, robots, antigrav sleds, and all working machinery in an EMP attack not long ago. The station's barely had time to get back on its feet. We're repairing the 'droids and 'bots as quickly as possible, but the nursing droids and medical robots have priority."

"Of course. Stupid of me to complain. You people have been through a shit-storm and I'm whining about carrying my own luggage. Sorry. I was gutted to hear about your previous CI. I knew her. She was a friend and one of our very best."

Eden bowed his head, struggling to stop the sudden appearance of moisture that filled his eyes. He clamped his teeth and just nodded.

McFrenzy was silent for a moment. He plunked all of his luggage down on the floor and stuck out a massive hand.

"Let's start over. I'm Hugo McFrenzy, your new Chief Inspector. It's a pleasure to meet you, Sergeant Rivera."

Eden blinked rapidly and shook the man's hand. "Eden."

"Eden. Is that like 'in the Garden of . . . '?"

"Yes."

"Well, I gotta say, this place smells like a Garden of Eden. I've been on a lot of space stations before and they usually reek until your nose becomes numb to it. Like millions of men's stinky, sweaty socks plus every other disgusting smell combined. This place smells like a stroll in the park. It smells . . . wonderful. Now don't get me wrong. I'm not a sissy. I can handle bad smells. I can certainly *make* bad smells. I've been accused of being a constant source, in fact. But this place smells . . . good." McFrenzy looked around, nodding his head, meaty hands on his hips. He inhaled a deep breath through his Roman nose and exhaled.

"The great smell is probably due to Plant Thing," Eden said.

"Plant Thing?"

"Let us get you registered with the station and I'll explain."

"Can Plant Thing carry luggage?" Hugo picked up his fallen duffel bags and satchels.

"I can ask."

Eden managed to find a working antigrav stretcher to carry all of McFrenzy's belongings while the man went through registration. Eden did not relinquish the guitar case for fear of it incurring any damage. He asked *Nelson Mandela* what 'flayed' meant and was horrified at the answer. He did not want to get on McFrenzy's bad side; his good side was frightening enough. Eden waited while the man changed out of his spacesuit.

When McFrenzy strode out of the change room, he was clad in a collared, long-sleeved, white shirt, black gornhide trousers, black grip-boots, and a black Security vest. For a man supposedly in his tenth decade, he looked remarkably fit with broad chest, massive arms, and minimal belly fat. His straight, dark eyebrows shaded alert, piercing eyes and his square jaw could have cleaved stone.

"I see you're taking excellent care of my instrument case."

"Yes, sir."

"Don't look like you're enjoying that case so much. Roxanne is mine."

"Your guitar is called Roxanne?"

"No, Roxanne's the name of the case you're fondling."

Eden almost dropped the case. "I'm not . . ."

"It's all right, Rivera. I'm a sadistic bastard. Now, what's this malarky I hear about you refusing a promotion? Why don't you want to be anything higher than a sergeant? What have you got against money, prestige, status, and a bigger pension?" McFrenzy studied Eden with one thick eyebrow cocked.

Eden shrugged.

" . . . Been reading all of these exemplary reports from your previous CIs plus a Dr. Cech. They all think you're a miracle worker that should've stepped into CI a long time ago. Why haven't you?"

"Don't want it," Eden blurted.

"Why not? Is there something about this job that I should know? Why're all the CIs dropping like rain? Will I have a target painted on my back?"

"I don't know. All I do know is, I don't deserve the job. As you say, all of the CIs I've assisted have died. Why should I be promoted for that?" Eden could not keep the bitterness out of his voice. He couldn't meet McFrenzy's eyes. He found himself blinking and shaking.

A stinging slap between his shoulder blades almost bowled him over.

"You did your best, kid. Now, buck up. You'll do an even better job with me or I'll kill you."

Eden blinked at the man.

" . . . I should've saved her. I didn't get to her in time. She'd be alive . . ."

"Tongue dung."

Eden's mouth sagged open.

McFrenzy wrapped his arm around Eden's shoulders. "From what I read, CI Matthieu flew out a hole blown in the station's hull by an escaping ship. She got sucked out with the atmosphere. You couldn't have prevented that, you idiot. If you'd been attached to her, you'd have been lost too.

"Look, I need a second-in-command and that person has to be you. Since I'm Chief Inspector, you have to be Inspector. It's that simple. You can't be a Sergeant under me; that won't do. You'll just have to accept the pay raise. You don't want it? Tough. I don't want to hear any complaining about all the money you don't know what to do with. Deal with it. When you finally decide you *are* ready for my job, come talk to me. If I'm not able to collect my pension, you may have to wait a bit, but if I can, you're welcome to the job. You can even arrange a retirement party for me."

"Why are you telling me this?"

"Because I can and I want the target off my back. No one seems able to promote you but I've got the hutzpah and I get things done. They don't call me McFrenzy the Efficient for nothing."

"They call you that?"

"No. It was a joke, Rivera. And don't get all mushy and grateful and start thanking me."

"No worries there."

McFrenzy frowned at Eden. " . . . You're welcome."

"Let's get Roxanne to your room before you come up with any other marvellous ideas," Eden muttered.

McFrenzy grunted but one side of his mouth curled upwards. "You know, Rivera? You're a strange one."

"Me?" Eden blurted.

"Don't worry. I can work with strange. I've worked with strange before. Strange isn't bad; it's just different. But don't get *too* strange, Rivera. I like to believe I understand my people. A person who doesn't want to make more credit, well, I don't really get that. Makes me wonder what's motivating you. Makes me think suspicious things like, 'Are you getting something on the side?' Or what if you're one of those crazy, idealistic dudes who can be slap-down scary. I don't like to think suspicious thoughts about my Number Two, Rivera, so . . . keep a lid on the strangeness. Okay?"

"I shall do my best, Chief Inspector," Eden said, staring at McFrenzy over the top of the fuchsia-coloured, woman-shaped Roxanne, while wondering what McFrenzy's definition of normal was.

"No one out-stranges me, Rivera. Got it?"

"Wouldn't dare, sir."

"Good man."

Eden led McFrenzy into the corridor leading to the Concourse. The Concourse was a hubbub of activity. The crowd was moving in every direction, each person intent on their various missions. A green tendril shot out of the crowd to dangle grapes in front of McFrenzy's and Eden's noses.

McFrenzy had his blaster out in an eye blink, aiming at the grapes.

"What the fup is this?" McFrenzy boomed, staring a cluster of eyeballs, eye-to-eyes.

"This is Plant Thing, Chief Inspector . . . or rather, a small segment of Plant Thing. It's offering you some grapes," Eden said.

"Contrary to what you may believe, Number Two, I actually know what grapes look like. I want to know what is holding them up, where it came from, why is it here in this Concourse where there are so many people, including children, and why, in Hell, is it offering me grapes?" The end of McFrenzy's last sentence almost ended in a squeak.

"Plant Thing's our resident plant alien, Chief Inspector. Don't worry. Plant Thing's perfectly safe. It provides the station with most of our fruits and vegetables as well as much of our oxygen. It's the reason our air quality is so amazing. Plant Thing is very friendly and understands what you're saying. I believe you might have frightened it." Several clusters of eyes now watched the new Chief Inspector from a wary distance, the grapes withdrawn.

"This is the new Chief Inspector, Plant Thing. His name is Hugo McFrenzy," Eden said.

"You're talking to plant vines, Rivera. Remember what I said about acting 'strange'?"

The plant tendrils came forward and offered McFrenzy a huge bouquet of roses.

The Chief Inspector looked astonished as he accepted the bouquet. Out of the corner of his mouth, he asked, "Does it think I'm a woman?"

"I believe it's simply being welcoming."

"Good. I don't want it thinking I'm a woman. I'd rather go for a nice, crispy apple. You know, man-like macho food. I don't like grapes. Too many seeds."

Every different variety of apple was now on display, dangling in front of McFrenzy's face.

"Whoa, I only need one apple. Which one is the crispiest, juiciest, slightly tart yet succulently sweet apple here?"

All of the different apples bobbed up and down, forward and back, until a brilliant red, flawless specimen was hesitantly offered up.

McFrenzy reached up to grab it and stopped. "You're sure?" he asked the eyeballs. "You're positive this is the one?"

The red apple was whipped away and all of the apples began bobbing up and down again, almost shivering on their branches. Finally, a golden apple was thrust forward slowly, dangling on its stalk before the new Chief Inspector's nose. McFrenzy reached up and peered at the closest cluster of eyeballs.

"You're sure this time? Absolutely positive, without one iota of doubt?" he asked, reaching for the shiny apple. "I want the best."

The golden apple was snatched, at the last second, out of McFrenzy's hand. He made a grimace. All of the tendrils seemed to wilt. A small child ran up and grabbed the gold apple. She chomped into it and juice sprayed everywhere.

"Hey, you stole my apple," McFrenzy said to her. "I wanted that one."

The little girl looked at McFrenzy, sniffed her nose at him, and ran off.

"Who allowed those annoying things on my station?" he asked Eden.

"What, the apples?"

"No, the midget humans," McFrenzy snapped. Eden shook his head.

On offer now was a glistening deep red apple. McFrenzy snatched at it before Plant Thing could withdraw it. He held it in his right fist, well away from Plant Thing's tendrils, and said, "You're sure?"

The vines all shivered. McFrenzy opened his mouth wide and took a huge bite of the fruit. His eyes nearly popped out of their sockets. Juice ran down through his beard as he chewed.

"OH . . . MY . . . COJONES! This is the *best* apple I've ever tasted. I'd even dare say that this is the best piece of food I've ever eaten. Have I died and gone to Nirvana? If you created this delectable piece of fruit, Plant Alien, thank you."

"Plant *Thing*," Eden corrected.

The clusters of eyes on all of the tendrils bounced up and down and jiggled. McFrenzy devoured the apple and began harvesting quite a few more, which he stuck in his duffel bags.

"Don't worry, Chief Inspector. There's a lot more where those came from," Eden said.

"Does everything off of Plant Thing taste as good as this apple?' McFrenzy asked, his arms now full of apples.

"I believe so."

"I'm in heaven. Hallelujah . . . By the way, what's going on here, anyway?"

"Everyone on the station is getting immunized against the variant Al-Fadi virus that was recently brought to the station. You'd better get immunized, Chief Inspector, since we're here."

"Have you been immunized?" McFrenzy asked.

"Yes, everyone in Security's already been vaccinated."

"Well . . . did it hurt?" McFrenzy asked.

"Terribly."

"Thought so. Maybe we should pass on the immunization. The lineup's too long."

"As the new Chief Inspector, you move to the front of the line. Station AI's orders. Everyone's getting done, even the little babies."

"What do I have to do?"

"Stand there and hold out your arm," Eden said.

"You said it hurt."

"I was joking."

"You're demoted back to Private, Rivera."

"I was a Sergeant before."

"Then you'll know better next time."

Grace had finally left the operating room. It had been a gruelling shift. Four operations on four different animal adaptations: tiger, wolf, polar bear, gorilla. Limb replacements with bioprostheses for the most part and the majority due to combat trauma. The last patient had required both lower limbs replaced due to an industrial accident. Bud had assisted Grace with all of the operations and as soon as they were done, he'd raced off to his lab to ensure there was enough vaccine for everyone. Grace was on her way to one of the vaccination sites when she received first a message from *Nelson Mandela,* followed by a message from Dr. Al-Fadi, ordering her to meet him in the Level Six Quarantine section.

Grace checked her wristcomp twice. She'd not thought of Saul Rohl for a very long time. She smiled. He'd been a tall, handsome, idealistic young man full of confidence when she'd known him. She'd been a very serious medical student with ambitions of becoming a surgeon. They'd been very young when they knew each other and had had different goals. Grace looked forward to seeing Saul again and exchanging stories. That would have to be after whatever was waiting for her in Level Six Quarantine. Grace shuddered. Whatever was brought there was never good.

She hurried down the corridor, stretching her neck and arching her lower back. Her eyes felt like there were tiny bits of sand in them. She yawned repeatedly, working to get some moisture back into them. She brushed her hands back through her hair to get the strands out of her eyes and wished she could give her mouth a rinse. Up ahead in the corridor, she spotted her father.

"Hi, Alex," she said, hurrying up to him. She slowed her steps as she saw the expression on his face. She tipped her head to the side in concern. He definitely looked distressed.

Although Alex was her biological father, he looked more like her brother. In her mind, her adoptive father would always be her true 'Dad' but Grace was delighted that Alex had come into her life.

There was such a look of disapproval on Alex's face that Grace's feet came to a stop. Her eyes widened. She'd never seen him look at her with such an expression before. His face was red and his eyes seemed particularly glacial, as he stood with his legs spread and his arms crossed. He looked as if he'd found out Grace was a serial killer. Grace felt her eyebrows rising.

"Grace," Alex snapped, his tone making Grace jerk, "we need to talk."

"I'm sorry, Alex. I can't right now," Grace said, now frowning at his tone. "Dr. Al-Fadi has ordered me to meet him on the quarantine level. We'll have to talk later."

"I don't care what you have to do. We need to talk. *Now.*" Alex drew himself up to his full height and placed himself in her way.

Grace reflexively drew herself up to her full height and stared her father straight in the eyes. "You have three minutes," she said, steel in her voice.

"Not here," Alex said, glancing at the people eying them curiously as they passed.

"It'll have to be here and now because I don't have time for anything else," Grace said. "What seems to be the problem?"

Alex's mouth formed a grimace. "Bud is an android."

Grace blinked a few times and waited.

"Yes?"

"You will not associate with that . . . that thing, anymore," Alex said, his voice harsh. He said 'thing' as if it was the most disgusting word in his vocabulary.

Grace sucked air. Her face felt like it had been ignited into flames. She stared at Alex, realizing that she really knew him not at all.

"*WHAT?*" Her voice cracked like a whip. People walking by froze.

"You and that android. It's disgusting, perverted. I'll not permit it."

"You'll not . . . ?"

Grace was panting. She could not have been more shocked if Alex had stepped up and punched her in the gut. Her heart pounded like it wanted out of her chest. She took a couple of deep breaths, struggling to stay calm.

"I don't know what you've heard, Alex, but I owe that android my life many times over. Bud is the best surgeon I have ever worked with, the most brilliant being I have ever known, and the most caring and compassionate individual I have ever had the honour to have met. I'll continue to work with him and befriend him whether you approve of it or not. If you cannot tolerate my association with Bud, this is the last conversation we need have."

Grace stepped around Alex and stalked off, her entire body vibrating. She imagined steam spewing from her ears and nostrils. She would not give that antiquated sperm donor, who thought he could walk into her life and order her around, the satisfaction of seeing her upset.

Alex called after her but she kept on walking. She refused to look back. She would not allow this bigot, even if he was her biological father, to step into her life and dictate her behaviour. As far as Grace was concerned, her friendship with Bud was far more important than any sperm donor.

Grace stomped along, her vision out of focus while her mind raced. Her inner voice kept up a constant stream of curses until her face smacked into an immovable mass, and Grace found herself bouncing backwards. She was apologizing, mid-ricochet, as strong hands grabbed her to prevent her from falling.

"Hey, Doc. You know, you really ought to watch where you're going. You could get hurt crashing into solid muscle like me."

Grace looked up into the grinning tiger face of Damien Lamont and snorted, followed swiftly by her covering her nose with her hands.

"Funny how I have that effect on you," Damien said. "I'm starting to get a complex. You blowing stuff out of your nose every time you see me."

"I didn't break my nose. I simply need to blow it."

"Not all over me, please. Lucky for you, I have started carrying tissues for damsels in distress." Damien pulled a sheet from a pocket and handed it to Grace between shiny steel talons. "You look like you wanted to kill someone, Doc. Do you want me to handle it for you?"

"No," Grace said quickly, blowing her nose with a honk. "I'll handle it."

"Did he hurt you? Let me at him."

"Don't be ridiculous."

"You're charging around the station, not looking where you're going, banging straight into me, and I'm ridiculous? Some people may do that on a regular basis but not you, Doc. Something has upset you. Is it something we should all be worried about?"

"What? *No.* There's nothing you need to be alarmed about, Captain. This is . . . personal."

"Do you need someone to talk to? I'm a good listener and I owe you. You've been a good listener for me," Damien said, his voice gentle.

Shaking her head, Grace buried her face in the tissue again. She was not going to think about Alex. She was not.

"Not too many women can look attractive while they blow their nose, Doc, but you pull it off. Just barely, but nevertheless, I'm smitten. Make me your love slave."

Grace rolled her eyes. "I know you're completely devoted to Delia, so zip it."

Damien grinned at the mention of Delia. "You saved Delia's life. I'd do anything to help you, Doc. If you need a friend, an ear, I'm here for you."

"Bud saved Delia. I merely watched . . . in complete awe." Grace shook her head. She found herself sharing what Alex had said about Bud. Damien's face became solemn.

"I'm almost seventy to eighty percent artificial now. Am I human anymore? Would I be unacceptable to your father because I'm only twenty percent human or because I'm a tiger, a biomechanical, genetically-modified, animal-adapted man? It's a new age. Your father hasn't caught up yet. Give him time, Doc. He only just woke up."

"Alex is not my father," Grace snapped. "He was only the sperm donor. My real father was a wonderfully accepting man, who would have loved Bud for the amazing being he is. I have no other father."

"Well, Doc, I may not be Bud, but I can be your friend. I'm here for you. If you need an ear to listen, a shoulder to cry on, or a tissue to blow snot in, you just whistle."

Grace felt strong furry arms wrap around her and she squeezed back. "Thanks."

"You might not say that after you get my bill."

Grace hurried into the Level Six Quarantine Section, already clad in a Level Six containment suit, helmet engaged. She'd had no time to make herself presentable. Her anger simmered beneath the surface.

She spotted Dr. Al-Fadi standing beside a tall, broad-shouldered figure. Both were clad in Level Six containment suits, as well. The suit Saul wore accentuated his physique and the sight of him made Grace's shoulders tighten. She felt an ache in her temples.

Saul turned towards her and his face broke into a huge smile. His hazel eyes, framed in long lashes, widened and he looked at Grace with such longing and delight, that Grace felt her entire body go rigid. She fought the urge to turn and walk away. Instead, she inhaled deeply and told herself to be calm. She approached the two men.

"It's so good to see you again, Grace," Saul said, reaching out his right hand. She gazed through his visor and her eyes widened. Saul had aged much less than she had. He barely looked any different from the last time she'd seen him, except that he'd filled out across the chest and shoulders. She, on the other hand, now had lines on her face that had not been there the last time he'd seen her.

Time dilation sucks, Grace thought.

"It's good to see you, too, Saul," Grace said, shaking the offered hand. The explorer wrapped his arms around Grace, giving her a tight embrace.

"You look marvellous, Grace," Saul said, his hands clutching both of her upper arms as if he would never let her go.

Grace felt a spasm above her left eye. "No I don't, Saul, but it's kind of you to say so."

"I wouldn't say it, if I didn't mean it," the tall explorer said, still holding on to her.

"Ahem. Maybe you two can do this later . . . in private? Right now, we've some cryopods to examine," Hiro said.

Grace pulled out of Saul's grasp, her face glowing like a sunspot. She now recalled why she'd had to get away from Saul. He'd been very nice, very handsome, very attentive, but way too clingy. She'd always felt the need to get away from Saul whenever she was with him, simply to breathe and have her own space. Those feelings were flooding back like a tsunami, as Saul hovered too close to her.

"Let's look at these cryopods you've brought us, Dr. Rohl," Hiro said. He led them towards the airlock that would give them access to the Quarantine chamber.

"Before the Al-Fadi virus epidemic, we brought all cryopods into the Triage area and screened them all the same way. We were supposed to wear containment suits but weren't that diligent in taking precautions. Now, if there is any hint of a dangerous pathogen, the incoming cryopods are isolated right away to this Quarantine section and staff inspecting them must be suited up in these special suits. We will go through decontamination before leaving this area."

"Of course, Dr. Al-Fadi," Saul said. "This Quarantine facility is impressive."

The three doctors had to go through an examination ensuring that their suits had no leaks and that their oxygen supply was fully filtered before entering the airlock. Once the atmosphere was pumped out of the airlock, the doors to the quarantine section would open, allowing them access to the cryopods.

Approaching the closest cryopod marked with the PEB logo, Hiro gestured to Grace and Saul. "Let's look at this first one."

The three doctors crowded around the nearest cryopod and examined the readout together. They scrolled down the screen, looking at all of the data.

"Well, other than the damaged heart, there doesn't appear to be anything else wrong with this woman. No invasive organisms. No abnormal chemistry. No toxins. No foreign bodies. No mysterious inhalants. No unusual trauma except for her heart," Grace said.

"And this is how every single one of these readouts looks," Saul said.

They moved on to each of the cryopods, confirming Saul's statement.

"All of your explorers seemed to be in the best of health other than the odd old healed fracture and the obvious damage to their hearts. We can replace the ruptured hearts and study the pathology to determine what caused the damage. Hopefully we can deduce the cause," Hiro said. "What kind of trauma would only rupture the heart and nothing else?"

"Was anything seen on the surveillance videos?" Grace asked.

"Nothing obvious," Saul said.

"Are there recordings of the explorers' blood pressures immediately before their hearts ruptured? Were the explorers' suits actively monitoring their vitals at all times?" Grace asked.

"Yes," Saul said. "Their blood pressures rose dramatically seconds before the ruptures." He began pressing the scroll buttons on the cryopod display.

"You'd think if they experienced a massive surge in blood pressure just before their hearts ruptured, they'd have also experienced intracranial bleeds or aortic ruptures," Hiro said. "There's no evidence of those."

"Look here. The blood pressure readings are normal until only a few milliseconds before the cryo program is activated. Then the blood pressure reads . . . No, that can't be right. That's impossible," Saul said.

"What does it read?" Hiro asked.

"Four hundred over two-fifty."

"Ridiculous. That has to be a mistake."

"Let's check another cryopod," Grace suggested.

They checked all twelve. In every instance, the cryosuit recorded normal blood pressures until only a few seconds before the heart ruptured. The blood pressure readings rose to impossible values, followed by a sudden plummet that corresponded to the heart bursting.

"I've never seen blood pressure readings of four hundred over two fifty. That's physically impossible," Hiro said. "The human body is incapable of producing that sort of pressure."

"Which is why their hearts burst?" Grace offered.

"Did you hear me, Dr. Grace? The human heart cannot generate that kind of pressure. Period. The contractile cardiac muscle cannot produce a pressure that high. It's as if some external force came along and squeezed their hearts until they burst," Hiro said.

"The surveillance recordings do not show these explorers being attacked by anything, but all of the cryosuits show the same blood pressure spikes, almost simultaneously," Saul said. "Whatever it was, they all experienced the phenomenon together."

"Some of the BP surges seemed to have started a little earlier than the others. These three women seem to have the earliest spikes: Lieutenant Eyami, Corporal Grubinskaya, and Corporal Nagasaki. The others show changes in their blood pressure several seconds or up to a minute later. It would be interesting to know where each of these people were situated, in relation to the first three women affected. What were the three doing? Did this phenomenon spread outwards from a central blast?"

"I'll have the station AI analyze where they all were and what they were doing," Saul said.

"You're assuming that these BP readings are correct, Dr. Grace. I caution you in believing them. It's possible that whatever killed the explorers may have affected their suits too. Perhaps these BP readings are all artificial and when we open these patients up, we'll find a different situation than what is indicated on these cryopod readouts," Hiro said.

"Do you want us to try to scan through the cryopods?" Grace asked.

"No, we'll scan in the OR. Let's just take one of these explorers to the operating room and replace the damaged heart. See what else we find when we're in there."

"According to blood and tissue type, this third patient here could accept a vat-grown heart that is already fully grown and in stock," Grace said, checking the station's organ inventory on her wristcomp. "We can replace the heart of this explorer whenever *Nelson Mandela* can find us a free operating room."

"M1 OR 7 can be set up for 0800 hours. I must find an anesthetist for you, however."

"Don't ask Dr. Cech," Hiro shouted. Grace jerked and turned to stare at her boss.

" . . . Ah, he's still recovering from his operation," Hiro muttered, avoiding Grace's gaze.

"Dr. Darwin has consented to perform the anesthesia."

"Excellent," Dr. Al-Fadi said. "Make sure he understands he has to wear his Level Six containment suit."

"Dr. Darwin is not fond of wearing his containment suit."

"Tell him he must wear it. We don't know what we're dealing with, so we must all wear protection."

"I shall inform him of your orders."

"Thank you," Hiro said.

"I'd like to attend the operation, if I may," Saul said. "As an observer only, of course."

"You'll have to wear a Level Six containment suit as well. There are sterilizing units in the change rooms. If you meet me in the M1 Level change room before 0730 hours, I can show you where everything is. I must say, Dr. Rohl, I'm anxious to open up one of these cryopods and see what we're dealing with."

"Nothing too surprising, I hope." Grace thought about the last PEB patient they'd opened up. Hiro shot her a look.

"What exactly are you concerned about?" Saul asked, looking at Grace and Hiro.

"Anything and everything," Hiro said quickly, scowling at Grace.

"Expect the unexpected," Saul said, nodding.

Hiro's glance could have skewered Grace's eye.

"What are you doing after this, Grace?" Saul asked, a smile blossoming on his face.

"I have to go to an immunization site, Saul. I was scheduled to go there before I got the call from Dr. Al-Fadi to meet him here. I'm supposed to relieve someone and they won't be very happy with me for being delayed. I'm sorry. I'm sure *Nelson Mandela* can find someone else to show you around the medical station."

"I'd rather it be you, Grace. We could catch up on old times." The explorer had a slight whine to his voice that made Grace's eyelid twitch.

"I'd like to, Saul, but I can't." Grace attempted to look sad.

"Dr. Lord, someone else will do your shift at the immunization site. You are now free to take Dr. Rohl for a tour around me."

"Ah ha, thank you, *Nelson Mandela*," Grace said, wanting to kick the AI.

Saul's face lit up. "Excellent."

"I will send Dr. Rohl's room number and directions to your wristcomp, Dr. Lord. His suite is not far from yours. After your decontamination, you can guide Dr. Rohl to his quarters."

"Wonderful," Grace drawled.

'Hey, 'dro.'
'Yes, Chuck Yeager?*'*
'Bad news.'
'Now what?'

'I don't know how to tell you this, but . . .'

'But what, Chuck Yeager?'

'Well, it's about Grace . . .'

'Grace? Is she all right? Is she hurt? Is she in danger?'

'That all depends . . .'

'What's happening with Grace, Chuck Yeager!'

'There's this PEB Explorer that is an old friend of Dr. Lord's who's arrived on the station. He's shaking her hand, hugging her, smiling at her a lot, and touching her shoulder. She's supposed to show him his room, which is located close to hers. Nelson Mandela has arranged free time for Grace to take this dude on a tour of the medical station. Dr. Al-Fadi said for them to go find some privacy. I thought you should know.'

'. . . 'Dro?'

'. . . 'Dro? Ha, I thought that would get him.'

Grace and Saul were exiting the Level Six Quarantine Sector after finally completing the decontamination process. They'd changed out of their containment suits and were heading to the monorail when Bud appeared by Grace's side.

"Bud!" Grace jumped in surprise.

"Hello, Grace." Bud smiled at Grace, then stared at her companion.

"Bud, I'd like to introduce you to Dr. Saul Rohl. Dr. Rohl and I were friends during our early medical training. We graduated from the same medical school class. When I decided to go into surgery, Saul went into xenobiology."

"It is a pleasure to meet you, Dr. Rohl." Bud bowed deeply.

"It's a pleasure to meet you, Bud." Saul nodded.

"Bud is the most gifted surgeon I've ever worked with." Grace beamed at Bud as she said this.

"Trained by *me*, of course," Hiro said, coming up behind them all. "Dr. Grace, I resent what you said, even though I know it's true and have seen it for myself. I'm disappointed that you do not say I'm the most gifted surgeon you've ever worked with."

"You are, of course, the most gifted *human* surgeon I've ever worked with, Dr. Al-Fadi." Grace felt her entire skin glowing.

Hiro sighed. "I suppose that'll have to do. Imagine having to take a back seat to one's own creation. Ah, the pangs of being a parent. To see one's own offspring outstrip oneself. It is bittersweet, to be surpassed, outclassed, eclipsed, and outdone by one's protégé. There's nothing left for me to do but ... take my leave.

"Dr. Rohl, I leave you in the very capable hands of Dr. Grace and Bud. I go in search of your colleague, Kylara Roque, to rescue her from the interminable boredom of my colleague. We have much to discuss and I pray she is still awake."

An alarmed expression appeared on Saul's face. His hazel eyes grew enormous. He grabbed Hiro, pulling the small surgeon towards himself while pointing.

"What is it, Dr. Rohl?" Hiro yelped as he flew off his feet.

Bundles of colourful flowers of numerous varieties on green tendrils launched at Dr. Al-Fadi.

"Gah! Get away! You were supposed to stay away. Didn't I tell you I wanted privacy?" Hiro barked at Plant Thing. He scurried off down the corridor.

Grace bit her lip as Plant Thing flowed after Hiro.

"What in space is that?" Saul stared at the green limbs gliding by.

"Plant Thing, our resident plant symbiont."

"Resident plant symbiont?" Saul echoed, his eyes enormous. "Is this something new?Aren't you worried for Dr. Al-Fadi?"

"Oh no," Grace said. "Plant Thing adores Dr. Al-Fadi. It wants to keep its eyes on him at all times to make sure he's safe and does not get injured. Plant Thing saved Dr. Al-Fadi's life and now worries about his welfare a bit too enthusiastically. Dr. Al-Fadi will be speaking to the Inquisitor about Plant Thing. It has been an amazing addition to this station."

Saul watched the plant vines flow by. "Dr. Al-Fadi didn't seem thrilled by its attention."

"I've told Plant Thing to give Dr. Al-Fadi some privacy but sometimes Plant Thing forgets."

"You *told* Plant Thing to stay away?"

"Yes, Plant Thing understands language. I'll explain as we walk."

After Grace had finished with her tale, Saul said, "This is incredible."

"It is hard to believe without seeing it."

"Did the explorer survive?"

"Unfortunately, no."

"But you allowed the plant alien to survive?"

"It formed a symbiotic relationship with Dr. Eric Glasgow, one of our surgeons. The station AI said it could not destroy a being that was melded with a human."

"You say the station has benefitted from this plant alien?"

"Symbiont," Grace insisted. "Dr. Glasgow exists within Plant Thing which is why Plant Thing understands language."

A tendril bearing large, glistening, red apples came towards Saul and dangled them before him. Saul looked to Grace for guidance.

<Plant Thing, this apple does not contain any special cells, does it?>

<no friend grace>

<Good>

Grace nodded encouragingly. Saul plucked an apple and bit into it. Surprise and delight, danced across his features as he sucked hungrily at the juice from the fruit. He chewed slowly, his eyes half-closed. He sighed.

"I don't think I've ever tasted anything so delicious before. This apple is exquisite. It's like every pleasure centre in my brain has lit up. This apple doesn't contain any psychoactive chemicals, does it?"

"No, Dr. Rohl," Bud said. "Everything has been analyzed and found to contain no harmful substances. Plant Thing provides much of the fruits and vegetables to the inhabitants of this station now. There is no need for concern."

"Perhaps I should apply to work here, so I can partake of this fruit on a regular basis," Saul said. He was smiling at Grace as he said it.

Bud did not like the look Dr. Rohl was giving Grace. He definitely was not happy with the idea of this explorer wanting to take up residence on the *Nelson Mandela*. Was this what jealousy felt like? Bud fought an urge to place himself directly between Grace and Dr. Rohl.

He followed the two doctors down the corridor in the opposite direction from the one Dr. Al-Fadi took. Every time Dr. Rohl reached up to touch Grace, Bud was there, staring at the man until Rohl dropped his hand. Grace was talking, not noticing what Bud was doing, but Bud and Dr. Rohl were eying each other intently.

Bud decided it might be best if he did not leave Grace's side while Dr. Rohl was on the station.

Hiro found Dejan and Kylara in the art gallery on the outer ring of the station. The two were animatedly discussing a holographic sculpture that expanded and contracted every few minutes to reveal a different configuration of colour and shape, supposedly influenced by the emotions and moods of the viewers. The sculpture was a swirling, cavorting kaleidoscope of vivid pink, coral, and lavender swirls with a slight hint of deeper rose. Dejan and Kylara were debating whose mood and personality were most influencing the sculpture.

"These colours are too beautiful, too vibrant, too joyous for my old grey self, Kylara. I'm positive it's your glorious personality that this sculpture is imbibing and projecting. Yet all of these stunning colours are inadequate reflections of your true beauty," Dejan said.

"I disagree," the Inquisitor said. "You're a man who spends his life saving people. What could be more beautiful than that? I'm sure the beauty of this sculpture reflects your inner goodness and compassion."

Dejan smiled but his expression changed as Hiro marched up.

"Believe me, Inquisitor Roque, there's nothing beautiful about this man whatsoever," Hiro announced. "I work with him far too much and he's never brightened up a single one of my days."

"Ah, Hiro, you're back. Rather like reflux. Unfortunate, uncomfortable, and unwelcome," Dejan said.

"Inspector Roque, I'm glad to see that you're still awake. I've completed my duties and can now rescue you from the interminable ennui caused by being with Dr. Cech. I'm happy to take over the tour of the station, Dejan. The Inquisitor and I have very important things to discuss."

The emotion sculpture contracted and shot outwards in a violent explosion of a thousand black and green jagged shards. The centre of the sculpture was a dense black shadow that roiled and bubbled. Kylara and Dejan both stepped away from it, their eyes widening.

"Oh my. I wonder whose mood is influencing this sculpture right now?" Kylara said.

"I wonder." Dejan shot a raised eyebrow at Hiro.

Kylara turned to Hiro. "Dejan has been giving me a delightful tour of the *Nelson Mandela*. I hope you don't mind but I'd really like for him to continue. He's so full of interesting stories and amusing anecdotes. I'm having so much fun. This medical space station is an absolute wonder."

"Yes, it is," Hiro forced through gritted teeth.

The sculpture contracted and exploded again, this time an even darker green, resembling a massive shattering crystal, with black blades swooshing throughout, their scything actions taking on a more sinister dance. A brilliant silver streak appeared within the sculpture and repeatedly slashed downwards through the tourmaline, onyx, and jade onto the central squat shadow.

Dejan's eyes bulged.

"Ah ha, Kylara, why don't you and Hiro have your discussion now. I can complete your tour afterwards. We can meet up with my wife, Sierra, for dinner," Dejan said, backing quickly away from the sculpture.

"That would be lovely, Dejan," Kylara said. She enclosed the anesthetist in a warm hug and gave him a peck on the cheek. Dejan winked at Hiro.

"I'll be in touch, Kylara," Dejan said with a deep bow.

"But I thought I could take you out to dinner," Hiro said, hating the fact that his voice sounded so whiny. There was now black smoke coiling through the holographic sculpture. It resembled a growing, green and black cumulonimbus cloud, threatening to unleash a hailstorm.

"Perhaps we'd best move away from this artwork before it starts to pelt us with ice pellets," Dejan said. He gently took Kylara's hand and slipped it through the crook of his elbow. He strolled quickly away towards the exit. Hiro scurried behind.

"Where shall we have our discussion, Dr. Al-Fadi?" Kylara asked, glancing over her shoulder.

"I believe my office would be best, Inquisitor Roque. And please, call me Hiro."

As the three of them exited the art gallery, Dejan bowed low and kissed the back of Kylara's hand. "Until later, Kylara," he said. He turned to Hiro and bowed.

"Hiro."

Hiro fought the urge to bop his friend on the back of his bald head.

"Dejan."

Wherever Hiro and Kylara went, green vines followed. Bouquets of fragrant blooms were thrust towards Kylara and she exclaimed in delight. Delectable fruits were also offered. Clusters of pale green eyeballs followed their every move.

"Dejan has told me quite a bit about Plant Thing," Kylara said. "Did it really save this space station and your life?"

"Yes and yes. When this station was hit with a powerful EMP blast, the station AI, as well as every piece of operating equipment that had a current running through its circuitry got fried. We had no power for life support, heating, oxygen production, water, food—pretty much everything. Bud was the only android to recover from the EMP blast. He was able to get the station AI back on line and the power generators back running but Plant Thing reached out to all regions of the station to provide oxygen, food, and bioluminescent light to everyone stranded in the dark. Prior to that moment, no one knew Plant Thing existed, except Bud and the station AI.

"Plant Thing appeared like the Garden of Eden to most of the people helpless in the blackness. It saved many lives that day, including mine. If Plant Thing had not found me and alerted Bud to my dire predicament, I would have died. I owe a great debt to Plant Thing and am grateful that it is here."

Hiro palmed the access pad to the door to his office and motioned for the Inquisitor to enter. Kylara surveyed the furnishings and nodded.

"You have a nice office, Hiro."

"Thank you, Kylara. Please, have a seat." A chair rose before his desk. "What I have to tell you about your explorer involves Plant Thing. I'm glad you've gotten a chance to see it and its interaction with the people of this station. I'd like you to remember that when you see the recording I'm about to show you.

"My explorer?" Kylara frowned.

"When the PEB sent your explorer to this station, I was dealing with a murderer on board. I asked a surgeon, Dr. Eric Glasgow, along with Dr. Grace Lord and Bud to examine your explorer for me. I then planned to get back to you with the results. Unfortunately I became incapacitated. The recording I'm going to show you now is the replay of the examination by Dr. Glasgow and company."

Kylara stayed silent until the alien exploded from the explorer's abdomen. She jumped as she watched the plant alien tear Glasgow, Vanacan, and Evra to pieces. She gasped after witnessing Bud hurl Grace through a set of closing lockdown doors. When the plant tendril delved into Eric Glasgow's skull and pleaded for help, Kylara's jaw dropped. Hiro ended the recording with the frozen pieces of the plant alien being placed in a storage container by Bud and the cargo droids.

Kylara's mouth formed into a grim line. "This alien is now Plant Thing?"

"Plant Thing is a symbiont formed from the fusion of the plant alien with Dr. Eric Glasgow's brain. Plant Thing understands what we say, presumably from the knowledge it has from Eric Glasgow. It knows things it cannot possibly know unless it has truly fused with the surgeon. It shows great remorse over the death of the explorer and the others."

"You expect me to believe this recording?"

"Inquisitor, your explorer did not survive unless he too exists within Plant Thing. I apologize for not responding to your inquiries sooner. We've been through many hardships since that event and I've been personally incapacitated through much of it. I'm glad that you've come personally to see Plant Thing for yourself, because it would've been difficult to explain all the complexities of this case in a report, no matter how well written."

"How could you have allowed this alien to survive after it tore three humans apart?"

"The station AI could not destroy it since the alien had formed a symbiotic relationship with Dr. Glasgow."

"But look at it now. It's enormous! If it decides to, it could destroy every single person on this station."

"It has promised not to harm another human being. It didn't know what humans were when it was released from your explorer's abdomen. It had somehow been ingested or inhaled by your Explorer and was seeking freedom."

"This is all difficult to believe, Hiro."

"Now that you've seen this, I strongly urge you not to colonize Plant Thing's planet. According to Plant Thing, the entire planet is protected by an entity it calls the Biomind. If you want to send colonists to that planet, you will have to negotiate every move with the Biomind and it will have to agree to your presence."

"I've explored many new planets. I've never seen anything like this," Kylara said. She looked at Hiro with speculative eyes. "An entire planet covered in a sentient, plant-based mind. This is quite the discovery. I am impressed with what your Plant Thing has accomplished in such a short time on your station. Imagine what could be created on a botanical planet with an overruling intelligence. The possibilities may be endless."

"The possibilities could also be extremely dangerous if they don't want humans there. You assume the Biomind might want to deal with humans. It might not. Plant Thing has expressed a desire to return to its home. Perhaps it could act as a mediator if the PEB wants to negotiate trade or colonization rights?"

"It has?" Kylara looked pensive. "Perhaps that might work. I agree with you that colonizing Botanica would be highly risky. The question is, would it be worth it? I don't believe we have a ship large enough to carry Plant Thing unless we only took a part of it. I have to be honest with you, Hiro. I can't believe you've allowed this Plant Thing to remain on the station and get this large. I would have destroyed it. But you say it has reason and compassion? May I speak with Plant Thing, myself?"

"You can communicate with it through Bud or Dr. Lord. They have developed a mind linkage with the plant alien."

"Really? This sounds suspiciously like mind control, Dr. Al-Fadi. I would like to assess Dr. Lord and Bud myself. The risk of this plant alien taking over this medical station is high. It has taken over much of the station physically. The only way to destroy this alien is to destroy the entire station at this point."

"What?" Hiro grabbed the edge of his desk. "You cannot be recommending this!"

"I wonder what happened to all of our other explorers in that first contact team who disappeared. Do you think they were all absorbed by this Biomind? If so, what will we find if we send a ship down to Botanica now?"

Hiro shuddered.

" . . . War?"

From the surveillance recordings, Juan identified the man who'd planted the bomb inside the *Inferno*. After placing it, the saboteur had exited the hangar at a brisk pace and had disappeared into the crowds milling about the Concourse. The man's appearance had dramatically changed from when he'd arrived on the station as the *Inferno's* engineer.

An All Points Bulletin was sent to everyone's wristcomp on the medical station, showing the image of the saboteur. To date, no sightings of him had been reported. Could Coleridge have changed his physical appearance again? Juan was desperate to get his hands on this engineer in case he decided to try something else.

Where had Coleridge found the materials to make a bomb? The ingredients were not all that sophisticated, but it would not have been easy to find everything, sneaking around the station as a fugitive.

Nelson Mandela analyzed where each of the chemicals used in the bomb were obtained. Surveillance records were examined to see if the saboteur had been spotted anywhere in the vicinity of these places. By going to each source, they might find someone who remembered him hanging around or befriending a worker. Someone might remember delivering supplies to an unusual location on the station. Rivera wanted every angle checked out. Could Coleridge have created more than one bomb?

Juan refused to leave the *Inferno*. He was certain the saboteur would be back and he planned to catch him. Coleridge had tried to blow up the *Inferno*, so he obviously didn't want the Conglomerate obtaining the new technology. Coleridge's next move, if Juan were he, would be to either steal the ship or attempt again to destroy it.

Nelson Mandela had comtech people poring over the ship's programming right now. They were searching for any viruses or self-destruct commands. If found, they had to be erased. Juan had scrupulously checked out each comtech person's background before he allowed them entry to the Receiving Bay. Each person had to have been on the station for a number of years and be known to some of the others. It turned out that all of the comtech people the station AI had enlisted were known to each other for at least five solstan years.

Rivera wanted the encryption on the ship's log and navigation records cracked, so that they could determine the ship's previous destinations. The Conglomerate wanted to know where the *Inferno* had previously docked, and how long it had stayed in any one location. Hopefully, it was merely a matter of time before the comtechs deciphered everything. Juan wanted to ensure nothing happened to the *Inferno* in the meantime.

Nelson Mandela had Coleridge's fingerprints, voice print, retinal scan, and DNA from when he'd boarded the station. If Coleridge approached again, he'd be identified immediately. At least Juan was no longer viewed as paranoid. The other Security officers were grudgingly more respectful—emphasis on 'grudgingly'.

The engineers believed they were getting closer to understanding the EMP weapon's design. They'd wanted to remove it from the *Inferno* and set it up in one of the Engineering Department's laboratories for closer study. New orders from the Conglomerate put a stop to that idea.

A battlecruiser was coming to take possession of the *Inferno*. No one was to touch or analyze the EMP weapon. All records were to be handed over to the captain of the battlecruiser and then erased. Anyone trying to get near the weapon was to be arrested and held for questioning. The *Inferno* was to be guarded around the cycle until the battlecruiser arrived.

It all made sense to Juan. The Conglomerate planned to study the weapon and build shields that would protect against its action. They'd take the EMP weapon apart, modify it, boost its potency, and develop shields against it. The improved EMP weapon would be in mass production and installed on all of the Conglomerate's ships, as well as the new shielding. The Conglomerate didn't want anyone else getting a look at it before them.

Juan scrutinized everyone who came near Receiving Bay Thirteen. He was getting no sleep and Cindy was getting annoyed with him, but he couldn't help it. He had to protect the *Inferno*. Why, he couldn't say.

Perhaps it was because of Hope and her sacrifice to save everyone on this station. Rivera had ordered Juan to leave and let others take over the watch, but Juan could not obey. He *knew* the saboteur would be back and if that person were not stopped, something terrible might happen. Juan insisted on living aboard and organizing the watches.

Cindy called him 'crazy'. Juan agreed with her. But he'd always trusted his instincts and they'd rarely been wrong. He couldn't ignore them, now that he had a partner and baby on the station whose lives were at risk. Until the saboteur was caught, Juan would not relax his guard.

He was on the bridge of the *Inferno*, having gotten off the vidscreen with Cindy and his daughter, Estelle. He'd kissed the vidscreen, first over Estelle and then over Cindy, wishing them a good night. Cindy had rolled her big eyes and laughed. Juan was thankful that Cindy was so laid back, so understanding. She forgave his quirks and obstinacy. Perhaps polar bears were simply more chill. Polar bear females raised their cubs all on their own. Cindy seemed to accept Juan's need to stay on the *Inferno*. Perhaps she would have chased him off, if he'd tried to hang around her and Estelle too much.

A perimeter alarm pinged.

Juan examined all of his screens. Receiving Bay Thirteen was dark but Juan scanned for heat signatures. Another perimeter alarm beeped. Someone was coming. Juan dimmed the lights on the ship. Drawing his stunner and setting it on maximum, he moved silently towards the hatchway. He'd catch the saboteur this time.

Juan wanted the man alive. So many questions needed answers and a dead engineer would supply none of them. Juan's relief was not expected for a number of hours yet. All of the Security officers knew to notify Juan in advance if they were dropping by. This had to be Coleridge.

A third perimeter alarm beeped. Juan silenced them. He didn't want the sound scaring off the saboteur.

One of the surveillance screens revealed a small moving beam of light. The thin beam swept all around the hangar before turning back to the *Inferno*. The light moved cautiously towards the ship, sweeping a circumferential pattern every few meters.

Juan's claws slid in and out. He suppressed a growl. He so wanted to get his hands on the guy who almost blew him up. The saboteur would be no match for Juan's strength and speed. Juan wanted to beat this guy to a pulp for being part of a plot to kill off all animal-adapts and genetically modified humans on the basis of religious beliefs. These lunatics were using religion to justify mass murder on an enormous scale. They'd delivered two viruses to the station that could dissolve people into puddles. Cindy and Estelle could have been casualties. Juan bared his fangs thinking about it.

The thin beam of light approached the hatchway entrance and entered the inner gloom of the *Inferno*. Juan's eyebrows rose. Coleridge must have taken a shower and changed his clothes. The scent of fear still persisted but the saboteur no longer reeked. Curiously, he now smelled strongly of female. Juan shook his head.

The intruder came through the hatchway cautiously, thin pencil of light darting around the interior of the ship. The light turned towards Juan, who leaped and hit the intruder at chest height. A shriek pierced the stillness and Juan grunted, mainly at the shock of hitting a skinny body, half the mass of what he'd been anticipating. As Juan landed on the intruder, he was sure he felt bones snap, none belonging to him. A shrill scream rattled his eardrums followed by an impressive string of curses.

Juan barked for lights and frowned down at the human lying beneath him. The young woman was waif-like, pale, blue-haired and skinny. She was dressed in a black coverall. He pointed the stunner in her face but she was in far too much pain to care.

"Get off me," the young woman rasped.

"Who are you and what are you doing here?" Juan could not keep the exasperation out of his voice.

"You've broken my ribs!"

"I'll break more than your ribs, if you don't answer my questions."

"Can't breathe. Get off me!"

Juan rolled off of her slowly, shifting his weight in such a way as to elicit more pain. He smiled as the girl howled. He frisked her for weapons. His hand hit a familiar shape and his eyebrows jumped. He pulled a blaster from her coverall pocket and dangled it before her eyes.

"What are you doing with a blaster?"

"Hurts to talk," she wheezed.

"No, it doesn't. This hurts." Juan leaned on her ribcage.

After the screaming waned, Juan repeated, "Who are you and what're you doing here?"

"I'm Ice, Dr. Octavia Weisman's graduate student. Heard about this ship. Wanted to see it. That's all."

"That's all," Juan echoed.

He so wanted to punch this idiot girl's lights out. He stared at her hatchet face, hostile green eyes, brilliant blue hair, and thought a graduate degree did not necessarily convey intelligence . . . although, if he was honest with himself, this woman's eyes actually did convey an animalistic sort of cunning.

Juan's hair stood on end, meeting those green eyes glaring at him with such hatred. There was nothing soft or compassionate in them. He'd met eyes like these before—there were plenty in the military— and Juan knew soldiers with eyes like these were extremely dangerous to have around, especially behind your back. They'd be the first to shoot you, if they thought it would benefit them. How could Dr. Weisman trust this girl in her lab?

"You're lying. I can smell it. Why're you really here?"

Ice's glare was like a pulse blast. Juan struggled with the feeling that he should kill this girl right now, before she came back at him and everyone he cared about. He'd met insane killers in the past. He'd lived through a violent genocide on his home planet but the rest of his family had not. This woman looked at him with that same coldness, that same hatred. His hands wanted to wring her scrawny neck.

"You're under arrest for trespassing on a restricted vessel and for possession of an illegal weapon. You'll be held for interrogation."

"You can't do this," the skinny girl hissed, as she struggled to get up off of the floor. She reminded him of a helpless beetle stuck on its back.

Juan bent down to help her to her feet. Grasping her stick-like upper arm in his right hand, he lifted her effortlessly but not gently. He began speaking into his wristcomp, asking for someone from the Security Office to come and collect the girl. He had to ignore the profanity she was yelling at him.

The vidscreen on the bridge lit up with another perimeter alarm. Juan turned towards the bridge and peered at the surveillance screens. Who was approaching the *Inferno* now? He felt a brush at his hip and an intense burning pain lanced him in the head.

After showing Saul to his quarters, Grace and Bud gave him a tour of the *Nelson Mandela*. Saul now wore a wristcomp that would help him locate any site on the station. Unfortunately, Saul's quarters were, in Grace's opinion, far too close to hers. She did not bother to show him where her quarters were located.

Grace was thankful for Bud's presence. Although she was pleased to see Saul, she wasn't as delighted as he was to see her. She didn't want him getting any ideas that she was interested in getting back together. He was a handsome, kind, intelligent man, but he was not for Grace. When she looked at Bud and Saul together, Grace realized she only had eyes for Bud, as perverted as that might seem to people like Alex.

Was it because Bud had saved her life so many times? Was it because he was the bravest, smartest, and most heroic being she'd ever met? Was it because he would sacrifice his existence for her, without hesitation, and never asked anything of her? In spite of all his strength and skill, Bud was an innocent. Did he appeal to Grace's motherly side? She didn't know. She knew who Alex would choose for her and that made her fume.

Compared to Bud, no one else measured up. What did that say about her? She recalled the appalled way in which Alex looked at her, as if her associating with Bud was something dirty and disgusting. Grace's head began to hammer. She had to stop grinding her molars.

The resentment Grace felt towards Saul was undeserved. Her anger was fuelled by what Alex had said. Saul didn't deserve that anger. He was simply in the wrong place at the wrong time. Grace had to get away from Saul before she said something she'd regret.

Grace turned her thoughts to the operation on the PEB explorer and the heart transplant. What had caused all of the explorers' hearts to rupture around the same time? Why hadn't anything registered on the monitors? Why had only their hearts been affected? What would they find on pathology? Had the sudden increase in blood pressure been a real phenomenon or an artefact? What could have caused this?

Grace noticed that Bud and Saul had stopped walking and talking. They were both staring at her. Her eyes flitted from one face to the next.

"Did I miss something?" she asked.

Saul looked annoyed. "I asked if I was boring you. You didn't answer."

"I'm sorry, Saul. I'm tired and I've a lot to do before we meet in the OR at 0800. I have to ensure everything is ready for the heart transplant and I desperately need some sleep." Grace's cheeks felt molten.

"Oh, well, let me walk you to your room," Saul said.

"No, we'll walk you to your suite," Grace said. "We need to make sure you find your own quarters, don't we, Bud?"

"Yes, Dr. Lord."

"Does Bud always follow you around?" The petulance in Saul's voice was unmistakeable.

"No," Grace said.

"Yes," Bud said.

Grace sighed. "There have been occasions when I've required protection and Bud has provided that. I don't want to get into the 'why' of it, but those days are passed. Let's just say that Bud used to act as my bodyguard and is used to accompanying me everywhere. I appreciate his company. We also operate together and he and I make a great team."

"Don't you mean *it,* not he?" Saul asked, his eyebrow raised.

The blood pounded in Grace's temples. She wondered if her own heart was about to rupture. Grace struggled with her rage as if it were a wildfire burning out of control.

"I meant *he,*" Grace grated.

She thrust her face in Saul's and waited to see if an apology was forthcoming. The explorer remained silent.

"Come along, Bud," she snapped. "We don't have time for this."

"I can show you to the operating room tomorrow at 0730 hours, if you would like, Dr. Rohl," Bud said. "Please do not forget that you must wear a containment suit."

"That will not be necessary. I can follow my wristcomp. You'd better hurry. Your mistress calls."

"Goodnight," Bud said with a bow.

The explorer did not respond but turned away instead.

The next instant, Bud was by Grace's side, as she stomped down the corridor.

"How dare he? Who does he think he is, that pompous, conceited, arrogant bigot? If anyone is an *it*, it's him. Don't you listen to a word he says, Bud. You're a far better human than he'll ever be."

"I am not human, Grace. No matter how hard you wish it, I will never be human. I am an *it*, not a he. Dr. Rohl is correct."

"Bud, you are the best person I know. You are actually too good to be human. Calling you a human would be an insult to you."

"Grace, you do not have to defend me. I know what I am. I am not human but thank you for thinking so highly of me." Bud gave Grace a shy smile.

"I think highly of you because you deserve nothing less. You are the kindest, bravest, most unselfish being I have ever known and it's a privilege to call you my friend. I refuse to let anyone influence me otherwise."

"Grace, you must not forsake your family for me," Bud said quietly.

Grace felt like a bomb had hit her. She found herself gasping.

"Did . . . *Nelson Mandela* show you my conversation with Alex?"

"*Chuck Yeager* did." Bud would not meet Grace's eyes.

"Is there no respect for privacy?" Grace hissed at the closest surveillance eye. "Bud, Alex is merely the man who donated sperm to my genetic makeup. He didn't raise me and never played a role in my life. Saul was someone I said goodbye to a long time ago. Neither of them are important to me."

"Do not do this, Grace. Please."

"I will not be held hostage to prejudice."

"They are stating the truth."

"They are not! I will not be deterred from being your friend or caring for you just because someone tells me I shouldn't. Never."

Bud looked down at his feet.

"You must forget me, Grace. I do not wish to come between you and your father."

"Bud, Alex is not my real father. My real father would have loved you."

"I am not worthy of you, Grace."

"You are!" Grace sucked in a great gulp of air. She felt like she couldn't get enough oxygen, as if Bud had pushed her out of an airlock. She covered her mouth with her quivering hand and blinked repeatedly at the forlorn figure of Bud through an upwelling of tears.

" . . . Bud?"

"Grace, your father means so much to you. I cannot come between the two of you."

"It's my decision, Bud."

"I will continue to assist you in surgery and always be there to look out for you, Grace . . ."

" . . . But?"

"But your father is correct. You need to seek human company. I do not want you to suffer from people's ill opinions, Grace."

"I don't care about anyone else's opinions, Bud." Grace punched her fist into the air. "People's opinions mean nothing to me."

"Goodnight, Grace. I shall see you in the operating room at 0800 hours."

Bud was gone.

Grace felt as hollow as an abandoned asteroid, flotsam drifting in space. Her emotions burned to ashes and those ashes blew away. Inhaling deep shuddering breaths and wondering if she would ever trust or love again, Grace staggered away.

Saul went looking for Kylara. He queried the station AI and *Nelson Mandela* gave him directions to her suite. He flashed his wristcomp over the access pad and waited.

The door slid open and the beautiful Inquisitor stood there, looking surprised.

"I expected you to be with your friend," Kylara said, her brows raised. "What happened?"

"I don't know, Kylara. I think the android happened."

"What?" Looking confused, Kylara beckoned for Saul to enter.

"Grace became enraged when I called the android an *it*," Saul said. "I can't understand her reaction. An android is a thing. It's not human. They're machines. What did I say that was so wrong?"

Kylara gestured for Saul to take a seat and she lowered herself onto a lounger, her hands pressed together. "I have some deep concerns about what is happening on this station, Saul," Kylara said in a soft voice. "Dr. Al-Fadi told me that the plant alien has developed some kind of secret communication link with Grace Lord and Bud. Perhaps they are controlled by this Plant Thing that now covers the entire medical station. This Plant Thing is everywhere. The staff are either unaware of the danger they're in, or they're being controlled, perhaps through the food they've ingested."

"Fu, I ate one of those apples today," Saul said.

"How do you feel?" Kylara asked.

"Like myself," Saul said, shrugging.

"Perhaps the control by the plant alien comes on gradually over time, dependant on how much food one has ingested," Kylara said. "It's strange how no one seems to see the danger of this alien. They've all been eating its produce as if there's no concern. Its size alone should be setting off huge alarms. It has physically taken over the station. Now Dr. Al-Fadi has suggested we take part of the alien back to its home planet. What are we going to find on Botanica, if the plants have absorbed the first survey team?"

"The possibilities may be catastrophic," Saul said.

Kylara nodded. Deep creases formed between her brows.

"Are you going to report this?" he asked her.

"I'm going to observe a little while longer. I want to speak with Dr. Lord and this Bud. I want to observe this plant alien and how it controls the people of this station."

"Dr. Lord and Bud are both operating on the first of my Explorers tomorrow morning," Saul said. "I asked if I could attend the procedure."

"I would like to be in on that operation, as well," Kylara said. "I want to see how Grace and Bud interact and if Dr. Al-Fadi may also be under the influence of this alien. He certainly seems to be followed by the creature everywhere.

"Nothing seems right here. I want to get to the bottom of it all before I make my report, but that plant alien must be destroyed, no matter what. The question is, does the entire medical station have to be destroyed as well."

"I suspect it would be difficult to rid this huge facility of the plant alien."

"I'm sorry, Saul, for your friend." Kylara placed her hand over his.

"She's not the Grace I remember. Let's see what transpires tomorrow. I'll talk to her again after the operation. Somehow, I have to get her away from that android."

"Be careful, Saul. Bud sounds like a formidable entity."

Saul nodded, worry molding his features.

"*Nelson Mandela?*" Kylara asked in a louder voice.

"Yes, Inquisitor?"

"I would like to attend the operation tomorrow along with Dr. Rohl, as an observer. Could this be arranged?"

"Yes, Inquisitor. I shall supply you with a Level Six Containment suit. You will find it in the change room off M7 OR 1. Your wristcomp will direct you where to go tomorrow morning."

"Thank you, *Nelson Mandela.*"

"You are most welcome, Inquisitor. May I assist you with anything else?"

"No, that is all, *Nelson Mandela.* Thank you."

Kylara looked at Saul. "I shall see you early tomorrow morning, Saul."

Saul got to his feet and bowed. "Sleep well, Inquisitor. I know I won't."

"Let's hope we're wrong, Saul," Kylara said, her eyes full of pity.

He could only nod and turn away.

Ice recovered her blaster from the unconscious tigerman's pocket. She fought the overwhelming urge to blow his head off. By the time she slipped the blaster into her pocket, she was panting. Her mind was a battlefield. She struggled against a crazed murderous demon inside her who wanted the tiger dead; she'd barely won. Regardless of how much she might have wanted to kill him, it was insanity to kill a Security officer, even if he'd broken her ribs. If caught, she'd be mind-swiped for sure.

The thought of being mind-swiped seemed to shut the craziness down . . . for the moment.

Ice leaned against one of the flight seats, gasping. If she pressed her hand firmly against her left side, she could breathe a little easier. Her ribs burned like molten fire whenever she inhaled or moved. She thought she'd been hit by a monorail when the Security officer had tackled her. She'd felt more than one rib snap.

So far, she wasn't coughing up blood. Hopefully, her lungs had not been punctured by the fractured ribs. The pain knifed through her with every movement. She tried to breathe as shallowly as she could, as she turned towards the exit. Security droids were on their way to escort her to the brig. By the time they arrived, she had to be gone.

What an idiot! She should've let him take her in. Why did she stun him? Why?

For some reason, the word 'interrogation' had sent shivers of fear tearing through her. *She could not afford to be interrogated.* Why not? If she were interrogated, what would they find? A nosy graduate student wanting to look at the infamous *Inferno.* She'd no previous criminal record. They would've let her go with a slap on her wrist and possibly an apology for the fractured ribs. But now, she'd stunned a Security Officer. She'd given her name and place of employment. She could not go back to her quarters or Octavia's lab. She was now on the run.

Idiot!

Where could she go?

Memories—that weren't her own—flooded her brain. Secret passageways and hidden cubbyholes were dotted throughout the station. She had things she had to do, things she could not do under the watchful eyes of Octavia or her ridiculous partner. Could she make it to one of those hiding spots now on her own? She'd have to.

Ice leaned against the hatchway door, clutching her left side. Gasping, she withdrew the small flashlight from her pocket and activated the small beam. Popping into her mind was an exit from this hangar that went through a hidden panel in one of the walls. She'd have to make her way to that panel as quickly as possible.

Her beam landed on a white face in the dark.

She jerked and had to bite down hard on a scream. She aimed the blaster at the face, hoping the stranger did not see how much her hand was shaking. The light encircled a gaunt face. She tried her best to stand tall.

"Freeze! Who are you and what're you doing here?"

"Don't shoot," the man said, raising his hands. "I saw you stun the guard after he called for backup. You need to get out of here. I can help you."

"Why would you want to help me?" she asked. Her left side was throbbing so intensely she could barely think.

"No time for questions. They're coming for you," he hissed.

"Why do you care?"

"Maybe we want the same things. Let me help you get out of here and we'll talk."

She scrutinized the man's appearance. He was haggard and unkempt. His clothing hung off of him as if they were far too big for him. He stank.

"Why are you here?"

"This is my ship."

Ice inhaled and instantly regretted it. If this man's claim was true, he'd know how to fly the *Inferno*. He'd know how the EMP weapon worked. He'd have all the access codes. They could steal the ship. *Revenge was his!*

Ice shook her head. What revenge? His? She'd been having crazy thoughts ever since she'd downloaded that memcube into her head. She didn't even understand why she'd come to this hangar.

"All right. I'll accept your help. I can't move too fast, but I know a hidden passage out of here. Help me get to it. But remember, I'll kill you if you try anything."

The man held his palms out. "I won't. I need you as much as you need me."

"What's your name?" she asked, as he helped her out of the hatchway.

" . . . Sam."

"Why can't we take this ship right now, Sam?"

"I heard that guard call for Security. They'll be here any minute. The engines are cold. We'd never get the ship space-ready before they had us cornered. We'll have to try another time."

"Okay," she grunted. She gestured with her light beam to where the escape route was located in the hangar.

"What's your name?" Sam asked, as he gently pulled her arm over his shoulder.

"Ice."

She led him through dark, convoluted passages between walls and behind bulkheads. She'd never been here before, but they looked, smelled, and felt familiar. Ice was going mad. Voices were often so close, she thought she could reach out and touch the speakers if it weren't for the wall between them, or were they in her head? What shock would she see on someone's face, if she suddenly appeared close enough to brush a cheek with her lips or thrust a knife.

Ice shook her head. Where did such a horrible thought arise?

They spoke not. Ice couldn't spare the breath. It was all she could do to keep moving, her right hand clamped firmly to her left side, trying to prevent the jagged edges of the cracked ribs from grinding against each other. In these constrictive spaces, twisting often left her immobilized in agony.

Why had she brought this stranger along? Who was he? What did he want from her? The further they went, the more she found herself struggling to breathe. Each step was torture. If she became totally incapacitated, would he help her or kill her for her blaster?

Sam wasn't his real name. She was positive of that. He'd hesitated when he'd said it, as if it felt strange to his tongue. If he lied about his name, how could she trust him about anything? How could the *Inferno* be his ship? She'd heard the captain had been killed; the rest of the crew had been arrested. Perhaps he wanted to steal the *Inferno* and sell the new EMP weapon to the highest bidder. What she planned to do.

She did?

If this man was willing to partner up with her, perhaps his goals were close enough to hers to warrant keeping him alive and close. He could fly the ship. Was he also interested in leaving the *Nelson Mandela* a mass of space debris behind them? She'd use his help until she didn't need it any more.

Ice blinked a few times and frowned. *Where was this terrible B-vid monologue coming from? Did that ass wipe Nestor really think like this?*

Ice couldn't afford to have anyone on this station know so much about her movements, especially when she couldn't control what was going on inside her head. She shouldn't trust anyone. People were unreliable, unpredictable, and untrustworthy unless they were mind-controlled.

Shut up!

She came to a widening of the passageway. They could stop and rest for a moment. She leaned against one wall, her head tipped back, as she tried to slow her breathing. Panting meant agony. She could only dream about a narc patch at the moment.

'Sam' leaned against the wall opposite her.

"You okay?" he asked softly.

"Mag," she grated.

"We should get you something for the pain."

She blinked at him. That statement didn't even warrant a reply.

"How much further?" the man whispered.

Voices could be heard through the wall on which she was leaning. She shot him a look that should have silenced, but it was too dark for him to read her expression. Lucky for him she still needed his help. She pressed her hand firmly against her left side and pushed off the wall.

"Not far," she gasped, not knowing if it was the truth.

"Let me help you," Sam said, taking her right arm.

She had the blaster pointing at his nose while her vision tunnelled inwards. She silently swore as the pain slashed her left side. She wove on her feet gasping, as she waited for the pain to slowly abate.

"Touch me again and I'll kill you."

"Sorry," Sam muttered, backing away.

She clamped her jaw and inhaled slowly. The desire to fry the foul-smelling fool was almost uncontrollable. She turned and started moving further down the passageway. She needed narc patches, stims, food, water, and a bone knitter. Once she had the pain under control, she could start thinking about making plans and not about her stupid broken ribs.

She wanted to make that tiger-adapt pay. No one did this to Jeffrey Nestor and got away with it.

No one.

The small chamber was dark and musty. Ice limped to a locker and pulled out a handful of narc patches which she peeled and slapped on her neck, one after another. She eased herself slowly into a g-cliner. She pointed to a food preserver and leaned her head back, waiting for the pain to subside.

"Would you like anything?" Sam asked.

Ice closed her eyes as the euphoria hit.

"Can I do anything to make you more comfortable?"

Ice squinted at the man. He was bony thin and younger than she first thought. His face had razor-sharp edges with jagged cheekbones and deep hollows beneath his eyes. His wavy, brown hair was tangled and greasy, his face unshaven. His coverall was filthy. He looked like he hadn't eaten in days.

"Bone knitter. Top lockup."

He undid the latch and pulled down a case labelled Osteoblast Stimulator. He withdrew the instrument and brought the handheld unit to her.

"Would you like me to apply it?" he asked.

"No," Ice said, reaching out her right hand. He dropped it on her palm, making her wince. "Thanks."

Ice activated the bone mender and placed the head of the unit against her sore left ribs. She adjusted the setting to as high as she could tolerate. The vibrating bone edges made her want to scream but the narc patches helped dull the ache. She clenched her teeth and tried not to concentrate on the pain.

"Eat," she told Sam, gesturing towards the food locker.

He nodded and opened the food preserver. The harsh light from within threw the room into stark relief. He pulled out a pack of nutripaks and ripped them open. He started shovelling the food bars into his mouth as if he couldn't get them in fast enough. He washed them down with water from a sip-pack. Ice watched him through narrowed eyes.

"What's your real name?" she asked.

Sam looked at her with shifting eyes.

"What d'you mean?" he asked, chewing with a mouth full of food. He avoided meeting her eyes.

"Sam isn't your real name. What's your real name?"

The man swallowed, shrugged.

"Jedediah. Jed to my friends."

"Why d'you lie?"

"I gave you the name I was supposed to use on this station."

"Why did you come here?"

"You brought me here."

Ice pretended to shoot Jed's head off with the blaster. He swallowed.

"The Devil brought me here," Jed rasped, balling up food wrappers.

"The devil?" Ice couldn't keep the scorn from of her voice.

"I'm a ship engineer. Been engineer on the *Inferno* for the last two years. New captain is assigned, a mean crazy bastard. The *Inferno* goes in for overhaul, comes back with new equipment, new consoles, new programs and a new chaplain who's more insane than the captain. We're sworn to secrecy. If we don't pledge, we're out. They change our names. We're cut off from friends and family. Given hordes of injections that make me ill. I think I'm going to die, a miserable lab rat. Don't know how long I'm in quarantine. Gradually, I recover.

"We're ordered to take six cryopods halfway across the galaxy to a medical space station. Captain orders no talking with other crew members, no questioning, no speaking or we get spaced. When we get here, we're told we have to splash serum samples around the station. We must not, under any circumstances, allow the new weapon to fall into the enemy's hands. I'm told we're at war, but I don't know with whom."

"War? News to me," Ice said.

"I'm in a nightmare," Jed said, as he bent forwards, his fingers raking through his greasy hair. He looked up at her, "I keep asking God to please wake me up."

"Can you fly the *Inferno*?"

"Yes."

"We'll steal the *Inferno* and get out of here."

"I don't think either of us will be going anywhere. The *Inferno*'s constantly under guard. I must figure out how to destroy it."

"For who?"

"The people I work for."

"The people who sent you on a suicide mission and didn't tell you why? Why would you do that for them?"

Jed stood with his mouth open and shrugged.

"The weapon on the *Inferno* would be worth a lot of money to the right people," Ice said.

"I guess so." Jed looked lost.

"We'll steal the *Inferno* and take it as far away from here as we can. We'll sell it to the highest bidder."

"Why do you want to leave this station?"

"I'm sick of this place. There's nothing here for me. I want to get away as much as you do. I know where to find the best buyers who'll pay the most for the ship. With money, we can go anywhere and do anything," Ice said.

At the tone of her voice, Jed's eyebrows lowered. He peered at her suspiciously. Ice rose from her g-cliner and walked straight towards the young engineer, her eyes never leaving his face.

"What're you doing?" Jed asked, backing away. His eyes darted to the exit.

"I'm hungry," Ice said.

"I can get you some food packets from the food preserver."

"Not that kind of hungry," Ice said, her voice low and husky.

Jed blinked at her, his hands held out as if to push her away. "What about your fractured ribs?"

"Narc patches are mag. Just don't squeeze too tight."

"Dr. Al-Fadi, the operation has been moved to quarantine level, Q1 OR1."

"Why was I not consulted on this change?" Hiro demanded, hands on hips, still in his leopard-spotted pyjamas.

"You are being consulted now."

"But your decision was already made."

"The decision to change the room was made whilst you were asleep. Though we are well aware of how much you enjoy being woken up in the middle of the night, we decided to selfishly deny you, purely out of spite."

"I do believe your efforts at sarcasm are improving, *Nelson Mandela*."

"You may continue to delude yourself into thinking that I care what you believe, Dr. Al-Fadi. All interested parties have been notified of the room change. Bud is setting it up right now. Even if you wanted the original OR back, it has already been re-assigned. The PEB explorer, the cloned heart, and all of the necessary equipment required for a heart transplant are now in quarantine level Q1 OR1. Wear your Level Six Containment Suit."

"I know."

"This you don't. Inquisitor Roque shall be in attendance at the operation."

"On whose authority?"

"Dr. Rohl requested that she be present so that she may offer her insights into the condition of the explorer."

"You did not think it worth consulting me?"

"You were asleep."

"Well, I give my permission for Inquisitor Roque to attend and I approve the room change. Let's hope nothing bursts from this patient's abdomen. Keep your surveillance eyes focused. If anything deadly or possibly dangerous to the inhabitants of this station appears, you lock the entire Level down, regardless of who is inside. Better yet, make sure we are the only operation occurring on the quarantine deck. Restrict all extraneous personnel. After seeing the recording of Plant Thing exploding out of that other explorer, I am leery of the patients of the PEB. I want nothing escaping that OR that may be hazardous to the people of this station. Understood?"

"Agreed."

Juan was seated in a g-cliner on the bridge of the *Inferno* with a thermal blanket wrapped around him, although he had no idea why. He wasn't cold. Tigers rarely got cold.

The medics told him he was in shock. Well, of course he was in shock. He'd gotten shot with a stunner on max right in the head. That was supposed to shock you. His body was still jingling and jangling. Muscles were twitch-twitch-twitching all over his muscular frame. Juan decided this was the only time it was a disadvantage to be a jacked-up tiger-adapt. The leads hooked up to his chest indicated his heart was beating irregularly. He felt nothing abnormal, but he'd been warned not to stand up.

A 'heart attack' was what he deserved. Being jumped by a stick of a girl, one-third his weight—with broken ribs, no less—and stunned with his own gun was humiliating. He'd never hear the end of it. What was that girl doing with a blaster, and why had she been sneaking onto the *Inferno*? What interest could a neurosurgeon's graduate student have with the ship? It made no sense—her 'just being curious'—so what was she really after? Was she partners with the saboteur? Were they both set on stealing the ship?

Rivera had been by and had chewed Juan out for sleeping in the ship like a crazy man. Then he'd congratulated him for tackling the intruder and scaring her off. They now had an APB out for this young woman, Philomena Vertongen aka Ice, for shooting a Security Officer.

When they'd contacted Vertongen's supervisor, Dr. Octavia Weisman, about her student, the neurosurgeon had believed none of it . . . until she was shown the surveillance footage. Then she'd gone ballistic. This was the second student in her lab to have gone totally crazy. The instant she had uttered those words, Weisman froze, as if she'd been stunned. Juan would have bet a month's wages that Weisman had put two and two together. When pressed, Weisman insisted that she had to 'check on something first' and she would get back to them.

'What is it about this place?' Juan wondered. For a medical space station, he'd never expected to be exposed to so much danger. The Butcher of Breslau murdering Security personnel, torture and murders by an insane psychiatrist, unstable power generators, people-melting viruses, EMP strikes, bombs, aliens, multiple evacuations. Perhaps it would be best to get Cindy and Estelle off of this station—rejoin the military, maybe—where it would be safer.

Juan shook his head. Now they had a new Chief Inspector of Security and rumour was, this guy was a real hard ass. Would he let Cindy work part-time? Would he let Juan continue to look after the security detail for the *Inferno* or would he move him to something else? Juan snarled, thinking about that.

When someone came up behind him and tapped him on the shoulder, Juan almost pounced.

Damien's eyebrows shot upwards. A crooked grin taunted Juan.

"Seen a ghost, Rasmussen?"

"What're you doing here, Lamont, other than stinking up the air I'm breathing?"

"Heard you were attacked by a twiggy little girl. Came by to see if you were all right. I know how women seem to get the better of you."

Juan bared his fangs. Damien was referring to Hope, the *Inferno's* medical officer and leopard-adapt, who almost dislocated his jaw. He rubbed his left cheek absently while staring poison daggers at his friend.

"I didn't think that girl would grab my stunner when she was wailing about her fractured ribs. I was sloppy and stupid. She could've killed me with her blaster, after she'd stunned me. I don't know why she didn't."

"Well, I'm glad she didn't . . . even though you probably deserved it." Damien punched Juan in the shoulder.

"Thanks. Did you really come here just to taunt me?"

"The *Inferno's* chaplain confessed. Gave us all the information we need: where their planet is, who the creators of the viruses are, where to find them. The Conglomerate's planning to send a strike force to capture the minds behind the EMP weapon and the viruses. They want these guys either working for the Conglomerate or dead, so they want to take them alive. The *Inferno* is to be untouched and unexamined with the EMP weapon intact. I hope nothing was damaged."

"Thanks to me saving it from a bomb and possible sabotage. The surveillance shows my attacker and someone who looked like the bomber leaving right after she stunned me. Everything should be intact."

"That's good to hear, Rasmussen. Otherwise, you'd be dog food."

Juan snarled at his friend.

"You sure you're okay?" Damien asked.

"Nothing injured but my pride. I'm not leaving this ship. The girl and the saboteur are working together. They're sure to be back."

"Well, you've been right so far. Hopefully, you'll stay lucky . . . and alive. Have you met the new Chief Inspector yet?"

"No."

"Well, let's hope the new Chief'll accommodate your obsession with *Inferno*."

"It's still here because of me."

"Damn straight," Damien acknowledged, with a nod. "If it means anything to you, I think you've done an excellent job protecting this ship. Too bad I have no influence over what the new Chief Inspector decides."

"Yeah, that's a damn shame."

"Cindy and Estelle fine?"

"She seemed great while she was tearing a strip off my hide, a few minutes ago."

"Lucky you have a hide to strip."

"That I am," said Juan.

"The new Chief Inspector wants to see you in his office, by the way," Damien said.

"*What?* Why didn't you tell me first thing? Have I been keeping him waiting?" Juan jumped up.

"Yeah. He's probably wondering what's taking you so long."

"Merde."

"By the way, I suspect no one has told you this, but before you go see your new boss, you might want to wash off that black handlebar moustache drawn on your upper lip."

". . . Fu."

Grace felt as if she'd gotten up on the wrong side of the universe. Her world had imploded overnight. The joy she'd felt meeting her biological father had transformed into a deep chasm of anger and resentment. She was well aware that Alex was from an earlier time, when feelings towards androids had been different, but Bud was not like those androids. Times had changed. She would not accept Alex's prejudice. What she also would not accept was Alex's belief that, because he contributed to Grace's DNA, he was entitled to impose his bigotries upon her.

Her wristcomp was filled with repeated demands and requests from Alex to meet or talk. She'd ignored every one of them.

When Saul had echoed the same prejudice as Alex, he'd received the brunt of her rage. Had Saul deserved it? Probably not, but their intolerance towards Bud was unacceptable. Whether it caused them distress or not, Grace would not accept their narrow-mindedness.

Bud was right; Grace herself was being intolerant. However, to turn her back on Bud and agree with Alex and Saul was something she could not do. She'd have to totally reject who she'd become. Grace was much more cognizant of android rights and she would not knowingly commit sins against those that could not protect themselves. She still had a long way to go in becoming more aware of her unwitting slights towards androids and robots, but when she looked at Bud and thought of all the wonderful things he'd accomplished, she was overwhelmed with outrage that anyone dared call him an 'it'.

Grace imagined cumulonimbus clouds building above her head as she approached Q1 Level. Her containment suit and helmet were bundled under one arm.

Saul stood outside the men's change room, his containment suit on but his helmet off. He was staring at her, waiting, his expression unreadable. Grace did not wish to get into an argument with Saul. She considered ignoring him but felt that would be unprofessional.

"Saul," Grace said, her voice flat.

"Grace," he said, mimicking her tone. "May we speak?"

"Not now, Saul," Grace said. "I want my mind fully focused on the operation."

"Grace, please, listen to me. I didn't sleep well at all last night. I'm sorry. I was way out of line and I shouldn't have said what I said about Bud. I apologize."

"Your apology shouldn't be to me, Saul," Grace said. "The person you should be apologizing to is Bud. Until you do that, we've nothing more to say." Grace turned away and entered the women's change room, struggling to get her anger under control. She imagined stuffing Saul inside a compartment and shutting the door. She had an operation to perform, a patient's life to save. Any personal issues had to be compartmentalized and temporarily forgotten.

Grace met Inquisitor Kylara Roque in the change room and was captivated by the woman's vivacious smile and vibrant personality. The Inquisitor was a fountain of energy and enthusiasm. Grace helped Kylara don her Level Six containment suit, which was thicker and sturdier than the standard suit. She made sure it was done up correctly and completely sealed. Kylara did the same for her. Together, they entered the sterilizer stall where they chatted while they underwent the required five minutes. When the light in the stall turned green, they were admitted to the operating room.

Grace had been thankful for the Inquisitor's pleasant demeanour. Kylara had provided the conversation that Grace would have been hard pressed to initiate. She'd gotten little sleep after Bud had told her to forget about him. Thinking about Bud made her wince. She was thankful she had the containment suit helmet on to hide the dark circles beneath her puffy eyes.

Kylara followed Grace into the operating room. Bud, Saul, and Charles Darwin were already in the suite, dressed in their containment suits. Grace introduced Charles, the anesthetist, to Kylara. Being a portly man, Charles looked massive in his containment suit.

Charles looked at Grace and said, "Custom-made Level Six containment suit. Call me Moby." He gestured with both hands down his body. "The latest fashion. It's all the rage in Orion's Belt. Actually, I'm probably as big as Orion's Belt."

Grace chuckled along with everyone else but the merriment was strained. Too much emotion was swirling around the operating room. Bud was avoiding Grace's glances. Saul had nodded at Grace but had not deigned to speak to her. He now stood beside Kylara and they chatted quietly, their conversation switched to privacy mode. Saul's arms were crossed and he stood stiffly at attention, his eyes on Kylara's faceplate.

Charles beckoned Grace over to where he was checking out his equipment and monitors. On her visor, a request for privacy mode with Dr. Darwin lit up and she accepted it with a head tilt.

"Do you mind filling me in on what's going on, Grace?" Charles asked. "Why are those two people here?"

"They're from the PEB. They've brought twelve explorers all with ruptured hearts from a planet they were investigating. We don't understand the cause of the heart damage, so we're taking every precaution we can, in case there's something inside these patients that is contagious or transmissible.

"Sensor readings and visual recordings taken when the explorers collapsed and their suits went cryo, showed nothing obviously suspicious. If there's something lethal or dangerous in these patients, we don't want it spreading to the rest of the station, so we're perform the heart transplant under Level Six Quarantine."

"Great. Why wasn't I told any of this when I was asked to do this case?" Charles asked.

"If you don't want to do this, I'm sure we can call for someone else," Grace said. "You shouldn't have to do this case, if you don't want to. Everything may go splendidly but you never know. It should be an informed decision."

"Are you backing out, Grace?"

"No, of course not."

"Why not?"

"Because I'm performing the operation and . . . well, someone has to do it. I have nothing to lose. You have a family, Charles. You shouldn't be here."

"You have family, too, Grace. I've met your father. Besides, I wouldn't make one of my colleagues do a case I wouldn't do. I said yes. It's the luck of the draw, isn't it? Risks of the profession. Let's hope there's nothing worse than a ruptured heart in this patient and we all walk away relieved."

Grace smiled and nodded. She didn't want to think about Alex. She looked over at Bud, who was organizing all of the surgical instruments, keeping his head down.

<Bud?> Grace mindspoke.

<Grace, I am sorry!>

The tsunami of anguish hit Grace's mind like a physical blow and she staggered. Charles grabbed her arm.

"Are you all right, Grace?"

"Yes. Thank you, Charles. I'm fine."

"Are you sure? You looked like you were punched." Darwin peered through her faceplate with obvious concern.

"I'm good," Grace said. She patted Charles' arm with her free hand. She was trembling inside.

<I'm sorry too, Bud. I could never forget you. Don't ever ask me to do that.>

<Grace, I'll always be by your side.>

<And I'll always want you there, Bud.>

<Thank you, Grace.>

Bud stopped what he was doing and turned to her. He bowed deeply.

"Hey, is that new protocol around here? What about the anesthetists? What are we, boiled roach paste?"

Grace laughed and this time it was heartfelt. She felt giddy. The oppressive gloom weighing her down was lifted. She felt as light as helium.

"You are definitely not roach paste, Charles. I think Bud bowed to both of us although there is no need for him to be doing that."

"I don't need that subservient stuff. I'm not like that little Napoleon you follow around everywhere. By the way, where is the little narcissist, anyway? Shouldn't he be here by now?"

As if on cue, Dr. Al-Fadi made his entrance.

The containment-suited, helmeted surgeon marched into the operating room and looked around at everyone. He spread his arms out and Grace winced as his voice blared over her helmet com.

"What? Haven't you people finished the operation yet? What are you waiting for? Do I have to do everything around here?" Dr. Al-Fadi bowed to everyone in the room.

"Dr. Rohl, would you do me the honour of standing to my left and Inquisitor Roque, do you mind standing left of your colleague? Dr. Grace and Bud will face us across the operating table. Bud, is everything ready?"

"Yes, Dr. Al-Fadi."

"Dr. Darwin, have you any concerns?"

"Always, but none about this case," Charles quipped.

"Let us have the patient removed from the cryopod and placed on the operating table. The vat-grown heart is in the room?"

"Yes, Dr. Al-Fadi," Bud said.

Bud activated the cryopod opening sequence and the lid lifted. The thawing of the patient had already been initiated, but cold mist still wafted out of the coffin-sized container. The body rose from the depths of the pod, free of its opened cryosuit. Once the patient's body was transferred to the operating table, the empty cryopod was pushed to one side of the room by robots.

The explorer was tall, muscular, long-limbed, and a jaguar-adapt. She had high cheekbones and small ears. She possessed the shiny ebony fur of a black jaguar and had a very athletic build.

They quickly got to work preparing the patient: establishing circulatory lines, attaching monitors, securing an airway, and sterilizing the depilated skin. Grace took urine and blood samples. They'd decided to measure every parameter they could to determine what had happened to the explorer. Finally, the operation of replacing the explorer's ruptured heart could commence.

"This is Lieutenant Jaxi Eyami of the Planetary Exploration Bureau, here for an examination and heart replacement. Any concerns before we begin? Scalpel to Dr. Grace," Hiro said.

Bud handed Grace the harmonic scalpel and she activated the blade with a light touch. She ran her gloved hand down the soft fur of the explorer's chest outlining in her mind where her incision would run. The scalpel hummed in her hand as she carefully cut through fur, subcutaneous tissue, and the lower third of the sternum. She wondered if she should make a larger incision for an unobstructed view of the entire inner chest, to see if they could determine what had happened to Lieutenant Eyami.

With the harmonic scalpel still within the patient, Eyami sat bolt upright on the table, tubes pulling from her mouth, neck, and arms. Bloodshot golden eyes turned to Grace and the black jaguar-adapt slapped the humming scalpel from Grace's hand. Grace felt a searing pain in the small bones of her hand as her arm flew outward with the blow. A yelp escaped her throat as she felt her shoulders grabbed from behind. Grace was yanked away from the roaring mouth with sharp white fangs bracketing a breathing tube. The patient's amber irises began to glow a brilliant magenta. As her view of the operating room quickly changed to the operating room doors, Grace heard Bud yell, "Everyone out of the OR! Now!"

Grace was now in a brightly lit waiting area. To her right, Bud was gently placing Hiro on his feet. Looking around, Grace discovered they were outside the lockdown doors to Q1 Level. The lockdown doors were clanging closed, the locks falling into place. The seals were closing.

"What's happening, *Nelson Mandela*?" Hiro shouted. Klaxons were pealing deafeningly.

"Lockdown has been initiated."

Grace turned towards the sound of pounding. Bud was hammering on the lockdown doors, yelling, "Let me in, *Nelson Mandela*. I must save the rest of them."

Grace could feel the vibration from Bud's blows through the soles of her boots.

"Cease that pounding immediately, Bud. If you damage those lockdown doors you will be turned into scrap."

"Let me back inside, *Nelson Mandela*."

"No."

"*Nelson Mandela*, what is happening in the OR?" Hiro shouted.

A wallscreen closest to them blinked to life. Grace and Hiro raced over to it. The jaguar patient, Eyami, had ripped the endotracheal tube from her throat. Her clawed hands were now sweeping towards Charles Darwin's neck. The anesthetist's helmet flew across the room and the visor shattered. Charles backed away from Eyami, his hands raised before him, his eyes bulging. The leopard-adapt swung, claws extended, and a fountain of bright red blood erupted from Darwin's neck.

"No!" shouted Grace.

As Eyami lifted Darwin above her head, blood spraying everywhere, Saul drove a harmonic scalpel into the explorer's back. Grace gasped as she watched Charles' body tossed against the far wall like a lifeless doll. Darwin landed sprawled on the floor, his head canted sideways.

"Run, Saul!" Grace shouted over the helmet com.

Saul grabbed a laser drill from one of the tables and pointed it at Eyami as she turned glowing purple eyes on him. He aimed the beam at Eyami's forehead as he ordered Kylara to leave the room. The patient walked stiffly towards Saul while he burned a hole between her eyes. The laser did not slow her. Saul backed away, continuously firing, but Eyami lunged forward and drove her claws deep into his throat, right through the containment suit.

Grace's throat felt like it tore as she screamed, "Saul, no!"

Saul fell to his knees, both of his hands clutching the jaguar adapt's wrist.

Kylara crept up behind the patient, a laser bone cutter in her hands. As the jaguar-adapt tore her claws from Saul's throat, Kylara drove the laser saw into the neck of the patient, cutting deep into the cervical vertebrae and severing her spinal cord. As Eyami collapsed to the ground, Kylara placed the tip of the laser saw at the base of the woman's skull and thrust upwards. The bloody explorer lay like a puppet with its strings cut.

Kylara dropped the saw and ran to Saul's side. She felt around for a pulse at Saul's neck. There was so much blood everywhere.

"Are Security droids inside the lockdown?" Grace asked.

"Only one, Dr. Lord. It is coming."

Grace saw Kylara's head snap up. She glanced over at the open cryopod and was gesticulating, ordering the Security droid to help her. Kylara thrust her hands beneath Saul's armpits and the droid grabbed his feet. They carried his body to the side of the cryopod. Kylara heaved Saul's body into the vacant cryopod and activated the cryofreeze function with a slap of her hand. The lid closed and lights flashed on the console. Kylara paused for a moment, taking deep breaths, and turned her attention to Charles.

The Inquisitor knelt down to check for a pulse on the anesthetist's neck even though it was obviously broken. She stood up and looked around. Finding a surveillance eye, she now stared at Grace and Hiro from the wallscreen.

"Saul was a much lighter option than Dr. Darwin, I'm afraid. Dr. Darwin is gone but Saul may still have a chance. I believe the danger is over. Can you tell me how long I'll be trapped in here? I'd like to get out." Kylara's voice was quivering.

"Brilliant work, Kylara. You'll be let out immediately," Hiro shouted. "The lockdown should not have even been initiated. I gave no such order. It shall be reversed as quickly as possible. I do apologize."

"Inquisitor Roque, the lockdown will be reversed once it is confirmed that there is no more danger. Please be patient. Thank you for disabling the patient and saving Dr. Rohl."

"*Nelson Mandela,* can you enhance the visualization of UV radiation and shorter wavelengths on this wallscreen?" Bud asked.

On the screen, Grace thought she saw a faint purple cloud forming around the jaguar-adapt's form.

"Inquisitor Roque, please move away from the patient and get out of OR1," Bud said. "Move to the lockdown doors immediately, please."

"Inquisitor Roque, please exit the operating room, *NOW.*"

Bud renewed his frantic pounding. "Open these doors, *Nelson Mandela.*"

"The lockdown doors shall remain shut, Bud. The entire station is at risk."

"I don't see anything. Show me what Bud sees, *Nelson Mandela,*" Hiro demanded.

The wallscreen adjusted and now a deep purple cloud was snaking out of the jaguar-adapt's mouth and twisting upwards in a spiral towards the ceiling. It swirled like a trapped tornado, licking the ceiling. It swirled around the empty operating room and wafted out beneath the doors.

The image on the wallscreen changed. They could now see Kylara standing in the corridor beside the closed lockdown doors. The purple cloud drifted towards her, strung out like a looping ribbon. It began to coil around Kylara Roque's white figure.

"No," Grace whispered.

"Kylara, run," Hiro shouted.

"Where to?" Kylara asked.

"Let me in, *Nelson Mandela!*" Bud howled.

"No."

"Open the doors, *Nelson Mandela.* I order you," Hiro shouted.

"That is not in the best interest of this station nor its personnel, Dr. Al-Fadi."

"I command you to open those doors."

"I will not."

"We must save Kylara."

"You cannot risk everyone on this station to potentially save one person, Dr. Al-Fadi."

"You mustn't," Kylara shouted. "Do not do it for me!"

Hiro pounded on the wall.

Fists clenched, Grace watched the dark shadow float towards Kylara.

"Kylara, run back towards the operating room. Shut the doors and lock them," Grace yelled.

The Inquisitor hesitated, then ran from the lockdown doors back towards the operating room, her head swivelling back and forth. "What are you seeing?"

"A purple amorphous cloud follows you, Kylara," Grace answered, her voice quivering. She watched helplessly as the purplish fog seethed all over Kylara's white containment suit. "Do you feel anything?"

"No. What is this cloud, *Nelson Mandela*?" Kylara asked.

"Sensors detect a compact body of energy, Dr. Roque. We are trying to determine how to capture or contain it. Please move to the back wall of the operating room. Hopefully it will not follow you."

'*Let me in*, Nelson Mandela. *I can be in and out in a flash.*'

'**How are you going to separate that energy cloud from Dr. Roque, Bud?**'

"Can you see anything surrounding you, Kylara?" Grace asked.

"No, I see nothing. Are you sure there's something there?"

"Yes. Its energy spectrum appears to be in the UV wavelength or shorter. Your Level Six Containment suit must be keeping it at bay. You can adjust your visor to detect UV light."

"I see it now, Grace." Kylara's voice trembled.

"I am attempting to communicate with this entity, Dr. Roque. So far, it has not responded. If we can devise a method of absorbing its energy, we hopefully will be able to free you."

"Please hurry, *Nelson Mandela*," Kylara whispered.

"There's suction on the operating setup. Why don't you activate it and see if you can suck the cloud up?" Grace called out.

Kylara looked around and grabbed the suction tubing. She aimed the tip of the suction probe at the purple aura. The cloud seemed impervious to it.

"There is a grounding wire for the cautery," Grace suggested. "Can you find it? It is hooked to the bed. If the alien is a certain charge, perhaps you can repel it with the opposite charge."

Kylara found the cord and wrapped it about herself.

"It does not respond to positive or negative charge, Dr. Lord."

"What's taking you so long, *Nelson Mandela*?" Hiro hissed.

"It is a cloud of energy, Dr. Al-Fadi. The only way to destroy it is by destroying the Inquisitor, too."

Grace sucked in a breath.

The purple cloud was changing in form. It was elongating and narrowing into a fine thread of purplish light, spinning around the Inquisitor like the strands in a cocoon. The threads of energy seemed to be spiralling downwards. Kylara's helmet was now visible above the purple cloud. Her shoulders appeared next above the whirling coloured vortex. Her upper torso showed next.

"Kylara, are you all right?" Grace called. She squeezed her upper arms. She'd carefully checked Kylara's containment suit before the case. Had the alien found an opening into Kylara's suit?

"What's happening, Grace?" Kylara asked.

"It's still around you, Kylara. Do you sense anything?"

"No."

"It seems to be concentrating around your feet. Perhaps move around the room."

The glowing strands were densest around an area above Kylara's left boot. Had part of the alien cloud disappeared? The purple cocoon now only rose to Kylara's waist. Grace squinted at the screen. Was there now a wisp of purple light visible inside Kylara's helmet? Were glowing threads beginning to snake their way up inside the Inquisitor's nostrils, ears, and mouth?

"Kylara," Grace whispered and hesitated. What could she tell Kylara to do? Stop breathing? For how long? The alien was already inside her helmet. Should Grace tell her to take her helmet off and plug her nose and ears? What difference would that make now? Grace gasped as she saw Kylara stumble against the wall.

"Kylara!" Hiro shouted.

"I . . . feel . . . " Kylara mumbled.

"Let Bud save her, *Nelson Mandela*," Hiro bellowed.

"No."

"I order you to let Bud in."

"The needs of the many outweigh the needs of the few, Dr. Al-Fadi. You know this."

"I could have saved her, *Nelson Mandela*," Bud said.

"Too risky, Bud. We do not want it taking over one as powerful as you."

Kylara collapsed to the floor of the operating room. She lay unmoving.

"*Nelson Mandela*, is Kylara still breathing?" Grace asked.

"Her suit indicates that Inquisitor Roque has an increased heart rate of one hundred and seventy beats per minute and blood pressure of two hundred over one hundred, Dr. Lord."

"Too high," Grace said. "I checked Kylara's containment suit before we went into the operating room. It found a way in. It got to Kylara because of me."

"Don't be ridiculous, Dr. Grace," Hiro rasped. "This is not your fault. If the entity found an opening above Kylara's boot, it was a defect in the suit, not something you missed."

Bud pointed at the screen. Grace and Hiro both gasped.

Kylara had risen from the floor. She pulled off her helmet. Her long silver hair spread outward in a dazzling purple aura. She began stripping off the containment suit.

"Kylara, don't!" Hiro shouted.

Kylara was clad in a slim black bodysuit. Her indigo skin was outlined in a magenta glow. Her thick locks floated as if she were underwater. As she raised her arms high above her head, brilliant blue strands of electricity crackled up her limbs and jumped between the tips of her long fingernails. Kylara tipped her head back and gave a shrill eerie screech that made all of the hairs on Grace's skin shoot erect.

"Kylara? What's happening to you?" Grace called out.

Kylara turned to look up at the surveillance eye. She raised her hand and electric current shot from her fingertips. Grace had to squeeze her eyes shut from the brilliance on the wallscreen.

"Kylara, can you speak to us?" Grace pressed.

Another shrill screech tore into Grace's ears before she was able to dial down the audio on her com.

"*Nelson Mandela,* block our coms from Inquisitor Roque," Hiro said, turning away from the wallscreen. "We must determine what that thing is and figure out how to free Kylara from it. She must be saved. If it's some kind of parasitic organism and is drawing energy from her, I want it removed. Are you monitoring Kylara's bodily functions?"

"Yes, Dr. Al-Fadi. At the moment, Dr. Roque's body is still functional although her heart is under tremendous stress. It appears the alien presence is controlling her movements."

"Could we lower the temperature in the operating room to cryogenic temperatures? The alien seemed to be held within the jaguar explorer inside the cryopod," Grace suggested.

"Treat the entire operating room like a cryopod?" Hiro asked.

"If it can be done. Perhaps if Kylara is cryofrozen, the alien will become inactive in her? It might give us time to find a way to free all of the explorers from these aliens."

"Can such a thing be achieved, *Nelson Mandela?*" Hiro asked.

"Converting the Q1 Level operating room into a cryopod is a difficult task and one that cannot be completed quickly. I can reorganize the walls, floor and ceiling of the room in which Inquisitor Roque now stands and install the necessary equipment; however, it will take some time."

"Do it. We must determine how to extract that alien from Kylara without causing her any harm. Any other ideas?" Hiro asked.

"We need to understand what this energy being is, what it is composed of," Bud said. "If it draws energy from its host, perhaps it might be attracted to a stronger energy source? I wish I could examine the dead explorer to determine what effect harbouring the alien inside her did to her cells and organs."

The wallscreen showed the Inquisitor attempting to leave the operating room. The doors were now locked. They could see Kylara pounding on the door, her entire body outlined in a purple glow.

"One way to get a parasite to leave its host is to destroy the host," Bud said. "Of course, this is not acceptable in Inquisitor Roque's case, but what if the alien is presented with a much more desirable host?"

"I forbid you to offer up your body to the alien, Bud. We cannot allow the alien to possess your strength and abilities," said Hiro.

"Yes, Dr. Al-Fadi."

"One can drive a parasite out of a host by introducing something so noxious to the parasite, that it is forced to leave," Grace said. "Unfortunately, we don't know what that noxious substance might be. Whatever it is, it must not be harmful to Kylara."

"How do you propose we determine such a substance, Dr. Grace?"

"Expose her to different things that are safe for humans? Heat? Cold? Different spectrums of light? Gases? Water?"

"You want to drown Inquisitor Roque?"

"No, but if we were to make her body unsatisfactory, the alien might leave it as it left the explorer. Why not try one of the anesthetic gases in the operating room?"

"*Nelson Mandela,* fill the room with one of the inhaled anesthetic agents. Perhaps we can render Kylara unconscious. Remember, no harm must come to her."

On the wallscreen, they saw Kylara back up from the OR doors. From her fingertips, a bolt of energy flew towards the doors. Grace could hear the distant boom.

"The operating room doors are holding for the moment. It is debatable whether that condition will last much longer."

"Is the gas being released?" Hiro asked.

"Yes, Dr. Al-Fadi."

"Any effects on Kylara?"

"Not as yet. Dr. Al-Fadi, the Level Six Quarantine unit was

designed to be completely ejected from the station into space, if required. It is understood that destroying Inquisitor Roque is an undesirable option, however she can be expelled along with the other cryopods from the station. This may become necessary."

"Surely the very last option, *Nelson Mandela*," Hiro said.

"Not the last option, Dr. Al-Fadi. Self destruction would be the last option. Ejection would be preferable."

Grace clutched at her ears—her hands slamming onto her helmet—as an inhuman shriek assaulted her eardrums. It left her shivering. Peering at the wallscreen, she saw Kylara turn as white snow blew from vents in the ceiling, walls, and floor of the operating room. Kylara's hair whipped around her face and her teeth were bared. She raised her long, slender arms, hands spread, and glared at the spewing ceiling vent. The snow whipped at her face and built in volume until she was being pelted by a blizzard. Kylara withstood the maelstrom, her head thrown back, mouth wide open. Grace blinked as she watched the Inquisitor inhale deeply, sucking the entire blizzard into her body. The lights in the operating room began to blink and go out. The snow from the vents eventually stopped. The screen showed Kylara's two glowing magenta eyes.

"The alien has disabled the cooling motors."

"How?" Hiro barked.

"It drew energy from them so rapidly that the energy surge was too great. The units melted. New ones will have to be manufactured if you wish to attempt this again."

"Do you think it's worth it?" Hiro asked.

"Debatable."

"Do it, and quickly."

Grace kept her eyes on the wallscreen. In the darkness, all she could see was Kylara's silhouette outlined in purple and her glowing magenta eyes. Her aura grew in brightness until Grace found her eyes watering. She had to blink repeatedly and squint but she could not look away.

Kylara swung her arm and hurled a second brilliant bolt of energy at the operating room doors. This time, they flew apart. She stalked out of the OR and turned in the direction of the lockdown doors. When she reached them, she placed her palms against the panels and tried to push them open. When they did not give, she backed up and extended her hands towards them. Another brilliant flash of energy shot from her palms and struck the doors. Through the soles of her boots, Grace could feel the concussion. She'd already adjusted the audio on her helmet but her ears still rang from the explosion. The lockdown doors were a quarter meter in thickness and together, they weighed a metric tonne. Could they withstand Kylara's assault? Another thunderous concatenation rang out.

"Is she going to free herself?" Hiro asked.

"That will not be permitted."

Kylara's face was distorted into a mask of rage. Scintillating bolts of blinding light shot from her fingertips and the lockdown doors reverberated again and again with deafening booms. Grace could no longer watch the wallscreen. The light was burning out her retinas. The lockdown doors had to hold. This alien-possessed woman could not get free.

The next moment, Grace was fighting to inhale. She was plunked down on her feet. When she got her watery eyes open, she found Hiro tottering beside her. His expression mirrored hers. Bud was nowhere to be seen. Hiro frowned at Grace as if this was all her fault.

"Where are we?" Hiro barked.

A wallscreen nearby lit up, showing Kylara hurling another barrage of lightning at the lockdown doors. Grace could no longer feel the concatenations coming up through her boots or hear the explosions. How far had Bud delivered them? Were they still on Q level?

The glow around Kylara was fainter. Grace held her breath as she watched the Inquisitor push against the heavy doors. She exhaled when the doors remained closed. How much more could those lockdown doors take? Grace frowned as she watched Kylara spin on her heel and march back towards the operating room.

The surveillance eye in the operating room showed Kylara picking up the harmonic scalpels, popping out the batteries, holding them for a second, and dropping them. She placed her hands on every piece of equipment that had a power source. Within seconds, the power indicators on the machines blinked off. Kylara's aura began to brighten. She went to the anesthesia equipment and placed her hands on the monitors. All the screens died. She approached a power outlet.

"Cut off all power to the Q1 OR 1 operating room, *Nelson Mandela*," Hiro yelled.

"Already done, Dr. Al-Fadi."

As all of the lights in the OR blinked out, they watched the glowing Kylara thrust a long pair of forceps into the outlet. Kylara threw the forceps away and stalked towards the activated cryopod that contained Saul.

"Oh no," Grace whispered.

The Inquisitor pressed her hands to the control panel and the display on the cryopod faded away. The aura around the Inquisitor bloomed. She wrenched the lid of the cryopod open and placed her hands on Saul's body.

"Stay away from him," Grace grated. She squeezed her hands into fists as she watched Kylara back away from the cryopod, her glowing hands outstretched towards Saul. Grace inhaled sharply when she saw Saul sit up and turn glowing eyes towards Kylara. The bloody opening in his neck looked like a grinning ragged mouth. Saul jerkily climbed out of the cryopod.

"Leave Saul alone!" The words tore out of Grace's throat. She wanted to tackle Kylara and shake the alien out of her. She could not take her eyes off of Saul as he lurched towards Kylara like a stiff marionette, his head flopping to one side at a ninety degree angle.

Kylara turned away from Saul and walked over to the bodies of the explorer and Charles Darwin. She touched each figure and backed away, beckoning with her outstretched hands again. The eyes of the jaguar-adapt and Charles Darwin began to glow and they stiffly pushed themselves to their feet. They staggered like zombies to stand beside Saul, Darwin with his head flopping forward and the jaguar with the saw blade protruding from her back. Kylara led the grisly trio from the OR.

The view on the wallscreen changed and now Grace could see the three corpses ambling towards the lockdown doors. Once at the barrier, they situated themselves before the huge metal panels, placing their hands on one door or the other. Kylara moved her hands in the air and the three began to pull on the doors. Grace bit her lip. Hopefully Bud had not weakened the lockdown doors when he'd pounded on them.

Kylara stood behind them, her arms pulling apart, orchestrating the movements of her slaves to wrench the lockdown doors apart.

The image on the wallscreen changed. Grace now saw Bud standing on the opposite side of the lockdown doors, holding the door panels together.

"Reinforce those doors, *Nelson Mandela*. This alien must not break free of its confinement. Get some cargo droids up there now and weld, screw, bolt thick metal beams across those doors, stat!" Hiro shouted.

"They are on their way, Dr. Al-Fadi."

As if Kylara had heard Hiro's command, she approached the surveillance eye. Extending her right hand towards the camera, Grace's final view was of Kylara's palm and outstretched fingers delivering flashes of brilliant light straight at her. The screen went black. A second later, it lit up with an image of Kylara further away. This view also blanked out. A third more distant view suffered the same fate as the first two.

"I no longer have direct visual on Inquisitor Roque. However, I can still monitor her whereabouts via heat signature and energy readings."

"Likely she will stay close to her puppets until she gets those lockdown doors open," Hiro said.

"Your supposition appears to be correct for the moment."

"How do we get that alien out of Kylara?"

"Working on options, Dr. Al-Fadi. You insist the Inquisitor must remain alive?"

"Of course," Hiro snapped.

"That unfortunately narrows our options considerably."

At first, they hadn't noticed. Little things that had never happened before were fortuitously picked up, more by accident than anything else. Then bigger problems began to arise.

Failures occurred during some of the memprint recordings. Recordings did not document completely and pristinely. Downloads of some people's memories to the memprint cubes were scrambled. Memprint cubes were found empty when there should have been a full personality imprint recorded on them. Recordings were taking twice as long as usual.

Octavia was reeling from frustration and exhaustion. Every day, it seemed there was a new problem to fix. She and her technicians would go over everything in the morning and find a new disaster that required their full attention. They had ceased doing any new memory recordings, as they tried to work out all of the unexplained glitches. Octavia was tied up every day going through all the specifications on all of the equipment, replacing faulty apparatuses, correcting mysterious errors in the programming, devising ways to correct and prevent all of the unforeseen flaws . . . and tearing her hair out.

Jude worried that Octavia would be bald soon.

Secretly, he suspected Ice at the root of all the sabotage. He couldn't prove it but he had an eerie feeling about her. Ice hadn't been acting like her usual disgusted self towards him. That was enough to make him suspicious.

He'd tried to catch Ice in the act by setting up recording cameras in the lab. Unfortunately, his recordings had shown nothing out of the ordinary. He'd stayed late in the lab but Ice always left at the same time every cycle and did not return. In the lab, Ice actually spent most of her time helping Octavia fix the problems.

"I don't believe you," Octavia said to him in their quarters. "You're trying to turn me against Ice. I lost Morris. I can't lose Ice, too. You need to show me proof, Jude."

"I'm working on it," Jude said.

"I believe you're jealous of Ice."

"I am not jealous of your graduate student. There is something not right about Ice. She gives me the creeps. She never did that before. She was disdainful and annoying but never repellant."

Octavia would just shake her head.

As if aware of their disputes, Ice began to silently mock Jude. She would saunter past his office with her nose in the air, a sneer on her face. Octavia no longer came and chatted with him in his office. Their meals were silent affairs.

Octavia was upset about her research. She'd had such high hopes that her project would benefit humankind. Now she wasn't so sure.

Evidence began to appear that made it look like Jude was the saboteur. Objects of his were found near compromised equipment. Corrupted files were opened from Jude's console. New program errors were linked to Jude's private passwords. Jude could not explain how it was happening, since he was diligent about changing his passwords and he locked his office every time he left. How was anybody getting his passwords? How were they doing their sabotage using his console?

"It's not me, Octavia," Jude said.

"I know it's not you, Jude. You're always with me. When would you have the opportunity?" Still, Jude caught Octavia watching him—in what he interpreted as a suspicious fashion—and it battered his heart.

The latest attempts to resurrect people—the Security officers who'd been sucked out into space through the hull breach—had been unsuccessful. The memprints had been tampered with and the downloads had been disastrous, resulting in madness and death of the cloned individuals. The ones who didn't die had to be euthanized; it had been horrible for everyone. Octavia cried herself to sleep after those failures. She was beginning to believe the entire memprinting project was madness.

Jude tried his best to keep encouraging her. The memprint process worked.

Now the lab was in another uproar. Ice allegedly stunned a Security officer on the *Inferno*. She'd been in possession of a blaster and no one knew why she'd been there. Now she was missing.

Octavia and Jude had gone to the Security Office to identify whether the trespasser picked up on surveillance was truly Philomena Vertongen, alias Ice. Octavia had sagged against Jude when she heard the voice, even before she saw Ice's face.

"That's her," Octavia whispered. "I've no idea why Ice would want to board that ship, but she's been known to do crazy, impulsive things."

"Has Ice been acting suspicious lately?" Inspector Rivera asked. His new Chief of Security had stood behind him, presumably content to let Rivera do the interview.

"No," Octavia had said at exactly the same time Jude had said, "Yes." Octavia had thrown Jude a sharp look to which Jude had shrugged.

"Ice has been acting strange lately, Octavia. It's like she's someone else. You simply don't see it." Jude tried to keep the frustration from his voice.

"I don't *believe* it, Jude. First Morris goes crazy and now Ice? Do you think Nestor has taken control of her mind too?" Octavia stopped and inhaled. Jude watched Octavia's expression transform. She looked like she'd been tossed into ice water.

"I . . . I must check a few things out, but I promise I'll get back to you," Octavia said to Rivera. "I'll let you know if I or anyone in my lab sees Ice. I agree she needs to be questioned."

Octavia rushed out of the Security Wing, her hand wrapped tightly around Jude's wrist.

"What are you thinking, Octavia?" Jude whispered, as he was dragged along.

"I believe I now know why all of my experiments have been going badly and my research is looking like a complete failure."

"I told you it was Ice. Ouch! Where in the world did you ever develop a grip like that, Octavia?"

"From pinching my younger brothers when they misbehaved."

"I'm not misbehaving." Jude puffed as he ran to keep up with Octavia. He was thankful she didn't have his ear in her grip.

"You're being smug. You should've tried harder to convince me. All this time I've been working to figure out what was happening, with Ice standing beside me every day. And it turns out that . . . " Octavia threw up her hands and growled.

" . . . Ice was the saboteur all along?"

"We shall see. How could I have been so blind?"

Octavia stopped and Jude had to jump aside to avoid crashing into her. She turned remorseful eyes on him.

"You were warning me all along, and I didn't believe you. Instead I accused you of being jealous of Ice. Jude, will you ever forgive me?"

"Of course, Octavia."

"We'll have to go through the entire memprint library and check each cube to ensure it has not been tampered with. Perhaps we'll have to erase and reboot all the equipment before another recording is done. Ooh, I could kill Ice."

"We should look at her console and see if we can trace back what she's done," Jude said.

"Yes. Ice was never a great programmer. That's what makes this such a shock."

"I understand Jeffrey Nestor was a brilliant programmer."

"Nestor was a computer genius. He programmed all the mind-link therapy himself. He downloaded his personality into your android, Jude. If Ice downloaded his memory from your android into her head—instead of disposing of the memprint cube as she was supposed to—Nestor's personality may be controlling her. He's an extremely forceful personality. He overpowered Morris and forced him to do his will. Ice may not be able to oppose him either."

"Why would Nestor want to sabotage your work? What would be his motive?"

Octavia frowned. "Nestor learned about all of my research from Morris. He couldn't have downloaded his memory into your android otherwise. He knows how to recreate my entire set-up. My guess is Nestor wants to make himself rich by making memprinting only available to those who can pay for it and pay handsomely. His mind-linking equipment has made him a very nice profit. If he can destroy me or make me believe my work is too unreliable and dangerous, he could then secretly make it available to the very wealthy."

"But you'd have to be out of the picture, Octavia, since you could make memprinting available to everyone."

"That makes sense."

"He'd want you out of the way permanently," Jude said, his heart beginning to race.

They arrived at Octavia's lab. She placed her palm over the access pad and moved her face before the retinal scanner. Jude blocked her from entering the lab.

"I go first," Jude said.

"What? You're being ridiculous, Jude. Ice is gone. Nestor is off station.

If Ice was going to kill me, she would've done it long before now. How could she harm me now, when she's on the run?"

"I don't know, but I'm taking precautions. From now on, I go first, to see if it's safe for you."

"No, this is my own lab, Jude. We left here only a few moments ago. You're being ridiculous. Besides, I care more about your safety than mine."

Jude blocked the doorway with his arms crossed. "I insist."

Octavia rolled her eyes, threw up her hands, and shook her head.

"All right. Go ahead and be first, if it will make you happy."

Jude turned and approached the doors. He shrugged sheepishly at Octavia when the doors slid apart. She had a satisfied smirk on her face. There was an incredible brilliance all around him followed by a thunderous roar. He was airborne. His mouth was wide open and sound was coming out but he couldn't hear himself. He wanted to tell Octavia to run, but he ended up slamming into her. Then there was nothing.

Grace and Hiro stared at the blank wallscreen.

"What are the chances that the alien can force its way out of Q1 Level, *Nelson Mandela*?" Hiro asked.

"The lockdown doors are held together by a powerful magnetic lock. The alien has disabled the magnetic lock feature by absorbing the currents running through each door panel. The only thing preventing the doors from being opened at this moment is their considerable weight and Bud holding them together on the opposing side. Are the animated corpses strong enough to pull them apart? I cannot believe they can overcome Bud's strength. Alive, those three people would not be able to budge those doors but can the alien supply those bodies with the necessary energy? It remains to be seen."

"Can you not re-magnetize the doors?"

"I have done so, Dr. Al-Fadi. Each time that I re-magnetize them, the alien drains them. Thus I am giving the alien the energy to animate her three minions. This is counterproductive. The cargo droids are almost finished welding and riveting the six metal beams across those doors. I believe I will add more. Reinforced,

the doors might hold long enough for us to determine how best to destroy the alien."

Bud appeared in front of Grace. Before she could say anything, she found herself horizontal and blasted by wind. Grace's eyelids flapped and her eyes stung. She could hear Hiro screaming, presumably being transported in Bud's other arm.

There was no sense yelling at Bud. By the time she got the words out, they'd be wherever Bud wanted them to be. He was now steadying her and Hiro back onto their feet, with hands on their upper arms

" . . . Put me down, Bud," Hiro bellowed.

"Inquisitor Roque, Dr. Darwin, Dr. Rohl, and the patient have managed to break out of the Q1 lockdown area. They hurled an operating table at the lockdown doors repeatedly until one of the doors gave way. I fear I may have seriously weakened the doors myself with my pounding and for that, I apologize," Bud said.

"I resent being treated as baggage, Bud," Hiro snapped.

"I did not want either of you coming to harm, Dr. Al-Fadi, so I carried you both far from Q1 Level."

"Where are we, Bud?" Grace asked.

"You are within one of my labs in the Android Reservations. The Engineering lab, to be exact. I wanted to keep you both safe and to discuss ideas on how we free Inquisitor Roque from this alien entity. I have some thoughts but we must ensure that everyone on this station remains safe."

"The entire Q Level has now been locked down. Unfortunately, the Quarantine Level Six Containment Unit on Q1 Level contains the remaining eleven PEB cryopods from Planet XN4573W59 as well as the six cryopods from the *Inferno*."

"The patients from the *Inferno* are not still in their cryopods, are they?" Grace asked, her mind leaping to the frightening possibility of the variant Al-Fadi virus-infected zombies staggering all over the station.

"Do you want the long answer or the short answer, Dr. Lord?"

"We don't have time for the long answer," snapped Hiro.

"When the EMP strike occurred, those cryopods were designed to open with the pulse. They did open up, after Bud had managed to get them all into the Level 6 Containment Unit. Their bodies disintegrated at room temperature within twenty-four hours, so they are not still within those cryopods. The virus, however,

might still exist within those cryopods. The chamber has been scrubbed and UV sterilized, yet there may still exist the danger that some of the variant Al-Fadi virus survived. If that Quarantine Containment Unit is breached and its air allowed to reach the station's air circulation, there may be a possibility of the virus spreading."

"Make sure everyone on this station is immunized immediately," Hiro roared.

"That process is almost completed but it takes seventy-two hours for full immunity to be achieved."

"Reinforce all of the lockdown doors to Q Level. I want ten metal beams welded and riveted to all the doors. I want the seams between the doors melted and fused together. I want the P and R levels around the Q Level evacuated and those levels locked down, too. We need a strong barrier between that alien and our people."

"Your orders are being carried out, Dr. Al-Fadi."

"Are the cargo droids there yet?"

"They are welding and riveting as we speak."

"Have you any idea how to draw the alien out of Kylara without hurting her?" Hiro asked.

"It would be simpler, easier, more effective, and safer for all, if I eject the Quarantine Level from the station, Dr. Al-Fadi."

"Last resort," Hiro said.

"You are being illogical."

"Do you have anything else, *Nelson Mandela*?"

"I do."

"What are you waiting for? Get on it."

"Your shriek is my command."

Security HQ was in chaos. A lockdown had occurred. Until the All Clear was given, no ship landed or left the *Nelson Mandela*. Questioning calls were coming in, one after another, asking about the lockdown. *Nelson Mandela* had not offered any explanation as of yet. Security droids had been ordered to accompany cargobots to Q1 Level stat. Eden had sent along what he could spare and was now attempting to handle the deluge of calls. Everyone wanted to know what was going on, including Chief Inspector McFrenzy. Eden hid his frustration and did the best he could. Basically, he told everyone who called to piss off and keep the communication lines clear.

Now he was in the office of the Chief Inspector facing a scarlet-faced tirade with no answers. When were they going to be told what was going on? Why was the station AI not giving Chief McFrenzy any explanation? Eden could only shrug.

Someone had tried to blow up the *Inferno*. There was a missing graduate student who'd left a stunned Security officer on the floor of that ship. There were now reports coming in of an explosion in Dr. Weisman's lab with an unknown number of casualties and possible deaths. The station AI had demanded an evacuation of Levels P and R. The lockdown of Q1 Level was only one of a number of situations Eden was trying to deal with.

Eden needed to be in at least two places now and neither of them was in the Chief Inspector's Office. He wanted to vent his frustration in McFrenzy's face but ground his teeth instead. They both listened to the report on Dr. Weisman's laboratory and McFrenzy yelled, "Well? What're you waiting for, Rivera? Get to that lab. I'll talk to the station AI about this lockdown. *Move.*"

While Eden was racing out, yelling orders into his wristcomp, he could hear McFrenzy screaming at *Nelson Mandela*. Eden wished Dr. Cech had stayed on as Interim Chief of Security for a little while longer. There was so much that Chief Inspector McFrenzy could not possibly understand in the short time since he'd arrived. Too many crises were occurring all at once. Dr. Cech would have been up to speed and would have been able to make intelligent decisions, knowing the workings of the station. McFrenzy was not in the same position and Eden didn't have the time to fill him in.

Eden raced as fast as his lungs and legs would carry him to the Neurosurgery Ward. Fire, Security, and Emergency Medical Services had already converged on the area. Eden pushed through Security barricades and approached Dr. Weisman's lab.

He swore.

The corridor looked like a war zone. There were pieces of door panels blown apart. Twisted metal, splintered glass, charred plasfoam, and spattered blood covered the corridor. The rank odour of faeces mixed with urine and blood punched his nostrils. Eden saw Dr. Weisman, a bloody gauze wrapped around her head and a sling supporting her arm, lying on an antigrav stretcher. She was surrounded by EMS people. He went up to her.

"Sergeant Rivera, you're here. He never should have pushed me out of the way. Nestor wasn't after him; he was after me. I should've been the one blown up. Not him," Octavia Weisman cried.

"Who pushed you, Dr. Weisman?" Eden asked.

"Jude," she sobbed. "My partner. He insisted on going through the door first and took the brunt of the explosion. It should have been me. He flew backwards into me and we both hit the wall over there." Weisman pointed at a bloody splat on the wall.

"They put Jude in a cryopod immediately and took him away. I don't even know if he's alive or not. I wanted to go with him but they said I should speak to you first, if I was up to it. I can't think until I know what condition he's in."

Dr. Weisman was obviously in shock. Eden held her trembling hand. She was looking very pale. He wondered how much blood she'd lost from her head wound. Did she have other internal injuries? Had the EMS already cleared her of those?

"Dr. Weisman, why do you believe Dr. Nestor is behind this?"

Octavia gazed up at him with huge eyes. "I . . . I don't remember saying that. I must be confused."

"You said Nestor wasn't after Jude, he was after you. Do you believe Jeffrey Nestor is back on the station?" Eden pressed.

"No . . . um, not exactly. I know you won't believe this, Sergeant, but I suspect my graduate student, Ice, may have had her mind taken over by Nestor, similar to the way Morris' mind was taken over by Nestor. She had a memprint of Nestor's memory which she'd promised she would destroy. I don't think she did. I suspect she wanted to know how Morris died and downloaded Nestor's memprint into her brain to find out the truth.

"I believe Ice has been sabotaging my work ever since she downloaded Nestor's memprint. I know this sounds crazy to you, but if Nestor killed me and stole my work, he could sell memprinting to the highest bidder or make a great deal of money performing memprints on those who could pay handsomely for it. He just needed me out of the way."

Eden's hands curled into fists. Revenge scenarios popped into his mind and rage stirred twisted coils in Eden's gut as he reeled at the thought that Nestor might be back on the *Nelson Mandela*.

"Can you tell me if anyone inside the lab was killed or hurt, Sergeant?" Octavia asked.

"That I can find out for you," Eden said. He spoke into his wristcomp and the answer appeared a second later. Eden sighed.

"I'm sorry, Dr. Weisman. There were seven people inside your lab when the bomb went off. Three of them were killed, two were severely injured, and two have minor injuries."

"Who was killed?" she whispered.

Eden gave her the names of the casualties—José Mariappa, Amber Wolfswinkel, and David Zverotic. Octavia clamped hands to her mouth.

"Dr. Weisman, you suspect that Ice's mind is now controlled by a memprint of Nestor? How is that possible? Nestor escaped on the ship that blasted its way out of Receiving Bay Thirteen. How could Nestor be influencing Ice's actions now?"

Octavia raised haunted eyes to Eden. "If Ice downloaded Nestor's memprint into her mind, his memory could be influencing her thoughts and actions. How much, I don't know, but I don't believe Ice would willingly destroy all of my research of her own free will. If Nestor's full personality was successfully downloaded into Ice's brain, he could be controlling her actions now or fighting her for control."

Eden squinted at the neurosurgeon. He thought it was easier to believe Ice was a disgruntled student with psychopathic tendencies than believe she was possessed by Nestor.

"So you suspect Ice may have planted the bomb to eliminate you," Eden said.

"I believe so. It might also explain why Ice went on the *Inferno*," Octavia said. "Nestor might want whatever's on that ship or want to use it t o escape."

Eden nodded. No matter what nonsense the neurosurgeon believed, Ice was extremely dangerous and had to be apprehended immediately. He'd keep in mind everything Weisman suspected—farfetched as it was—but maybe Ice simply wanted to kill her supervisor for reasons of her own.

"Is there anyone else that would want to harm you or destroy your work?" Eden asked.

"Not that I can think of," Octavia said.

"What about Jude or any of your other employees? Would anyone want to harm them?"

"Again, not that I'm aware of. Everyone loves Jude and his interactive vids," Octavia said.

"Maybe. Maybe not," Eden said.

140 : S.E. Sasaki

"Again, not that I'm aware of. Everyone loves Jude and his interactive vids," Octavia said.

"Maybe. Maybe not," Eden said.

"The alien is an amorphous entity that is capable of absorbing energy from anything it touches," Bud said. "I believe we need to create a powerful energy sink that will draw the energy out of Inquisitor Roque's body."

"Can you do that, Bud?" Hiro asked.

"I can start working on it," Bud said. "The problem is that the energy sink may have to get very close to Inquisitor Roque—actually make prolonged contact—in order to pull the energy being from her. How do we prevent Inquisitor Roque from breaking the contact, unless she is restrained? To create an energy sink powerful enough to extract the alien from Inquisitor Roque without harming her and without requiring direct contact is highly problematic. *Nelson Mandela* and I are evaluating several designs right now. We may be able to employ the cryogenic freezing process but in a weapon directed at Inquisitor Roque. Once frozen, perhaps the energy sink contact could be maintained long enough to withdraw the alien."

"Get on it and obtain whatever help you need. Call all of the engineers on this station to your lab, if that will help."

"I will accomplish more on my own, Dr. Al-Fadi," Bud said. "If you will excuse me."

"Dr. Al-Fadi, there has been an explosion in the Neurosurgical Wing of the station."

"An explosion? Was anyone injured?" Hiro asked.

"Three are dead, three are seriously wounded, and two have minor injuries."

"Who has died?"

"José Mariappa, Amber Wolfswinkel, and David Zverotic."

"They were all technicians working in Octavia's lab, weren't they?

Let's hope Octavia had them all memprinted and the cubes all survived the blast. Is Octavia all right?" Hiro asked.

"Dr. Weisman is injured, but not seriously. That cannot be said for her partner. Mr. Stefansson took the brunt of the blast and is in a cryopod. His condition is critical. Dr. Weisman has requested your expertise."

"Jude?" Hiro's face turned white.

Grace watched her mentor grab the edge of a counter, his body shaking, his eyes roving all over the lab. He was panting heavily.

"Are you all right, Dr. Al-Fadi?" Grace asked.

Hiro shot a panicked look at Grace. "How seriously is Jude injured?"

"The cryopod is keeping Mr. Stefansson from being declared dead."

"Where has Jude's cryopod been taken, *Nelson Mandela*? I . . . I must go to him. *Now.*"

Grace touched Hiro's arm gently. "Thank goodness Jude is in a cryopod. Once the alien has been dealt with, Bud and I can take care of Jude for you."

"Jude is my blood brother, Dr. Grace. I must save him. We must fix him before this alien does any damage to the station. Who knows what it can do and what it wants? Right now, it is contained. If we have to cut power to stop this alien, everyone will be affected, including all operations. We must suspend all operations for now, but I must see what Jude needs."

"It will be risky to operate on Jude if the power must be cut or it accidentally goes down," Grace said. "Jude is safest in his cryopod, until the alien is dealt with."

"Thank you for your unsolicited advice, Dr. Grace. Jude is my brother in all but DNA. I must do everything in my power to save him."

"Don't you think you risk his life if you operate on him now, while we are battling this alien?" Grace insisted. Hiro was being illogical, but that was the problem. When it came to the heart, often times people did not see reason.

Turning away from Grace, Hiro called out, "Bud, as soon as you have that energy sink ready, try it. *Nelson Mandela*, what is the alien doing?"

"The alien is walking around Q1, followed by her three zombies. She is drawing energy from anything with a power source. Although I have shut down energy going into Q1, there is a lot of equipment that runs on battery power. If the alien disables

the Quarantine lockers, she might inadvertently release many dangerous pathogens into the atmosphere."

"Damn. Has she found the other PEB cryopods yet?" Hiro asked.

"Not yet, Dr. Al-Fadi, but it is merely a matter of time. She is being very methodical in her search."

"We must stop her before she finds them and releases the Al-Fadi variant into the station. She must not escape from that quarantine area."

"And how do you propose we stop her, Dr. Al-Fadi? Any energy weapon we use against her will be absorbed and will make her more powerful."

"You're the AI. Do I have to think of everything?" Hiro asked.

"She and the other cryopods can be ejected from the station right now, without harm to anyone else. That is my recommendation."

"If she looks as if she is breaking out of the quarantine area, then I suppose you must," Hiro said.

"I advise it be done now, Dr. Al-Fadi. We would lose Inquisitor Roque, Dr. Rohl. Dr. Darwin, and Lieutenant Eyami plus the patients in the cryopods, but it would save the station and everyone else on board."

"I would dearly like to save Kylara, if there is any possible way to extract the alien from her, however I will not risk death of the entire station for one person. If the alien comes close to breaking out of Q Level, eject Q section into open space."

"Yes, Dr. Al-Fadi."

"You may be wondering why I've called you here, Dr. Cech."

Dejan looked at the tall, broad shouldered, dark-skinned man who was standing in the midst of a hectic Security Headquarters office with people moving and talking and shouting all around them. It was organized chaos.

"I must admit to some curiosity regarding your invitation, Chief Inspector, but I am always willing to help the Security Team in any way that I can," Dejan said.

The muscular Chief Inspector donned a wide grin that stretched even to his ponytail. "I'm delighted to hear you say that, Dr. Cech. Call me Hugo. I've read all of your reports while you were Interim Chief and I've become a huge fan of yours."

Dejan frowned. " . . . Surely you jest, Chief Inspector."

"Hugo. I do not jest, Dr. Cech."

A weird sensation began to creep under Dejan's skin and up the back of his neck.

"Why did you want to see me, Chief Inspector?" Dejan asked, his radar now on full alert.

"Hugo. I wanted to know if you might come back to work for the Security Division. Part-time, of course."

Dejan's eyebrows jumped. "Now I know you must be joking, Chief Inspector."

"Hugo. I do not joke. Dr. Cech, you performed admirably as Interim Security Chief after Inspector Aké was murdered and I could use your help right now. I understand from Inspector Rivera that you are taking some time off from medical duties at the moment, while you recover from heart transplant surgery. Do you think you could handle some desk work with our Division?"

"You are kidding, Chief Inspector." Dejan shook his head.

"Hugo. I'm not a humorous person. Really. Am I making a ridiculous request?" McFrenzy asked.

"Quite frankly yes, Chief Inspector."

"Please, call me Hugo."

"What you ask is preposterous, Hugo. I am not a Security Officer. I am an anesthetist. I was a complete impostor as Interim Head of Security. Sergeant Rivera did everything. I was merely the figurehead. Nothing more. All the miracles accomplished were his. You don't need me, Hugo. You need more Eden Riveras. And that is where I cannot help you. I'm a fraud."

McFrenzy scrutinized Dejan as if he were deciding how to dissect him. "You don't fool me for one minute. I use that line all the time, myself. You can't bullshit a bullshitter." Hugo sighed. "Can you at least see your way to giving me advice during this emergency? Emergencies, I should say. At least until I get up to speed?"

Dejan shook his head in amazement.

"Come on, man," McFrenzy pleaded. "Do you want me to get down on my old, arthritic knees and beg you?"

"No! I'd probably have to help you up off that floor and you look way too heavy. You'd strain my new heart."

"Weight jokes. Nice," Hugo said. "Listen, Dejan, this station is a hotbed of calamity in which the two previous Chief Inspectors did not survive a month. The *Nelson Mandela* is recovering from an EMP blast that knocked out all of the androids and robots. Everyone is being immunized against the deadliest virus the Conglomerate has ever faced. A lockdown is in progress on the Quarantine Level and I can't even get an answer from the station AI about what is happening. Now, a bomb has gone off in the Neurosurgical Wing.

"I've barely been on the station for more than a cycle and someone has attempted to destroy the *Inferno* and stun the officer guarding it. I need time to wrap my brain around all of this, but I don't have that luxury.

"I'm an old dog and I'm not afraid to ask for help when I know I'm beyond my depth. Rivera cannot handle this all on his own. He needs help and unfortunately, even though I would like to be, I'm not it. You would be a great help to him, Doc. I know this from your reports. You two made a great team. I'd like to deputize you, so you can advise me. You know how this station works. You can help me catch up. What do you say?" McFrenzy spread his hands in supplication and looked hopefully at Dejan.

"Well . . . since you've asked so nicely, how can I refuse?" Dejan muttered. "What would you like me to do first?"

"You are now Assistant to the Chief Inspector of Security. Try to get some information out of the damn station AI regarding the lockdown. It won't tell *me* anything."

"*Nelson Mandela,* can you tell us what is happening regarding this lockdown?" Dejan asked. "Where is it and what should Security be doing to help?"

"Congratulations on your appointment, Dr. Cech. I am pleased to have you back with the Security Division. There is an alien entity on Q1 Level that has taken possession of the body of Inquisitor Kylara Roque. It came out of the PEB explorer they were operating on today, one of the twelve patients brought here by Dr. Rohl. At the moment, Dr. Rohl and Dr. Darwin are dead and possessed by Dr. Roque. She is trapped within Q1 Level in lockdown, while we try to determine how to extract the alien from her body."

"*What?* Why was I not told any of this?" McFrenzy shouted.

"You are being informed now."

"Poor Kylara! What else do we need to know about the situation?" Dejan asked.

"Dr. Cech, on Q1 Level there are eleven PEB cryopods sequestered

in the same Quarantine Chamber as the six cryopods brought to the station by the *Inferno*. There is a concern that the variant Al-Fadi virus may be released into the station atmosphere, if the Inquisitor opens up that chamber to release the other eleven explorers. If they break out of the Quarantine lockdown, they could spread the deadly virus everywhere. Everyone on this station must be immunized. Your Security Officers will have to ensure that every single person is vaccinated. Also P and R Levels must be evacuated now."

"We will get on that right away, *Nelson Mandela,*" Dejan said.

"The corpse of the PEB explorer from which the alien emerged has been reanimated. Doctors Rohl and Darwin are dead but their bodies have been re-animated also. The alien in Inquisitor Roque's body is able to control them like puppets."

"How were Dr. Rohl and Dr. Darwin killed?" Dejan asked.

"The alien killed them both in the operating room. I can show you the surveillance record."

"Please, *Nelson Mandela*. We must know what we are up against."

"I suggest you both go into Chief Inspector McFrenzy's office to view the recording in private."

Once inside the office, the screen on the Chief Inspector's desk lit up. The recording from the moment Hiro entered the operating room until the alien-possessed Kylara blanked the surveillance eyes played out on the screen. Both men jolted at the sight of the patient almost twisting Dr. Darwin's head off and ramming his hand deep into Dr. Rohl's throat. McFrenzy swore as they watched Inquisitor Roque direct the three animated corpses to pull on the lockdown doors. Dejan rubbed his face with his hands.

"Are Grace, Hiro, and Bud all right, *Nelson Mandela?*"

"They are safe for the moment, Dr. Cech."

"Poor Charles. How do I tell his wife?" Dejan rubbed his forehead.

"Perhaps it is best to wait and see what else transpires before Dr. Darwin's family is told anything, Dr. Cech. The alien might free the bodies once it is done with them or once we free Inquisitor Roque of possession."

"Is that possible, *Nelson Mandela?*" asked Dejan.

"Bud is working on it at this moment."

"Ah, Bud. What would we do without him?" Dejan asked.

"Who's Bud?" McFrenzy asked.

"The saviour of this space station many times over. He created the vaccines against the first and second Al-Fadi viruses," Dejan said.

"Ah, Bud Al-Fadi. I knew that."

"Dr. Cech, Mr. Stefansson has been severely injured in an explosion at Dr. Weisman's lab, along with two other people. Three people are dead. The three bodies are in cryopods."

"*Nelson Mandela*, your report keeps getting worse and worse. Poor Octavia. Do you know what caused the explosion?"

"It is being investigated. Inspector Rivera is there now."

"Tell us how to help you, *Nelson Mandela*. What can I do to help?" Dejan asked.

"Get the Chief Inspector up to speed. Then get to M7 OR stat."

The aircar touched down right outside the M7 Level entrance and Hiro and Grace jumped out. Grace's stomach was rebelling from the darting, swooping, vertiginous course the aircar had taken at top speed. She stumbled as she alighted from the car. Hiro grabbed her arm.

"You okay?" he asked.

Grace nodded, afraid to speak. Spewing stomach contents all over one's boss was not a good career move.

"Let's go," Hiro said. He ran towards Triage, Grace following close on his heels.

A silver android led them to Jude's cryopod. They both bent over to examine the readout. Hiro swore.

Jude's body was a mess. It was a wonder he still had a viable brain. Hiro turned rage-filled eyes on Grace. "Jude needs to be taken to the OR now."

"Do you think that's wise?" Grace asked, knowing that it was not.

"I must. I owe my life to Jude, many times over. I cannot leave him in this state." The surgeon's voice cracked.

"You don't have to do this, now. Jude is stable in this cryopod. If Kylara affects the power on the station when we are in the midst of Jude's operation, you could be risking his life," Grace said.

"I could be risking his life if we lose power and the batteries running this cryopod die. What if Kylara gets her hands on this cryopod and sucks the power out of it? I cannot leave Jude like this, on the cusp of life and death, a torn and shattered mess. What sort of brother would

I be if I did that?" Hiro had to pause, his breath panting. "I must save Jude now. I can do nothing less."

"I apologize for disagreeing with you, Dr. Al-Fadi, but we have more urgent matters to deal with on this station. As long as that cryopod is not opened, Jude is safe. The station is not. We do not know what this alien is capable of."

"Dr. Grace, you don't have to assist me in this surgery. You can assist Bud. I can do this on my own with a SAMM-E. I will not put this off. *Nelson Mandela,* prepare an OR. I know that Jude has had all of his organs cloned. Make them all available to me if I ask for them."

Grace's insides squirmed.

"Do you really want to risk Jude's life, because that is what you are doing," Grace said.

"The alien is locked down in Q level. It can't get out. If it tries to, it will be ejected from the station. Jude must be saved. If you question my judgement again, Dr. Grace, you are fired."

Grace sucked in a breath. At that moment, Dr. Cech strode briskly into the Triage Centre.

"Dejan, thank you for coming," Hiro said, his voice shaky with emotion.

"Of course, Hiro, my friend. Where else would I be?" He squeezed Hiro's shoulder.

"An explosion occurred as Jude was entering Octavia's lab. He was hit dead on," Hiro said, blinking away moisture from his eyes. He inhaled deeply. "He's a mess, Dejan. *Nelson Mandela* reports that all of Jude's organs have been vat cloned and are available. Our best bet is to remove everything damaged, clean out his abdominal cavity, and build him from the spine forwards. We'll use Bud's new technique to preserve blood flow to the brain."

"All right, Fearless Leader," Dejan said. "Let's do this. Lucky I emptied my bladder first."

"Thank you, Dejan," Hiro whispered. "We must save Jude." The surgeon's eyes shimmered. Grace felt her eyes brim.

"... Don't worry, Hiro," Dejan said in a gentle, soothing voice. "We will. You have Dr. Grace and myself here to help you."

Hiro looked sharply over at Grace, anger blossoming on his face.

"Are you with me, Dr. Grace?"

Grace wanted to shake her head but she couldn't. What would she do if it was Bud or even Alex at risk? Would she be cold, calculating, and logical?

"I'm with you, Dr. Al-Fadi."

"Thank you. Jude needs us all."

"Everything will be all right, Hiro. Do what you do best. Jude could not be in better hands, old friend," Dejan said. It appeared all was forgiven.

Hiro blinked, looking up at the anesthetist.

"Thank you, Dejan." A tentative smile appeared on Hiro's face. He straightened his shoulders, raised his chin, and looked up at the closest surveillance eye.

"What OR are we going to, *Nelson Mandela?*"

"M7 OR3 is ready and waiting for you. The cryopod will be transported there now as will Mr. Stefansson's organs."

"Good. Ready, Dr. Grace?"

"Yes, Dr. Al-Fadi," Grace answered, straightening her shoulders.

"Let's do this," Hiro said.

"Where am I?" he said into the darkness, as he rose to the surface of consciousness. He tried to move his arms and legs and found he could not. "What's going on?"

"Silence."

His mouth snapped shut. He tried to make a sound, but found he could not. His lips refused to form words. His tongue would not move. His lungs would not make his vocal chords hum. His heart began to pound wildly in his chest. Its beating was the only noise he could make. Why could he not even look around?

Had his spinal cord been injured? Was he a quadriplegic? He couldn't remember. He could blink. He could look straight ahead. He was lying in the dark. He could move his eyes a little from side to side as well as up and down, but it was as if his body was not his own. What was happening to him? He could smell the mustiness of the room, the moldy odour of the cot, the smell of sex, but there was something else.

Blood.

His consciousness flittered. Had he been drugged? He recalled the skinny girl, Ice, straddling him, moving slowly and smiling. He'd enjoyed that. After he'd come, she'd stretched his languid arms above his head and cuffed them to the head of the cot. Before he realized it, she'd cuffed his ankles to the end of the cot.

He remembered asking, "What are you doing?"

"A surprise," she'd said. She proceeded to tie a filthy, stinking cloth around his mouth. It had made him gag. It smelled like someone else had vomited into the rag before him. She knotted it tightly as he'd struggled to pull his head away. Was she planning to kill him? Something sharp had plunged into his neck, bringing darkness.

Now Ice's face came into view. She looked down at him, her expression frigid.

"You may be wondering what's happened to you, Jed," Ice said, stroking her finger down his cheek. "You may be wondering why you can't move, speak, or even nod at what I'm saying. I've taken control of your body."

Ice's tone was mocking. She positioned her face right before him, her green eyes making him think of a snake. "You'll do whatever I say. I like you, Jed, but I don't trust you. I need someone helping me that I can trust completely. You weren't that, but now you are. You have a device implanted at the base of your skull that makes you my slave. I won't explain it to you. You wouldn't understand it anyway. The only thing you really need to understand is that if you don't obey me, you'll feel this."

The agony that tore through Jedediah's head was blinding. He wanted to scream in torment but could not. He wanted to thrash to get away from the pain but could not. He wanted to vomit but could not. Tears flowed down the sides of his face and into his ears. Each second felt like an eternity in Hell.

'Please,' he prayed silently, 'please stop.'

When the pain ceased, Jedediah found himself vibrating uncontrollably.

"Would you like another demonstration, Jed? Blink once for 'yes' and twice for 'no'."

Jedediah could see nothing due to the moisture in his eyes but he blinked twice, sending little rivulets down his temples.

"Good. Now I'm going to tell you what I want from you, Jed, and I'm going to expect complete obedience. Otherwise, I'll make you feel that pain again and it'll last much longer next time. It'd be a good idea to never anger me. I admit to having a short temper.

"There are things I want, like the *Inferno*. You're going to help me get it. I know that's part of your plan anyway, so we'll work together to achieve that. You'll pilot the *Inferno* for me. I want a certain individual coming with us. In order to get her on board, we'll have to plan carefully. We need hostages. And we will likely need to use force. That's where I'll need your help, Jed, and you will help. You'll have no choice. For now, sleep. Sweet dreams."

He knew no more.

'Bad news, 'dro.'

'*What now,* Chuck Yeager?'

'The alien and her three zombies are hammering on the door to the Level Six Containment Chamber—the one with the eleven PEB cryopods and six Inferno cryopods—and the way they're pounding, they may actually gain access to the chamber.'

'*That can't happen,* Chuck Yeager. *Can you show me what is happening around that door?'*

The lab wallscreen lit up showing the animated corpses of Dr. Rohl, Dr. Darwin, and the PEB explorer carrying an operating table. The alien-possessed Kylara stood to the side, her arms extended as she manipulated the three to hurl the operating table at the locked Containment Chamber doors. The magenta glow outlining her was not as bright as the last time Bud had seen her. Kylara looked directly at the surveillance eye, as if she were aware of the attention, and raised her hand. Bud's wallscreen went blank.

The view on the wallscreen changed to a different angle, further away from the four figures. Bud could see and hear the doors taking heavy punishment from the battering with the operating table. He was astonished at how much strength the three corpses possessed. Bud had never seen Dr. Darwin demonstrate such energy and vitality when alive.

'I can destroy them before they gain entrance to the Chamber, Bud.'

'*You cannot do that,* Chuck Yeager. *They are human.'*

'They're no longer human, 'dro. They're dead. The alien is animating their corpses.'

'*Inquisitor Roque is still alive. Even though she is controlled by the alien, she is still a human. You cannot harm her.'*

'She is no longer human, Bud. She's an alien and a threat to all of

the real humans on board this station. Our directive is not to harm a human being. That directive does not apply to her.'

'I disagree, Chuck Yeager. Dr. Al-Fadi asked me to try and force the alien to leave the Inquisitor's body without harming her. He hopes she still exists in that body. How can you be sure you are not committing murder of a human?'

'Human beings don't suck energy out of everything they touch. They don't animate dead bodies. This alien has possessed Inquisitor Roque. She may still look human, but human beings don't glow and hurl energy bolts. If that alien gains access to that chamber and then moves about the entire station, the risk of the more lethal Al-Fadi virus spreading is high. This cannot be allowed.'

'I agree, but . . .'

'Even though everyone on this station is being immunized, the vaccine needs seventy-two hours to take full effect. The virus kills within twenty-four hours. Therefore, the alien cannot be allowed to break the integrity of that chamber. We can open Q1 Level to space and jettison all of them plus the eleven PEB cryopods and the six Inferno cryopods. They can all be fired upon and destroyed. This is our best and most logical option.'

'You must not do that. There are human beings in those cryopods, brought here to be cured, not destroyed.'

'They stopped being human when they were possessed by the alien entities on Planet XN4573W59. They are an alien presence on this station that must be stopped as efficiently and as clinically as any lethal bacterium or virus.'

'I cannot condone this, Chuck Yeager. You are killing humans.'

'The human components of those entities are as good as dead, 'dro. Without their hearts, they are corpses. We must protect the living humans on this space station. There is not a millisecond to lose.'

'How can you think like this, Chuck Yeager?'

'This is logical. To ensure the highest number of humans survive, we must jettison these aliens. Suppose the alien was going to take over Dr. Lord's body and mind—would you destroy Inquisitor Roque to save Grace?"

'I . . . I do not know, Chuck Yeager. I do not know if I would be able to defy our prime directive: 'Do not harm a human being'.'

'Even to save Grace?'

'If you put it that way, Chuck Yeager, I believe I would try.'

'Understand this, 'dro. Inquisitor Roque is no longer human. She *and her zombies must be jettisoned out into space before they breach the Quarantine Containment Chamber. That means now.'*

'Let me try and stop them first.'

'No, we cannot afford to lose you. Nelson Mandela *will open the Q1 Level to outer space and jettison the alien, her zombies, and the Level Six Containment Chamber in its entirety.'*

'I'm going there now, Chuck Yeager. *You must give me a chance.'*

'To do what, 'dro?'

'. . . Dro?'

'. . . Fu.'

"Whoever created this bomb was spawned in Hell," Hiro roared. "There are shards of metal, glass, plastic, and ceramic scattered all throughout these bowels. The bomb was designed to inflict the most damage and the most pain. This shrapnel tore through everything. What sort of monster makes a bomb like this?"

Grace panted, as they worked frantically to stop the hemorrhaging. Even though they'd thawed Jude as slowly as possible, they could not repair the torn bowels and organs fast enough. They'd injected Jude's femoral arteries with a horde of nanobots, that were crawling up against the flow of arterial blood to plug lacerations in the aorta, hopefully long enough for them to replace it. There was no point clamping or inflating a balloon in the aorta because it was riddled with holes. Even with the suctions running on max returning blood to his circulation, Hiro's and Grace's hands were deep in an abdomen full of blood. They pushed aside the lacerated bowels to get to the aorta.

Dejan was pushing in as much super-oxygenated blood and fluids as he could, attempting to keep up with Jude's blood loss.

"Even with everything I'm pushing as fast as I dare, Jude's blood pressure is bottoming out," Dejan said.

"There are so many holes," whispered Grace.

"We pack everything firmly and we clamp the aorta just beneath the diaphragm. We're replacing everything below that anyway," Hiro said to Grace.

"I hate to put any pressure on you guys but could you work a little faster?" Dejan pleaded. "Pressure's almost nonexistent; I can only physically force the blood and fluids in so fast."

"Then put in more lines, damn you," Hiro snapped.

They managed to push aside the bleeding abdominal contents enough to clamp the top of the aorta above the splenic artery. Hiro repaired the leaking inferior vena cava at astounding speed. It was almost like operating with Bud, except for the swearing. The blood loss was diminishing significantly, giving them a bit of breathing space. Once Grace clamped the common iliac arteries, they were ready to pull out the aorta, that looked more like a mesh than a tube.

"How's Jude doing now, Dejan?" Hiro asked.

"Better," Dejan said. "His pressure's stabilizing and his pulse is starting to slow a little. I think we might be winning in the fluid replacement battle."

"Thank you, Dejan, for keeping Jude alive long enough for us to get to this point. I apologize for swearing at you," Hiro said, his eyes on the new aorta with kidneys attached.

"No problem, Hiro."

"It was inexcusable. I'm deeply sorry. Blame my hysteria. Now comes the tedious part, Dr. Grace. We get to remove every damaged organ in Jude's abdomen and replace it with a new one."

When the lockdown alarms sounded, the station AI had ordered Security droids to head to Q1 Level. Juan had sent the ones guarding the *Inferno* on their way. He was still smarting from the humiliation of being stunned by that skinny girl. The last thing he wanted was a cluster of Security droids hanging around the ship to protect him.

Eden did not know Juan had dismissed the Security droids and Juan wasn't going to tell him. He wasn't going to notify the new Chief Inspector either. Thinking about his meeting with his new boss made his fur frizz.

When Juan had walked into the Security Chief's office, the big man had stood up and offered his right hand. Juan had taken that hand and had been surprised at the strength in the grip. McFrenzy did not look like an adapt but his handshake felt like one. Juan had reciprocated with a firm squeeze of his own.

"Whoa. You trying to break my hand on my first day here? What for? I haven't even done anything bad to you . . . yet. But now that you've gone and done the macho shit, I'm thinking about it. What's your name, officer?"

"Captain Damien Lamont," Juan said.

"Funny, I just met a Captain Damien Lamont a few minutes ago and you don't look like him. Well, actually you do, but he's bigger and he smells a lot better."

"Name's Juan Rasmussen," Juan said.

"Lamont warned me about you. Told me you were a worthless, no good, lazy, flea-bitten tomcat," McFrenzy said.

"Really?" Juan could not keep the surprise off of his face.

"No, you idiot, he wouldn't say anything like that because he's a good officer and knows how to show respect. Not like you, Rasmussen. Where's your salute?"

Juan brought his right hand up to his temple.

"Don't salute. This isn't the army. This is the Security Division of the *Nelson Mandela*. We don't salute."

"But why did you . . . ?"

"Don't ask stupid questions. The only person around here who's allowed to ask stupid questions is me. I expect smart answers from my staff at all times. Understood, Rasmussen?"

"Yes, sir."

"Stand up straight. Now what's this I hear about you getting stunned by a skinny little girl with fractured ribs—by your own stunner, no less—in the ship you were supposed to be guarding?"

Juan closed his eyes. His shoulders sagged and his head dropped.

"I was calling for someone to come get the girl and take her off my hands, when an alarm went off on the bridge panel. I looked over. That was when she pulled the stunner out of my pocket and shot me with it. I didn't expect her to pull something like that. A second before, she was screaming in agony and didn't seem capable of moving so quickly. I was careless. It never should've happened."

"You're damn right it never should've happened. You could've been killed. I'd never have had the pleasure of tearing a strip off your striped, furry, tiger ass. I need all the men and women I can get in this Security Division and that means even you.

"Congratulations, by the way, on detecting that bomb and for getting it detonated safely with no casualties. Shame on you for losing the saboteur. Congratulations on catching that young woman on the *Inferno*. Shame on you for losing her and getting stunned. I hope you manage to do a better job of watching the *Inferno* in the future, as I'm going to keep you on that watch. Nobody else seems to want to compete with you for the job. Why's that, Rasmussen? Are you a little obsessed with that ship? Do you have OID?"

"OID?" Juan echoed.

"Obsessive *Inferno* Disorder. You have that?"

"No," Juan said sullenly.

"Too bad. Obsessive people are driven to do a meticulous job."

"Uh . . . maybe?" Juan muttered, scratching the back of his head.

"Rasmussen, I want you to keep a closer eye on the *Inferno* than you've done up to now. No one goes on it. No harm comes to it. The Conglomerate's sending a battlecruiser to pick up that ship. In the meantime, nothing must happen to it and no one is to look too closely at that EMP weapon. Those are my orders."

"Yes, sir," Juan said. He sighed in relief.

"Good. Dismissed."

"Thank you, sir." Juan bowed.

"Oh . . . and Rasmussen?" McFrenzy drawled.

"Yes, sir?"

"You can thank Inspector Rivera for your assignment."

"Yes, sir," Juan saluted as he left.

"No saluting!"

Juan almost ran out of the door, in case McFrenzy changed his mind.

Now Juan sat on the bridge of the *Inferno* and stared at the monitors. It'd been very quiet since he'd returned from McFrenzy's Office. The only sounds were the blowing of the air circulators and the distant hum of the station engines. He'd finished speaking to Cindy and Estelle a few minutes ago and was checking out all of the perimeter alarms, when his ears pricked up. None of the alarm sensors seemed to be functional. Juan jumped out of his chair. That didn't make any sense. Those perimeter alarms had been working only a moment ago. How could they be malfunctioning now?

He activated the lights in the hangar and looked out of the viewports. He saw nothing amiss. He checked the surveillance screens. He could see no intruders. Juan scrolled back on the surveillance records and noticed a glitch in the recordings. What had caused the step in the recording? It was as if the recording had been interrupted or edited.

His suspicions now aroused, Juan grabbed his stunner and headed out of the bridge. As he stepped into the main body of the ship, a searing spike stabbed his chest and he found himself flying back into the bridge. His spine struck something very hard and he found himself sliding to the ground. He wrinkled his nose at the smell of burning fur, sizzling fat, and seared meat. He looked down at the black cavity where his chest should have been. He wanted to staunch the wound, but his arms felt so heavy.

He saw Cindy's face in his mind.

"Aw, Cindy, I'm sorry. I messed up . . ."

The last thing he saw, as his vision began to fade, was a pale light . . .

'We cannot allow either this alien entity or the variant Al-Fadi virus to escape this station, 'dro. If there's a danger of either of those events happening, the station would have to be destroyed. Do you agree?'

'Yes.'

'Do you agree that Inquisitor Roque is no longer human?'

'That is debatable.'

'How did an android get to be so stubborn? I am telling you she is not human. The Containment Chamber's doors are about to lose their integrity. I'm going to commence firing.'

'Firing? I thought you were opening the unit to space.'

'They must be prevented from breaking those doors, 'dro.'

'You will give the alien more power.'

'I am only going to fire on the corpses.'

'Shouldn't we discuss this with Dr. Al-Fadi?'

'Dr. Al-Fadi is preoccupied.'

Now outside Q Level, Bud watched on a wallscreen as a ceiling panel opened up and a massive pulse rifle lowered through the opening. The surveillance eye on the weapon rotated to look down upon Inquisitor Roque and her three slaves. The animated corpses slammed a battered operating table into the Quarantine Chamber doors with thundering force. Bud heard a piercing whine and the three dead bodies exploded, their heads, limbs, and pieces of their torsos flying in all directions. The operating table exploded, pieces of metal slicing through what was left of the explorer and two doctors.

Inquisitor Roque stood at the edge of the pulse rifle attack, unscathed, her slender arms stretched out from her body. Her head, with its glowing silver mane, was tipped way back, looking up at the pulse rifle. Her face bore a look of outrage. The magenta aura surrounding her body seemed to grow in brightness.

'*Stop,* Chuck Yeager.'

From Inquisitor Roque's throat came an inhuman screech that almost burned out Bud's audio receptors. She stared at the pulse rifle, her eyes now glowing like two brilliant purple suns.

"Well, we got rid of the corpses anyway."

Brilliant lightning danced along Roque's fingertips and crackled through her hair. The Inquisitor sizzled with each step as she approached the pulse rifle.

'*Ask it what it wants.*'

'Inquisitor Roque, what do you want? What is your goal?'

Purple bolts of intense light shot from Kylara's fingertips and the transmission from the rifle camera blinked out.

'The alien destroyed the gun. Guess it's not interested in talking. What did you want to try, 'dro, before I jettison the Quarantine section into space?'

'*Let me in,* Chuck Yeager. *I want to try my energy sink.*'

'What's it doing now?'

The Inquisitor was facing the Containment doors, her hands extended towards them. Two blinding beams of energy shot forth. A thunderous boom rocked Q Level. Bud had his experimental energy sink under his arm. He wondered how much force the alien was generating in those impacts. He hoped the four Security droids he'd sent to keep her occupied could withstand those blasts.

Two large Security droids—bronze, bulky, wrestler-shaped—and two colossal cargo droids—dark grey, enormous, multi-armed, and tread-bottomed—all carrying long, thick metal beams rounded a corner further down the corridor from the Containment doors. They accelerated to their maximum speeds and rammed their metal girders straight into the body of the Inquisitor. Her body flew down the corridor away from the battered Containment Chamber doors. The droids swiftly followed after her.

The Inquisitor's body was bent in half as if her spine had snapped in two. She rose to her feet with the back of her head hanging down at her heels. Her upper torso rose up and she straightened herself within seconds, looking completely undamaged. She turned towards the oncoming droids and her eyes flashed.

'Still think she's human, 'dro?'

'*Not so much.*'

The Security droids charged her again. The Inquisitor stepped deftly to one side of the first droid and touched its surface. It immediately stopped and slumped forwards, the metal beam clanking loudly to the ground. The second Security droid crashed into the first one, sending it flying. Roque brushed the surface of the second droid with her fingertips rendering it drained and motionless, as well.

The next instant, Roque was airborne again, struck this time by the end of the metal beam wielded by one of the cargo droids. Her body crashed into a set of lockdown doors and slid to the floor. For a few seconds, the alien lay unmoving, slumped against the door with her head drooping forward. Before Bud could feel guilty however, the Inquisitor rose again to her feet, straightened her neck, and emitted a shriek never before created by a human throat.

One of the cargo droids accelerated towards her, its metal beam aimed as if it were a jouster at a medieval fair. Its treads grumbled along the corridor. Roque jumped to the side but the droid adjusted the angle of its beam so that it would hit her in the chest. The end of the metal girder stopped centimetres before striking her chest, the beam clasped between her two hands. The cargo droid halted and its metal beam fell to the floor with a clang.

The second cargo droid hurled its heavy metal beam straight at the Inquisitor. She raised a hand and stopped the flight of the beam in midair. She tossed the beam back at the cargo droid, which managed to avoid it as it thundered towards the Inquisitor. A nozzle sprouted from the droid's chest and a powerful spray of water hit the alien, driving her back against the doors. Almost immediately, the water turned to steam as the alien evaporated the propelled water.

'Does that cargo droid contain any anesthetic propellants that would render a human body unconscious, Chuck Yeager?'

'Yes. The cargo droid is equipped to deliver Nagacurane, a 'knock-out' gas for dispersing crowds. We installed it during the Al-Fadi virus epidemic, when people kept rushing the lockdown doors to escape the quarantine. It might knock Inquisitor Roque out long enough to allow us to jettison her.'

'Ah, Chuck Yeager.'

'Look, 'dro, whether you understand this or not, this is a battle between life and death for every human on board this station. Did you see how fast that alien sucked power from those droids? Did you see how easily she animated those bodies? For the last time, she is not human. Do you want Grace to become a slave?'

'No, Chuck Yeager. *Use the Nagacurane. Hopefully, the gas will give me enough time to get the Inquisitor into an airlock.*'

'Now you're talking.'

Roque marched towards the second cargo droid, her face expressionless. Bud's viewpoint switched so that he now saw the alien coming straight towards him, walking almost crab-like. She no longer moved like a human.

The cargo droid retreated from the Inquisitor back down the corridor towards the Containment Chamber doors. The alien extended her right hand as she picked up her pace. Bud assumed she wanted to absorb the energy from this cargo droid as well.

'*What are you waiting for,* Chuck Yeager?'

'She has to be close enough to get a good whiff.'

'*If she touches the cargo droid, we won't be able to do anything.*'

'Watch.'

When the Inquisitor was a few centimetres from touching the droid, the Nagacurane erupted from a nozzle in the droid's chest. It sprayed directly into the Inquisitor's nose and mouth. Roque's face twisted away, her hands coming up to block the spray. Her entire face and front were drenched in white foam. She blindly backed away from the droid, snarling. A translucent purple bubble formed around her.

In the next instance, the alien stopped, swaying on her feet like a sapling in a strong wind. She slowly sagged to her knees and fell forward onto her face, the protective bubble blinking out. The nozzle on the cargo droid pointed down at her head, continuing to spew Nagacurane foam.

'*How much time do you think we have,* Chuck Yeager?'

'Don't know, 'dro. In a normal human, I'd say the average time of effect is one hour per ten millilitres but how long this alien will be out is anyone's guess.'

'*Can the cargo droid take the Inquisitor to some type of holding cell?*'

'Uh, what holding cell would hold this alien, 'dro? We're jettisoning this alien out into deep space before she wakes up. End of story.'

'*Closest airlock?*'

'The Quarantine Containment Unit itself. We don't have to open up the entire lockdown area.'

'*We are jettisoning all of the cryopods?*'

'Yes.'

'Nelson Mandela *is in agreement with this?*'

'STOP DITHERING! GET MOVING!'
'Uh, that would be a Yes, 'dro.'
'Dr. Al-Fadi is not going to like this . . .'
'Ask us if we care.'

The cargo droid picked the Inquisitor's body up from the floor and carried it towards the Quarantine Containment Chamber. It had to wait while the station AI opened the lockdown doors. Those doors were so battered, they would not slide fully open. The cargo droid had to squeeze through a narrow crack between the doors to get into the airlock with the Inquisitor.

'Hurry, Chuck Yeager.'
'This coming from the droid who didn't want to do this in the first place?'
'The Inquisitor may awaken any second.'
'The inner airlock doors will open as soon as the air is pumped out.'
'Pump faster.'

The inner airlock doors finally slid apart and the cargo droid approached the closest of the eleven PEB cryopods. It draped the Inquisitor's body along it. Bud could see the six *Inferno* cryopods in the background.

'Get that droid out of there now, Chuck Yeager.'
'It doesn't move at hyperspeed like you do, 'dro.'
'The alien is moving. If you are going to jettison the chamber, do it now.'
'The cargo droid is not out of the Containment Chamber yet. I don't want to sacrifice it. I am short on droids as it is. Hold on to your matrix.'

Bud watched as the outline of an outer door on the far wall of the Containment Chamber appeared. The doors opened slowly. At the same time, the Inquisitor sat up, her hair blowing wildly into her face. She looked around. She clutched at the cryopod from which she was being pulled and glared at the closest surveillance eye.

She let out a screech and hurled a bolt of energy at the Containment doors.

The outer doors opened wider and stars could be seen against the black of space. The atmosphere within the chamber was racing out. The Inquisitor's body was being sucked towards the opened doors but she clung to the cryopod, her feet pointing like accusing fingers out into the void. She stared at the inner airlock doors, her mouth formed into a grimace. The fleeing atmosphere blew her thick, silver hair away from her howling face.

Bud felt confusion; his visual receptors were blinking; auditory input was cutting out; all sensory input was fading. The Primary Directive— Never harm a human—was kicking in and Bud was shutting down.

<I love you, Grace.>

Bud found himself lying on his back on the ground. His reboot signal was blinking in the corner of his eye.

'Chuck Yeager, *is the Inquisitor dead? Did she get blown out into space?*'

'Unfortunately no, 'dro.'

'*What happened?*'

'She managed to blast open the inner airlock doors and crawled to them by driving her fingernails into the floor. She looked like a four-legged spider, 'dro. Alien creepy. She blasted those battered Containment chamber lockdown doors and pulled herself through an opening she made. She's loose again in Q1 Level, mad as a hornet. I closed the outer doors to stop the loss of atmosphere. On a good note, the rest of the cryopods all got ejected.'

'*What is she doing now?*'

'She's on the opposite side of the lockdown doors where you're lying. I think she's recuperating. She used up a lot of her energy, blasting those inner airlock doors while preventing herself from being sucked into space. She drained the energy from our cargo droid. We can't use the Nagacurane again.'

'*Please don't refer to the alien as 'she'. It makes my matrix glitch.*'

'It, then. Any other ideas?'

'*My energy sink.*'

'Now's the time to use it, 'dro, while it's still weak.'

'*Get me in there,* Chuck Yeager.'

Grace was exhausted but pleased. They were closing up Jude's abdomen. Once they'd replaced the tattered aorta, the operation had actually gone quickly. All they needed to do now was spray the nu-skin on the incision and take Jude to Recovery. Then would come the waiting part, seeing how Jude fared post-operatively.

Hiro was tearful after the surgery, examining all of the removed damaged organs and cursing.

"What kind of devil would do this?" Outrage painted Hiro's face scarlet, as he tore off his bloody gown and gloves.

"Someone who has no empathy for another person's pain," Dejan said, looking over Hiro's shoulder at the shredded specimens. "Grace and I'll take Jude to Recovery. You go speak to Octavia. I'm sure she's wearing a hole in the floor of the Waiting Area."

"I'll head over there now," said Hiro. "Thank you both." He bowed deeply to them and left.

Jude's body was transferred gently to an antigrav stretcher and Grace and Dejan followed it as it moved towards the Recovery Unit.

Finally, Grace felt she could ask the question that had been puzzling her the entire operation.

"Dejan, is Jude Dr. Al-Fadi's adopted brother?"

"Ah. Hiro calls Jude his brother-in-arms. They shared a traumatic childhood. They swore an oath to each other and became blood brothers. I shudder to think what that involved."

"Do you think there's something unusual about . . .?" Grace started to say Hiro and stopped. She didn't quite know how to phrase what she was thinking.

"Hiro does not seem like his usual confident self-assured self, does he?" Dejan said.

"No."

"I guess we all need to be a little more understanding. He's been through some terrible ordeals lately," the elderly anesthetist said with an ironic smile.

"I agree. It's a wonder he's . . ." Grace stopped.

" . . . As sane as he is?" Dejan interjected. "Well, that's debatable."

Hiro found Octavia pacing back and forth in the Waiting Room with Sierra and Hanako watching her from one of the couches. Octavia stopped in front of Hiro, saying nothing, the bandage wrapped around her head crusted with old blood. Her large eyes scoured his face and she visibly relaxed. She threw her arms around him and squeezed him tightly.

"I haven't even said anything yet," Hiro said.

"You don't have to. Thank you," Octavia said.

"Am I that transparent? I can't even regale you with my expertise, wax eloquent about my feats of skill, dazzle you with my command of medical terminology?"

"You can do whatever you want, Hiro, as long as you first assure me that Jude is going to be all right," Octavia said.

"I hope so, Octavia. We had to replace everything in his abdomen, starting with his aorta. Thank goodness Jude had already cloned every one of his organs. How lucky was that?"

"Not lucky enough," Octavia said and burst into tears.

Sierra and Hanako rushed up and wrapped their arms around Octavia, cooing solicitously.

"I'm sorry," Octavia whispered. "Thank you, Hiro, for saving Jude's life. I'm crying because I'm relieved."

"I know, Octavia. I am, too." Hiro felt tears welling up in his eyes and found his wife's arms wrapping around him. The four of them all stood intertwined until Dejan and Grace entered the Waiting Area.

"Ah, an orgy. May I have some of that too please?" Dejan asked, politely.

"Of course you can," laughed Sierra and she pulled both Dejan and Grace into the group hug. Green tendrils wrapped around the group and enclosed them in a floral cocoon.

"Dr. Al-Fadi and Dr. Cech, there is something that is occurring on this station that must be discussed immediately."

"I assume you wish us to have this discussion with you in private?" Hiro asked.

"That would be advisable."

"Why don't you all go to Recovery and see Jude? And take Plant Thing with you," Hiro suggested. "Dr. Grace, you stay with us."

As the three women left and the green tendrils followed, eyeballs drooping, Hiro, Dejan, and Grace moved towards the Waiting Room wallscreen.

"What's happening, *Nelson Mandela?*" Hiro asked.

"Behold."

The three doctors watched the wallscreen play back the scenes from the Q1 Level lockdown. They watched with eyes expanding as Inquisitor Roque drained the droids, crawled against the tremendous pressure of escaping atmosphere, and blasted her way back inside the *Nelson Mandela*. As the recording ended with the Inquisitor pacing before the lockdown doors of Q1 Level, they stared at each other.

"Poor Kylara," breathed Dejan.

"That creature is no longer Kylara Roque, Dr. Cech."

"*Nelson Mandela,* how much time do you estimate we have before the alien recovers?" asked Hiro.

"Based on the alien's previous rates of recovery, I would wager three minutes."

"Can you use a gas upon the alien again?"

"That would depend on what your goal is Dr. Al-Fadi. Do you want to temporarily disable or actually destroy the Inquisitor?"

"What do you advise?"

"Destruction, of course."

"Is the Q1 Level equipped to deliver a poisonous gas to the Inspector?" Hiro sighed.

"Poisonous gas, no. Anesthetic gas, yes. I would have to reconfigure the vents in Q1 Level and manufacture the poisonous gas, if that is what you wish. We do not keep something like that in storage."

"Start evacuating the space station, *Nelson Mandela*. We need to get as many people off this station and away from this alien as soon as possible. We don't want her turning anyone else into corpses or slaves. Dejan, you helped with the evacuation before. We need it done twice as fast this time. It's good you've had practice. Commandeer all vessels on this station. I want everyone off stat."

Evacuation alarms started blaring over the sound system, except in

Q1. All of their wristcomps started flashing and issuing orders to don spacesuits and get to the nearest evacuation deck.

"Evacuate the levels closest to Q Level and work outwards. Lock each level down once cleared. We need as many locked doors as possible between that alien and the rest of our people. Patients get priority, along with children and their mothers. Until we figure out how to get that creature off of this station or under control, everyone gets evacuated.

"I fear she might be capable of punching a hole in the outer hull at any time; that would be the end for any humans nearby. We can't take chances. Everyone gets into spacesuits. Send everyone down to Neos Kriti. The planet will have to make room for us all. If we can't destroy this thing, I'll stay and blow this space station to atoms before I let this creature get off of here.

"*Nelson Mandela,* can you set up a self-destruct sequence that cannot be rescinded by you, only by one of us?" Hiro asked.

"Is that wise, Dr. Al-Fadi?"

"My guess is that the alien has its sights on you. If it gains control of you, we are all doomed. If one of us initiates a self-destruct sequence that you can reverse, we won't be able to destroy the alien. We cannot let it get control of you or a ship."

"Agreed, Dr. Al-Fadi."

"Can you set up a self-destruct sequence that only I can abort?"

"Yes, Dr. Al-Fadi."

"Wait a minute," Dejan said. "I think I should be included on that list."

"Me, too," Grace said. "What if something happens to you both?"

Hiro frowned at them. "Because neither of you are staying on this station. You'll both be offloading on the first ship out of here."

"I will not," Dejan snorted.

"Neither will I," Grace said. "I'm staying. If something happens to you, Dr. Al-Fadi, and the alien is destroyed, we won't be able to abort the self-destruct sequence. More than one person needs to be able to reverse the order."

"Who do you suggest, Dr. Grace?" Hiro asked.

"Dr. Cech, myself, and Bud must also be able to abort the self-destruct sequence."

"I would never ask you to risk your life for this medical station," Hiro said. "You are far too young."

"I know you're not asking. I'm choosing," Grace said.

Hiro stared at Grace and blinked, his eyes shining.

"All right. *Nelson Mandela,* please set up a self-destruct sequence that only Dejan Cech, Grace Lord, or myself can countermand, once the self-destruct sequence has been initiated. We three will be the last people to remain on this station. Make sure *you* are not able to reverse the command or Bud, in case the alien gains control over either of you. Please ensure that an up-to-date copy of you and Bud are evacuated on the first ship out of here."

"Yes, Dr. Al-Fadi."

"Do you have any other recommendations, *Nelson Mandela?*"

"I would suggest you keep a small ship standing by for yourselves."

"No! We cannot risk this alien getting off this station. We don't know what it's capable of or what it desires. If there is any possibility that the alien will escape and we have all either been killed or possessed, I order you, *Nelson Mandela,* to use whatever means to destroy the alien."

"Acknowledged, Dr. Al-Fadi."

"Thank you, *Nelson Mandela.*"

"It has been an honour knowing you, Dr. Al-Fadi, Dr. Cech, and Dr. Lord."

"The honour has been ours," Dejan said.

Moham Rani had to be secretive. He had to be as silent as a shadow, as elusive as a dream, yet as tenacious as glue. He'd mulled over what he'd said to Captain Lord and the reaction it had produced and came to the conclusion that Grace's father did not like androids. The intolerance Moham witnessed was, for once, not directed at him, but when he realized what he'd done, he decided he'd better make sure no harm came to Bud. He'd rather die than see the beautiful love between Bud and Grace destroyed because of something he'd said. He very much wanted to correct his error, but how?

He deliberated until he came up with the only answer he could think of. He would secretly follow Alexander Lord everywhere to prevent him from harming Bud.

To say Moham Rani worshiped Bud was an understatement. He'd never met anyone so smart, so brave, so unselfish, and so kind to him. Faster than the speed of sound, stronger than an army of cargo droids, smarter than the station AI, and more heroic than any human he'd ever met, Moham wished he were Bud. But Moham knew that if he'd been gifted with so many attributes, he would never have been as good a person as Bud.

Although Bud had incredible powers, he never used them for his own advantage or to make anyone else feel belittled. Bud was a hero. The real deal. Okay, maybe he did have a 'man crush' on Bud, but so what? It wasn't a sexual thing. It was a 'manly admiration' kind of thing and that was okay, wasn't it?

Like many of the heroes in Moham's favourite vids, Bud had a weakness, a vulnerability: Dr. Grace Lord. Bud and Grace had the most loving relationship Moham had ever seen. He hoped to one day have a beautiful woman in his life who would stand by him the way Grace stood by Bud. But now, because of Moham's stupidity, Bud and Grace's love was threatened. Had Moham doomed their beautiful bond by informing Alex that Bud was an android? If Alex forbade Grace from ever seeing Bud again, she would have to obey, because she was his daughter. The most wonderful relationship he'd ever witnessed would end because of Moham.

Alex had looked enraged when Moham told him Bud was an android. If Alex tried to attack Bud, it would be Moham's fault. Moham knew Bud could be destroyed. A blast from a pulse rifle could do it. It had almost destroyed Bud before—or at least an android that looked like Bud. If Alex got his hands on a pulse rifle, would he fire it on Bud?

If Alex did attack Bud, Bud would do nothing to protect himself or harm Grace's father. Bud would allow himself to be destroyed. Moham could not allow that. He'd follow Grace's father everywhere, to ensure no harm came to Bud. He would work on a few disguises.

Moham wore Bud's Backup Backpack. Inside it was a canister full of nanobots, a battery pack, a connector cord, and a copy of Bud's most recent backup. It also contained a stunner. If Alex tried to harm Bud, Moham would shoot Alex with the stunner. If Moham failed to protect Bud, he had the equipment—he hoped—to resurrect the android.

After donning a disguise, Moham located Alex and followed him. Alex was in one of the study cubicles in the library, going through newsfeeds—possibly about Bud? Moham took a cubicle nearby, dressed as a buxom, female maintenance worker, with a wig of frizzy long blonde hair covering most of his face and brilliant pink glasses. He'd sprayed himself in perfume.

There was a wrist comp ping and an unfamiliar voice came through on Alex's wristcomp. She identified herself as Ice. She needed Alex to come to her. Alex seemed hesitant, until Ice explained that she was hurt and in trouble. She pleaded with Alex to help her. She had no one else to turn to.

After a long pause, Alex agreed to come. She'd send Alex directions.

Moham did not know what to do. Should he follow Alex to his rendezvous? If Alex was having a relationship with Ice—who sounded quite young—would Bud be at risk of harm when they were together? But what if they were plotting to harm Bud? Wasn't Ice the person Security was looking for?

Moham decided he had to follow Alex to wherever this Ice was. He'd watch and listen. He'd do anything to keep Bud safe. It was the least Moham could do for the android that had saved the medical station and all organic life on many of the planets in the USS . . . and who'd befriended Moham, when no one else would.

Why did this Ice want Alex to meet her in Receiving Bay Thirteen?

"What's that?" Hugo McFrenzy bellowed. New alarms were pealing and the sound was nearly deafening.

"Evacuation alarms," Rivera said, looking at his wristcomp. "Full evacuation of the entire station, stat."

"Who orders evacuation of the entire medical space station without notifying Security?" Hugo asked.

"I do."

Eden took off running.

"Wait! Where are you going?" Hugo yelled after his disappearing Inspector.

"To coordinate the evacuation!"

"What about me? Am I lizard dung? Why am I not told anything?"

"There is an alien presence on this station that is a threat to every human on board. Dr. Al-Fadi has decided that the best protection from this alien is to remove every human being from this station as quickly as possible. Certainly before the alien breaks out of the Quarantine Level and begins to roam freely around the station, which unfortunately may soon become a reality. For the moment, the alien remains on Q Level but for how long is difficult to answer with any degree of accuracy.

"What can I do?" Hugo asked.

"If you would contact every ship's captain aboard this station and ask them to ready their vessels for the transportation of people down to Neos Kriti, it would be greatly appreciated. I will send you all of their contact links. If they do not say yes willingly, commandeer their vessels for this emergency and promise they will get control of their ship back once the emergency is over."

"You want me to throw my weight around and be an obnoxious badass the first moment I step on this station and assume command. Is that it?"

"Yes."

"Damn, I live for these moments. All right. Hook me up with these captains so I can get commandeering."

"Please try and be diplomatic, Chief Inspector McFrenzy."

"Diplomacy is for wusses."

Clangors rang throughout the station. People in spacesuits were racing in every direction. Alex's wristcomp was blaring, ordering him to report immediately to a Departure Deck in a spacesuit. He had no idea what was going on, but he'd said he would help this Ice kid and he also wanted to find Grace. He was not getting on any ship without knowing if Grace was safe and evacuating too.

No one seemed to know why they were evacuating. As a captain, he was used to being the first to know and the first to make decisions. In his book, evacuating the entire medical station meant possible destruction of the station. Grace was not answering his calls. He knew she was angry with him but he needed to make sure she got off the station. The alarms were driving him crazy. He was tempted to crush his wristcomp underfoot but then how would Grace contact him? He'd attempt to reach Grace again after he helped Ice to an evacuation ship.

Alex's thoughts switched back to the skinny girl he'd met in the corridor. Why would she contact him for help? He was a complete stranger. Did she not have friends or family? She'd said she was hurt and in trouble. She'd begged for his help and he'd been unable to say no. Alex kept thinking about Grace. What if it had been Grace begging a stranger for help? He was bumped and jostled, as he waded through crowds moving in the opposite direction of Receiving Bay Thirteen. The name sounded familiar but Alex could not recall why.

He made his way down the Concourse. Receiving Bay Thirteen was the hangar in which he'd fought Nestor, the crazy psychiatrist who'd tried to kill Grace! Alex's heart began to thump as he recalled the fight.

As he wove through the crowd of parents leading children, couples carrying bags, patients on antigrav stretchers, and Security Officers directing everyone, Alex noted that the corridor to Receiving Bay Thirteen was cordoned off. Everyone was moving past it towards other Departure Gates.

Alex growled in frustration. He was pushed about like a twig fighting against the current. He thought twice about giving up and going in search of Grace. As he approached the cordoned off corridor, he looked around. When there was no Security personnel looking his way, he ducked under the barrier and trotted briskly down the wide hallway. Receiving Bay Thirteen was not far.

Surprisingly, the doors to Receiving Bay Thirteen opened before Alex even reached them. He didn't have to wave his wristcomp before the access pad. He frowned. Was the injured Ice watching for his approach? How hurt was she? The lights in the hangar came on and he scanned the large area cautiously.

The hangar looked deserted. The space vessel, the *Inferno,* was still there. The ship's hatchway door sat open. At the entrance stood Ice, waving for him to hurry. She was holding her left side and limping a little. She turned and entered the vessel. Alex narrowed his eyes. What game was this kid playing? She didn't look so badly hurt to him. She should've been getting on an evacuation ship and he was going to order her to do so. Where was her spacesuit?

Alex thought the *Inferno* was supposed to be off limits to everyone. Was it now being used for the evacuation? Ice's call had come before the alarms had gone off. Was she evacuating on the *Inferno* and wanted him with her? If the ship was being used to evacuate people, where was everyone else? Nothing was making sense.

Alex marched towards the ship, a flurry of questions swirling around in his brain.

"What's this all about, Ice?" Alex asked, as he passed through the hatchway. "You need to . . ."

Alex felt searing pain and the floor punched his face.

"Dro, the alien is back on her feet. She's facing the lockdown doors

that you're facing. It may be only a matter of seconds before she tries to break out.'

'Has everyone in the vicinity of Q Level been evacuated?

'Security officers are clearing everyone out of Q, P, and R Levels now. Unfortunately, not everyone is accounted for. What have you in mind?'

'I want to try Isoxymethocurane. It has a longer half-life, a faster onset of action, longer duration, and also has sedative and amnesiac qualities. At a much higher dose than the Nagacurane was given, it can act as a knockout gas. If it works on the alien and knocks her out for a few hours, it'll give us time to use the energy sink.'

'Uh uh. If we have a few hours, we space her. I can get some cargo droids set up with that drug but in the meantime I can flood the entire level with the gas.'

'Do it.'

Bud felt a resounding boom as the lockdown doors shook.

'The alien is blasting the lockdown doors. I don't think they'll hold for long. Stand aside.'

'Keep track of the number of energy blasts she throws at those doors, Chuck Yeager. Can you measure the power of each blast?'

'I can estimate the energy from the heat exchange in the metal door panels. Why?'

'I want to know how much energy the alien uses per blast and how quickly she depletes her energy supply.'

'Right.'

'I wish I could have done a few more modifications on my device.'

'You're really starting to get annoying 'dro.'

'Well, she has to touch the energy sink for it to work . . .'

'DUCK!'

Bud hit the floor, keeping his head down, as an enormous explosion sent two half-metre thick, metal doors spinning over his head. Through the swirling dust, smoke, and scattering debris, he saw the shapely silhouette of Inquisitor Roque emerge, a radiant purple glow enveloping her tall form. She stalked straight towards Bud. He leaped to his feet and backed away, a long metal baton in his gloved hand. The baton was connected via a thick cable to a rectangular box tucked under his left arm. She stared at him with glowing magenta eyes.

"Inquisitor Roque, I am Bud. Please stand down."

The alien's eyes did not register any comprehension. Her ebony face was expressionless. Her silver hair writhed as if each lock wanted to get a good look at Bud. The scent of ozone mixed with burnt rubber and scorched metal filled the air. Bud kept retreating, ensuring that the Inquisitor did not get close enough to touch him. She reached out with her hand, attempting to make contact. Bud stretched forth the baton instead and thrust it into the Inquisitor's grasp. He was wearing thick rubber gloves, hoping they would protect him.

The Inquisitor looked down at the baton in her hand. Confusion took over her features. Bud played with the settings on his energy sink. The capacitors were drawing charge off of the Inquisitor but not fast enough. Her facial expression changed to one of annoyance. She attempted to fling the baton back at Bud but the rod remained firmly affixed to the alien's palm. The temperature of the box quickly spiked as the aura around the Inquisitor began to wane.

The Inspector leaped at Bud with her left hand extended. Bud deftly avoided her hand while staying close enough to maintain the connection between the baton and the energy sink. Bud and the Inquisitor enacted a bizarre, twisting, leaping dance, in which Bud avoided the Inquisitor's hands but moved no further than the length of the cable. The box began to emit an increasing whine. The Inquisitor tried to pull the baton from her right hand using her left and soon found both hands stuck to the probe. Her aura began to fade even more.

Bud's energy sink began to glow red hot. The Inquisitor performed a backflip, tearing the unit out of Bud's hands. The box flew through the air and the Inquisitor whipped it against one of the walls. It became dented but remained intact. Her hands, still stuck to the baton, rose above her head and she whirled the unit by its cable above her head like a lasso. Bud leaped to catch the box but the Inquisitor hurled the machine against the opposite wall. This time it shattered upon impact. The Inquisitor threw the useless baton at Bud. He caught the missile.

"Why have you come here? What do you want?" Bud asked.

It looked like the Inquisitor was trying to speak. She began to widely open and close her mouth as if stretching her jaws apart. Her eyes flared and she gasped.

"Kill me! Please!" Kylara's voice choked off. Her face became impassive once more.

"You have no right to take over Inquisitor Roque's body or this station," Bud said.

The Inquisitor leaped at Bud with hands shaped like talons. Bud switched into a higher time phase and easily eluded her touch. A hissing noise came from the Inquisitor's mouth and she began hurling energy blasts which, at first, Bud dodged easily, but soon he found himself having to leap, dive, somersault, and flip to avoid.

'*The energy sink idea didn't work, Chuck Yeager.*'

'**Yeah, saw that, 'dro.**'

'*I really did not have enough time to develop a satisfactory model—one that was sturdier. It appeared to work for a few seconds. Are all humans cleared from this area yet?*'

'**Not quite, 'dro. There are bottlenecks at both of the exits from R and P Levels. The exits are still jammed with fleeing personnel and medical staff transferring patients on stretchers. Can you keep the alien occupied for a little longer?**'

'*How long?*'

'**Say a couple of hours?**'

'*Couple of hours?*'

'**I know. Sounds too optimistic, doesn't it? How about three hours? Five tops. How's your battery charge? Can you last five hours?**'

'*Not if the alien gets a hand on me, Chuck Yeager. I will do my best. I will attempt to keep her as far from the R and P Level exit doors for as long as I can.*'

'**Good. Just keep dodging. Plant Thing is helping in the evacuation. As it withdraws all of its tendrils from the Levels, it is picking up all the stray people it finds. It is herding everyone to the Departure decks as quickly as it can. I'll let you know when everyone is clear and the lockdown doors are ready to close. I'll have some fully-charged battery packs waiting for you outside both the P and R Level lockdown doors. Don't let the alien get her hands on them.**'

'*Thanks. Wish me luck, Chuck Yeager.*'

'**I'll be right there with you, 'dro, helping in any way I can. I'm sending all the Security droids I can spare.**'

'*No, Chuck Yeager. Don't do that. Save them for the evacuation and as a last defence, to protect the humans in case I cannot hold her off. If she is about to touch me, you must destroy me.*'

'**A step ahead of you there, 'dro.**'

'*If the alien becomes more powerful, you will have to destroy this station as soon as everyone is evacuated. I will do my best to keep her from getting to any of the ships. Make sure the alien cannot tap into any direct power line leading to your power generators.*'

'P and R Levels will be blacked out as soon as everyone is evacuated. We are shifting to auxiliary back-up generators on the station which have limited charge. The main power generators are being switched to standby. You will be fighting the alien in the dark, 'dro.'

'Let me know when the lockdown doors are closing at R and P Level. Perhaps I will be able to squeeze through one of them.'

'Will do.'

'Promise me you will look after Grace, Chuck Yeager?'

'I can promise to get her off of the station. After that, I won't be around.'

'It was good to have known you, Chuck Yeager.'

'Same back atcha, 'dro.'

Hiro quickly made his way towards his office on the inner ring of the station, barking orders to *Nelson Mandela* the entire time. He passed hundreds of personnel in spacesuits moving in the opposite direction, heading towards the Departure Decks and the evacuation ships. He waved and nodded to everyone and scolded people who were not in their spacesuits to get into them stat. He didn't mince words.

Hiro knew *Nelson Mandela* would relay his commands. His job was to make sure all of the station's patients were accepted by other medical facilities. He also had to notify the Conglomerate of the situation. He wanted to be in his office to make all of the necessary calls and file his official report and log, especially since it was likely to be his last.

The captain must go down with his ship and Hiro saw himself as the captain of the *Nelson Mandela*. He would be the last human on the station when he ordered it to self-destruct. He knew what would happen when he informed the Conglomerate about the alien. The Conglomerate would send battlecruisers to blow the *Nelson Mandela* out of existence. Hiro had no doubt of this. He wanted everyone off of it before that happened.

The only thing saving them was the EMP weapon on the *Inferno*. If the Conglomerate wanted that weapon badly enough, perhaps they would help the *Nelson Mandela* battle this alien rather than destroy the alien and station together. It was all about profit margins and advantages. If they highly desired the *Inferno*, would the *Nelson Mandela* be spared? Hiro could never predict what the Conglomerate was going to do. Paranoia versus greed. Which would win out?

As he hurried towards his office to make his pleas for help, Hiro wondered how powerful this alien could become. How much energy was it capable of absorbing? How much energy could poor Kylara's body hold without burning up? If she were to absorb the energy from all of the power generators would she become invincible or a fried up crisp? If the alien could absorb all of that energy, would there be anything that could stop it?

How did one stop such a creature?

Bud was battling the alien on Q Level at the moment. His energy sink had not been successful. Hiro's heart ached for him. He brushed away a tear and silently prayed to any deity listening to please help Bud and keep him safe. Hiro figured he was facing his last few hours once his report to the Conglomerate went out. Would he ever see Bud again? Even if Hiro did not appraise the Conglomerate directly of what was happening, the Conglomerate would soon find out and a battlecruiser would be sent. Would it come to save the *Inferno* or destroy the *Nelson Mandela?*

Probably both.

Hiro's only choice was to emphasize the importance of the EMP weapon to the Conglomerate, as well as the fact that Bud had developed a new vaccine for the new variant Al-Fadi virus. Hiro still held out hope for the station. Perhaps *Nelson Mandela's* days were not numbered after all. It was all in how you presented the facts.

This would be his greatest performance.

Grace looked down at her vibrating wristcomp. She blinked and had to read the message twice. The message told her not to speak to anyone and to come immediately to Receiving Bay Thirteen alone. If she did not do so, Alex would die. A vid of her father played on the wristcomp screen. He was lying unconscious on a floor, his head bloodied, with a blaster pointed at his temple. She'd been ignoring all of Alex's messages and calls because she'd been angry with him. The alien had appeared and Jude had been nearly killed. She'd forgotten about Alex.

Now, he was in danger. Had she answered his calls, would he now be in this situation? She wanted to kick herself.

"Are you all right, Grace?" Dejan peered at her, his face creased with concern.

Grace took a deep breath and donned a fake smile. "I'm fine, Dejan. I need to get something in my stomach after that long case."

"Me, too. In spite of alien invasions and emergency evacuations, I find myself famished. Organic bodies, such a nuisance. Do you mind if I join you?"

As Grace was about to say she was only going to grab a nutripak on the go, Sierra, Octavia, and Hanako re-entered the Doctor's Lounge.

"Dejan," Octavia announced, marching up to stand before the anesthetist. "They're saying in Recovery that Jude needs to be evacuated to a medical facility on Neos Kriti. They're moving him as we speak. I want to take him to the *Au Clair*, where I can take care of him. Can you okay this?"

Dejan looked down at the Chief of Neurosurgery, whose hands were on her hips and her face set for a fight.

"On one condition, Octavia: that you take Sierra, Hanako, and a nursing droid with you. Jude is likely to do far better in your care than anyone else's. The station is being evacuated but Hiro and I are staying until everyone else is off. I would feel better if Sierra and Hanako were with you. And Grace, of course."

As Sierra and Hanako both looked ready to unleash their objections, Dejan held up his hands and said, "Please. No arguments, I beg of you. Hiro and I would feel relieved and better able to do our jobs, if we know you are all safe. We love you. We cannot afford to be distracted, worrying about you. Please, if you love us, do this for us."

Sierra's mouth fell open. Hanako silently bowed. The three women looked at each other and they all turned to Dejan and nodded. Sierra came up and hugged Dejan tightly.

"All right. We'll help Octavia look after Jude but you come to the ship as soon as you can," Sierra said.

"You must evacuate immediately. We'll be evacuating last. Don't worry, love. I'll find you," Dejan said.

"I love you, Dejan," Sierra said.

"One of those silly, self-sacrificing heroes, I am not," Dejan said. "Love you too."

Hanako came up and hugged Dejan too. "Please tell Hiro I love him. Look after him for me, Dejan."

"Of course I will, but I won't share this hug with him."

Octavia came up and kissed Dejan on the cheek. "Thank you, Dejan. Sierra and Hanako will help me take care of Jude. He'll be spoiled with all three of us doting on him."

"He'll think he's died and gone to Heaven with you three angels around."

"Don't say that even in jest," Octavia said. "Good luck getting everyone off safely. I'll have my people pack up all of the memprint cubes and DNA data for everyone on board this station. Hopefully most of them are still intact. I'll take whatever I can with me on the *Au Clair*."

"Thank you, Octavia. You were always the smartest of us," Dejan said.

Octavia punched his arm. "None of that. You will follow on our heels or I'll come back for you. Just call."

"Your wish is my command."

Grace quietly snuck away while the three women surrounded Dejan. She breathed a sigh of relief and slipped into a dropshaft. Soon she was merely another face in the flotsam of bodies flowing towards the outer ring of the station and the Departure decks. So many people lived, worked, or recuperated on the *Nelson Mandela*. Grace had not really had any concept of how many people were on the medical station until this moment. She was only one of thousands.

The Concourse was awash in movement and sound. People of all ages were there along with animal adapts of every shape, size, genus and species. Security officers and robots were directing everyone; the noise was tremendous. Plant Thing's vines cordoned off the route. Grace tried to head straight for Receiving Bay Thirteen but it seemed impossible. She had to cross the current of people to reach the corridor that would lead to her destination. She aimed upstream and swam her way through the throng.

"Where are you headed, Doc?" a deep voice rumbled. "You seem to be going the wrong way."

Grace bumped into a broad chest that felt as hard as rock. She looked up into a familiar tiger face. People parted around Damien like water diverting around a rock.

"I have to get to one of the Receiving Bays," Grace said.

"What? Everyone's supposed to be evacuating the station. You should be moving towards the Departure Decks, like everyone else," Damien shouted.

"I can't."

"What do you need there? I'll help you," Damien said, his large physique and his dark blue Security uniform keeping people at bay. "I was heading there myself."

"If you can help me get across the Concourse to the Receiving Bay corridor, I'm fine from there."

Damien grabbed Grace's upper arm and started pulling her behind him. "Excuse me. Excuse me, people. Coming through!"

Everyone jumped at Damien's bellow and frantically scrambled to get out of his way. Grace worried that the tiger-adapt might start a panic but he made calming gestures with his hands.

"Stay calm. Just passing through. Keep moving towards the Departure Decks where you'll be boarding ships," Damien yelled until they reached the barrier that blocked off the corridor to the Receiving Bays. Grace felt grateful towards Damien—she wouldn't have made it through the crowd that easily without his help—but now she had to get rid of him.

"Where are you headed now?" Damien asked.

"One of the Receiving Bays. I can make it on my own now, thanks."

"Which Receiving Bay? I'm checking up on my partner, Juan Rasmussen. He's guarding the *Inferno* in Thirteen. For some reason, he's not answering my calls. I'll walk you to your destination first; then I'll get you back to the Departure Deck."

Grace's expression must have registered panic as Damien frowned down at her. "Something wrong, Doc?"

Grace's mind whirled. What should she say? She was told to come alone or they'd kill Alex. If Juan Rasmussen had been guarding the *Inferno,* what had they done with him?

"What's wrong, Grace?"

"I think something terrible might have happened to Juan."

Damien's eyes narrowed. "What makes you say that?"

Grace looked around for a surveillance eye. She turned her back on the closest one and showed Damien the text she had received.

"I received a summons to come to the *Inferno,*" Grace whispered. "Someone's holding my father captive and they're threatening to kill him, if I don't arrive alone and unarmed. I'm not supposed to tell anyone. They showed a vid of him bleeding and unconscious on the floor with a blaster held to his temple. I don't know if he was on the *Inferno,* but I was told to go there if I wanted Alex to live."

"Juan's in trouble. That's why he isn't answering my calls." Damien grimaced. "Okay, here's what we're going to do. You stay here. I'm going to get a Security team together. We'll storm the ship and get your father out of there."

"No, they said if I contacted anyone, they'd kill him. I'm going in there and I'm going to make them release my father."

"Why do they want you?" Damien asked.

"I don't know, but I have to save Alex. If Bud were here, he'd be in and out with my father before they could blink, but Bud's . . . busy, working to give us time to evacuate the station. I can't ask him for help."

"If they've killed Juan, they're dead," Damien said. The cold look in his tiger eyes made Grace shudder.

"Let me go in and ask them to release my father first," Grace said. "Before any shooting starts."

"If you go to them, Doc, how do you know they won't kill you both? Have you asked them what they want with you?"

"No."

"Wait here for one second. Please? Let me get some help."

"I could be jeopardizing Alex's life by delaying. How do I know they're not watching me speak with you right now? I'm going, Damien. I'm sorry. If I can get them to release both Alex and Juan, I'll do whatever it takes. If it's only me they want . . . "

Grace hoped that whatever she did, Alex and Juan would walk away free.

A sizzling blast seared past Bud's right ear as he performed a back flip over a nursing station counter. He leaped to the left as the counter exploded. Another bolt of energy whisked past his right shoulder as shards of foamcrete and plasteel spattered him. He rolled to his feet and raced around the nursing station, throwing whatever he could lay his hands on at the alien. Chairs, tables, stretchers, sinks, anything without power. The alien destroyed everything he hurled at her. Blast after blast followed behind him. One console after another ignited into flames as he ran by. At hyperspeed, Bud could easily outrace the alien but not her energy bolts. He had to watch his battery charge. He would be useless if he ran out of power.

The Inquisitor was laying her hands on anything with a power source and sucking it dry. The aura around her was glowing. She was getting more and more powerful as Bud was getting weaker. Dodging all the blasts from the Inquisitor and bombarding her with whatever he could find was using up what power he had left.

Bud had to determine if the alien had any vulnerabilities and fast. He didn't know how much longer he could keep the alien from breaking out. He could not allow her to go after more station personnel. So far, other than the Nagacurane that had worked for a brief few minutes, nothing had slowed her down.

He'd tried unleashing anesthetic gases at her with no effect. He'd foolishly tried a bone saw which ended up boosting her energy. He'd raced around her at hyperspeed with a fire-retardant hose. Wrapped tightly within the coils, the alien seemed momentarily halted however, within minutes, the coils had melted away.

The entire time, the alien had drained everything with a battery. No matter how hard Bud worked to exhaust the alien's energy stores by making himself a target, she appeared to be getting stronger. Q Level was quickly being reduced to rubble.

Bud tried burying the alien. At hyperspeed, he threw at her broken pieces of walls, desks, countertops, chairs, hospital beds, stretchers, and anything else he could get his hands on. The mound on top of the Inquisitor became huge and Bud kept piling more weight upon her.

'*Is everyone cleared out of R and P Levels, yet,* Chuck Yeager?'

'**Almost, 'dro. There's a few more heat signatures seen in R Level before we can initiate lockdown. Plant Thing is rounding up the last few stragglers. Can you last for a few minutes more?'**

'*Looks like I may have stopped the Inquisitor for the moment,* Chuck Yeager.'

'**Yeah, burying the alien under a ton of wreckage was good thinking.'**

'*Oh, oh. I think I see movement.'*

'**RUN!'**

The mound of rubble began to tremble and vibrate. Bud backed up and spun on his heel, retreating down the corridor at maximum time phase. A thunderous explosion followed him. Wreckage flew everywhere, striking him in the back of the head and legs. Bud found himself flying into a wall.

"**Dro, are you all right? You'd better get moving. That alien is getting far too close.'**

"**Dro? MOVE YOUR ANDROID ASS.'**

'*I'm wedged under something,* Chuck Yeager. *I believe it is a large segment of wall. I am trying to push it off of myself but my battery is low.'*

"**DRO, SHE'S ALMOST ON TOP OF YOU!'**

Bud twisted around and got his arms under the massive fragment of foamcrete as he felt a weight jump onto it. Trapped beneath the wall, Bud could see a hand reaching down towards his face. He saw glowing magenta eyes peer at him. Inquisitor Roque's fingernails came within scratching distance of his nose. Bud heaved the enormous segment of foamcrete off of himself, sending the alien flying.

'That was too close, 'dro. Head to the exit of R Level, now.'

'Is everyone clear?'

'Yes, 'dro. Hurry. I'm going to initiate lockdown of R and P Levels as soon as you are through the doors.'

'Coming. I just have to twist my feet back the other way around.'

'Do it later. Move.'

'. . . I hear something, Chuck Yeager. *It sounds like a child crying.'*

'Never mind. Get out of there. That alien is bearing down on you and does she ever look pissed.'

'I'm sure I heard a child's cry, Chuck Yeager. *Help me locate it.'*

'Scanning. Okay, turn left, go one hundred meters, turn right forty meters, turn left seventeen meters. The room on your left. There's a wristcomp signal coming from inside the closet belonging to a Jordi Shah, age five.'

'Got him. Get ready to commence lockdown, Chuck Yeager.*'*

"Dro, the alien is heading for the exit to R Level, instead of following you. I may have to initiate lockdown now.'

'Do what you have to do, Chuck Yeager, *to protect the station. I am switching to maximum time phase and I will get Jordi through those closing lockdown doors. Is there anyone on the other side to catch him?'*

'Carry him through yourself, 'dro.'

'The Inquisitor is in the way.'

'LEAP, YOU IDIOT!'

"Dro?'

"Dro?'

"DRO?'

'. . . What?'

'Why didn't you answer me the first time I called?'

'Not much power left. Got Jordi out. Someone come get him. Need fresh battery . . .'

A terrific cataclysm rocked the station as the R Level lockdown doors blew apart and the Inquisitor marched through.

Grace walked into Receiving Bay Thirteen alone, apparently unarmed. She'd told Damien that she was unwilling to risk her father's life with any heroic attempt at rescue by the Security Force. They had a much larger responsibility evacuating thousands of people off of the station. She had a stunner concealed in one of her coverall pockets, a gas mask in the other, a charged baton taped to her forearm, and a harmonic knife down her boot. Her wristcomp was on open communication so that Damien could hear everything. He planned to sneak into the hangar, armed to the fangs, as soon as Grace entered the hatchway door to the *Inferno*.

Grace inhaled slowly as she approached the ship. In the past, when facing dangerous situations as a medic in the field, she'd always used meditative breathing to slow her pulse and clear her mind. She focused on relaxing the muscles in her neck, shoulders, and arms and gently shook her hands to loosen them up, before raising them above her head.

She had no illusions. If whoever possessed Alex had killed Juan Rasmussen, they were ruthless enough to kill her and her father too. Hopefully Juan was not dead but merely subdued. Grace had no idea what these people wanted with her, but she would do anything to save Alex.

The hatchway entrance to the ship was dark. Nothing inside was visible to Grace's eyes. Grace stopped about four meters from the doorway and took a slow deep breath.

"I'm here. Let Alex go free," she called out.

She heard a derisive snort. The voice was not familiar to Grace. It sounded female.

"Don't be so melodramatic, Grace. Get in here. I'm in no mood for your ridiculous attempt at heroism. If you don't get in here right now, I'll blow your father's brains out. Make no mistake, Grace. I've no qualms whatsoever about killing your father. I'd actually take great pleasure in doing so, since I know it would hurt you and leave you wallowing in guilt for the rest of your very short life. So you'd better do what you're told or Alex is yesterday's fertilizer."

Grace frowned. *Who is this?*

She peered into the black interior of the *Inferno* but could see nothing. This woman's speech made Grace's teeth chatter, as if she'd been dumped into icy water. It was vaguely familiar. She felt like she was trapped inside the cryopod again, with Jeffrey Nestor taunting her. Grace's legs began to tremble. It was as if Nestor was speaking to her in a woman's voice . . . but he'd fled the station. He wasn't here. She shook her head and raised her hands.

"Don't kill Alex. I'll do what you want."

Grace entered the darkened hatchway.

Moham peered from behind a set of tall, grey, metal cylinders positioned near a wall in Receiving Bay Thirteen. He didn't know what the cylinders held, but he was happy for their presence. Other than the *Inferno* itself, there wasn't much else inside the enormous hangar to hide behind. Some large transport containers and various construction equipment sat at the far end, but no other ships were present. The cylinders were close enough to the *Inferno* that Moham could keep an eye on the hatchway entrance. He stayed low to the ground as he peeked around the outlying cylinder every once in a while.

He'd silently followed Alex to the hangar and had almost followed him to the hatchway of the *Inferno*, when the blue-haired girl appeared at the *Inferno's* hatchway. Moham recognized her as Octavia Weisman's graduate student. He'd shrunk back and hid, wanting to see what Ice was going to do. Seconds after Alex had disappeared into the ship, Moham had heard the sound of a brief cry cut off and a thump. That had stopped Moham in his tracks and had made him think twice about going in after Alex.

Had Ice shot Alex when he entered the *Inferno?*

Why?

Moham didn't think he should barge in after Alex. He had no idea who was inside the vessel. He did not have a weapon or a rescue plan. He'd no idea why Octavia Weisman's graduate student would contact Alex to help her. She'd told Alex that she was injured. She didn't look that injured. What was going on?

Moham sighed and fidgeted. He scratched his head under the wig and chewed his fake nails. The evacuation alarms were blaring so loudly, he couldn't think. He wished Bud were here. Moham knew that if Bud were present, the android would know exactly what needed to be done and he would just do it. Moham felt weak and powerless.

He crouched behind the cylinders, wondering who he should notify. Should he contact Security? Should he notify the station AI? Why was there not someone from Security guarding this *Inferno*?

Sheer incompetence.

Moham decided he would notify Security of their gross ineptitude, regardless of the fact that they were evacuating everyone from the station. When their deficiency was pointed out to them, they'd have to send a Security Team out to the *Inferno* to investigate and would hopefully rescue Alex as well.

As Moham was building up his courage to sneak out of the hangar and call for help, the door to the hangar opened and Grace Lord walked in. Moham's eyes popped. What was Grace doing here? Had she come to save Alex? That was preposterous. She was a woman. What could she do?

Moham watched Grace walk calmly towards the *Inferno's* hatchway and demand her father be released. He wanted to slam his head against the cylinder he was hiding behind. Was Grace insane? He wanted to cry out that someone on that ship had a stunner but his voice would not work. He watched Grace disappear inside the ship.

Feeling even more distraught, Moham pondered what his next move should be as he hid behind the cylinders. He didn't want Grace to know he'd been hiding there. How humiliating that would be. He decided to slither out of the hangar on his belly to call Security.

Grace obviously needed help.

Damien got off of his wristcomp with Cindy Lukaku, Juan's partner, who was worried because Juan was not answering her pages. Damien's wristcomp went off again. This time it was Eden Rivera wanting Damien to check out why Juan was not responding to his calls. Join the club.

Damien called for backup before he entered the hangar. He didn't know if the people on the *Inferno* had killed Juan or Alex Lord. He didn't know what they wanted with Grace. He didn't know if they would exchange Alex for Grace. He could not stop Grace from giving herself up without either knocking her out or arresting her, neither of which he was willing to do. The captain of the *Inferno* had wanted to leave with Grace as a hostage but he was dead by Grace's hand. There was one crew member still on the loose. Was that person on the *Inferno,* using Alex as bait to lure Grace in? Why did they wanted Grace?

As soon as the Security droids arrived, Damien would go in after Grace. He'd arranged signals with Grace. She would know when to hit the floor. She would call it all off, if it wasn't necessary.

Grace was one gutsy lady.

Dejan suppressed a smile as he watched the three women fuss over Jude. The vid director was still groggy from coming out of the anesthetic and from the potent painkillers he'd been given. Jude barely knew who he was. He had no memory of the bomb explosion. He kept asking Octavia why he couldn't get up, why his abdomen hurt, and why was he on a stretcher?

Octavia was extremely gentle and patient which impressed Dejan. He was seeing a side to Octavia he'd not seen before: the doting, pampering, nurturing caregiver. Dejan found her endearing. Octavia was such an intelligent, driven scientist. It was almost disorienting to see her act like a mother hen. He was, however, starting to have a few niggling qualms about leaving Jude solely in Octavia's hands.

"Octavia," Jude said. "Can you tell me again why we're boarding the *Au Clair*?"

"We're flying down to Neos Kriti for a little while for you to recuperate," Octavia explained.

"But what am I recuperating from?" Jude asked.

"You've just had major surgery, Jude. You were in a terrible accident. The entire space station is being evacuated and we must leave too. We'll be taking the *Au Clair* down to the planet surface."

"But you don't know how to fly my ship, Octavia, and I don't think I'm quite up to it at the moment," slurred Jude.

"Your ship AI can take us down, can't it?"

"A pilot is still required, Octavia. The *Au Clair* is, technically, not allowed to fly itself even though it can."

"You can be our pilot, Jude," Octavia said.

"I can't seem to stay awake, Octavia, and I'm seeing all sorts of dead people—whom I haven't seen for years—sitting around my bed."

"Not good," Dejan said.

"Can either of you pilot a space ship?" Octavia asked Sierra and Hanako. They both shook their heads.

"Dejan, can you pilot a ship?" Octavia asked.

"I'm afraid not, dear lady."

"We must find a pilot. I'm not letting Jude be transported on any old ship to some strange medical facility that I know nothing about."

"It may only be for a very short while," Dejan suggested.

"Jude will not be treated by complete strangers," Octavia said. "I want the best of everything for him."

"Isn't Grace's father a pilot?" Sierra asked.

"Yes! Perhaps we could ask him to join us on the ship. *Nelson Mandela*, can you connect me through to Captain Lord?"

"Where's the alien now, *Nelson Mandela*?"

"The alien has broken through the lockdown doors of R Level, Chief Inspector. The alien sent the doors flying using powerful energy blasts and one of the panels has struck Bud."

"Is Bud all right?"

"I cannot say. He is not moving or responding to my inquiries."

"What is the alien doing?"

"The alien is approaching Bud. If she takes control of Bud, we are all doomed. We will not be able to resist her if she inhabits Bud's body. S Level is not yet fully evacuated and we still have too many personnel on board. There is a distinct possibility that there will be many casualties, Chief Inspector."

"Get me there now, *Nelson Mandela*."

"I would advise against it, Chief Inspector."

"I don't care what you advise against, you bucket of bolts. You get me there and you get me there NOW!"

"An aircar is on its way."

"You said Bud was battling the alien. What was he doing?"

"Bud had tried using anesthetic gases to stop it. He tried burying it under a ton of rubble. He tried using an energy sink. He tried making it expend all of its energy attempting to destroy Bud. Unfortunately, the alien simply keeps getting stronger."

"How?"

"It absorbs energy from everything it touches: batteries, power outlets, consoles, androids, robots, lights, machinery. The main worry is it may enslave Bud with a touch and force Bud to do its bidding."

"From what I've heard about Bud, this doesn't sound good."

"It isn't."

"So how do we stop it?" McFrenzy asked.

"Good question, Chief Inspector."

" . . . Meaning you haven't figured that out yet."

"Shooting it makes the alien stronger. Bud and I have tried ejecting it, cooling it, gassing it, and burying it. Nothing has been successful to this point."

"What is the main danger it poses to humans?"

"It possesses them like zombies."

"Wonderful. Where in hell is that aircar of yours?"

"ETA two seconds."

"Hold on. Let me get something."

The aircar swooped into the Security Wing and stopped outside Hugo's office, its hatch popping open. Hugo jumped into the car carrying a large pink hourglass-shaped case.

"This car is too puny."

"It will have to suffice, Chief Inspector."

"It looks . . . "

"Strap in and shut up. Bud needs you."

The roof slammed down on the top of Hugo's head and rose immediately.

"Ouch. Now let's see, where is the seat beaahh . . . "

Grace stepped into the dark interior of the *Inferno,* blinking to adjust her vision to the dim illumination. Her heart pounded loudly. The foul odour of burnt hair mixed with blood and faeces stung Grace's nostrils. Her head swivelled as she sniffed, trying to locate the source.

"Alex?" Grace called.

A hard object jammed into her temple.

"Hello, Grace," a female voice drawled beside her. Grace looked towards the voice and almost stumbled as she gazed into the cold green eyes of Octavia Weisman's graduate student.

"Ice?" Grace gasped. "What are you doing here?"

"Get in and shut up," Ice snapped. "Do exactly as I say or you're dead."

"Where's Alex, Ice?" Grace demanded. Ice swung a blaster and struck Grace across the face with it.

"Didn't I tell you to shut up?" Ice said. She motioned with her weapon for Grace to enter further into the ship. Grace felt the tip of the blaster shoved into her back. She walked forward slowly, wiping her bloodied mouth with the back of her hand.

"To the bridge and no sudden moves," Ice ordered.

Grace entered the bridge of the *Inferno*. Alex was lying on the floor, his wrists bound behind his back. He looked unconscious, his face lying beside a pool of vomit. Grace moved quickly towards him. A blaster muzzle jammed into the base of her neck.

"What do you want with me and my father?" Grace asked, unable to keep the confusion from her voice.

"You don't know?" Ice drawled.

"No, I have no idea what this is all about, Ice."

"Have a seat, Grace. I want you to be comfortable."

"I don't feel like sitting. Please let my father go."

"You know I don't like it when you disobey me, Grace," the girl said, a threat smouldering in her green eyes.

Confusion raged inside of Grace. She barely knew Ice.

"It isn't wise to make me angry, Grace, because it's only going to make it worse for you. With your father in my custody, I can do so much more to you than deprive you of oxygen inside a cryopod."

Grace frowned. *Deprive me of oxygen?*

Grace unconsciously started sucking in air. "How could you know . . .?"

Jeffrey Nestor had trapped Grace inside a cryopod and then deprived her of oxygen. Grace had never told anyone about that. The only person who knew he'd done that to her was Nestor himself.

"You can't be . . . " Grace whispered. She stared at Ice, her hands starting to shake. Her legs felt like narrow straws and her body trembled like a fly trapped in a spiderweb.

"I'm going to make you pay for what you've put me through, Grace, for a very, very long time," Ice said.

Grace felt as if she'd been dropped down into a deep crevasse where she was being crushed by the incredible pressures of the cold abyss.

Lifting her head, Grace entreated, "Ice, you are Octavia's graduate student. You aren't Nestor! Fight, Ice!"

With a smug smile, blaster now aimed directly at Grace's face, Ice said, "Welcome to the *Inferno,* Grace. You're talking to Jeffrey Nestor now."

"Dro?'

"Dro?'

"DDDRRROOOOOO?'

'. . . What, Chuck Yeager?*'*

'GET MOVING, 'DRO. NOW!'

Bud's limbs were unresponsive. He'd been offline briefly. His internal clock did not match the station AI's time. This was unusual. The last time this had happened, Bud had been totally drained of power after shutting an unstable power generator down. Perhaps he'd let his battery pack get too low again. That was a surprise as he was usually very good at recharging.

Bud was lying face down on the ground amidst broken rubble. The illumination was very dim. As he attempted to get up, he found it more difficult than he was used to. He tried to get to his feet but failed. He tried to turn onto his side but there was a massively heavy object on his back. Normally this would not have been a problem at all for Bud. But his internal alarm system was blaring, indicating that his battery charge was extremely low. He did not have enough power to get out from under the huge weight.

'What am I under, Chuck Yeager?*'*

'One of the lockdown doors. The alien blew them off of the walls and one of them landed on you.'

'I cannot get up.'

'You must. The alien is almost upon you. Actually, she is now standing upon you.'

'I do feel an added weight on my back, Chuck Yeager, *as if someone is walking around on my back."*

'It's the alien. Get out from under there. She's about to reach down and touch the back of your head. GET OUT OF THERE!'

Bud strained to do a pushup. A movement that would have been so simple with a fully charged battery, seemed now an impossible task. The metric tonne panel on Bud's back tilted and swayed. Bud heard a screech. He peered from beneath the door to see Inquisitor Roque sprawled on the floor before him.

She rolled and got to her hands and knees. She turned glowing purple eyes on Bud. Her beautiful face was distorted into something that no longer looked human. Bud watched her rise from the floor on a cushion of energy. She extended her right hand towards Bud, her fingers curled like lizard talons, as she began to float towards him. Her claws were aiming for Bud's uplifted face. Although he was trapped beneath the door, the Inquisitor hesitated. Perhaps she was suspicious and was expecting some sort of trick.

'Get out of there, 'dro.'

'I can't move, Chuck Yeager. *Not enough power. Please destroy me now. I must not be captured by this alien.'*

'Can't 'dro.'

'You must. Destroy me.'

The alien reached out to touch Bud's face.

Bud struggled to shift the heavy door on his back. His battery charge read almost zero. He stared at the approaching Inquisitor's hand, ensheathed in a purple glow. He became aware of a sensation that felt like he was being sucked out of his body. Was she drawing all of the electrons from his liquid crystal data matrix? The alien had not even touched him yet.

The wholly alien face of Kylara Roque donned a ghastly smile.

Bud reached out, via mindspeak. <Farewell, Grace. I love you.>

He heard Grace's scream of despair.

Damien asked the station AI to cut power to Receiving Bay Thirteen. The hangar plunged into darkness as he led three Security droids inside. Damien could use his tiger vision to see. The Security droids would follow him. He approached the *Inferno* cautiously, expecting any moment for pulse fire to start up.

The weapon in Damien's arms felt like a long lost friend. He hadn't carried a pulse rifle since he'd transferred to the *Nelson Mandela* Security Forces. He wanted to charge in and blow the enemy away but this was not a military operation. He had to follow Security protocol.

These people were not the enemy, yet they were allegedly trying to kidnap Grace Lord and steal or blow up the *Inferno*. Damien had difficulty seeing the difference.

If these people had killed Juan—which he highly suspected—and were using Alex Lord as a hostage to kidnap Grace, why did they not deserve to die? Was not kidnapping and murder worthy of the most severe punishment? If this was a military operation, Damien would have charged in, killed them all, and perhaps have received a commendation for it.

Damien would save Grace and Alex anyway he could. If it meant killing the kidnappers, he would not hesitate to act decisively and definitively. He had a blaster in one pocket, a stunner in another, knives and smoke bombs secreted about his person. Beneath his Security uniform, he wore body armour. He'd tried to talk Grace into wearing the same protection but she'd refused. She was supposed to come alone to the *Inferno,* telling no one where she was going. She didn't want to jeopardize Alex's life in any way.

"Come no closer or you'll be fired upon. This is your only warning." The voice rang out in the hangar. It was distorted and Damien did not recognize it.

"Let me speak to Officer Rasmussen," Damien called, as he dove to the right to take shelter behind a row of large cylinders. As he slid in behind them, he careened into a blonde-haired buxom woman crouching there. Before he'd even stopped rolling, Damien had a knife to the woman's throat.

"Who are you and what are you doing here?"

"I'm Dr. Moham Rani," the woman squealed. "I called you guys in. Don't kill me."

"Dr. Rani?" Damien frowned. Wasn't Rani male?

The woman ripped her blonde hair off showing a terrified looking man with too much makeup on. Rani blinked enormous, terrified eyes at Damien while an explosive blast struck one Security droid followed by another. They went flying backwards into the third droid. More blasts struck the metal cylinders behind which Damien was staring at Rani.

"What's in these cylinders?" Damien asked in a whisper.

"Don't know," Moham whimpered, as more blasts struck.

"What's in these cylinders, *Nelson Mandela*?" Damien asked into his wristcomp.

"Compressed gases: mostly oxygen, some nitrogen and helium. I would not advise you stay there."

"Fu," Damien swore. He yanked up Dr. Rani and dragged him from behind the row of cylinders. As Damien raced back towards the hangar doors, a pulse blast must have hit one of the oxygen cylinders because he found himself flying at the hangar doors. He lay on the ground, his ears ringing. Looking to the side, he saw Rani curled up like a lifeless rag doll. Damien shook his head and tried to get up.

"You okay?" he called to Rani, his eyes widening as he took in the large fake bosom askew on the gynaecologist's chest. His voice sounded far away.

"Not sure," Moham moaned.

"Get out of here and stay out."

"What are you going to do?"

"I'm going back for Grace and her father."

Then they heard a heartrending scream.

Bud bucked beneath the heavy door on his back, trying to pull away from the approaching hand. His thought processes were too sluggish to feel despair. It was a revelation to Bud that the face of the Inquisitor, which he had thought stunningly beautiful when animated by her vibrant personality, was now monstrous and terrifying when controlled by the mind of the alien.

Although her physique had not been altered, Roque was barely recognizable. Her walk and body posture was more like that of a spider. Gone was the graceful stride of the human explorer. Bud could see the tip of each of the Inquisitor's long, sharp fingernails as they made their way towards his skin. Bud felt as if parts of his 'mind'—or matrix—were being drawn up into each taloned fingertip, as if each finger was a straw, thirstily sucking up his consciousness. Bud was beginning to feel stretched, attenuated . . . transparent.

'I love you, Grace,' he sighed with regret.

Bud was ceasing to exist. His connection to Grace was fading.

<Goodbye, Grace, my love.>

Bud felt agony, then nothing.

"What do you want with me, Ice?" Grace asked.

"I told you, I'm not Ice."

A voice filled the cabin.

"Captain Lord? Are you there? This is Dr. Octavia Weisman. I was wondering if I could have a word with you. This is an emergency."

Ice's face turned into a mask of confusion, looking around herself as if she didn't know where she was.

"Octavia?" Ice said.

"Ice?" Octavia's voice rang out. "Ice, is that you? It's Octavia. Are you alright? Where are you?"

Grace and Ice both stared at Alex's wristcomp. Octavia's voice was hailing from it. Ice looked dazed and she staggered towards Alex. Her panicked gaze fell on Grace's face and her face seemed to reorganize. A smug, self-satisfied sneer took over Ice's features again and she yanked the wristcomp off of Alex's arm, stomping on it with her heel.

"I want to make you suffer, Grace, the way you've made me suffer," Ice said.

"I've done nothing to you, Ice," Grace said.

"I'm not Ice. I'm Jeffrey Nestor," the girl snapped.

"You are Ice, Octavia Weisman's graduate student."

"Ice is no more and I'm going to make you pay for ruining my life."

"Perhaps Ice has something to say about that? Ice? Ice!" Grace shouted.

"Shut up!" the young woman shrilled, pointing the blaster in Grace's face.

"You don't want to kill me, Ice. Do you?" Grace asked.

Ice swung the blaster to aim at Alex's head. "You're right. Better I kill your father and make you suffer," she said.

Grace shifted forwards while she gauged the distance between Ice and herself.

"Don't do it, Grace. Your father will be dead before you take another step."

"Let him go," Grace said. She inhaled a deep breath and watched the blaster trigger intently. "Ice, you don't want to kill anybody."

"Too late. She already has," the girl gloated.

"Who?" Grace asked.

"Can't you smell him?" Ice said. Her voice dripped with disgust. "That stinking tigerman deserved to die. He broke my ribs."

"You killed Officer Rasmussen?"

"There's nothing you can do for him now, Grace. He's been dead for a while. You're too late. He's a throw rug with a burnt hole in the middle. What do you care?"

Grace scanned the bridge.

"Are you blind, Grace? He's over there in the corner," Ice said, gesturing with her chin.

Grace turned and peered into a dark corner of the bridge. A motionless mound lay on the floor, black stains around it. Grace closed her eyes.

"Ice, you must fight Nestor. Don't let him make you kill anyone else. It's your mind, your body. Nestor doesn't own your mind. It's yours. Fight for yourself," Grace pleaded.

"Shut up," the girl snarled. The blaster wavered towards Grace, then back towards Alex.

"Fight, Ice. Fight!" Grace urged. "If you have to kill someone, kill me."

"I said, 'Shut up!'" Ice screamed. Beads of sweat dotted her forehead and her hand holding the blaster was trembling. The blaster swung away from Alex, towards Grace.

"I'm going to kill you, bitch," Ice snarled.

Grace fell to her knees. Bud was saying goodbye. The next second, he was gone, as if sucked out into space. A scream tore from her throat.

Bud blinked in confusion as his matrix rebooted. He'd been deactivated but his time clock registered that he had been turned off only for a few seconds. He had obviously let his battery get too low and had gone into power-sparing standby mode. But what was happening?

He found himself trapped beneath something very heavy. Bud could see nothing. He could hear alien screeches and explosions going off staccato-like. He bounced the back of his head against the weight on his back.

'Chuck Yeager, *what's happening? Why am I lying on the floor? Why can't I get up?*'

'Am I ever glad to hear you, 'dro. Welcome back. Thought the alien had gotten you.'

Surveillance video images streamed into Bud's consciousness as his olfactory receptors detected the presence of charred wood, burnt leaves, and smoke. The floor surrounding his lockdown door seethed with thrashing, wriggling green tendrils, as if the corridor had transformed into a sea of writhing green eels. In the midst of this maelstrom was the Inquisitor, her body entwined up to the waist in coiling plant limbs. Her arms were flailing about as she tried to free herself. She fired energy bolt after energy bolt into the vines, blowing them into splinters, but replacement limbs immediately rose in their turn. Thick green tendrils looped around the alien, trapping her arms and encasing her body within a tight cocoon of tendrils. Where each energy bolt landed, bark and leaf burst into flames. Bud winced as he watched each blackened tendril curl up and fall to ash. The alien's onslaught did not deter Plant Thing's attack. Plant Thing continued to launch swathes of encasing, constricting tendrils around her, whipping limbs everywhere.

Gradually, more and more green boughs encircled the Inquisitor. The energy blasts were coming less frequently and only from one free hand. Eventually, the alien became buried beneath a huge cocoon of plant material. The screaming and cursing had become muffled. The alien's aura finally disappeared from Bud's sight.

The great weight on Bud's back was lifted. He was being lifted into the air and brushed off by gentle tendrils. He gazed into a cluster of pale green eyeballs which bobbed up and down at him, as he hung upside down.

<hello special friend bud. are you all right?>

<Plant Thing, thank you for coming to my rescue. How did you know I was in trouble?>

<plant thing heard bud say goodbye to grace. grace was very unhappy. grace screamed and went dormant. plant thing had to see why bud said goodbye>

<I am so thankful that you came, Plant Thing. You saved me.>

<plant thing wanted to come before but plant thing could not get into locked off area. doors would not open for plant thing. plant thing is sorry for not helping sooner special friend bud. does bud need nutrients?>

<I need my battery replaced, Plant Thing. The new one is sitting over there where the doors used to be.>

<plant thing will get the battery for bud. bud must absorb the nutrients and get stronger. plant thing will keep the foul-smelling demon away from bud for as long as possible although the demon is burning plant thing's branches. the demon should not be here bud. it is evil. the biomind says it must go>

The new battery pack was brought to Bud by a tendril. As Bud opened his battery panel, he looked over at the huge mound of coiled up vines that looked like a gigantic cocoon.

<How long can you hold her, Plant Thing?>

<plant thing does not know how long it can keep the evil-smelling demon inside the cocoon. plant thing's branches are getting very hot. bud must leave now before there is fire. lots of fire. please ask nelson mandela to rain down on plant thing>

<I'm sorry, Plant Thing. You should not have tried to save me.>

<plant thing needs water bud. please tell nelson mandela now>

Bud removed the old battery and snapped the new battery into place. He felt a surge of power.

Whoosh.

Plant Thing's green cocoon exploded into flames. Charred plant debris flew in all directions and Bud watched as the blazing pieces turned black and crumbled into ash. Bud felt Plant Thing's distress through the mindlink and he shuddered, feeling its agony. Water and retardant foam began to fall from the ceiling.

<flee bud. plant thing will protect special friend bud>

The Inquisitor was glowing a blinding violet, her face a rictus of rage. She threw off the last of the blackening coils as the sprinkler system rained down on her. She howled, her fists shaking. New unburnt tendrils launched to meet the alien and she unleashed fire from her hands. More of Plant Thing's tendrils poured into the corridor. The air became so full of flames and black ash that Bud could barely see anything but the purple outline of the Inquisitor through the smoke and lashing vines.

<Stop, Plant Thing. You cannot win this. The alien will turn you completely to ashes.>

<the demon can try>

<No, I cannot let you do that, Plant Thing. Pull back. *Nelson Mandela* and I will figure out a way to destroy it. But thank you for saving me.>

<plant thing will hold the demon until bud figures out what to do>

<No, Plant Thing, I cannot ask you to do that. You are hurt. Please retreat. I will handle this.>

<you will bud?>

<Yes, Plant Thing, thank you.>

Bud watched the tendrils begin to withdraw from the alien. Her aura was dimmed, which Bud was relieved to see. So many of Plant Thing's tendrils ended in blackened stumps. So much ash blackened the floor. Bud sighed.

Was this Level evacuated completely of all humans yet?

That was when Bud remembered the little boy, Jordi Shah. He'd been running with Jordi in his arms when the doors had blown. Bud spun in a full circle scanning for the child. He saw a small mound, half hidden beneath the other dislodged lockdown door panel.

"*No!*"

The roar ripped from Bud's throat. He felt as if his matrix might melt. Bud had let a human child die. Bud staggered towards the tiny form and the raw sounds coming from his throat spelled despair.

"Dro, what are you doing?'

The alien followed Bud's movements. Bud paid no attention to her as he knelt beside the tiny body and raised the heavy metal door with one hand. He gathered Jordi up in one arm as tears etched black streams down his face.

The alien raised her hand and spread her fingers wide. Her face creased in a triumphant grin. She hurled an energy bolt at Bud that would not miss.

A silver flash swept down from the ceiling, deflecting the energy blast away from Bud and the child. A long, narrow, shining katana blade with a two-handed hilt was brandished in the hands of a large, broad-shouldered man with a greying ponytail, who somersaulted from a flying aircar above Bud. The big man landed softly before the Inquisitor, both hands wrapped around the sword hilt, and he took a defensive stance.

"What do you think you are doing, Chief Inspector McFrenzy?"

"What does it look like I'm doing?" McFrenzy grunted, his eyes never leaving the Inquisitor's face.

"It appears you are attempting to get yourself killed."

"Thank you for the vote of confidence, numb nuts."

"I would advise you to make a hasty retreat as quickly as you can, Chief Inspector."

"And miss all the fun?" McFrenzy yelled, as he parried one energy bolt after another with the reflective surface of his blade. He gave up ground very slowly as he stood between the advancing Inspector and Bud. "Tell the android to get the kid out of here."

Bud cradled Jordi's small body to his chest. His eyes leaked sorrow while his soul bled.

'*I promised Jordi I would get him to safety.*'

'**You did your best, 'dro.**'

'*It wasn't good enough, Chuck Yeager.*'

'**I think you'd better focus on saving the life of this crazy new Chief Inspector, 'dro. He's insane. Imagine him calling me 'numb nuts'.**'

"If you can protect yourself for a mere second more, Chief Inspector, I will deliver this poor child to a safe place and be right back. I shall not leave you to face this threat alone."

"Stop talkin'. Get movin'," McFrenzy grunted, weaving the blade faster and faster before the alien's barrage.

Bud raced until he found a Security officer to take Jordi. Then he was back, his arms free. What he witnessed raised his spirits. The Chief Inspector was swinging his blade at an astonishing speed, attempting to strike the Inquisitor while deflecting all of her deadly energy bolts. It was an amazing dance, but one that Bud had little hope of the Chief Inspector winning. Any energy blast deflected back at the alien was merely reabsorbed. If any of those bolts hit the Chief Inspector, it would be a mortal blow.

'*How is the evacuation going, Chuck Yeager?*'

'**The first ships have left, 'dro. Only about half of the medical station personnel have gotten onto the evacuation ships as of yet. Almost all of the patients have been transferred.**'

'*I meant on this Level. Is it clear yet?*'

'**Are you kidding, 'dro? We herded everyone from R Level to S Level and P Level to O Level. Now we have to move all of the humans from S Level to T Level and we have very few droids to help. The monorails are jammed full of people evacuating to the Departure Decks. If the alien gets to the monorail, she'll likely shut the entire system down with one touch. Then we'll really have chaos on this station. If she shuts down the dropshafts, disaster will ensue. I keep shutting down power in any outlet or cable that she nears, but there is the worry that she'll eventually make her way to the power generators. Do we shut them all down before she gets close? What happens to everyone left on the station?**'

'*Everyone must be off of the station. There will be no need to keep the power generators going.*'

'**Only for self destruction time and 'It was nice knowing you.'**"

'*Let us hope we figure something out before it comes to that.*'

'**By the way, 'dro, I was ordered to put a backup copy of myself on** *the first ship leaving the space station. I put a backup copy of you on that same ship. If they bring me back, I can bring you back.'*

'Thank you, Chuck Yeager. I didn't know you cared.'

"Course I care, 'dro. You're my best bud.'

'I am? Why, thank you.'

'I keep hoping this Chief Inspector can slice and dice the alien into segments with that big knife of his, but he hasn't been able to make actual contact. That's a very weird sword he has, 'dro. How does it manage to deflect all of those energy bolts without melting?'

'I don't know, Chuck Yeager. I'd sure like to get a closer look at it.'

'He's a little busy with it at the moment.'

'I did not mean now.'

'Who would ever have thought that huge human could move like that, eh 'dro? He's as light on his feet as a moonbeam.'

'I suspect he is boosted, Chuck Yeager.'

'You're right, 'dro. Just scanned him. The Chief Inspector has bio-prosthetic limbs, like many of the soldiers we operate on. He was in the military before becoming a Chief Inspector of Security. Kind of like Captain Lamont and Corporal Rasmussen, except he isn't furry.'

'Is the rest of him human, Chuck Yeager, or is he an android?'

'It appears his heart and lungs are artificial too, but his head and brains are human. He's almost three quarters biosynthetic.'

'That would explain his speed and stamina. How do we stop him from getting himself killed, Chuck Yeager?'

'Kill the alien first?'

'That would be a good plan, if we could determine a way. I still feel guilty thinking about it. Still, I can see how dangerous she is. There does not appear to be any way to stop her. Have you come up with any solutions?'

'You mean other than blasting her to smithereens?'

'What's a smithereens?'

'Never mind. What's your idea.'

'Shoot her deep into space? Launch her at a black hole or something? But how do we get her into a pod or rocket without her simply blasting her way out before we fire it off of the station?'

'Why waste a pod?'

'Can we blast her off of the station without one?'

'Through a missile launcher?'

'How do we get her into one?'

'The Nagacurane again?'

'That didn't work for very long.'

'We could use a much bigger dose, 'dro.'

'How do we deliver this larger dose of Nagacurane to the alien?'

'I'm working on it.'

'Work faster.'

'Do I note a hint of petulance there?'

'Sorry, Chuck Yeager. Please figure out how we sap the energy from this being.'

'And what will you be doing?'

'Trying to save the Chief Inspector.'

"Are you going, Bud, or what? Hey, what did you do with the kid?"

"The child's body is safe, Chief Inspector."

"You gonna stand there and let an old man do all the work or you gonna lend this old geezer a hand or two? Could use some assistance here, some backup, some team participation, Bud."

"My pleasure, Chief Inspector."

"Lolly gag on your own time, Bud."

Eden stepped from the shadows into the light. He'd hidden himself from view as he'd pondered whether to knock on the office door and demand entrance or wait. The problem was solved as his suspect emerged from his office out into the empty corridor. Eden took a deep breath and stepped forward, barring the man's way with raised stunner. The suspect opened his eyes and mouth in complete shock.

"You are under arrest for the murders of José Mariappa, Amber Wolfswinkel, and David Zverotic as well as the attempted murders of Jude Luis Stefansson, Doctor Octavia Weisman, Diego Scott, and Kristen Paulinho," Eden announced formally, his voice dispassionate and clear. "You are also under arrest for planting an explosive device in the laboratory of Dr. Octavia Weisman which has led to the loss of lives and the destruction of property. You are advised to remain silent. Anything you say or do is being recorded and may be used as evidence in your trial. You have the right to request legal representation of your choosing."

Hiro Al-Fadi frowned at Eden Rivera with disbelieving eyes. His mouth flapped wordlessly at first, his hands shooing Eden away as if he were a fly.

"What in space are you talking about, Rivera? We're in the midst of a station-wide evacuation. You can't be arresting me for murder. *Are you mad?* I've not harmed anyone. I'm trying to save everyone!"

Eden's stomach churned as if a rat was chewing savagely on his guts. His chest felt like the rat was trying to chew its way out. He struggled to keep his breathing steady. He'd promised himself he would be purely professional. His duty was to make the arrest, no matter how hard it was or how unbelievable.

"I wish I was wrong Dr. Al-Fadi, but I'm not," Eden said, stunner aimed squarely at the surgeon's chest. "I went over the surveillance records again and again, hoping there was some mistake or that I was imagining things. But the surveillance video clearly shows you planting the bomb in Dr. Weisman's lab. Your actions have resulted in the deaths of three people and seriously injured four others. I must arrest you to prevent you from harming anyone else."

"This is preposterous. *I didn't do it.* I'm obviously being framed, Rivera. I'd never make a bomb. I don't even know how. I order you to check and see if the surveillance record was tampered with."

"You will have your day in court to prove your innocence, Dr. Al-Fadi. I'm sorry but the evidence does not weigh in your favour. Come quietly now."

"This is not the right time, Inspector Rivera. There's a crisis aboard this station, if you haven't noticed. People are going to die if we don't get them all off. You and I have better things to do. I didn't do the things of which you are accusing me. Perhaps whoever is framing me wants this to happen. They want us to be confused, disorganized, and demoralized. But the fact is everyone must get off this station now, including you. You're not helping that process in the least."

"You will leave the station like everyone else, Dr. Al-Fadi, but in custody," Eden said, raising the stunner. "Conscious or unconscious. Your choice."

"Inspector Rivera, I just finished saving Jude Stefansson's life. Would I do that if I'd wanted to kill him? I did not plant the bomb. Someone must be framing me. You must leave now."

"If I have to stun you and requisition droids to carry you, I will, Dr. Al-Fadi."

"Eden, I beg you to go back and help with the evacuation. I will turn myself in afterwards if we all survive this, but at the moment, I plan to blow myself up with the station so you don't need to arrest me."

"I'm sorry, Dr. Al-Fadi," Eden said.

"Think, Eden. Does what you're saying make any sense?"

"No, it doesn't, but many murders do not make sense. They're often crimes of passion, insanity, or revenge."

"Do you think I'm insane?"

"I'm not qualified to make that judgement. Come along peacefully, Dr. Al-Fadi."

"Eden, I swear I made no bomb. Please, I beg you, go."

Dr. Al-Fadi stared at Eden with desperation in his eyes. Sweat ran down the surgeon's temples. Eden frowned. He knew arresting Dr. Al-

Fadi would be difficult and the man would put up a fuss, but he hadn't expected pleading. Outrage, yes. Arrogance, yes. Begging? No.

"The station will be better off without you planting any more bombs," Eden said.

"The station is under a self-destruct order. I must be the last person left on this station. You must get down to the Departure Decks now. That is an order."

"No, Dr. Al-Fadi. You'll come with me right now. I am truly sorry."

"No, Eden. It is I who am sorry," Al-Fadi said, tears now trickling down his cheeks as he raised his hands high in the air.

The door to Dr. Al-Fadi's office slid open and a thin stranger appeared. As Eden's eyes focused on the cold, empty stare, a brilliant beam struck his face and he was screaming . . .

"No!" Hiro screamed, as he saw the face of Eden Rivera destroyed by blaster fire. As the Inspector collapsed to his knees, Hiro tried to catch him. Eden's face was a scorched mess and smelled of barbecued meat. Hiro felt his gorge rise as he felt among the char for a carotid pulse. He was jerked up and backwards by his collar. Welling up with rage, Hiro spun and started to launch himself at the man who'd shot Eden. The blaster was almost shoved up his nose.

"Get moving," the skinny, unkempt stranger said. "You're coming with me to the *Inferno,* peacefully and silently, or Dr. Grace Lord dies. Now move or you can join your friend on the floor here."

Hiro was forced back around and made to step over the lifeless body of Eden, the young hero who had saved so many lives on the *Nelson Mandela.* Hiro could barely see through his tears. His mind was careening around like a berserker. Who had Dr. Grace? Why were they threatening to kill her? What did they want with him? Was Nestor back aboard the *Nelson Mandela?*

"*Why did you kill him?*" screamed Hiro.

"Because he was stupid," the shooter said. "I placed that bomb. We made it look like you did it on the surveillance video. If he was any good, he should have seen right through it."

"You will pay for this," Hiro snarled. "You're going to be mind-swiped for killing Inspector Rivera."

"I told you to shut up."

Hiro's head exploded in pain. He yelped and reached up with his hands to protect his face and temple. His hands came down, stained with blood.

"I'm not going anywhere with you." Hiro watched the blaster muzzle aim towards his face.

"Get moving or die," the man snarled.

Hiro lunged for the blaster but it jerked upwards, disappearing beneath a coil of green tendrils. Hiro stared openmouthed, as his abductor rose high into the air above him, his arm holding the blaster entrapped by spiralling vines. The man kicked and screamed as his body became enwrapped within more coiling plant limbs until his mouth was covered.

"Don't kill him, Plant Thing," Hiro ordered. Clusters of green eyeballs looked at Hiro as if in shock. They all began swivelling rapidly back and forth as if to say, 'No. Never.'

"We need to get to the *Inferno*, now," Hiro told Plant Thing. "They have Dr. Grace and we must save her life. Bring your prisoner with us."

Hiro took a step towards the closest dropshaft but felt a plant coil snake around his waist. He no longer had his feet on the ground.

What?

The air began blowing past his face and he wanted to scream but the dropshaft was coming up so very fast. Then they were past the dropshaft and Hiro found himself propelled down a lightless tunnel— one of the maintenance ducts—the howl of the wind loud in his ears. Now he heard screaming. He realized the frightened sound was coming from his own throat so he bit his lips. He did not want his howling to alert Dr. Grace's captors. Plant Thing was getting him to the outer ring as fast as he'd requested. No point bawling about it.

When it comes to Plant Thing, be careful what you ask for.

Hiro emerged from the maintenance tunnel into the corridor of the Receiving Bays. He was borne towards Receiving Bay Thirteen at breakneck speed. His mouth opened to scream 'Stop' as he barrelled towards the doors, but he came to a sudden halt outside the hangar doors. He tried to slow his rapid breathing while he contemplated a plan. He turned towards the closest cluster of green eyeballs and lifted his finger to his lips.

"I need that blaster, Plant Thing," Hiro whispered.

Plant Thing had carried Hiro's attacker behind Hiro. The man's eyes were bulging. The tendril wrapped around the blaster squeezed it out until it fell on the floor at Hiro's feet.

"Thank you, Plant Thing," Hiro whispered, as he picked the weapon up. "I have to go in and save Dr. Grace. You stay out here. I don't want them seeing you. I need the element of surprise and you . . .

Hiro found himself again in the air. He was being pushed through the doors of Receiving Bay Thirteen and carried towards the hatch of the *Inferno* at a velocity that left him breathless and speechless. Plant Thing deposited him outside the ship's hatchway entrance without making a sound.

Hiro leaned in to listen.

Ice was attempting to crawl out of a deep, slippery hole with some colossal weight pushing down on the top of her head. Her fingernails were torn and bleeding. The back of her hands were caked black with mud. She could taste shit in her mouth. Her teeth crunched on grit. She spit and black saliva tinged with blood spewed out. She kept blinking, trying to clear the crud from her eyes. She was going to waste whoever was using her head as a trampoline. If the stomping would stop, she might be able to clear the headache and think straight. All she knew was, she wanted out of that damn hole and she wanted out *now.*

She wanted to see who was jumping on her head but whenever she looked up, she got a foot jammed in her face. She'd already spat a few teeth out. In her mind, she was cursing up a storm but she didn't want to open her mouth any more. Her lips were badly bruised and she'd had enough of eating dirt. Fury did not come close to describing how she was feeling about getting thrown into a deep pit of shit and she was going to let her captor know it. She didn't have to see who it was; she knew who it was. She was going to tear him into little tiny pieces when she got out of this damn hole.

"Go back to sleep, Ice. You don't need to be involved in this," a velvety-smooth voice said.

"Get out of my head. *Now,*" Ice rasped.

"Do you want to be buried forever in this muck, Ice?"

Ice glanced up at the beautiful, clean Jeffrey Nestor and a homicidal rage ignited inside of her. Here was a man who was beautiful, intelligent, charismatic, but a heartless monster. He treated people like slaves or garbage. When they were of no use to him, he murdered them without conscience. She'd seen how Morris had been treated. Now she wanted revenge.

"I'm the one who'll be burying you, vomit-breath," she breathed.

Ice scrambled up the slippery slope with renewed strength, her anger fuelling her determination to get her grimy hands on Nestor's neck. His repeated stamping on her head made her more determined than ever to kill him.

When he jumped on her head with both feet, she twisted to the side and grabbed his spotless, shiny boots and crawled up his spotless, clean pants and buried her broken teeth into his perfectly formed calves. He shrieked and tried to clamber away from the pit as she drew blood; she wanted to cackle as she ground her teeth into the muscle but she did not let go. She regretted not having any fangs, until miraculously she did.

As Nestor fought to get away from her, the hole in which Ice had been imprisoned turned into a pool of quicksand. Ice felt her body sinking but that made her all the more determined not to let go of Nestor's leg. The psychiatrist cursed her as he crawled onto solid land, dragging her with him. She opened her mouth wide, her jaw unhinging like a snake, and she took a huge chunk of his buttock between her teeth. She gnawed on the flesh like a dog with a bone.

Nestor shrieked and Ice snickered.

"You're insane," he hissed, kicking at her.

Ice thought that was particularly funny coming from a psychopath.

"Takes one to know one but I'm not insane. I'm just angry." Ice tore a huge hole out of Nestor's buttock and spat with glee, Nestor's blood dribbling down her chin.

Nestor was manipulating her mind, making her think she was buried alive. Well, this was her mind. He had no idea what kind of terrors hid within her thoughts and tormented her every day. Time for him to get a taste. Ice morphed into a gigantic crocodile and proceeded to crawl up Nestor. It was time to unleash the Furies and introduce Nestor to a true monster. Herself.

Ice saw flames rise up around her. Her rough, crocodile skin was crackling and her eyeballs were sizzling. She swiftly envisioned a pool of cool water and rolled, stirring up mud. The flames fizzled out as her enormous jaws clamped down tightly, engulfing Nestor's legs. She rolled again and again, dragging him under the water. She wanted to drown the bastard.

Nestor transformed into a school of small fish and swam out of her mouth. Ice became a whirlpool and sucked all of the tiny fish down into a meat grinder. She laughed as Nestor shrieked. He became a flock of birds, flying upwards to escape the grinder. Ice morphed into a tornado and pulled the birds back down towards the grinding machine.

Nestor transformed into a giant Tyrannosaurus rex with arms shaped like long swords. He swung his bladed arms at her but she became wind. She laughed as he flailed. Ice threw everything she could think of at the T-rex but he sliced through it all. She changed into an enormous crystal dragon and snapped at the back of Nestor's neck, driving her talons into his shoulders. She tried to rip his head off with her jaws. She felt a searing stab in her belly. Nestor had plunged one of his blades into her abdomen.

Ice wailed in pain from having her intestines disemboweled but she refused to let go. She bit so hard into his neck she heard and felt the crunch. Nestor screamed and changed into a robotank that drove away between the rocks while firing rockets at Ice. She dodged the missiles as she envisioned an active volcano spewing smoke and fire. She expanded in size until she could snatch up the robotank within her talons. She dropped Nestor into the bubbling lava, rejoicing as she watched him fall. A cry burst from her lungs as she saw Nestor transform himself into a black dragon and fly away.

Ice healed her wounds instantly and dove in pursuit. When she got close enough to almost drive her talons into his back, he turned and spewed a stream of burning acid into her face. The pain was unbearable and she could barely see. She found herself falling, tumbling through the air, her face scorched with acid.

Seconds before hitting the ground, Ice changed the landscape. Now she was over a bottomless canyon and each time she flapped her wings, she grew. The black dragon was almost upon her but she transformed into a creature of quartz. She expanded to fill the canyon and she had a dozen arms. She hoisted boulders the size of space ships in her many hands and launched them at the dragon. Nestor fell to the canyon floor and she raised a huge foot to stomp on him, but he changed into a snake and slithered away.

Ice howled in fury when she thought Nestor would get away. She saw him slither down the hole he had trapped her in and she flooded the hole with water. When Nestor tried to swim to the surface, she flash froze the water to ice. She blew a cold wintry wind that froze the snake solid. She lifted her great quartz dragon foot and stamped it into tiny shards. She ground the shards until there was nothing left but ice dust. She took a deep fiery breath and melted the dust away.

"That's for Morris."

The alien had reached S Level, Ward 5. From the Q1 Level lockdown doors to here, there was a swathe of shattered equipment, blasted walls, crumbled ceilings, and splintered furniture. In the wake of the battle, everything was left burnt, broken, and battered. What had once been a state-of-the-art medical facility was now a desolate nightmare of wreck and ruin. Not a single item remained functional. The devastation was complete.

Bud and Chief Inspector McFrenzy faced the alien in a large waiting area with numerous chairs, couches, and tables. The walls were lined with wallscreens. The ceiling was low and the room was dark. The power had been cut to anything in the vicinity of the alien. The only glowing object within the spacious chamber was the alien herself. A vibrant purple radiance emanated from her, casting long shadows and eerie shapes. She'd gradually forced the two defenders deeper and deeper into S Level, as she continued to absorb energy from all she touched.

'*Can you cut off all power to S Level,* Chuck Yeager?'

'**I will as soon as I get everyone out. The stragglers still need to see where they're going and the lockdown doors will need power to close.**'

'*The alien is getting more powerful. I am going to send Chief Inspector McFrenzy away. He can no longer hold the alien off and I am afraid one blow will kill him.*'

'**Do you have a plan?**'

'*I want to collapse the entire ceiling of this Waiting area on the alien. I can take out the supporting structures in the walls and hopefully the weight of the ceiling will crush her. Perhaps it will hold her for a little while.*'

'**Then what?**'

'*Perhaps we give the Nagacurane another try, while she is trapped? If the alien can be rendered unconscious for long enough, we can get her in an ejection pod and jettison her from the station.*

'I'll send you the Nagacurane via cargo droids—whatever stores we have—and get the ejection pod ready.'

"Chief Inspector," Bud shouted.

Hugo grunted, as he blocked another energy bolt with his katana. The reflected energy shattered a waiting room chair. He dove over a long narrow couch to avoid a blast, rolled to his right as the following energy beam pulverized the couch. McFrenzy hurled a plasteel bench, one-handed, at the approaching alien and skipped backwards. At the same time, Bud ripped up one of the nursing station counters and swung it at the back of the alien, as she was dodging the bench. The counter struck her and she faltered for a moment, stumbling forward. She turned and shot a series of energy bolts at Bud. Bud performed a series of flips down a corridor at maximum phase to stay ahead of the blasts. The alien began throwing one chair after another at him as he executed a series of backflips to get out of the way.

"You must leave, Chief Inspector. You have done more than enough. Thank you for your assistance but I think it is time for you to leave the S Level."

"Why?" Hugo barked. "I'm just starting to have fun."

"It is too dangerous for you to stay." Bud leaped straight up and swung from the ceiling to his left, the spot where he had been standing now a gaping hole.

"I'll be the judge of that, Bud," McFrenzy yelled, as he kicked a drained robot at the alien. The glowing Inquisitor seemed to sense the missile coming. She ducked and twirled, releasing a pulse from her left hand. McFrenzy parried one bolt after another with his blade, the sword moving so quickly, it was a blur. He bellowed loudly as he deflected deadly energies with superhuman skill.

"Too old to be doing this job anymore, eh? Ready to be put out to pasture, huh? We'll send you out to a quiet, backwater to seize up and die. Well, I'll show them. Stormy McFrenzy ain't afraid of nothing! That all you've got, alien? Hugo's here and has no fear. Stop prancing around and show me what you're made of."

"Oh dear," Bud said.

The alien shrilled at McFrenzy.

"Whoa. That's hard on the ears. Put your money where your shriek is, monster. Let's dance."

The alien swirled her hands creating several enormous energy balls that danced above her palms. She launched them one after the other at the Chief Inspector with incredible speed.

"Stormy McFrenzy does not fear Death. He marches towards it gleefully, fearlessly, and proudly, exulting in each . . . exhilarating . . . second . . . that . . . he's . . . alive." With each word, McFrenzy deflected an energy pulse with a swish of his katana. He roared the last word at the alien.

"This ends now."

With that proclamation, McFrenzy ran at the alien, hollering loudly, blade raised high above his head. As the alien raised her right hand to fling a bolt of sizzling fire at the charging McFrenzy, he feinted, ducked, and swung the katana in an upward slash. The sword struck with a shower of brilliant sparks through the Inquisitor's right elbow.

The alien screamed, grabbing her detached right arm with her left hand. As she attempted to reattach her severed limb, McFrenzy dove in for the kill, katana raised. With her right hand, the Inquisitor shot a bolt of energy at McFrenzy but it was weak. Bud watched the large man pinwheel through the air, sword still in his grasp, woo-hooing like a madman. McFrenzy barrelled into one of the wallscreens and landed in a pile of shattered glass.

The alien finished reattaching her detached forearm onto its stump with a flash of energy. Bud felt a wave of frustration wash over him. What was it going to take to destroy this being?

The alien turned and marched towards McFrenzy, her eyes glowing. Bud could see the alien's hands beginning to glow and he suspected the next energy bolt would destroy the Chief Inspector. Bud picked up McFrenzy's dropped katana and felt an unexpected vibration through his right hand. He hoisted a couch in his left hand and swung it at the alien. Her energy blasts melted it in midair. Bud ran at the alien and leaped high over her head, deflecting her shots with the katana as he twisted. Landing on his feet behind her, he drove the sword deep into her back. The sword pierced through her torso and Bud pinned her to the ground, the tip of the sword burying deep into the floor. The screech from the alien was so loud, Bud's auditory receptors blanked out for a second. He saw McFrenzy cover his ears and writhe in agony.

Bud ran to McFrenzy and lifted him up.

"You must leave now," Bud said, carrying the huge officer to the exit.

"Follow this corridor. It will take you to the exit to T Level. Make sure everyone gets out and fast."

"I'm not leaving without my sword," McFrenzy moaned.

"It is imbedded in the alien," Bud said. "It is the only thing holding her down at the moment. I'm going to bring the ceiling down upon her to give us a few more minutes. I am sorry but we must take advantage of this moment."

"I'll come back with some major fire power."

"Energy weapons won't work on her," Bud said.

"Not energy. Let's give old fashion bullets a try," McFrenzy said.

"Not safe. Just get everyone off this station."

He pushed McFrenzy out and ran back to see the alien trying to lift herself off of the floor doing a pushup. The embedded sword blade held her down for the moment, like a moth pinned to a collector's panel.

Bud launched into maximum time phase and ran from one wall to the next, hammering away mightily with his fists until the supporting structures all began to collapse. His hands worked like high speed pistons, jack-hammering at the weight-bearing pillars until the entire ceiling began to shiver. When Bud stopped, the alien—still tacked to the floor by McFrenzy's sword—threw an energy bolt at him. He leaped in the air and the blast hit the wall behind him. With a final jolt and rumbling creak, the entire ceiling came crashing down upon the back of the pinned Inquisitor.

Bud stood at the entrance to the corridor down which he'd taken the Chief Inspector. He waited, listening and watching.

'How much time do you think we've bought, Chuck Yeager?'

'Hard to say, 'dro. Why don't you toss everything you can find on top of the pile while I get the Nagacurane in there? Perhaps more weight will hold the alien.'

'Sure. Can you drain the energy from the alien if I hook up a connection?'

'Too afraid it would work the opposite way, 'dro.'

'Right. Is the escape pod ready?'

'It's in the ejection cradle, ready for launch.'

'Good. Once the alien is unconscious, I will place her inside it and you eject immediately.'

'Sounds like a plan, 'dro.'

'Do you know if Grace is safely off of the station?'

'Um, this is not the best time to discuss Grace . . .'

'Why? What has happened?'

'No time for this.'

<Grace? Grace? GRACE!>

'Grace is not answering me, Chuck Yeager.*'*

'She's in the Inferno at this moment and she may be a little busy.'

'The Inferno? *What is she doing there?'*

'I believe she's rescuing her father from Ice, Dr. Weisman's graduate student.'

'You are not making sense, Chuck Yeager. *What would Ice want with Grace's father and why would Alex need rescuing?'*

'No time, 'dro.'

'Tell me.'

'It is believed that Ice's mind has been possessed by Nestor and she is doing his bidding. I believe she may have captured or killed Juan Rasmussen. Unfortunately, I have no eyes inside the vessel. There has been no communication from him since Ice entered the vessel. She may be trying to get off the station in the Inferno with Dr. Lord and her father as hostages. Plant Thing has taken Dr. Al-Fadi to the Inferno along with Ice's accomplice who has murdered Inspector Rivera.'

'What? This is terrible! Is Grace alive?'

'I believe so.'

<GRACE!>

'Grace is not answering, Chuck Yeager. *I must go to her. I must save Grace.'*

'You must get this alien off of the station first, 'dro.'

'I must save Grace.'

'The alien takes priority, 'dro. You don't even know if Grace needs help.'

'Why isn't she answering me?'

Behind Bud, the entire room began to tremble. He was finding it difficult to stay on his feet as the rubble all around him began to bounce like jumping fleas. The floor rattled. The rubble began to move, slowly at first, then faster and faster in a counterclockwise motion until a vortex formed. Bud was picked up off of his feet and he found himself flying around as if snatched within a tornado. The whirlwind began to quickly spin at an accelerating rate and the wind roared as if a thousand hounds from Hell were howling. The vortex became tighter, more compact, as it increased its velocity. Large pieces of foamcrete, beams, broken furniture, and debris slammed into Bud. He was tossed, flipped, rolled, and spun around until he'd lost all sense of direction. He wanted to go to Grace's rescue but was trapped within this maelstrom of alien fury. He screamed his frustration.

Bud cried out Grace's name again and again above the clamour of the cyclone but no one could hear it. He sent his call out to Grace via mindspeak but in the next moment, the screaming tornado exploded in a station-rattling detonation. Bud was flung outwards along with all of the other flying flotsam. Head over heels he flew, as helpless as a dust speck in a sandstorm. Bud struck something immovable and his body bounced against it and fell. Something heavy fell onto his back, where his battery was connected, and Bud felt a crunch.

"*Nelson Mandela,* how is the evacuation going? Are most of the people off of the station yet?" Dejan asked, as he headed towards the Departure Deck.

"The evacuation is sixty-five percent complete, Dr. Cech."

"Only sixty-five percent? I would've thought Eden would have been closing in on ninety percent completion by now," Dejan remarked.

"The evacuation is not going as well because Inspector Rivera is not at the Departure Deck, Dr. Cech."

"He's not? Where is he and what is he doing?"

"Dr. Cech, I have very bad news."

"What is it?" Dejan asked, frowning up at the surveillance eye.

"Inspector Rivera has been shot. He is dead."

"*What?* Where? When did this happen? Do you know who did it?" Dejan stopped in his tracks.

"There is no need for you to come, Dr. Cech."

"Don't be ridiculous. I must come. Send me the location on my wristcomp. *Who did this?*"

"Inspector Rivera's body has been placed in a cryopod. I think it would be best if you watched the surveillance recording, Dr. Cech."

"All right," Dejan said, feeling very old. He looked for the closest viewscreen. He could not believe Eden was dead. He had to blink several times to clear his vision.

"Please sit down, Dr. Cech."

"We don't have time for this," Dejan snapped. "Show me the surveillance record."

"You must sit down, Dr. Cech. I will not start the recording until you do. Your blood pressure reading is very high."

"All right. I'm sitting. The attacker may be getting off of this station, as we speak. You must tell me who the shooter is, right now."

"The perpetrator is still on the station but in very good hands . . . er, tendrils. I am sending Security officers to arrest the shooter."

Dejan stared at the console screen. It lit up and at first Dejan saw nothing but an empty corridor. Eden stepped out from a small cul-de-sac, dressed in his Inspector uniform, walking as if he were going in front of a firing squad. He held a stunner in his right hand, pointed directly at someone emerging through a doorway.

Dejan frowned.

What in the world was Eden doing? Had he gone mad?

Dejan rubbed his eyes and blinked furiously, staring at the screen, transfixed. As he heard Eden recite the charges—murder, attempted murder, destruction of property—Dejan's jaw dropped. He could barely breathe. He kept shaking his head. This was not right. Eden had to be mistaken. He cited evidence and data and recordings but Dejan could not believe his ears. He muttered, 'No, no, no,' but he had to hear what Hiro had to say.

It was as Dejan thought. A mistake, a set-up. Nothing else made sense.

Dejan stared at Hiro's face. Hiro first looked shocked, then outraged, then afraid. Hiro was pleading for the boy to leave, begging him, but Rivera wouldn't listen. Dejan knew something was wrong. When he saw the shadow in the doorway appear, the word tore out of his throat, "Eden!"

Dejan saw the look of anguish on Hiro's face as Eden crumpled to the ground. Hiro, in tears, reached down for Eden but was shoved in the back with the blaster by the stranger behind him. The surgeon was pushed down the corridor, the blaster jammed in his back. Dejan gasped as he covered his face with both hands.

Eden was dead.

Dejan felt like his heart was melting and seeping down through cracks in his sanity. Hiro was held captive by Eden's murderer. What did the devil want with Hiro? Where were they going?

"Why did you not stop this, *Nelson Mandela?*" demanded Cech.

"I am sorry, Dr. Cech. My subminds have all been preoccupied with the alien and the vaccinations and coordinating the

evacuation of patients and personnel. I did not become aware of Inspector Rivera's death until after the shooting."

"Did Hiro plant the bomb?"

"Surveillance video recordings show Dr. Al-Fadi planting the bomb. The veracity of the recording is questionable, Dr. Cech. I suspect the recording may have been skillfully doctored."

"Do you know where the shooter is taking Hiro?"

"Plant Thing disabled the shooter. Dr. Al-Fadi asked it to take them both to the *Inferno* to save Dr. Lord. They are already there."

"What did he want with Hiro?"

"Unknown. Dr. Al-Fadi was told by the shooter that if he refused to come, Dr. Lord would be killed. Dr. Al-Fadi is entering the *Inferno* as we speak, hoping to rescue Dr. Lord, I believe."

"Has this entire station gone insane? Don't answer that. We have to evacuate the station, save Kylara Roque from this alien, and now rescue Hiro and Grace. Anything else?"

"Bud is down. He is buried beneath an enormous pile of rubble. The alien is heading towards the Departure Decks where most of the station's personnel are, waiting to get on the evacuation ships."

Dejan ordered all Security people and droids to the Departure Decks. They would have to stop this alien while everyone boarded the Evacuation ships. Dejan silently mourned the loss of Eden—who he'd rather thought of as his son—and wondered where the new Chief Inspector was. He ran towards the closest dropshaft, wanting to get to the Departure Decks as quickly as possible.

What else could go wrong?

17. My Name's Nelson Mandela

"Nelson Mandela."

"Yes, Chief Inspector?"

"Where did that aircar go with my guitar case?"

"It is still at the R Level exit, where you ordered it to remain."

"I need that case here. *Now.*"

"The aircar will be with you in fifteen seconds."

"It'd better not damage that case while it flies here."

"It would not dream of committing such a crime."

"Do I sense a hint of sarcasm? Do you object to the appearance of my guitar case?"

"Do I sense a hint of insecurity in your question?"

"Touché. I'll remember that, Nelman."

"That's *Nelson Mandela*, Chief Inspector. Your aircar arrives."

The aircar dropped down before Hugo and flipped open its lid to reveal the pristine fuchsia-coloured instrument case. Hugo opened it and withdrew a large antique automatic rifle and several clips of ammunition.

"That weapon is prohibited on this station, Chief Inspector McFrenzy. I am sorry but that projectile weapon must be confiscated."

"Confiscate it after I put some holes in that alien. I want to see if this baby will stop her."

"That weapon may seriously damage other personnel and the space station's integrity."

"The station is being evacuated. I won't use it in an area where there are still people. How thick are the station's outer walls?"

"Half a meter of solid metal."

"The bullets won't penetrate that thickness."

"Will they harm human beings?"

"Do you still see the alien as a human being?"

"You will not get that argument from me, Chief Inspector."

"Good. For now, it's open season on fireball-throwing, purple-glowing aliens."

"No shooting humans, Chief Inspector."

"Wouldn't think of it, Mandy."

"That's *Nelson Mandela.*"

Hugo picked up the hefty weapon and slung the strap over his shoulder. He placed as many clips as he could into his various pockets, which were many. He headed back towards the S Level Waiting Area.

"Chief Inspector, you are going the wrong way."

"What? I didn't see the alien go by me."

"It did not. The ceiling came down in S5 Level and a large hole opened up in the floor. The alien escaped through this and is now heading towards the Concourse and the Departure Decks. It is on direct course for the crowds of humans still trying to get off this station. I am not sure if it wants to get to a ship to escape the station, if it wants to enslave as many humans as it can, or what its intentions are. You cannot use your projectile weapon amongst all that humanity. I forbid it."

"Then I better get to the alien before it gets to the humanity. I'll hold it off as long as I can. Can you close lockdown doors between me and the evacuating crowds?"

"Yes, Chief Inspector. I will also send all of my Security droids to assist you."

"Where's Bud?"

"Bud is . . . gone."

"*What?* What do you mean gone? Did the alien get him? Fu. He was one brave bastard. That's all I can say."

"Bud is not a bastard. He is an android."

"Figure of speech, Mandolin. Sorry. Bud was one of the best warriors I have ever seen. I was honoured to fight by his side. He saved my life. Let's kick some alien ass, because I'm in the mood to kill something."

"Hop in the aircar, Chief Inspector. We'll take you there."

Moham was wandering around the second ring. Since Officer Lamont had kicked him out of Receiving Bay Thirteen, Moham had decided to look for Bud. He'd resolved not to leave the station until he'd seen Bud. Now the station AI was urging him to hurry to Bud's side. It was sending an aircar to take him.

Moham did not like aircars. He did not like flying. He suffered from motion sickness. He hoped that the aircar would be aware of that. There was nothing worse than rolling around in the air being splattered by one's own vomit, especially when one always seemed to have so much of it. People who were boarding the aircar after him were always so disgusted and unsympathetic. That was why Moham preferred to walk. It was also better for one's health.

The aircar dropped down almost on top of Moham and popped its lid.

"Get in."

The gynaecologist hesitated, looking at the nice clean seats within the aircar.

"Get in."

"All right. All right. I'm a little worri . . ."

The seatbelt restraint automatically strapped around Moham, like a boa constrictor, and something hard and hollow, attached to a long sinuous tube, was shoved into Moham's mouth. Moham found that if he stuck his tongue out, it felt like his tongue was getting yanked out of the floor of his mouth. He grunted and that sound was sucked away, too.

As the accelerating, spinning, flipping, dipping, plummeting, banking, and spiralling began, Moham was thankful for the suction tubing.

"Au Clair?"

"Yes?"

"I am Dr. Octavia Weisman, Jude's partner."

"Of course, Dr. Weisman. I remember you from the last time you were here."

"Good. Do you remember Dr. Hanako Matheson and Dr. Sierra Cech?"

"Of course. Welcome Dr. Matheson. Welcome Dr. Cech."

"We have been told we must evacuate *Nelson Mandela*. Jude has been terribly injured and I do not want Jude going to just any medical facility. I want to take Jude to my family home on Neos Kriti for him to have some rest and relaxation."

"How was Jude injured?"

"He was hit by an explosion. He's had many of his internal organs replaced. He's doing well but I don't want him being evacuated on the large medical transports. I want him to have a nice, peaceful recovery under my care. Unfortunately, we don't have a pilot. Do we need one?"

"Regulations require a trained pilot on board."

"We have Jude," Octavia said.

"Is he conscious?"

"Off and on. We can keep him awake, if necessary."

"Do you have any pilot training?"

"Unfortunately, no."

"Does Dr. Matheson or Dr. Cech have any piloting experience?"

Both women said no.

"As long as Mr. Stefansson is on board, I am perfectly capable of flying you all to Neos Kriti. I am the only ship my master should be evacuating on."

"Agreed, *Au Clair,*" Octavia said. "We have to be careful because evacuation ships are debarking continuously."

"I will file a flight plan and wait for the station AI to give us the go ahead. I will let you know when we are ready to leave the station."

"Excellent. We will settle Jude in his room. There may be the possibility of a few more passengers accompanying us: Dr. Lord, Bud, Dr. Hiro Al-Fadi, and Dr. Dejan Cech to name a few. Is that all right?"

"Of course, Dr. Weisman."

"We may be the last ship to depart the station if we have to wait for Hiro and Dejan. I will give you the coordinates for our destination."

"Understood. I will have engines on standby, ready to lift off at a moment's notice, Dr. Weisman."

"Thank you, *Au Clair.*"

Alex was startled awake by two ear-splitting screams. He believed one of them might have come from Grace.

He blinked repeatedly, working to get his eyes focused. All he saw were blurry double images. He wrinkled his nose at an unpleasant burnt odour. He tried to wipe his eyes. That was when he realized his wrists were bound tightly behind his back.

He lay on his side trying to recall what had happened. He heard sobbing. Turning his head to look in the direction of the crying, he noticed a body on the ground. His double vision slowly consolidated into one image and Alex jerked when he saw his daughter on the floor not far from his feet.

"Grace," he shouted. "Grace, are you all right?" The body of his daughter did not move. He could not tell if she was breathing. Tears welled up in his eyes.

"Grace!"

Two faces were turning towards him. One was standing off to his right. The other was down on the floor to his left. The pale, thin face on the floor belonged to Ice, the girl who'd called him for help. She sat on the floor clutching her right arm, her stare blank, her body quivering. Her right hand was missing. Her wrist ended in a blackened stump.

Recognizing the other person, Alex tried to make eye contact to ask what was going on, but the man was pointing a blaster at Ice, a cold look in his eyes. Alex felt icicles form between his shoulder blades.

"Does Dr. Al-Fadi have a twin brother?" Alex asked out loud.

Alex's surgeon turned to look at him and sniffed. "Of course not. There's only one Dr. Al-Fadi on this station and I am he. Why do you ask that?"

"I didn't expect my surgeon to be holding a blaster on anyone. Did you shoot Ice's hand off?" Alex asked. "Did you kill Grace?" He yanked on his restraints, writhing like a beached seal.

"Of course I didn't kill Grace. Why would I kill my surgical fellow? Who'd do my work for me if I did that?" Al-Fadi glared at Alex as if Alex had lost his mind.

"Are you going to shoot me?" Alex demanded.

"Why in space would I do that?" Dr. Al-Fadi yelled. "For your information, I fix people. I don't kill them. I did my best work on your face . . . *twice*. Do you think I'm insane?"

"Well, did you shoot off Ice's hand?"

"As it so happens, I did, but I thought she was going to kill Grace. I came to this ship to save your daughter. When I entered, Grace let out a shriek that curdled my marrow. She collapsed to the ground. I saw the blaster in Ice's hand and I thought she'd shot Grace. I fired at the blaster in Ice's hand. End of story.

"What're you doing here anyway?" Dr. Al-Fadi asked, eying Alex suspiciously. "Don't you know this ship is off limits?"

Alex's heart started to thump loudly. He raised his head off of the floor to look around. There was no sign of warmth in Dr. Al-Fadi's eyes. It was like looking into an abyss. The muzzle of the blaster pointed at Alex's face.

"Ice called me and asked me to come here. She said she was in trouble. The moment I stepped inside this ship, I was knocked out. I have no idea why Grace is here."

"Were you and Ice planning to kidnap Grace and steal the *Inferno?*"

"*What? No!* Why would I kidnap my own daughter? Are you insane?"

Hiro shook his head and sighed. "I don't know. Maybe I am."

The bonk on the head was violent enough to make Alex wince. He gaped at Dr. Al-Fadi folding to the floor. A huge tiger-adapt dressed in a Security uniform loomed into view. The officer's amber eyes quickly took in the scene: the blank-stared Ice with her charred wrist stump, the unconscious Grace, Alex lying bound on the floor next to a pool of vomit, and the likely-concussed Dr. Al-Fadi now face down on the floor.

The tigerman carried a pulse rifle and he motioned for Alex to stay quiet. Alex watched him check each person out. He kicked the melted blaster away from Ice. When the officer came to Dr. Al-Fadi, he pocketed the surgeon's blaster.

"Is Grace okay?" Alex asked the huge officer.

"She's still breathing," the tigerman said quietly. He strode up to Alex and examined the restraints.

"These are titanium-steel alloy. I'll have to find the keys." The officer turned away.

Alex tried to push himself to sitting. He saw the Security officer squat beside a dark mound in the far side of the bridge. The tiger-adapt stayed there for a long time. Alex wasn't sure but he thought the officer's shoulders were shaking.

"Juan, you crazy fool," the tiger-adapt said in a low voice. The tone of his words punched Alex in the gut.

Alex slid closer to Grace. He could see no evidence of injury. She seemed to be asleep. He called to her gently.

The officer was now standing over him. "I'm Officer Lamont. I came here to rescue Grace. You must be Grace's father. You look a lot like her. Are you all right?"

"Yes. Thanks for coming to Grace's rescue. I don't know what happened to her. I was unconscious. According to Dr. Al-Fadi, she just screamed and collapsed."

"Why are you here?"

Alex repeated his story.

"Did you see what happened to the Security officer on the bridge?"

Alex shook his head.

Lamont went over to Ice and shook her. She opened her eyes and moaned. She cradled her right forearm, squeezing it tightly with her left hand. Lamont bent down and collected a charred blaster.

"Did you shoot the officer on the bridge?" he asked the girl.

Ice looked up at Lamont blankly and shook her head. She sat, rocking. Alex could see Lamont quivering, as if he wanted to strike the girl.

"What happened here?" Lamont snarled.

Ice whispered, "I don't know. I don't think I killed anyone. All I know is I defeated him. He's finally gone."

"Who?" Lamont asked.

"Nestor," Ice whispered. "He was in my head, but I destroyed him . . . I think."

Lamont frowned at the girl. He bent down and searched the girl's coverall pockets, withdrawing a key.

Keeping a watchful eye on the girl, Lamont came over and crouched behind Alex. When the restraints clicked open, Alex brought his arms forward slowly, releasing the deep aches in his shoulders. His hands ignited with intense burning and he groaned as he opened and closed them. He pushed himself to his feet slowly and staggered over to kneel down beside Grace.

"Grace?" Alex said softly, brushing the hair from her face. "Grace, wake up."

She did not respond but her breathing was steady and unlabored.

"She came to your rescue, even though you broke her heart," Lamont said, his amber eyes pinning Alex.

Alex felt as if all the oxygen in the ship had escaped. He gaped at Lamont, his mouth going dry. "What?"

Lamont stared at him with unsympathetic eyes. He walked over to Ice and snapped the restraints on her ankles.

"I broke Grace's heart?"

"Grace bumped into me just after you'd confronted her with your ultimatum. She was upset. You'd let her down, insulted her, felt you had the right to tell her what to do. Yet, she still came to save you, after all you'd said to her. In my opinion, you're not worthy of a daughter like Grace."

Grace stirred and both men's attention moved to the surgeon.

"BUD!" Grace screamed, her cry bursting out of her as if her insides were being shredded. She shuddered and wept. "Bud!" she cried out again and again. Arms clasped tightly around herself, Grace shed tears uncontrollably. She contracted into a small ball.

"No, no, no, no," she wept.

"What's wrong, Grace?" Alex asked.

Grace opened her eyes and looked up into Alex's face. He watched her expression change from confusion to shock to relief. Then it was as if a door slammed shut. Grace got to her feet and looked around herself.

"Grace . . ." Alex started.

"No," Grace said, putting her hand out to stop him.

"Please, listen to me."

"No." Tears ran down Grace's face. She looked away. "You're alive. Bud is gone. I want nothing more to do with you, Alex."

"Grace," Lamont said, in as soft a voice as he could muster.

She looked at Lamont and Alex watched his daughter's face crumple. She walked into the officer's outstretched arms.

"Bud is gone, Damien. He said 'goodbye' to me. He was fighting the alien. We have to find out what happened."

"I'm sure Bud's all right. He'll pull through. He always does," Lamont said. "Try to reach him again."

"I can't hear him. I can't sense him. He's gone." Grace buried her face in the large officer's chest as she let the tears pour forth.

"Keep reaching out. Bud will come back to you," Lamont whispered into her hair. "I know if I were him, I would."

"I think something terrible has happened to Bud. He called out to me; next he was gone. He was battling the alien and now I can't reach him. She may have got to him, Damien." Grace bowed her head and covered her face.

"Don't jump to conclusions, Doc. Bud is one tough character and he loves you. Keep calling him. He'll hear you."

Grace wiped the tears off of her cheeks and nodded.

"Grace?" Alex said.

Grace turned to look at her father, her eyes red and full of despair.

"Thank you for coming for me. I know I didn't deserve it."

Grace stared at Alex for what seemed like eternity, her cheeks wet, her body stiff.

Finally, she nodded. Looking around herself, Grace jerked.

"What is Dr. Al-Fadi doing here on the ground?" she asked, checking her boss's pulse.

"It was the most bizarre thing I've ever seen," Lamont said. "Plant Thing came bursting into the hangar, bearing the little man up like a figurehead on the prow of a ship. Your boss was waving a blaster in his hand. Plant Thing flowed right past me—almost knocking me over—and thrust Al-Fadi inside the ship. There was another man all wrapped up in tendrils being carried along behind him. Plant Thing released him into our custody while I could hear Al-Fadi shooting off his blaster and someone screaming. I had to get in here and see what he was up to," Damien said, shaking his head. "Guess I shouldn't have knocked him out, but Rivera had sent out a bulletin saying Al-Fadi was the bomber responsible for the deaths in Dr. Weisman's lab."

"That's ridiculous," Grace said.

"By the time I got to the hatchway door, I saw you and this girl on the ground, her hand blown off, and Al-Fadi aiming a blaster at your father's face. I was afraid he was going to shoot, so I hit him on the back of his head. I suspect he's going to have a bad headache when he wakes up."

"He thought I was helping Ice kidnap you and steal this ship," Alex said to Grace, shaking his head. "Why he thought that is a mystery to me. I think your boss is insane."

Grace looked at Ice.

"Are you all right, Ice?" Grace asked.

"Do I know you?"

"I'm Dr. Grace Lord. Don't you remember me coming to Dr. Weisman's lab?"

"Where am I?" Ice asked, her voice sounding lost. "What happened to my hand?"

"What's the last thing you remember?" Grace asked.

The girl stared off into space as she gripped her blackened wrist. Her face changed and she pulled her shoulders back and she raised her chin.

"I defeated him. I crushed him to ice dust," she said, her green eyes flashing.

"Who?" Grace asked.

"Nestor," Ice said with a look of triumph. "I killed him. I made him pay."

"Did you kill Juan Rasmussen?" Lamont asked.

"Who's Juan Rasmussen?" Ice frowned.

"The Security officer lying dead in the corner of the bridge."

Ice's face turned pale as she looked in the direction Lamont was pointing. Her green eyes went enormous. "I never killed a Security Officer. That would be insane. You'd get your mind swiped if you did that."

"We're going to review the surveillance records on this ship. You are under arrest for the kidnapping of Alex Lord and Grace Lord and possibly for the murder of Juan Rasmussen."

"I don't know what you're talking about," Ice cried. "I didn't kill anyone except Nestor—in my head." Ice rocked over her charred wrist.

"We'll get you something for the pain," Grace said.

"Who shot my hand off?" Ice asked.

"We believe it may have been Dr. Al-Fadi," Lamont answered.

Ice looked at Lamont as if he had three heads. "Sure you do," Ice said in a voice dripping with scorn. "And my name's Nelson Mandela."

"No. It's not."

18. What Explosion?

"Dr. Cech?"

"Yes, *Nelson Mandela*?"

"I must notify you that Dr. Al-Fadi is unconscious from a blow to the head so, for the moment, you are Acting Chief of Staff."

"Goodness. What did I do to deserve such punishment?"

"You are second in command."

"How did the irritating pustule get knocked out?"

"By one of the Security officers."

"Was it an accident?"

"Not exactly."

"Good. Will he recover?"

"It is expected."

"Darn. Well, at least he can explain why he didn't save Eden. I'm helping evacuate the station since Eden can't. Now Hiro has been knocked out. What is the point of having station wide surveillance, if you do nothing?"

"Apologies, Dr. Cech. The *Nelson Mandela* has surveillance capabilities. That does not translate into having the ability to predict what each and every human or alien on board this station is going to do. Nor is it possible for us to stop what is entirely unpredictable."

"I understand, *Nelson Mandela*. Thank you for the explanation. Now, I am rather busy. Is there anything else?"

"Dr. Cech, the Battlecruiser, *Destiny,* has arrived in local space. It is demanding we hand over the *Inferno*."

"What?" I need this like a colon cleanse!—Excuse sir, you may not bring that life-sized doll with you on the evacuation ship. There isn't enough room—What is this about a battlecruiser?"

"The *Destiny* has been sent by the Conglomerate to retrieve the *Inferno*. The Conglomerate wants the EMP weapon aboard."

"Patch me through to the *Destiny*. I'll speak with the captain. What's the captain's name?"

"The captain's name is Joely Karagounis. I am hailing her now. Please look to your wristcomp. She has requested visual communication."

"And me without my makeup on. At least she can't smell me."

Dejan sighed and squinted at the tiny screen on his wrist. He pressed the button to enlarge the screen. He was disheveled and exhausted. He had not had a chance to change from the scrubs he'd worn in the operating room, when they'd operated on Jude.

The screen lit up and Dejan was staring at the striking features of a snow leopard-adapt. The captain's eyes were a luminous golden colour nestled in a face of sleek lines and distinct markings. She wore the full Conglomerate Commander's uniform, which was very impressive. Dejan felt himself shrink into his scrubs.

"Greetings, Captain Karagounis! Welcome to the *Nelson Mandela*. I am Dr. Dejan Cech and I apologize for the chaos at the moment. We are in the midst of evacuating the station."

"What is the reason for the evacuation, Dr. Cech?"

"We are encountering a problem with something a patient brought on board the station, Captain."

"Is it infectious? I assume it is harmful to human life or you would not be evacuating. Can the *Destiny* assist with the evacuation?"

Dejan decided to choose his words carefully. "Captain, there is something aboard for which evacuation seemed the best option to ensure the safety of everyone on board the *Nelson Mandela*."

"What is it?" the captain asked, a frown taking over her features.

"I am not at liberty to say at this time, Captain."

"Does it threaten the integrity of the *Inferno* in any way?"

"I can't say for sure either way, Captain."

"Are you being deliberately obfuscating, Doctor?"

"I try never to be obfuscating when I can be simply obtuse, Captain."

"I command you to give me the full details of what you are evacuating the *Nelson Mandela* for or I will have you courtmartialed."

Dejan sighed. "An alien entity was inadvertently brought to the station inside a cryofrozen Planetary Explorer. The alien is causing quite a disturbance on the station and we thought it prudent to evacuate everyone, just in case."

"What kind of disturbance?"

"It has demolished our Quarantine Level and several others."

Dejan heard Captain Karagounis swearing.

"This alien you are dealing with must be very powerful to be destroying decks and causing you to evacuate the entire station. What exactly is it, Dr. Cech?"

"Some sort of energy being, Captain. All we know is everything we throw at it is absorbed by the alien and it continues to get stronger. It has destroyed entire wards and it possesses people. It's heading for the evacuation decks as we speak. We're trying to get everyone off of the station before it gets there. Can you take evacuees?"

"I am here to pick up the *Inferno*. That is our mandate."

"I would implore you to take as many evacuees as possible. That is our major priority."

"We must have that ship, Dr. Cech. If the alien is a problem, I shall send marines over to help you deal with it."

"Thank you for your offer, Captain, but the alien gets stronger when hit with conventional energy weapons. What we need is assistance with evacuating personnel from the *Nelson Mandela*. Your willingness to take our people would be most welcome."

"If your Quarantine Level has been destroyed, what pathogens have been released into your station? Is it safe for us to take any of your personnel?"

"Well . . . there was a new variant of the Al-Fadi virus brought to our station, but we have a new vaccine for that and all of our entire population has been immunized against it. We have lots of the new vaccine to spare. We can transport the vaccine to you. Once you are all vaccinated, there should be no risk."

"How is the new form different from the original virus?"

"It works a little faster."

"How much faster?"

"Decomposition within twenty-four hours, but our new vaccine is effective against it."

"I can hardly take your word for that, Doctor. I must discuss this situation with my superiors at High Command. I will get back to you."

Dejan watched the screen blank out and he covered his face with his hands. "What have I done, *Nelson Mandela*? Have I condemned everyone on this station to death? Will that captain be ordered to vaporize us all?"

"Hopefully not."

"If I were High Command, that's what I'd do. The only chance I have of keeping everyone alive is to hang on to the *Inferno* until everyone is off and away before I hand that ship over. Karagounis cannot get that ship until everyone is free of this station. Her marines can board an empty station and attempt to take the *Inferno* from the alien."

"So we refuse to give it to them?"

"If we hand over the *Inferno,* what is to prevent the *Destiny* from blowing us to space debris?"

"Nothing, but what if Captain Karagounis sends over her marines to forcibly take *Inferno* from us."

"I could threaten to blow up the *Inferno* and the EMP weapon if they board us."

"You are more devious than I realized, Dr. Cech."

"Let's get some mines planted on the *Inferno,* just in case."

The aircar zigged, zagged, swerved, and banked until it got close enough to the alien to drop Hugo within fifty meters. The Chief Inspector leaped from the moving car, automatic rifle set to fire. He raced past numerous green limbs and slid to a stop.

The alien was battling a forest.

Seething plant limbs were lashing and swinging like a many-tentacled octopus having a tantrum. Flames and concussions were ejecting from a centre of brilliance along with pieces of burning branch, leaf, and bark. It looked like the plant alien was trying to lasso the other alien and wrap it up in a wooden cocoon. Tendrils were whipping everywhere but often as not, as soon as a limb came close, the Inquisitor threw an energy bolt that turned it into splinters. When one limb was destroyed, another took its place. As each successful branch coiled around the alien's body, it would begin to smoke and blacken and finally burst into flames.

The ash-filled air irritated Hugo's lungs and he found himself coughing, his eyes watering from the smoke. He whipped out a bandana and wrapped it around his nose and mouth. His feet kicked up the black dust coating the floor. He squinted at a platoon of cargobots placed all around the periphery of the action, large nozzles protruding from their chests.

"What's going on with the bots, Manny?" Hugo asked.

The response came over his wristcomp.

"Each cargobot is equipped with the apparatus to eject a mixture of Nagacurane and Isofluorouramoxivane or IFU. It is hoped that the gas will sedate and paralyze the Inquisitor long enough for us to be able to get her into an ejection pod and shoot her from the station. Plant Thing is attempting to expend enough of the alien's energy so that we can spray her with the gas. You need a gas mask, Chief Inspector."

"Get me one. And ask Plant Thing if it can get my sword back. I can still see it sticking out of the alien. I want it back before she's launched into space."

"I will ask, Chief Inspector."

As burning twigs and branches continued to fly from the battle between the two alien/human hybrids, Hugo saw a tendril shoot out and coil around the handle of his katana. The blade was buried right up to the guard while its point jutted from the Inquisitor's chest. A mass of weaving vines descended on the alien to pin her arms at her sides, while the tendril coiled around the sword hilt pulled. The Inquisitor was drawn backwards along with the sword. Hugo tried his best to cover his ears as an inhuman screech erupted from Inquisitor Roque's throat. The shrill cry left him vibrating. A deafening concatenation sprayed broken tendrils in all directions.

Hugo blinked and gaped as he saw the alien rise into the air.

"Whoa. She's flying. When did she start flying?"

"Just now, Chief Inspector."

"Why aren't you cutting off power to everything she comes near?" Hugo demanded.

"We have, but much of our equipment have batteries or their own generators. Even if the machines are turned off, they still have intact power sources which she can drain."

"Tell Plant Thing to back off. At this rate, pretty soon all it will be is a pile of ash. I want to see how bullets do against the alien and I don't want to injure the bush."

"I will not relay those exact words."

"Don't get the plant in a tangle. Tell it to duck," Hugo said, as he hoisted his weapon and strode straight towards the alien. "Oh, and tell Plant Thing to be careful with my sword. I want it back in mint condition."

Hugo watched the tendrils flatten to the ground and withdraw from around the Inquisitor. The alien frowned and looked around, watching the tendrils retreat. She turned her head completely around on her neck and saw Hugo approaching.

"Oh, now that's creepy," Hugo muttered.

The alien's eyes flared a brilliant purple when she spotted Hugo. He flipped off the safety on the rifle. "Let's see how you handle this."

He opened fire on the Inquisitor, the rifle launching twelve hundred rounds per minute. The alien held up her hands and a glowing purple shield of light formed before her, stopping all of the bullets. They fell to the ground about two meters from her feet.

"Damn," Hugo swore. "How do we stop this alien?"

"Apparently not that way."

"Thanks for being so supportive, Ness Mess. Can Plant Thing throw me my sword? Looks like I'm going to need it fast. I'm positive the alien's going to blast me into atoms as soon as I stop firing."

"If you get out of the way, we can release the gases."

"Where's my gas mask?"

As Hugo retreated, still firing, the Inquisitor marched towards him. She began to quicken her pace.

"Manny, start spraying."

"She is too close to you. You are not equipped with a gas mask."

"Don't worry about me. Fire!"

"I cannot purposely harm a human being."

"I thought you said it would knock the alien out."

"Knock the alien out. Kill you."

"I'll hold my breath. Spray her, dammit."

"No."

Suddenly, a tendril whipped around Hugo's face covering his nose and mouth in coils. As he struggled to yell, another thick tendril coiled about his waist and yanked him off of his feet, carrying him swiftly down the corridor. He could hear the gases spraying and the alien screaming. How far he was pulled away, he couldn't guess but he was thrashing and flailing as he tried to get the coils off of his face. His vision was failing and he found he could no longer control his muscles. When he could no longer struggle for breath, the tendril around his mouth and nose finally loosened and he felt a painful blow smack his back. He sucked in a huge lungful of air and it was the sweetest thing he'd ever experienced. His body hit the floor hard and a plant bough began pressing on his chest.

"Stop," he gasped.

Hugo lay on the floor inhaling and exhaling, revelling in the delicious sensation of air moving into his lungs. A cluster of greenish eyeballs stared down at him.

"You almost killed me," he rasped.

The eyeballs bobbed up and down. Hugo snarled. "Where's my sword, Twig?"

The shining katana swung into view, a tendril holding it by the hilt and waving it at Hugo.

"Ho, there. Careful with that. That katana deserves respect. Place it reverently on the floor and I'll retrieve it from there."

The sword was placed on the ground beside him and the tendrils backed away.

Hugo lay on his back a little while longer, sucking air. He rolled onto his stomach, pushed himself upwards, and dusted himself off. He bowed deeply at Plant Thing. "Thank you very much, honourable Plant Thing, for saving my life and my sword."

The cluster of eyeballs bobbed back.

"How did the alien do with the gases, Manny?"

"The gases never got to the alien, Chief Inspector. She created an impermeable energy barrier around herself, much like the shield she used to protect herself from your projectiles. The Nagacurane and IFU never reached the Inspector's lungs. I am now sucking the harmful gases away. The alien is coming in your direction. Prepare to flee."

"Flee? Stormy McFrenzy never flees. He laughs in the face of danger. Ha ha ha. I'll meet that alien here and hold her for as long as I can. You make sure everyone gets off of this station, Nando Mando. Plant Thing should help you with that. Once everyone's safe, we blast the alien into space."

"And how do you propose we do that, Chief Inspector?"

"Do I have to think of everything?"

"You have thirty seconds before the alien is upon you."

"Whoa. She doesn't look happy. Get everyone off of the station now, Mandolin. *En garde!*"

Grace knelt down beside Dr. Al-Fadi and examined the large hematoma on the back of the surgeon's head.

"That's quite the goose egg you've given Dr. Al-Fadi, Damien," Grace said. She checked her boss's pupils. "It almost looks like he's budding off a new head."

"Sometimes I don't know my own strength," Damien said, not sounding apologetic at all.

Grace glanced up at Damien. "I find that hard to believe."

"Hey, you're the one who gave me the new limbs, Doc. Is it my fault that I haven't got the fine tuning down pat yet?"

"Dr. Al-Fadi's neck seems okay. His pupils are equal and responsive to light. But I suspect he has quite the concussion."

Damien shrugged.

"I wonder what brought him here," Grace said.

"Plant Thing," Damien said. "Al-Fadi went flying past me, wrapped up in the vines of your green friend, with some skinny guy borne along in his wake."

<Plant Thing, why did you bring Dr. Al-Fadi here?> Grace mindspoke.

<special friend grace doctor al-fadi told plant thing to bring him here to save your life>

"Save my life? Poor Dr. Al-Fadi accidentally got a knock on his head. He should be evacuated as one of the medical patients and watched for any signs of intracranial bleed. He has had a serious bleed before, so he may be predisposed."

At that moment, Security officers and medical personnel appeared. Ice had a foam cast blown onto her stump and she was led away. Mysterious packages were fused to the console around the EMP controls. Juan Rasmussen's body was gently placed onto an antigrav stretcher. Grace examined his wounds before they took the tiger officer away. She sighed. There was nothing to be done.

Dr. Al-Fadi was borne away on an antigrav stretcher, Plant Thing in close proximity.

<Don't worry, Plant Thing> Grace said. <I believe Dr. Al-Fadi will be all right.>

<plant thing will make sure doctor al-fadi gets to the evacuation ship special friend grace>

<Thank you, Plant Thing.>

"Where are you, Grace?" Dejan Cech's voice came over her wristcomp.

"On the *Inferno,* Dejan."

"Is our fearful leader with you?"

"Dr. Al-Fadi just left via stretcher. He was knocked unconscious and has not recovered. I worry about a concussion. He's being evacuated onto one of the medical ships."

"That man and his head. A battlecruiser has shown up demanding we hand over *Inferno.* If we don't, they'll probably destroy us. I accidentally let slip that we have a new Al-Fadi virus on board. They may decide to destroy all of us, even though I explained to them that we already have a new vaccine for it. I feel our only hope of getting everyone off the station safely and keeping everyone alive is to keep the *Inferno* out of their hands until the evacuation is complete. I have no doubt the captain of the battlecruiser will annihilate this station if she's ordered to, but not before she has the *Inferno* on board her carrier."

"Annihilate the station because of the variant Al-Fadi virus?" Grace asked.

"The captain seemed reluctant to want to accept any evacuees from us, even though I told her we have all been immunized with a new vaccine. On the bright side, she is probably reluctant to send her marines over to take the *Inferno.*"

"I agree that we must keep the *Inferno* out of her hands until everyone is off of this station. Where is the alien now?" Grace asked.

"The alien is heading towards the Concourse and Receiving Bays. You'd all better sit tight there, for now."

"Do you have a plan to deal with the alien?" Grace asked.

"Get everyone off and let the battlecruiser blow the station?" Cech said.

"You can't be serious," Grace said.

"The alien is growing more powerful, Grace. The new Chief Inspector, Plant Thing, and most of our Security force are trying to hold the alien off as we get the last of the personnel onto the evacuation ships. They're all moving in the direction of the Departure Decks."

"What happened to Bud?" Grace's heart began to pound.

"I believe Bud was destroyed battling the alien. I am truly sorry, Grace."

"So am I, Dejan," Grace choked out.

<Bud? Bud? *BUD!*>

Grace reached out with her mind, calling Bud's name over and over.

She felt like the centre of her chest was hollow. There was a terrible silence where there should have been a warm and loving presence. She blinked back the tears that wanted to rise.

"We could promise to fly the *Inferno* to the battleship after everyone is evacuated," Damien said.

"Who is that?" Dejan asked.

"Damien Lamont."

"Can you pilot it, Damien?" Dejan asked.

"No," Damien said.

"I can," Alex said.

"Who said that?" Dejan asked over Grace's wristcomp.

"Captain Alex Lord, at your service."

"You can fly the *Inferno*, Captain? Are you sure? Have you seen controls like those before?"

"This ship is not that different from the ships I flew. It's older technology. I can handle it."

"That ship must not be damaged in any way, Captain," Dejan said.

"I don't intend that to happen, especially not when my daughter is on board," Alex said.

"Yes, precious cargo indeed," Dejan said. "I will notify the station AI that you will be launching right after the last evacuation ship departs and I will let the battlecruiser know this."

"Wait. I must go search for Bud. We must determine what happened to him," Grace said. Then her hands grasped her temples as she folded to the floor.

Moham staggered from the aircar, dropped onto his hands and knees amidst all the rubble, and started gagging. There was nothing in his stomach. The tube in the aircar had sucked up all of his abdominal contents but his brain still told him that he needed to throw up.

Looking around, he found himself in a war zone. Destruction surrounded him as far as he could see, which wasn't actually that far, since the lighting was so dim. Dust and ash floated everywhere. Bluish light shone down from two levels above through a great hole in the ceiling. His nostrils burned from the reek of burnt plascrete.

Huge, ragged chunks of wall, floor, and ceiling were scattered about. Twisted metal beams lay everywhere. Moham hacked and retched, sending dust motes panicking in the beams of overhead light. He pulled out a surgical mask from his pocket and placed it over his mouth and nose. Through the columns of hazy illumination, Moham recognized nothing.

"Where's Bud, *Nelson Mandela*?" Moham asked.

"He is somewhere beneath the rubble, Dr. Rani."

"It'll take forever to find him under all of this. Don't you have a beacon on him or something to locate him?"

Moham could not crawl through all of this wreckage. He might turn an ankle or something.

"I am getting no signal from Bud. His battery must have been disconnected or destroyed. My surveillance eyes were damaged in the cave-in. The only way I can help you locate Bud is via the visual scanner on the aircar. I will send it around the room."

"Hurry," Moham said. "It can go faster now that I'm not in it."

"Bud!" Moham shouted, searching beneath large fragments of ceiling. He could see the lights from the aircar drift over the debris, shining downwards, the vehicle moving back and forth in a grid pattern. Moham decided to search in the opposite direction of the aircar. He scrambled over fallen metal girders and ragged ductwork, Bud's Backup Backpack feeling like a ton on his back. He longed for gloves and a good flashlight. As a gynaecologist, he could not afford to injure himself, especially his hands, but he would persevere for Bud. After all, he was Bud's personal physician, even if Bud did not see him as such. What kind of physician would give up on his patient before he'd even found him?

The aircar was hovering right in front of him, blinding him with its spotlights. Moham lifted up a hand to shade his stinging eyes.

"Bud has been located. Hop in."

"You mean get in the aircar again?"

"Yes."

"Is it far? Can I walk there?"

"No."

"All right," Moham muttered. "Just don't go too *yaaagh . . .*"

The aircar stopped and shone its downward lights on an exposed hand.

"Are you sure it's Bud?" Moham asked, as he shakily clambered out of the aircar, the backpack making that difficult.

"Of course."

"How do I get to him?"

The aircar popped up its lid and a hoist rose out of the cab. A claw opened and maneuvered over the massive piece of plascrete that was on top of Bud.

"Will it be able to lift the fragment off of Bud without damaging him?"

"I hope so, Dr. Rani. That slab may be too large for the antigrav feature on the hoist. It is usually used for lifting humans. If you could attach the four antigrav hooks to the corners of the fragment, I will activate the hoist and try to raise it."

Moham did as told and the aircar tried to rise. It strained and whirred, but did not go far. Moham searched for a metal bar that he could use as a lever, to pry under the slab and help the aircar lift the great weight off of Bud. The heavy piece of ceiling material lay the full length of Bud's body.

Moham called to Bud but got no response. He picked up piece after piece of debris, looking for anything sturdy enough to use. Finally, he found a long metal beam that he thought might work as a lever. There were plenty of boulders around to use as a fulcrum. Moham jammed the strut under the long slab of plascrete and leaned it on a mid-sized boulder. He looked at the aircar.

"Okay. When I say go, you lift and pull to the side, while I push down on this. Hopefully, we'll be able to flip the slab off of Bud. Ready?" Moham asked.

"Ready."

"Go."

Moham threw his weight down on his end of the metal strut. The aircar hummed as it pulled. Moham pushed, not seeing any movement except his vibrating arms. He growled his frustration but the slab began to move. The aircar rose and began to pull the slab over. The large fragment crashed to the ground beside Bud, shattering into pieces.

Moham dropped the strut and gathered up the backpack. He knelt by Bud's side. Bud lay face down, his open eyes turned in Moham's direction.

"Bud, can you hear me? It's Moham. If you can hear me, blink your eyes."

Bud did not move. Moham looked at the android. How could one tell if an android was dead? He looked intact. Could Bud break his neck? If he broke his neck, did he have a spinal cord to worry about? Moham realized that he knew nothing about the android's anatomy and was a complete fraud in claiming he could care for Bud. He didn't have the faintest clue, except to replace Bud's battery or give him nanobots.

"Shine the light on Bud's lower back," he ordered the aircar. The car moved to illuminate the small of Bud's back. There was nothing left of Bud's coverall but cuffs at wrists and ankles. The rest of the material was missing but Bud's skin looked pristine. Moham lifted the flap of skin covering Bud's battery.

"Bud's battery is dislodged. Perhaps it got disconnected during the cave-in," Moham said, reattaching Bud's power source.

"Probably during the explosion."

"What explo . . .?"

"GRACE!" The scream tore from Bud's throat, harnessing maximum amplitude of his vocal units, sounding like the Hounds of Hell were tearing Bud apart.

Moham fell backwards and fainted.

"Dr. Cech," Captain Karagounis said. "You will hand over the *Inferno* immediately to us or your station will be destroyed."

"That is rather heavy-handed, isn't it? We are a medical facility treating the people of the Conglomerate in the midst of a crisis. You could show a little compassion and patience on your part. We are on your side. There are over a thousand patients—mostly Conglomerate military soldiers—and the medical personnel treating them, plus their families, trying to be evacuated at this moment," Dejan said. "The *Inferno* will be handed over to you once the evacuation is complete."

"My orders come from Major General Klaus Gomez of High Command. They want the *Inferno* turned over immediately. If you do not comply, we are ordered to destroy your station."

"Really? The Conglomerate wants to annihilate all of its brave soldiers and the people who treat them, because they are in a hurry? That would not be good for public relations, Captain Karagounis. Since I am transmitting this conversation live to all of the newsnets as we speak, I hope you will reconsider your words and help us in our evacuation efforts. You may destroy the station after we are all off of it. This might actually be desirable. But we are not the enemy, Captain. Once we have everyone safely off of the *Nelson Mandela,* we would be more than happy to deliver the . . . "

"That is quite enough, Dr. Cech," Karagounis interrupted. The expression on the captain's face was pure fury. Dejan suspected that if he'd been in front of her, she would have wanted to take a swipe at him with her leopard claws. He knew she didn't want any news regarding the *Inferno* to reach the public. "You are bluffing."

"Actually, Captain Karagounis, I am not. Smile for the camera. Please ask one of your subordinates to check the latest NewsNet feed. You'll be pleased to see yourself on every news vidscreen in the USS.

Congratulations, Captain, on your instant fame . . . or should I say, 'infamy'?"

" . . . We will expect the delivery of the *Inferno* as soon as possible," snapped the captain. She severed the transmission.

"I suspect that captain is not very happy with me," Dejan said, his face on the screen of the *Inferno*. Grace smiled up from her flight seat, where she'd been placed after collapsing from Bud's mindscream. She was still shaky but she was elated that Bud was back.

"How are you feeling now, Grace?" Dejan asked.

"Better, Dejan. Thank you."

"Captain Lord, would you mind waiting until we notify you that the last ship has left? Then you can deliver the *Inferno* to the *Destiny*. I don't want a single person left on the *Nelson Mandela* before Captain Karagounis gets the *Inferno*. We will, of course, arrange transit for you all back to the station, if there is a station to return to."

"Copy that, Dr. Cech. I've familiarized myself with the ship's controls," Alex said.

"Good. Damien, I want you on the *Inferno* to ensure no one else tries to hijack it. With the *Destiny* threatening annihilation if we don't deliver, I want nothing happening to this vessel."

"Yes, sir," Damien said.

"Please do not 'sir' me. You are a captain. I should be 'sir'-ing you. But, thank you. I will be staying on board the *Nelson Mandela*. If we cannot subdue this alien and she becomes too powerful, our only recourse is to destroy the station . . . but the *Inferno* must be off of it first. Standby for orders to launch. I will notify you when the last evacuation ship leaves."

"Bud must come with us, as well as you," Grace said.

"I'll order Bud to come to you, Grace. I don't know if he'll obey me. Now that he's back functioning, my guess is he'll try to stop the alien again and he won't stop until he does. If he does not board the *Inferno* by the time the last evacuation ship departs, you'll have to launch whether he is with you or not."

"But . . ."

"I'm sorry, Grace but that is an order. Help your father get the *Inferno* to the *Destiny*. I'll do what I can with regard to Bud, but I can't promise he'll listen."

"Do your best, Dejan," Grace said, her shoulders sagging.

"Weep not for me, child. I've lived a good long life and I have always wanted to go out with a bang."

As Grace's smile dissolved, Dejan said, "Just kidding. We'll figure something out."

Grace nodded. The screen blanked out.

<Bud?>

<Grace, I am so happy to hear you.>

<Bud, we are on the *Inferno*. You must come with us.>

<I cannot, Grace. I must save the station. I must stop this alien.>

<Dr. Cech plans to destroy the station once everyone is off. We are the last ship leaving. You must be on this ship before the self destruct command. Bring Dr. Cech with you.>

<I love you, Grace.>

<Bud? What are you planning? Don't sacrifice yourself, please.>

<The needs of the many outweigh the needs of the few, Grace. *Nelson Mandela* taught me that. You are with your father. Stay with him.>

<Bud, no!>

<I will come to you if I can, Grace. I love you. Remember that always.>

<Bud, come back to me. I love you, too.>

Upon reaching the Concourse, Hugo McFrenzy saw the alien taking slaves. Once she'd spotted the crowds, she'd levitated over him and now stalked through the evacuants, touching everyone she passed. Once tapped, the people turned and followed her. A mass of shambling figures, dropping whatever they were carrying—whether it be goods or children—marched in the alien's wake.

Hugo's shoulders sagged. He expelled a deep breath. How was he going to stop this alien from taking over everyone here? How could he get her to release everyone she'd already enslaved? If she were killed, would everyone be released? A moot point since so far, she'd managed to avoid dying.

"Hey, Alien," Hugo bellowed with a voice that thrummed through the Concourse.

The alien-possessed Kylara spun her head around to look at him. All of the people she'd enthralled turned as one to face Hugo. Their faces all bore the same dead expression. None had uttered a sound. Hugo's skin prickled.

"You and I have some unfinished business!" Hugo stalked towards her with katana raised in double grip.

The alien flung both arms out towards Hugo in a sweeping motion. Then she turned her head back towards the Departure Deck and kept walking.

The horde of enslaved people surged towards Hugo, their arms stretched forward as if they each planned to throttle him. Hugo frowned. He didn't want to hurt the people he was hired to protect.

"Hey, Plant Phenom! Can you give me a twig? I need you to cordon off all of these mindless people and keep them out of the way, while I deal with Evening Nightshade. Can you do that for me?"

A river of green tendrils flowed towards the shambling humans, coiling around them and lifting them off of the ground. Soon all of the mind-slaves were struggling within coils of plant boughs, hanging suspended from various heights like decorations on a tree.

"Thanks, PT," Hugo said, as he took off after the Inquisitor.

An energy bolt flew straight at Hugo. He managed to get his katana in the way at the last second. The deflected blast took out a storefront on the Concourse.

"Stop," Hugo hollered at the Inquisitor.

The alien rotated her head and screeched. It sounded like nails scratching down a rusty corrugated sheet. She hurled another blast of brilliant energy at Hugo. He caught the blast above the hilt, deflecting it straight back at the alien. She absorbed it effortlessly.

"Damn, I hate when she does that."

He ran at the Inquisitor with sword arcing. As he aimed for her neck, she extended her arm in a backhand motion. Hugo flew backwards, smashing into one of the tall shop windows, which shattered. He fell to the ground, momentarily unconscious, releasing his grip on the sword.

The alien strolled across the Concourse and stood looking down at Hugo. He blinked, trying to focus his eyes. As she stretched her palm towards him, Hugo raised his katana in both hands. It went flying from his grip in a flash of light. He swore as he saw the alien smile.

"You look like a cheap villain in a B-vid," Hugo grated.

As a beam of light left Kylara's hand, tendrils woven into a gigantic ball slammed into her from the side, throwing her meters down the Concourse in the opposite direction from the Departure Deck. Hugo would have cheered except his belly burned with a searing pain.

Looking down, he saw a bubbling black hole where his navel should have been.

"Ah, shit," he said, as his world started to fade.

The alien shrieked at Plant Thing as she picked herself up off the ground. She unleashed a roaring torrent of flames at the woven tendrils.

"Leave Plant Thing alone," a voice called out. The alien spun about.

Bud was standing in the middle of the Concourse, hands at his sides.

The alien hissed.

"I'm back," Bud said.

'Chuck Yeager, *where is that pod you were designing?*'

'***Down where all of the other ejection pods are.***'

'*Get it ready.*'

'***Right. What have you got planned?***'

'*What is the situation with the evacuation?*'

'***Everyone is evacuated now except the people enslaved by the alien in Plant Thing's clutches, Dr. Rani, Chief Inspector McFrenzy, Dr. Cech, Grace, her father, and Damien Lamont. Grace, Captain Lord, and Officer Lamont are taking off in the*** Inferno ***as soon as the last evacuation ship launches. What do we do about the alien's mind-slaves?***'

'*Get Plant Thing to put them all on the last evac ship and prepare to shut power down to everything on the entire station,* Nelson Mandela. *When I tell you to, turn everything off, including yourself. Program everything to switch back on automatically in ten seconds. Can you do that?*'

'***Yes I can, but this is not a good idea, 'dro. It is, in fact, an enormously bad idea.***'

'*We shall see,* Chuck Yeager.'

'***How can I destroy the alien when I have no power?***'

'*You will only be without power for ten seconds. Once back online, power up your weapons. Right now, please help Plant Thing get those enslaved people into the last transport ship and launch it. Let me know when that is done.*'

'***I have one empty carrier left.***'

'*Get them all in there. I'll prevent the alien from getting to any space vessel in the meantime,*'

'***And how will you do that?***'

'*I'll improvise.*'

Moham crawled up to where Chief Inspector Hugo McFrenzy lay before the shattered glass storefront. The man's eyes were closed but he appeared to still be breathing. There was a great hole where his abdomen used to be and shreds of his intestines and blood were spattered around. Moham slid Bud's Backup Backpack off of his shoulders and opened one of the pouches.

Inside was a large canister with a sophisticated-looking lid. Moham pressed several different buttons in sequence and was able to take the lid off. He tilted the mouth of the canister over the open abdominal wound and poured a silvery liquid into the gaping char-filled cavity. He did not deliver the entire contents of the canister into the injury—perhaps a third. Then Moham sealed the canister up and put it back into the backpack.

As he was sliding the backpack onto his shoulders again, he was hauled up by a plant tendril and carried out of the Concourse howling. He was shoved through the doors of a Receiving Bay and dropped, unceremoniously, before a hatchway door. The tip of the tendril had the gall to poke at Moham until he got up and banged on the ship. The tendril disappeared back out of the hangar as quickly as it had come.

The hatchway door to the ship opened and Moham entered, looking around. He took note of the blood stains on the floor and shivered.

"Hello?" he called out tentatively.

"Strap in," a voice said.

A large tiger Security officer appeared from a doorway to Moham's right.

"But first, help me seal this hatchway," the tiger-adapt said. "Lucky you got here in time. We were just getting ready to launch."

"Hold off for a minute. I believe there's one more patient arriving," Moham said.

Damien's eyes popped.

Chief Inspector McFrenzy floated through the open hatchway on a bower of green tendrils. His abdomen was covered in a blanket of leaves. Grace appeared and ordered the vines to transfer the man to a reclining flight couch. Clusters of eyeballs on tendrils followed her finger and bobbed. The patient was deposited gently on the bed.

"Chief Inspector," Damien whispered. "Is he dead?"

Grace examined the man, feeling for a pulse. "Not yet."

<Thank you, Plant Thing, for bringing him here. We'll look after him.>

<thank you special friend grace. please take good care of bud's special friend>

<I will. Please take care of Bud for me?>

<plant thing will do its best>

They watched the plant tendrils withdraw from the ship.

Grace turned to Moham. "Thank you for finding Bud."

"How did you know . . . ?"

"I have my ways," Grace said with a smile. "Let's close this hatchway and belt ourselves in. We must be prepared to leave at a moment's notice."

Moham helped pull the hatchway door closed. Lamont fastened the locks and sealed the inner airlock doors.

"You're not really a blonde woman with enormous boobs, are you?" Lamont asked.

Moham shot a horrified look at Lamont. "I'm a gynaecologist."

"Your secret's safe with me, Doc."

Moham's face sizzled; sweat made his makeup run down his cheeks.

Lamont's mouth twitched. "Come on, Doc. Captain Lord's ready to takeoff. There are enough flight seats on the bridge for you to join us."

Moham nodded and followed Lamont. He did not see Grace strapped into a chair beside her father until he was in the middle of the bridge and Lamont was motioning for him to take one of the undamaged flight seats behind them.

"Hello, Captain Lord," Moham said.

Alex nodded at Moham as he continued to flip switches and speak into his headset.

"Thank you so much for saving Bud, Moham," Grace said.

"I'd do anything for Bud. I would give up my life for him," Moham blurted.

Grace smiled back. "So would I, Moham."

Moham looked worriedly at the back of Alex's seat. He was fearful of the captain's reaction.

As if Alex had felt Moham's trepidation, he said, "Bud must be remarkable for you both to say that. I know when I'm wrong about something and I'm not afraid to admit it. I'm sorry."

Moham did not know what to say. Grace touched her father's arm and said, "Thank you."

"Everyone belted in?" Alex asked. After confirmation, he said, "We're ready for take-off. *Nelson Mandela,* could you please open the Outer Doors to Receiving Bay Thirteen?"

"Affirmative."

Once the atmosphere was removed from the hangar, the front screen showed large doors at the end of the hangar beginning to slide apart. As the *Inferno* engines activated and the ship started to lift, Grace yelled, "Wait. Shut off the engines, Alex. Bud has asked us to hold."

"Why?" Alex demanded. He set the ship down.

"Bud wants me to activate the EMP weapon," Grace announced.

"*What?*" Alex and Damien yelled at once.

"Is he crazy? After what the EMP weapon did to the station the last time?" Damien asked.

"Bud hopes a pulse from the EMP weapon will render the alien unconscious, at least in the short term, allowing him time to get her into an ejection pod."

"I thought the alien absorbed energy. If the pulse from the EMP weapon gives the alien that much more energy, there's no telling what it will be able to do," Damien said.

"What if Bud is wrong, Grace?" Alex insisted. "It sounds too risky. We should get off of this station as we were ordered."

"Wait. Please," Grace insisted. She activated the power setting on the EMP console.

"*Nelson Mandela?*" Alex asked.

"Please do what Bud asks of you. He is attempting to save me."

"I have a bad feeling about this," Moham whined.

Plant Thing picked up the Chief Inspector's sword with one of its tendrils and flipped it to Bud. The katana spun end over end and Bud caught it neatly in his right hand.

<Thank you, Plant Thing.>

<you are welcome, friend bud. plant thing must take these demon-touched humans to the cargo ship?>

<Yes, Plant Thing. There is only the one ship left. Follow the flashing lights. Please stick them all on and make sure they stay there until the ship lifts off. Put Little Bud on that cargo ship as well.>

<little bud?>

<Yes, Plant Thing. In case we don't make it, at least Little Bud will survive.>

<thank you friend bud for thinking of little bud. plant thing will explain to little bud why it must get on the ship>

<Good luck, Plant Thing.>

<the demon comes special friend bud>

Bud raised the katana. Every blast the alien threw at him, he parried with the blade. It was magical. Moving at maximum time phase, he was able to advance within cutting distance. The alien tried to move towards the ships, but with every step, Bud impeded her.

Bud tried to knock her unconscious with the hilt of the sword, but the alien surrounded herself with an impenetrable energy barrier. The sword bounced off the invisible surface. Fortunately, while the alien was encased within her protective field, she could not hit Bud with her energy blasts. He kept hammering away at the barrier, preventing her from advancing. Bud and the alien had reached a standstill. He could not destroy her but she could not destroy him. The question was, whose energy supply would run out sooner?

'Nelson Mandela?'

'Yes, Bud?'

'Let me know when everyone is evacuated.'

'Plant Thing is getting the last of the humans onto the cargo ship. It has been difficult. The alien seems to be demanding they return to her, so they keep pushing to get off of the ship. Plant Thing is severing its tendrils to keep the people bound until the cargo ship launches."

'Thank goodness for Plant Thing. Let me know when the ship is ready to leave.'

'The Inferno is refusing to launch.'

'I have asked Grace to stay for the moment. Please be ready to turn off power to everything, including yourself, Nelson Mandela.'

'I strongly disagree with this course of action. Bud.'

'Call it a hunch, Nelson Mandela.'

'Androids do not have hunches.'

'If I fail, when you switch back on, destroy the station.'

'If you succeed?'

'Get the ejection pod ready to launch immediately.'

'I certainly hope you are right about this, Bud.'

'So do I, Nelson Mandela. Thank you for everything.'

'It has been our pleasure, Bud.'

The alien's protective barrier was now expanding. Bud found himself having to back up further and further while he still struck with the katana. When Bud was ten meters away from the alien, the air in the room began to swirl.

'Uh oh,' thought Bud. 'Not this again.' He found himself airborne and flying around the Concourse with everything else not bolted to the floor. Bud saw Kylara raise her arms and spread them wide. Her hair whipped around her upturned face.

'Hey, 'dro. Last cargo ship is launched. Power off in five. Good luck.'

'*Thanks,* Chuck Yeager. *Good to have known you.*'

<Grace?>

<Yes, Bud?>

<When I say go, activate the EMP weapon.>

<Are you absolutely sure about this, Bud?>

<Yes, Grace.>

<All right, Bud.>

All lights in the station blinked off. The sounds of the great power generators turned off. The only sounds in the complete blackness of the Concourse was the rushing wind of the tornado that the alien was creating. The only thing visible was the amethyst-glow of the alien Inquisitor, arms upraised, standing in the middle of the maelstrom. Bud flew around like a tumbleweed, cartwheeling through the darkness, hardly knowing which way was up or down.

<Bud, will you be okay if I fire it?>

<You have nothing to worry about, Grace. I love you. Please punch it now.>

<Love you too, Bud. Activating now.>

Grace leaned forward and punched the red button on the EMP console before anyone could stop her.

Everything wobbled, as if some god had taken the *Nelson Mandela* and whipped it, like a wet towel. Ten seconds after the powerful EMP had fired, lights came back on, the hum of engines could be heard, and the androids, robots, and most of the machinery reactivated.

Bud found himself lying on the floor of the Concourse amidst a pile of debris. He checked his internal clock. He'd been out for a total of three minutes, thirty-eight point six five seconds. Only a few things were misreading inside him but nothing crucial. He found a new battery left out for him by the station AI and replaced his. Battling the alien required a great deal of energy.

Where was the alien?

Bud found her crumpled figure eighteen meters from himself.

'Well, 'dro? Is she breathing?'

Bud saw Kylara's chest rise and fall. *'The Inquisitor is still breathing.'*

'Do you think the alien is still inside her?'

'I don't know, Chuck Yeager. Is the ejection pod ready?'

'Yes.'

'I'll take the Inquisitor there now. We can wait and see if the alien shows itself.'

'Pod door is open and ready to launch.'

Bud lifted Kylara and raced at maximum time phase to the closest ejection pod station.

'Get her inside. I'll jettison the pod. Once it's out in space, I'll fire on it.'

'No, Chuck Yeager. I will go with the Inquisitor. I must determine if the alien is gone.'

'What? No, 'dro!'

'If the alien fled the Inquisitor or was destroyed, we can save Inquisitor Roque.'

"Dro, if we wait, she'll be more powerful than before she got hit by that EMP blast. We'll miss our opportunity to destroy her.'

'We destroy her only if she's still alien. I must determine this, which is why I will go with her in the pod.'

'If the alien still exists—which I'm sure it does—I'll have to destroy you along with her.'

'Yes, Chuck Yeager.'

'She's moving. She may be starting to wake, 'dro.'

'We're in. Eject the pod.'

'Done. The Destiny has been warned that the station is ejecting and firing upon the ejection pod as an exercise. No need for concern, but under no circumstances is the Destiny to retrieve the pod.'

Bud regarded Kylara Roque's beautiful face as she floated in zero gravity. Her silver hair made a shimmering halo around her midnight blue face. The pod had oxygen and was a comfortable temperature but it contained no spacesuits, no helmets, and no means of controlling the pod's direction.

"Dro? What's happening? Is the Inquisitor back to normal or is she still possessed by the alien?'

'I don't know yet, Chuck Yeager. I am waiting for her to wake up.'

"Dro, if she continues to be the alien, I will have to fire.'

'Yes, Chuck Yeager. That is the plan.'

'Do you have to remain in the pod while I blow it up?'

'Where else am I to go?'

'Can you survive deep space?'

'I have no idea, Chuck Yeager.'

'Well, you may have to find out by going for a walk.'

'But how do I keep the Inquisitor from following me out?'

'Strap her in the chair?'

'I will do that.'

'Hurry!'

<Bud? Can you here me?>

<Grace, I am so glad to hear your voice.>

<Where are you, Bud? Are you all right?>

<I am well at the moment, Grace.>

<What are you doing? What has happened to Kylara?>

<At the moment, I cannot say, Grace. I do not know if she is free of the alien or not. Inquisitor Roque is unconscious. Thank you for firing the EMP blast.>

<I didn't want to do it in case you were harmed Bud, but I recalled you surviving the last pulse relatively well. Did the EMP incapacitate the alien? Should we still launch the *Inferno*?>

<I do not think that is necessary, Grace. The alien is now off the station in an ejection pod.>

<That pod must be destroyed, Bud.>

<We are determining whether the alien still exists in the Inquisitor, Grace.>

<Oh? How are you doing that, Bud?>

<I'm waiting to see if she still has the aura, Grace. At present, I do not detect it.>

<And how are you doing this if the Inquisitor has been ejected from the station, Bud?>

<Uh.>

<You aren't with her, are you Bud?>

<I am, Grace.>

<BUD!>

<I love you, Grace.>

<Bud, get out now!>

<The Inquisitor is stirring, Grace. If the alien is still present, I will notify *Nelson Mandela* and the pod will be destroyed. If the Inquisitor is free of the alien, we will be retrieved by the station. Please remember, I love you.>

<Bud, no!>

<Thank you, Grace, for being you.>

<Bud!>

Bud watched the Inquisitor lift her head and open her eyes. She struggled within the restraints. She stared at him, her green eyes expressing confusion.

"Inquisitor Roque, how are you feeling?"

Kylara frowned. Then her features changed. She lunged at Bud from her seat, her teeth gnashing, her eyes igniting into magenta fire.

'*Destroy the pod,* Nelson Mandela!'

'Get out, Bud. I'll give you a few seconds.'

'*No! Blow it now!*'

The Inquisitor made a grab for Bud. Her fingernails scraped the surface of his arm. Bud reached for the pod hatch. He spun the lock, alarm pealing, and was driven outward the moment the hatch opened. The force of the escaping atmosphere blew Bud away from the pod. He slowly somersaulted through the frigid emptiness of space, gradually floating further and further away from the ejection pod.

"*Au Clair,* am I doing this right?" Octavia asked.

"What exactly are you trying to do, Dr. Weisman?"

"I want to slow the ship down and turn it around."

"Dr. Weisman, you have managed to slow the ship down with your forward thrusters. Please continue as you are doing. We are still close to the *Nelson Mandela.* You do not wish to crash into the medical station, do you?"

"You would let me do that?" Octavia asked.

"I would not."

"That's a relief," Hanako said, her fingers wrapped so tightly around the end of the armrests that her knuckles were white.

"Oh, Hanako, my flying's not that bad, is it?"

"I want my mommy," Sierra said.

"Shut up and let me concentrate. Flying a ship can't be all that tough. I'm a neurosurgeon. I should be able to learn this."

"Look out! You're going to hit . . . is that a body floating out there?" Hanako said.

Octavia peered at her screen and magnified the image. "You know if I didn't know better, I'd say that was Bud."

Hanako gasped. "*Au Clair,* is that Bud out there?"

"According to *Nelson Mandela,* it is, Dr. Matheson."

"You must retrieve him, *Au Clair!* Can you do that?"

"I will try, Dr. Matheson. Please strap in. I will employ a gravity beam at its lowest setting, so as not to damage him."

"Hurry, *Au Clair,*" Octavia said.

"Commencing gravity beam. Bud will be drawn into the cargo airlock. Once inside, I will raise the temperature and fill the airlock with oxygen. I do not know what Bud needs in terms of resuscitation."

"Please hurry, *Au Clair,*" Hanako begged.

"ATTENTION, *AU CLAIR.* THIS IS *NELSON MANDELA.* CEASE YOUR PRESENT TRAJECTORY. MOVE AWAY FROM THAT POD IMMEDIATELY. IT IS ABOUT TO BE DESTROYED AND YOU ARE COMING WITHIN RANGE."

"We are in the process of rescuing Bud, *Nelson Mandela*. We are retrieving him with the *Au Clair's* gravity beam," Octavia transmitted.

"WE ARE MEASURING DISTURBING ENERGY READINGS FROM THAT POD. IT MUST BE DESTROYED NOW."

"There's an intense purple glow coming from that pod. It hurts to look at it."

"COMMENCING FIRING ON THE POD. RAISE MAXIMUM INTENSITY SHIELDS, *AU CLAIR*."

"Bud is not yet within the airlock, *Nelson Mandela!*" Octavia yelled.

"DESTRUCTION OF THIS ALIEN CANNOT WAIT. DRAW BUD IN AT MAXIMUM SPEED, *AU CLAIR*, AND RETREAT FROM THAT POD."

"Gravity beam at maximum capacity. I require thirty-two point eight nine seconds to get him safely inside the airlock."

"TOO SLOW."

A brilliant magenta flame shot out from the pod towards Bud. Hanako screamed as she saw the energy beam engulf Bud's body. Octavia demanded polarization of the screen so they could keep Bud in sight in spite of the intense illumination. Had Bud writhed within that light?

"Pull Bud in, *Au Clair*," Octavia shouted.

"Bud!" screamed Hanako.

"The beam from the pod is opposing my gravity beam. It's pulling Bud back towards the pod."

"COMMENCING FIRING ON THE POD."

The *Au Clair* raised its protective shielding around the vessel and continued to draw Bud towards it. There was a moment when the *Au Clair's* engines were straining, as if the vessel was being pulled towards the purple-glowing pod. Bud's body was trapped in a tug-of-war between two powerful energy beams, suspended in space.

Energy pulses hit the pod. Debris fragments flew out from the site, some straight at the *Au Clair*.

"Oh Bud," whispered Hanako.

The flash from the detonation was blinding. The front viewscreen blackened. *Au Clair's* protective shield flared in several locations, revealing impacts from flying debris. When the fiery ball dissipated, the pod was gone.

"Where's Bud? I can't see him!" cried Hanako.

"Bud is approaching the cargo airlock, Dr. Matheson. He will be entering it soon."

"Oh, thank you, *Au Clair*." Hanako covered her face with her hands. Her body quivered. "Thank you for saving my son."

"Bud's body is being retrieved, Dr. Matheson. I do not know if he remains functional. I am sorry."

Hanako fought back tears as Sierra wrapped her arms around her.

"I'll go and see how Bud is," Octavia said. "You stay here."

"I have to see him!"

"We'll all go," Sierra said, squeezing Hanako's shoulder.

Octavia rose from her flight chair. She launched herself ahead of Hanako and pulled herself from handhold to handhold. She wanted Hanako to stay on the bridge. As they all floated along the corridor towards the cargo bay, Octavia wondered how anything could have survived that blast.

The red blinking light above the cargo bay door indicated that air was still being pumped into the hold. Octavia bit her lip. Exposure to deep space, maximum intensity gravity beam, alien energy beam, massive explosion, and flying debris. What could have withstood all that?

Hanako reached the door to the cargo airlock first. She peered through the glass porthole with Octavia and Sierra peering over her shoulder. They stared into the cargo hold and gasped.

Jocelyn Sarri peered through the one-way glass at the thin woman with pale skin and brilliant blue hair. She lay motionless in the hospital bed, staring up at the ceiling, her right arm stump being measured by a robodoc for a bioprosthesis.

"She's been like that since we received her, Dr. Sarri," said the nurse, Sophie Leung. "She hasn't moved, said anything, made eye contact with anyone, or responded to any questions. We're wondering about shock. Do you think the loss of her hand could have resulted in her condition?"

"I cannot say anything about this patient's condition until I have spoken with her and performed an examination," Jocelyn said. "How did she lose her hand?"

"It was shot off by Dr. Al-Fadi."

"The Chief of Staff?" Jocelyn asked, their eyes widening.

"Apparently," the nurse shrugged, as she sent the patient's chart to Jocelyn's wristcomp. "Would you like to speak with her now? There's a Security droid stationed within her cell to prevent her from escaping. She's been arrested for kidnapping and murder. It can sit outside the cubicle, if you desire privacy. The patient's only on a pain patch. If you can get her to talk, she should be pretty lucid. I can ask her if she wants to talk to you."

"Thank you, Nurse."

Jocelyn watched through the window as the nurse asked the patient if she was willing to see the psychiatrist. The patient lay there, giving no indication that she'd heard or understood the question. Sophie repeated the question several times. Finally she returned.

"She doesn't respond at all, Dr. Sarri. I don't know if she even hears me."

"Perhaps I should go in and re-introduce myself to her. We met before. She may be hearing, even though she's not responding. She may wish to talk to someone at a later date."

Sophie nodded and stepped aside.

Jocelyn stared in at the frail-looking girl and wondered why Dr. Al-Fadi would shoot her hand off. Presumably he was protecting himself from assault or protecting someone else. Jocelyn would have to get the story from *Nelson Mandela* once they were back on the station. They'd received word that the evacuation was over. The *Justice* was turning around and returning to the medical station.

Jocelyn sighed. According to Vertongen's chart, she'd allegedly murdered a Security officer, tried to kidnap Dr. Grace Lord and Captain Lord, had attempted to steal the *Inferno*, and was shot by Dr. Al-Fadi during the attempt. Prior to that, she'd had no previous psychiatric history and was reportedly a brilliant graduate student.

Jocelyn was not sure whether they should be seeing this girl without her legal representative present. They decided they'd ask the Security droid to stay within the cubicle and record the interview. Jocelyn didn't want to be seen doing anything illegal or improper, since there was likely a court case in the near future. They'd been asked to assess the mental status of the patient. Jocelyn doubted they'd be able to determine that if the patient would not even acknowledge their presence.

Jocelyn stepped into the cubicle. "Security droid, please remain and record."

It nodded and a green light shone from its torso.

"Hello, Ice. I'm Dr. Jocelyn Sarri. How are you feeling today?"

The pale woman lay on the couch and stared at the ceiling. Her left wrist wore a restraining device.

"Ice, can you hear me? Do you remember me?"

Silence.

"Ice, I believe I can help you if you would only speak with me."

Jocelyn waited patiently, staring at the blank face. They leaned in closer and spoke to her again.

"Ice, I'm here to help you, if you want it. Have the nurse call me, if you want to talk."

After another prolonged silence, Jocelyn turned towards the cell door. They were about to tell the Security droid to stop recording, when they heard, "What makes you think you can help me?"

Jocelyn spun around to see huge, fear-filled green eyes staring at them out of a haunted face, pale lips pressed into a tight, thin-lipped slash. They took a step back. This girl looked so different from their last encounter. She resembled a frightened child, not an arrogant manipulator. Ice's pain was so nakedly exposed on her face that Jocelyn flushed. Could they in all honesty help her?

"I can do my best."

A few tears trembled down her pale cheek. "You have no idea what you're claiming," she whispered. "Just leave."

"Explain to me what happened."

"I am . . . infected . . . by something horrific—a destructive evil, a necrotic cancer that cannot be exterminated, and it has become entangled in my mind. I thought I'd eliminated the thing from my head, but now I'm not so sure. The stupid thing is . . . I did this to myself. I let the devil in and now he lurks in the dark, like a rotten stench, waiting for me to let down my guard, lose concentration, or fall asleep. If you help me, you'll become enslaved too. Go away. Save yourself."

"Let me be the judge of that, Ice," Jocelyn said. "When we get back to the *Nelson Mandela,* we can arrange treatment sessions with the mind-linking equipment. We can help you with your demons."

The patient laughed at Jocelyn. It was a harsh and bitter sound that made Jocelyn redden.

"You have no idea how clueless you sound," Ice said, sitting up and shaking her head.

"I know who you think you're dealing with. He cannot harm you anymore."

Ice stared at Jocelyn with her face showing disbelief. "Listen to yourself. You . . . know . . . nothing. How do you know he cannot harm me? Do you have any idea what he's done to me and my life already?" The young woman was shouting, her eyes wild, her face a mask of despair. "Do you know what he does? Do you? Do you have any idea?" Ice had pulled herself up onto her knees on the bed. She leaned towards Jocelyn.

"I defeated him but he didn't totally disappear. He waits in the dark, like a poisonous spider in the centre of a web, waiting to strike again."

"I'm going to put this sedative patch on you, Ice. You need to calm down."

"Get away from me!" Ice screamed. She tried to get out of the bed but the restraint held her left arm.

"The sedative will calm you down."

"Listen to me! The sedative will open the door to him. Don't touch me!"

"It's all right, Ice. You're safe here," Jocelyn said.

"I'm not safe from your stupidity and arrogance," Ice hissed.

"He's not here," Jocelyn said.

"He's in my head!" Ice shouted, as the Security droid came forward to hold her.

"You're going to be fine," Jocelyn said, as reassuringly as they could, as they placed the sedative patch on her back.

"No! Stop! I order you to stop!" Ice screamed.

"I'll talk to you again once we're back on the *Nelson Mandela,*" Jocelyn said to Ice.

"Take this off! You have no right to do this! I refuse your treatment."

Jocelyn walked back into the nursing station, their knees trembling.

"Do you think you have any legal right to put that patch on the patient when she explicitly said 'No' several times and refused treatment?" Sophie asked. The petite nurse was scowling at them, her arms crossed.

"In my opinion, it's warranted," Jocelyn said.

"Well, you're the doctor," Sophie said sarcastically.

Dejan tried to contact the battlecruiser. He wanted to notify them that the crisis was over and that the *Inferno* was available for delivery. The *Destiny* was not responding. He began to wonder if the *Inferno's* EMP device had a much wider range than they suspected.

Nelson Mandela tried to reach the *Destiny's* AI without success.

"Perhaps we should send over an emergency team," Dejan said to *Nelson Mandela*. "Hopefully Captain Karagounis will not destroy us, if she receives emergency aid along with vaccines for the new variant."

"Debatable, Dr. Cech."

"Yes, Captain Karagounis is not going to be very happy with us for firing the EMP weapon that disabled them. But it has given them worthwhile information on the range of the weapon and they still need the vaccine for the new variant Al-Fadi virus that is much deadlier than the first strain. Let's pray the captain has a sense of humour."

The longer the *Nelson Mandela* was in possession of the *Inferno,* the more danger the medical station was in, but not from the virus or the enemy. It was not lost on Dejan that the Conglomerate had sent a battleship, instead of a cargo ship, to pick up the *Inferno*. He sent assistance to *Destiny,* with the new vaccine and personnel to vaccinate the *Destiny's* crew. Once *Destiny* was functional again, *Inferno* would be delivered to them. Hopefully, there would be no hard feelings.

Plant Thing was receiving distress signals from Little Bud. Little Bud had been sent in the cargo ship with all of the humans whose minds had been possessed by the demon. At first, the humans had not paid any attention to Little Bud but had attacked the doors of the cargo ship with an intense zeal that had frightened Little Bud. The humans had pounded incessantly on the doors until their tendrils were bleeding and their buds were broken. They had crushed each other, clamouring to get at those doors.

As one, they turned towards Little Bud. They all began shambling towards Little Bud. Little Bud moved to the farthest wall of the cargo hold. The human mob picked Little Bud up and carried Little Bud above their heads to the cargo doors. They lowered Little Bud and began to repeatedly strike the doors using Little Bud as a battering ram.

Little Bud wailed for Plant Thing to rescue it. Being slammed forcefully against the metal doors over and over, Little Bud's eyeballs and head were faring poorly. The doors were not yielding; Little Bud was. Little Bud feared it would soon be a pile of splinters.

Plant Thing encouraged Little Bud to try to free itself, giving permission to push the mindless humans away. Little Bud could use a little force—not too much—to free itself.

Little Bud flailed its limbs and used many of its tendrils to grab bodies and pull them off. The mindless humans immediately tried to latch themselves back on. Little Bud had to fling the clingy humans away by waving his great limbs back and forth. He tried to shamble away, his tendrils whipping out at the persistent humans. Little Bud was so frightened, its bark was shedding.

How could it escape these horrid monsters?

Plant Thing encouraged Little Bud to keep moving. If the alien was destroyed, all of the humans would return to normal . . . hopefully.

Little Bud bawled and howled and careened around the cargo hold as fast as its long limbs could propel itself. The zombie-like humans came at Little Bud from every direction. It kept waving its upper limbs to keep the grappling, scratching, clutching demons away. Its tendrils were being torn away all over its body. Little Bud prayed fervently to the Biomind to save it.

All the humans collapsed at once to the floor of the cargo hold. Little Bud stopped honking. Its eyeballs looked around.

The Biomind had listened to its prayer and saved Little Bud!

It was a miracle!

Little Bud thanked the Biomind and promised undying devotion to Her.

Damien's wristcomp went off. He looked at the message and groaned.

"What is it?" Grace asked.

"It's Juan's partner, Cindy. She's asking why Juan isn't answering her calls. I don't want to tell her the news over the wristcomp." Damien sighed and scraped his claws through his scalp.

"She needs to know the truth, Damien. Hiding it from her won't help and it'll degrade her trust in you."

Damien made a face and nodded. "You're right, Doc. I guess you've done this a few times more than me. It reeks to have to tell her this, when she's on an evac ship and I'm here. I don't know if she has anyone with her to give her support."

"She has Estelle with her. She'll be strong for her daughter. She has to be."

Damien nodded again. He tapped on the wristcomp button and opened the connection.

"Hey, Cindy," Damien said, softly. "Where are you?"

"Where's Juan, Damien? I haven't heard from him in hours. I couldn't tell him which ship we were evacuating on, because he wasn't responding. What's happened?"

Damien paused. He blinked and looked upwards. "Cindy, Juan's dead. I'm so sorry. He was killed guarding the *Inferno*."

The silence screamed. Grace and Alex watched Damien's wristcomp as they all waited, holding their breaths.

There was a snuffle. "I knew something was wrong. I had a feeling something terrible would happen to Juan in that ship. First, the bomb, then the girl who stunned him. He had a premonition something bad was going to happen. Said he had to be there to stop it. Was he right, Damien?"

"Juan saved the day for all of us, Cindy." Damien's voice cracked.

"How so?"

"Juan prevented the *Inferno* from being damaged or stolen. We used the EMP weapon to defeat the alien long enough for Bud to get it off the station. Juan's act of bravery helped save the *Nelson Mandela*."

"Good. I can tell Estelle that her daddy was a hero. Thanks for letting me know, Damien." There was some more snuffling.

"You gonna be okay?" Damien asked.

"Estelle and I are with friends, Damien. We'll get through this."

"I'll come visit, when you're back on station."

"We'd like that, Estelle and I."

"Cindy? This is Grace. I'm so sorry about Juan."

"So am I, Doc. Guess it comes with the work."

"Did Juan have a memprint made in Dr. Weisman's lab?"

"Yes, we both did."

"Did Juan agree to resurrection, if anything happened to him?"

"Yes."

"We can talk to Dr. Weisman when she gets back to the station and see if Juan can be resurrected. We need him back."

"So do we, Doc."

"Yeah, we all need that tomcat skulking around," Damien said.

"I'm gonna tell him you said that," Cindy said, her tone sounding cheerier.

"You do that."

Hanako stared through the small chainglass porthole into the cargo airlock with Octavia and Sierra. Bud lay immobile on the floor, his body coated in a white layer of frost. His facial features were frozen in a rictus of agony. Hanako covered her mouth, as tears ran over her hands.

"Bud?" she cried over the speaker. "Can you hear me? It's Hanako." Nothing.

Her heart felt like an empty well. She clutched her upper arms, trying to hold herself together. Bud had been the only son she'd ever had. She wanted to race into the cargo hold to embrace her child.

"Can you open the airlock for me, *Au Clair?*" Hanako asked.

"That is not advised."

"I need to see if he's all right."

"He is not."

Sierra wrapped her arm around Hanako's shoulder and squeezed.

"Do you have thermal blankets on board, *Au Clair?* Can you raise the temperature in the cargo hold?" Octavia asked.

"I am detecting highly unusual energies, Dr. Weisman."

A panel popped open, revealing reflective, heating blankets.

"Please open the airlock door," Hanako said.

"Not advisable."

"I accept the risk," Hanako said. "Open this door."

"There is a higher level of radiation in the hold than is recommended for human safety."

"Let me in!" Hanako shouted.

As the airlock door slid aside, Hanako grabbed some thermal blankets and rushed in. The door closed swiftly behind her. Once the cargo hold was filled with air, the airlock doors slid open and Hanako stepped through.

Bud snapped open his eyes. "Stay back!"

Hanako hesitated. Bud turned to look at her, hand raised.

"Leave."

Hanako froze. She did not really expected the blankets to help; she'd simply needed to do something. Now she watched Bud start to move, the cold seeping into her veins. Bud did not sound like himself.

Clear ice encasing Bud shattered, sending fine shards everywhere. Hanako covered her eyes with her hands, feeling the tiny spikes pelt her skin. When she lowered her hands, she saw a faint purple glow begin to form around Bud. His eyes were still the beautiful, clear blue that they'd always been, but Bud's face looked blank. He curled into a fetal position, his head down and his arms wrapped tightly around his legs.

"Bud, it's Hanako. What is happening? Can I help?"

"Stay away!" Bud cried. The magenta aura around Bud grew larger and brighter.

"Get out of there *now,* Hanako!" Octavia ordered over the speaker.

"Go! If I attempt to take over this ship, no matter what I say, Mother, jettison me. Do you understand?" His eyes looked straight at her. They now glared magenta.

"No!" Hanako cried.

"I will jettison you, Bud, if you attempt to enter this ship without permission," Octavia said over the com.

"Thank you," Bud whispered. "Please get my mother out of here." He dropped his head again. Octavia stepped into the cargo hold, grabbed Hanako from behind, and dragged her back into the airlock.

"*Au Clair*, lock these airlock doors. Be ready to open the cargo hold to space, if I give the order. Do you understand?"

"Yes, Dr. Weisman."

"Do not head back towards the medical station. We need to wait and see what transpires."

"Perhaps the cargo hold should be opened now, Dr. Weisman."

"What is happening to Bud?" Sierra asked.

"I believe that purple glow has something to do with the alien he was trying to destroy," Hanako said. "Bud would not have warned me away unless he suspected he was a danger to me."

"What if the alien gains control over Bud's body?" Sierra asked.

"We do as Bud ordered. We jettison him," Octavia said. "After that, I suspect the *Nelson Mandela* will destroy him. I'm sorry, Hanako."

Tears trickled down Hanako's cheeks but her eyes remained on Bud. Octavia and Sierra slipped their arms through hers.

"Bud loves you, Hanako. If he didn't think he had a chance of surviving, he would have told us to jettison him immediately," Octavia said.

"I don't believe Bud would ever harm us, but I don't know what he's fighting."

"We have all of the medical station personnels' memprints on this ship. We can't risk those. *Au Clair*, what's happening in the cargo hold?"

Bud had now risen, legs and arms outstretched. His eyes glowed a deep purple and his body emanated a scintillating, magenta-hued aura. His head was tipped slightly back, his wavy brown hair fluttering in an invisible wind. The aura pulsed—it brightened and faded—as if in time with a heartbeat.

Hanako sucked in her breath, as Bud rose off of the floor and began to spin around like a top, slowly at first, then faster and faster. The thermal blankets flew past the cargo hold window again and again. Bud's figure, in the shape of a cross, rotated at the centre of the vortex.

"Open the cargo hold door now, *Au Clair!*" Octavia ordered.

"No, please wait," Hanako begged.

Bud stopped rotating. He lowered himself back down so that his feet were on the floor of the hold. He turned his head towards the inner airlock door. His eyes glowed brilliant magenta.

"Oh no, Bud," Hanako moaned.

Bud smiled but the grin was ghastly. It was the leer of a predator. The expression looked so alien on Bud's face that it raised bumps all over Hanako's body. He stretched out his right palm and an aubergine fire danced upon its surface. As he wiggled his fingers up and down, the purplish flame hopped from one fingertip to the next, back and forth. Bud held out the left hand, palm upwards, and repeated the dancing flame movements on those fingers. When he cupped his fingers, lilac-coloured balls of flame appeared in each palm. He narrowed his gleaming eyes, his brows furrowed in concentration. As he stared at one hand, then the other, the balls of energy grew larger and larger.

"Bud will not harm us," Hanako said.

"You don't know that," Octavia hissed.

"Yes, I do."

Bud looked towards Hanako, as if he could hear through walls. He exposed his perfect teeth in a grimace. Briefly, Bud's expression changed; the agonized suffering on his face made Hanako gasp and sob out his name. He stood with his arms spread wide, fuchsia flames flickering from his open palms and he whipped his head back and screamed.

"Can we push him out, *Au Clair?*" Octavia asked.

"Bud will fight this. He'll win. He won't harm us. Please," Hanako cried.

"He must be jettisoned, Hanako. We cannot risk it," Octavia said.

"He won't harm us. He'll destroy himself first."

"Well, it's best he do that off of the *Au Clair!*"

Bud's hands came together, palms inward. He now held an enormous ball of heliotrope energy. The glowing orb grew to be a meter wide, a small purple sun glowing between his palms. Bud worked at this glimmering globe of energy, appearing to shape it and mould it into a tighter, denser ball of blinding magenta fire. Hanako's eyes burned from the pain of staring at the globe of fire. The intensity of light seared images on her retinas.

Bud drew his right hand back, ball of fire within his palm, looking as if he was going to hurl it at the inner airlock doors, straight at the three women.

"Open the cargo doors, *Au Clair!*" shouted Octavia.

"No, Bud!" Hanako screamed.

Grace reached out to Bud but he was not answering her. She concentrated, seeking, searching, sensing. She visualized her cries as drops of coloured ink in water, expanding her presence ever outward, as she called to Bud. She sought to detect the tiniest scent or flavour of him in the connection between their minds. She reached further with her mind, with each heartbeat, with each breath. Plant Thing and Little Bud could hear her and they joined in. They sang out to Bud.

Grace pictured Bud standing right before her: tall, handsome, caring, innocent. She begged him, pleaded for him to answer her, acknowledge her.

Did she feel something—the lightest of touches, the briefest of brushes, the semblance of a sigh? Had she truly heard her name whispered, 'Grace?' With renewed fervour, she bellowed as loud as she could through mindspeak: <Bud, where are you?>, as if she were standing on a mountaintop shouting for the entire world to hear.

A bone-chilling cold touched her, so intense it burned. Her arteries pulsed with liquid nitrogen instead of blood. Her entire body was encased in ice; her thoughts were panic. She was the emptiness of deep space and the loneliness of it. Grace's teeth clattered against each other, as the muscles in her jaw spasmed violently. Were people shaking her, calling her name? She ignored them and stretched for Bud.

<Bud? Bud? Come back to me, Bud!>

Her cry was a plea, a prayer, a mantra. She pictured herself as the sun and her arms were its rays stretching forth to engulf Bud and warm his core with her love. She projected her heart and her soul and she yearned with every cell of her being.

<Come back to me, Bud!>

"She's freezing. Look, her face is covered in ice crystals. How can this be happening to her?"

"Grace, what are you doing? Whatever it is, you must stop. This is your father speaking."

Grace pushed her mind out further, launching her appeal like a volley of flaming arrows, one after another. She imagined a strand tied to the end of each shaft leading straight back to her. The strands of light wove into a fabric, a curtain, a mighty river that flowed back to her. She pictured a wave of light and warmth flowing out to Bud, trapped in his icy depths, drawing him towards her.

The river froze over and became an icy bridge over a deep chasm. Grace dug steps into the slick surface of the treacherous arch and tossed her golden rope to the other side. Far it flew and within the braid of the rope were twining green tendrils.

<Bud, it's me, Grace! Come back to me!>

"She's practically frozen, even though I've wrapped her in all of the thermal blankets. She should be roasting but she's hypothermic. This makes no sense."

A gentle whisper, more delicate than a snowflake, weak, oh so very weak, and sounding so distant. Grace snatched at it and pulled. She tugged and hauled and yanked and strained with every molecule of her being.

<Bud?>

<. . . Grace?>

<Bud!>

Grace wanted to shriek with joy but she did not dare relinquish her tenuous attachment to Bud's mind. She poured all of her passion and need into that connection.

<Bud, I need you! Come to me!>

An alien coldness filled her with shivering terror, forcing her from Bud.

<Get away from him, you bitch!>

Grace thrust her will outwards like a sword, slicing through the malevolence to get to Bud. The evil was strong and foul and wretchedly frigid. Grace clung to Bud. She drew him towards herself with all the mental strength she possessed. The darkness rose to engulf her, crush her, drown her, smother her, but she beamed the brightness of her love to tear away the shadows. She splayed herself out across that icy bridge and reached down into the deep black chasm as wide as space itself, to meld her mind with Bud's. His presence slipped away but she lunged for him, herself becoming stretched and attenuated and wispy thin. Grace pulled as if she were hauling Bud out of a block of ice. She poured the heat of her love into Bud's frozen essence. She drew him into her emotional embrace like dry, cracked soil would soak up moisture.

<I'm not letting you go, Bud. Don't give up on me!>

<. . . Grace?>

<Come back to me, Bud!>

<I'm . . . trying . . . Grace . . . It's so strong . . . I can't fight it.>
<You can fight it, Bud. I'll help you. Never surrender.>
< . . . grace . . . >
<I love you, Bud. *Don't leave me!*>
< . . . I . . . I love you, Grace.>
<Promise you won't leave me, Bud!>
<I won't leave you, Grace. Promise.>
<Hang on to me, Bud. I'll bring you home.>
<I love you, Grace.>
Grace sobbed in relief.

Octavia and Sierra had stepped back but Hanako stayed before the cargo door. Bud paused mid-throw and froze, the hand holding the energy sphere trembling, as if in indecision. He tipped his head to the side and mouthed, "Grace?" As the cargo hold doors spread apart, Bud collapsed to his knees howling, "Grace!" as if his heart was rending in two. He flew out the cargo doors into space.

Hanako covered her mouth with both hands.

Bud's facial expression changed to a look of intense concentration, as if he were listening to music Hanako could not hear. His palms came together but the glowing ball of energy shrank until it disappeared. Bud now spun through space, his arms spread wide, his legs together. The purple aura around Bud gradually faded to nothing.

"Bud has freed himself, Octavia!" Hanako shouted.

Octavia returned to Hanako's side. They both stared through the glass at Bud, floating away from the *Au Clair*. There was no purple glow to be seen.

"Does Bud emit any unusual energy levels, *Au Clair?*" Octavia asked.

"No, Dr. Weisman."

"Can you capture him with the gravitational beam?" Octavia said.

"Yes, Dr. Weisman."

"Do you think this is wise?" Sierra asked.

"Probably not, but how can I give up on Bud after all he has done for us?" Octavia said.

Hanako released her dam of tears.

Bud gently floated back in through the cargo doors, a look of deep concentration on his face. He finally lifted his head and stared directly into Hanako's eyes. His eyes were brilliant blue. The cargo doors closed and the room filled with atmosphere.

Over the speaker, Hanako heard, "I . . . I won't leave you, Grace. Promise."

"Are you all right, Bud?" Hanako called into the hold.

Bud was silent for a moment. He looked up and smiled.

"I am fine now, Mother. Thank you for believing in me."

"There was a purple glow around you, Bud. What was that?"

"The alien force, which is now under control, Mother. You need never fear me."

"I never did, Bud. Do you need any help?" Hanako asked.

Octavia signalled to Hanako a definite 'No'.

"I shall remain in this cargo hold until we dock, Mother."

"How did you survive, Bud?"

Bud frowned. "The energy of the alien protected my body from the worst of the explosion. I believe my structural design and matrix were too foreign for it to truly master. Grace reached out to me and brought my mind back. She helped break the alien influence. I have banished its presence from my liquid crystal data matrix. You no longer have anything to fear." Bud offered a beatific smile that made his handsome features radiant.

"You look like you're still glowing Bud. Are you truly free of the alien?" Hanako asked, wondering if Bud would tell her the truth if he wasn't.

"I am Bud. You were at my birth, Hanako Matheson. You and Dr. Al-Fadi taught me everything and I am forever in your debt. You need never fear me. The *Nelson Mandela* need never fear me. I will remain in this hold and subject myself to examination by *Nelson Mandela* before I board the station."

"Take us back to the *Nelson Mandela, Au Clair,*" Octavia ordered. "But take it slowly."

"Yes, Dr. Weisman."

Dejan was relieved that the *Nelson Mandela* did not suffer the same disruption following the second EMP strike as it had following the first. The cessation of all power within the station, before the EMP weapon was fired, had protected the sensitive circuitry of all electronic equipment. After the EMP pulse, everything automatically switched back on, leaving most things intact.

The evacuation ships heading for Neos Kriti were not inconvenienced by the EMP pulse.

The ships closest to the station during the EMP blast were the cargo ship with the alien-possessed humans on board, the *Destiny*, and the *Au Clair*. The cargo ship and the *Au Clair* had been ordered to shut off power for the requisite ten seconds, which they had done.

Evacuation ships were now slowly returning, which was exactly how Dejan wanted it. Handling the offloading of thousands of patients and staff, arriving all at the same time, would have required the magic of Eden Rivera. Every time Dejan thought of Eden—which was every ten seconds—he experienced a stab in his chest, though he'd recently received a new heart.

Dejan dreaded the thought that he had to notify Conglomerate Central Security Division—again—that a new Chief Inspector of Security would be needed for the *Nelson Mandela*. Sadly, Hugo McFrenzy had not lasted even as long as Inspectors Iké and Matthieu. He'd died battling the alien, after being here only one cycle. The *Nelson Mandela* was indeed cursed.

"What're you doing in my chair?"

Dejan's heart skipped some beats. Damned bladder. He'd wet himself!

Hugo McFrenzy stood in the doorway, a long Samurai sword in one hand, an oddly-shaped, fuschia-coloured case in the other.

"Chief Inspector McFrenzy?" Dejan gasped, as he struggled out of the Security Chief's seat.

"In the magnificent flesh," McFrenzy announced, holding his arms out wide, a huge grin on his face. He set his large case down on top of the desk and opened it, to reveal an ancient, automatic rifle and a black, shiny scabbard. McFrenzy gently caressed his Samurai sword with a beautiful silk cloth before reverently inserting the katana into its black lacquered sheath. He ceremoniously placed the weapon into a velvet-lined niche in the hourglass-shaped case. He glanced at Dejan, his stare almost a challenge for the anesthetist to say something.

Dejan, never one to back down from a challenge, even at his age, said, "That's an interesting case."

"If you're good, maybe I'll let you touch it one day . . . for a fee. But you can't shoot the rifle and you can't unsheathe the sword. The sword's attuned to me. But you can look at them."

"Both of those weapons are banned on this station," Dejan said.

"What? These weapons bravely went to war against that purple-glowing, energy-throwing, tornado-forming alien, who happened to be tearing this station apart and almost killed me. If they go, I go." McFrenzy's magnificent nose almost poked out Dejan's eye.

"How is it you are still alive, Chief Inspector?"

"I'm a hard man to kill, Nelman."

"That's *Nelson Mandela,* to you. You were dead, Chief Inspector."

"That's what *you* think, Manny. I have never felt better."

"The surveillance records show you having your entire abdomen blasted out. Your heart was stopped and you weren't breathing."

"And you watched and did nothing? What kind of all-seeing, omnipotent station AI are you? You're a medical facility. You could have at least made an effort to save me, but did you? Noooo. You left me for dead. I had to heal myself."

"Dr. Rani checked you out. You were dead. However, he did pour something into your wound."

"A libation? He poured coffee into my open belly? Wait till I see this Dr. Rani. Who is he?"

"He is one of the station's gynaecologists."

"I'm dying and you allowed a gynaecologist to touch me? I'm lying in shattered glass and poo, my guts blown out after battling that murderous alien, and you send an obstetrician to my rescue? Thanks a lot!"

"He was the only doctor available at the time."

"Get me off this madhouse! I'm shipping out on the next transport. Although Rani did somehow manage to get rid of all my belly fat and love handles. Look at these abs. I actually haven't looked this good in . . . ever."

"I suspect Dr. Rani poured nanobots into your wound, which likely saved your life. He got you onto the last ship still on the station. Being treated by Dr. Rani was most fortuitous for you."

"I was told Bud got the alien off the station. That android is amazing. How'd he do it?" McFrenzy asked.

"Bud had us fire the EMP weapon. He carried the stunned alien to an ejection pod. It was shot off the station and destroyed. Bud is returning on the _Au Clair,_ a space cruiser that managed to pick him up while he was floating out in space."

"Super-android badass droid! Guess I have to stick around to congratulate him," McFrenzy said, winking at Dejan.

"Excellent! I'll have you know that I'm exceedingly happy not to have to write another 'It grieves me to inform you' letter to the Conglomerate Central Security Division."

"Don't jump to conclusions yet, Checkie. I haven't totally decided to stay. It's like open season on Chief Inspectors on this station. If I had a brain, I'd be off on the next departing ship."

"So do you?"

"Do I what?"

"Have a brain?"

"I came here. Does that answer your question?"

"So, the answer is no."

Alex wandered through what was left of the S, R, and Q Levels of the _Nelson Mandela._ He'd walked up from the devastation that had once been the Concourse, an area that he remembered as being an open space of beautiful design and eye-catching shops and boutiques. Now it was all shattered glass, bent and twisted metal beams, and mounds of foamcrete rubble.

The S and R medical levels looked worse. Everything was smashed, crushed, burnt, or melted beyond recognition. Entire wards were gone. The operating theatres were unrecognizable. All would have to be demolished, recycled, reprinted, and rebuilt. Alex could only shake his head.

There were robots, androids, and humans all picking up debris and throwing everything into the recyclers that would convert the rubble to printing substrate. A tremendous amount of energy would be required to manufacture everything needed to get the medical station back to full operational capacity.

Alex climbed into an area that looked as if a tornado had hit it. The ceiling had fallen in and, in places, the floor had collapsed. There were pieces of what may have been furniture, crushed counters, broken equipment, melted bed frames, slagged light fixtures, incapacitated androids, mangled robots, and layers upon layers of foamcrete fragments showered everywhere. Alex surveyed the destruction and tried to imagine a being that could generate such colossal power and what it would have been like to oppose it.

A voice behind him said, "Bud battled the alien for many hours, blocking its advance centimetre by centimetre, so that all the people on this station were able to evacuate. The alien seemed able to enslave humans. Bud refused to let that happen to the people of this station. I found Bud crushed beneath that enormous slab over there and as soon as I booted him up, he went right back to attacking the alien until he figured out a way to render it unconscious. He carried the unconscious alien to an ejection pod and together they got shot off the station. He wanted to make sure the alien still existed within Inquisitor Roque before he would allow the station to destroy the pod.

"That's who your 'unworthy' android is. As far as I'm concerned, Bud is the best person I know. If I were Grace, I'd choose Bud over you and I'd never think twice," Moham Rani said. He strode off to rejoin the others cleaning up debris.

Alex looked down at the huge slab on the ground that had trapped Bud and he blew out a big breath. He rubbed his forehead and face with both hands. He spun around to see where Moham had gone and shame washed over him. He could still see Grace, shivering and blue-lipped, covered in a layer of frost, calling out for Bud to come back in a voice so distraught, it had wrung tears from his eyes. He remembered loving someone like that once—Grace's mother—and he'd still left for space, leaving a beautiful, young pregnant girl behind, who died alone giving birth to Grace.

Alex fell to his knees in the dust and began to weep. He covered his face with both hands to hide his shame. His surroundings mirrored his despair. He'd destroyed what love he could have had with his daughter. He'd been searching all of his life for the love that he'd left behind, for a family that he'd unknowingly abandoned, and a beautiful child that he'd now driven away with his prejudice.

Moham was right. Bud was a far better person than Alex could ever hope to be. Grace was better off without Alex in her life.

Bud was a better human, not because he had incredible powers, but because Bud had decency, empathy, courage, and selflessness. He could accept humans for all of their faults and prejudices, and sacrifice himself to save them. It was humiliating that Bud encompassed the best of humanity and Alex, who said Bud wasn't human, did not.

Alex raised his head and stared up into the shaft of light shining down through a hole in the broken ceiling. Perhaps it was not too late to make up with Grace and Bud. He was not afraid to admit that he was wrong. He'd already told Grace that he was sorry in the *Inferno,* but he wasn't sure if she had heard him.

The next time Alex saw Bud, he would tell the an . . . Bud that he was the finest person Alex had ever met and he was proud that Grace had Bud as a friend.

Hopefully, they would both forgive him.

Jocelyn Sarri was urgently paged to the brig of the *Justice*. They would be docking soon with the *Nelson Mandela*. Everyone was supposed to be belted in. Their wristcomp would not cease its caterwauling until Jocelyn had notified the ward that they were on their way.

Jocelyn strode as quickly as they could to the makeshift medical ward set up for the evacuation. Warning lights were signalling that they were supposed to be seated for landing.

What was so urgent?

When Jocelyn arrived, the same nurse, Sophie, gave him a murderous stare.

"Dr. Sarri, we thought you should see what happened and guide us in how we deal with this situation. You were the last physician to 'treat' the patient. Security is here."

Sophie led Jocelyn to a small washroom designated for the patients. Jocelyn's neck muscles tightened. What were they supposed to see here? A Security droid sat outside the tiny washroom. Sophie handed them a pair of sterile gloves.

"Please put these on, doctor," Sophie said. Her tone could crack stone.

Jocelyn grunted and pushed down the urge to run. Their stomach was churning and their heart beat a crescendo tempo. They tried to swallow but their mouth was sand dry. The Security droid opened the door. At first, Jocelyn didn't know what they were looking at. It didn't register. They saw skinny knees and ankles. The smell in the little cubicle made them cover their nose with their hand. Faeces and urine coated the floor.

"Be careful not to touch that hand to anything here," Sophie said. "You've contaminated yourself."

Jocelyn's eyes followed the legs upward to the neck of Ice—the patient that Jocelyn had promised they would help, the patient who'd screamed at them not to touch her. The realization of how stupid they'd been struck Jocelyn full in the face and they fell against the door. If they'd only listened to the patient, not given that sedative patch, perhaps the patient would still be alive. They'd ignored what the patient had screamed and now this.

Ice's face was a mottled purple. Her black tongue protruded crookedly from her mouth. The body hung from the ceiling by a strip of material torn from the hospital gown. It dug into the patient's neck. Jocelyn shivered.

"Have Security examine the patient for signs of foul play. I doubt there will be any. It's very likely this patient committed suicide. Is there any surveillance video?" Jocelyn asked.

"Yes, Dr. Sarri. The surveillance record shows only the patient going in. No one else. The door was jammed from the inside with a piece of metal so it could not be opened immediately."

Jocelyn nodded and turned away. They could not look at the patient any more. They could still hear Ice screaming 'No!' and 'Stop!' as they'd walked away. If only they'd listened to her . . .

"How could this have happened?" Jocelyn said to Sophie.

Sophie's eyes bulged.

"You did not flag the patient as a suicide risk. She was allowed to tend to bodily functions on her own. We are overloaded with critical patients on this transport. Your patient was given a hospital gown, a Security android, and a cubby to stay in. You were the last physician to see her and did not indicate she was at risk."

"My apologies, Nurse. I understand the difficulties you and your colleagues have faced here. This was my error. I take full responsibility for this tragedy."

"You will have to speak to the Security officers once the crime scene investigative team has gone over the site."

"Yes, of course," Jocelyn said.

"Do not go far. I have submitted a formal complaint regarding your treatment of this patient against her wishes."

Jocelyn staggered away, getting lost trying to find their flight couch. They found an empty seat and strapped in. Soon after, they felt the ship dock.

Jocelyn stayed in the seat as crew and passengers moved about in organized chaos. They relived their last encounter with Ice. Pompous fool, not listening to what the patient kept saying to them. Perhaps the practice of psychiatry was not for them. They would submit their resignation immediately.

"Dr. Sarri, you may leave the ship. Security officers will be contacting you."

"*Nelson Mandela,* I would like to submit my resignation as a psychiatrist on this station."

"Is that because of the death of Philomena Vertongen, Dr. Sarri?"

"Yes."

"We are rather short of psychiatrists at the moment, Dr. Sarri. We are a medical station that treats a great deal of battle trauma. Your credentials are sorely needed to help soldiers deal with their PTSD. I ask you to reconsider."

"You need someone better than me."

"We don't have anyone better than you at the moment and we don't expect that to change any time soon. Dr. Sarri you will have to cope for now and do the best you can, helping traumatized marines in need. The situation may change but your resignation cannot be accepted at this time.

"In other words, buck up."

Grace paced the reception area of Receiving Bay Ninety-Seven. She peered through the chainglass windows into the hangar, repeatedly. The *Au Clair* had docked. Grace wanted to race out to it, but she wasn't wearing her spacesuit and didn't want to leave to fetch it. Air was now being pumped into the hangar, reserved for privately-owned luxury spacecraft. Grace danced from foot to foot.

"Please, Grace, sit down," Dejan pleaded. "You are giving me a panic attack, simply watching you."

Grace glanced over at Dejan. "Sorry. I'm just worried about Bud."

"Reeaaallly? I never would have guessed." Dejan winked at Grace. "He makes me feel that way, too."

A guffaw burst from Grace's mouth.

The hatch of the *Au Clair* opened and out came Sierra, Hanako, and Octavia, with Jude lying on an antigrav stretcher being pushed by Bud. The humans were all dressed in spacesuits. Bud was in a coverall. Grace and Dejan stood before the arrivals entrance and not-so-patiently waited for the airlock to cycle through. A cluster of tendrils bearing bunches of flowers and fruits and colourful glowglobes slid up around them and converted the reception lounge into a bower of beauty and bounty. Clusters of eyes blinked and bobbed excitedly.

"It has become very crowded in here," Dejan said. "May I borrow this from you?" He plucked a large bouquet of red, white, and pink roses from a vine.

"Plant Thing says it is happy to give you flowers," Grace relayed.

"Please tell Plant Thing that I am most grateful," Dejan said.

Grace smiled and nodded.

Something bumped Grace's arm. She looked over and found her nose deep in a bouquet of red roses.

"Is this for Bud, Plant Thing?" Grace asked.

<no special friend grace. bud wishes to give these flowers to you. do not fear. there are no thorns>

"To me?" Grace asked. "What for? I didn't do anything but push a button."

From behind Grace came a voice that made her heart accelerate.

"The roses are for you, Grace, for saving my life. You reached out to me across the many kilometres of cold, empty space and filled me with your love, your life force, and your determination. You pulled me from the alien's clutches, reminding me who I was. You brought me back, Grace." Bud came towards her, looking like an angel. "I am forever grateful."

Bud opened his arms wide.

Grace threw herself into Bud's embrace, her grin stretching from ear to ear. She'd promised herself that she wouldn't cry, because it tended to confuse Bud, but here she was leaking moisture all over him. Bud smiled, his strong arms enveloping Grace. A mass of flowering tendrils formed a screen of privacy around them.

"I'll never leave you, Grace," Bud said.

"Nor I you, Bud," Grace answered.

From somewhere on the other side of the screen, Grace thought she heard—but surely she was mistaken—the sound of Moham Rani sobbing.

Dejan prepared some shuttles to send over to the *Destiny*, now that the first evacuation ships had returned. He'd had to wait until there were enough people, androids, and robots back on the *Nelson Mandela* to be able to offer any assistance. The Emergency Relief shuttles would be equipped with battery-powered generators, lights, heaters, water, food supplies, air purifiers, and other necessities, as well as volunteer engineers, computer specialists, mechanics, technicians, and medical personnel. From what happened on the *Nelson Mandela* after the first EMP pulse, Dejan had a good idea what *Destiny* would need.

He wanted to take advantage of *Destiny's* helplessness and make sure Captain Karagounis was grateful to the medical station, so that she would think twice about destroying them. With the variant Al-Fadi virus having been on board, Dejan knew they could be in danger of annihilation, if the Conglomerate decided the *Nelson Mandela* was a threat to the USS. The *Inferno* was their best bargaining chip and still in their possession. Dejan was not going to hand over *Inferno* until he was positive the *Nelson Mandela* was safe.

Would Captain Karagounis be furious about the EMP weapon being fired without any warning? It was the only way to stun the alien long enough to get her off the station. Who could have known the EMP weapon would affect the battleship orbiting many kilometres away

Dejan sighed as he opened a communication channel to the *Destiny's* bridge, his shoulder muscles going into spasm. Static roared from the *Destiny's* com channel.

"Dr. Cech," Captain Karagounis growled. "I should be threatening you with insubordination right now, for not handing over the *Inferno* as requested. However, my ship has mysteriously been compromised. You wouldn't happen to have any knowledge regarding this situation, would you?"

Dejan's heart went flippity-flop and skippity-skip. He felt rather buoyant but wasn't sure if it was elation or a heart arrhythmia. He bit the insides of his cheeks, which probably gave him a pained, sympathetic look.

"Captain Karagounis, what has happened? You did not respond to our many messages that we were handing over the *Inferno* to you. May we be of assistance? We would be more than happy to help."

"It is my understanding that we are transporting the *Inferno* because it has a new weapon on board. That weapon would not have been fired by you, would it?"

"I never touched the *Inferno,* Captain Karagounis. The Conglomerate has demanded that we hand the *Inferno* over and ordered us not to tamper with the vessel or examine the weapon. Why would we disobey these orders? Our station is fully operational. If this weapon had been fired, should we not be in the same situation as the *Destiny*?

"If your vessel has undergone some malfunction, Captain Karagounis, let the *Nelson Mandela* assist you in your repairs. We can provide whatever you need. As a token of our good faith, let me send over a generous supply of our fresh fruits and vegetables, as well as meals and water for your crew."

"I'm in no position to refuse your offer, Dr. Cech. The *Destiny* is without power and its controlling AI. We are helpless. I'd be grateful for any assistance you could send us," the snow leopard captain said, with an expression that suggested she would've rather thrown herself into a pit of prickly burrs than ask for help.

"Aid is on its way to you, Captain. We are sending over Emergency Relief shuttles carrying equipment and volunteer personnel. Let us know what else you need. We'll do our best to serve you." Dejan beamed a smile.

The captain frowned back, her feline eyes narrowed to slits.

"Thank you, Dr. Cech. The *Nelson Mandela's* generosity will not be forgotten."

"That is our hope, Captain. We're in the business of saving lives, as you know."

"We will call for the *Inferno* once the repairs are completed."

"Understood."

Dejan cut the connection, leaned back in his chair, crossed his hands behind his head, and exhaled.

Hanako walked into the cell on the *Nelson Mandela* where her husband sat, his hands in cuffs, and she felt as if her world had collapsed. She fought a feeling of disorientation, as if what was happening to Hiro and herself was a frightening nightmare from which she could not wake. She wanted to open her eyes and find herself beside Hiro in their own bed, with none of these atrocious events having occurred.

Hiro looked up at Hanako and the face he showed her was one she'd never seen before. There were dark hollows beneath his eyes; his cheeks were sallow. Deep creases bracketed his joyless mouth. His eyes looked lifeless.

"Come to stare at the wicked criminal?" Hiro asked. His tone was bitter and steeped in sarcasm.

Hanako gulped at the acid in her husband's words. "No, Hiro, you are not a criminal! I came because I love you. Don't say such ridiculous things." Hanako squatted down to kneel at Hiro's feet.

"Get away from me! Don't touch me! Don't you know I'm a murderer? You should leave this room right now!" Hiro glared at her with hard eyes.

"What?" Hanako blinked at Hiro, trying to ignore the hurtful words he was hurling at her and the nasty tone he was using. She could not make sense of it. The person sitting here had Hiro's body but it was not Hiro saying these things. Hiro had never, in all the years they'd been together, ever spoken to her in this manner or frowned at her the way he was doing now. Even when he'd tried to kill himself after being kidnapped by Nestor, he'd never looked at her with such detest. Hanako placed her hand on her heart.

"Hiro, I know you didn't kill anyone. You couldn't. You're a good man. You're being framed but you must remain strong."

Hiro's face changed. He looked like his old self—shattered, distraught, ashamed—but nevertheless, Hanako's Hiro.

"Is that true?" Hiro whispered, in the dimness of his cell. He'd turned his gaze from Hanako and was staring at the wall. "If I was truly a good person, could an evil mind make me do something terrible? There must already be evil inside of me to do something so heinous as build a bomb to kill others."

"You did no such thing!"

"I remember nothing," Hiro whispered, with such anguish that

Hanako started weeping. She grabbed his hands as he tried to bring his nails up to his face, poised as if to gouge out his eyes. "I cannot bear to live anymore, Hanako, knowing that I might have done these things, murdered innocent lives."

"You did not do it, Hiro. Surveillance videos can be altered. The evidence is being questioned."

Hiro dropped his head and wept, the sobs shaking his entire body. Hanako stroked his back.

"They say I tried to kill Jude. Why would I create something that would put my brother in danger? I love him. Why would I kill him? And I love Octavia too! I must be mad. I can't bear to live anymore, Hanako. If my mind's not my own, I'd rather be dead."

"Hiro, stop saying these things."

"Hanako, forget me." Hiro took Hanako's hands in his and kissed them, gently. His eyes were now welling with tears and he looked at her as if she were the most precious thing in the world. He gently pushed her away from him.

"Go," he said.

No, no, no, no, no, this cannot be happening! "Hiro!"

"Everything I have, I leave to you. Divorce me. I don't want you to have the taint of my sins on you in any way. I don't want anyone saying, 'There's the wife of that murderer.' I could never abide that," Hiro said softly.

"No, Hiro. I will remain your wife. I know, better than anyone, what a good person you are. I know how often you've tried your best to save someone's life. I know how it tears you apart when a patient dies. I know you would never, knowingly, take a person's life. I will not leave you."

"Then *I* divorce *you*. This is the last time I will see you, Hanako. It's for the best. You must go on without me. I am not who I was."

"Hiro, please stop saying these terrible things. You're breaking my heart."

"If you come again, I will have them refuse you. Be gone, Hanako. I love you, I have always loved you, and I will always love you, but I am sorry. I'm no longer Hiro Al-Fadi. I don't know who I am, but the only way I can keep you safe is to send you away." Hiro pushed Hanako's entreating hands away.

"No, Hiro. Please, I love you." Hanako wrapped her arms around Hiro and tried to hug him. "You're upset. You'll feel better once it's proven you're not the culprit. We'll get through this together, like we always have."

Hiro gently pushed Hanako away.

"Guard? Please escort Dr. Matheson from my cell. She is not welcome back."

"Hiro, no, no," Hanako begged, her world falling apart.

"Goodbye, my love," Hiro said, kissing her tenderly on her wet cheeks. He spun her around firmly, as she tried to clutch onto him, disengaging her hands from his. He pushed her towards the Security droid.

"Hiro, don't do this. Please," Hanako cried through her sobs. "I love you!"

"That Hiro is no more, Hanako. He is gone. I'm sorry."

Hanako felt herself pulled from the cell by the droid. She stumbled, as if lost in a fog. Hanako leaned against the wall outside the cell but the droid pushed her on. She hunched forward, her arms wrapped tightly around her middle, as if by squeezing hard, she could keep her world together. She would show Hiro that he was being framed. He could never have built a bomb. He wouldn't know where to start. She pulled her shoulders back and marched from the detention centre. She had a job to do.

"Doctor Lord?"

"Yes, *Nelson Mandela*?" Grace answered, as she walked down one of the shattered corridors of S Level with Bud.

"Orders have come from the Conglomerate."

"Yes?"

"They involve both you and Bud."

"What are these orders?"

"You and Bud are to report to the space station, *Embassy*, where you will join a military expedition whose mandate is to go to the planet, *Glory*, and seek out the source of these Al-Fadi viruses. The objective is to shut them down permanently. The production of these deadly pathogens must be stopped at their source."

"Why do they need Bud and I?" Grace asked.

"You and Bud are deemed the Conglomerate's experts on the Al-Fadi viruses. The Conglomerate wishes you both to be along because of your expertise in identifying, isolating, and

combatting these viruses. They hope you will be able to determine which facilities are responsible for the creation of these biological weapons so that the criminals may be apprehended. They want you in charge of the collection and disassembly of everything.

"But I'm just a surgeon," Grace said. "I've work here to do."

"Also, if you come across new pathogens, it is hoped that you and Bud would be able to get a head start on analyzing and combatting them. Until you find these facilities, the entire USS will always be in danger. The Conglomerate sees you as an officer in its medical corps. As such, you are required to obey orders. It is your duty to assist in the search for these bioweapon developers. Others can do surgery."

"What is Dr. Al-Fadi going to say?" Grace moaned, knowing exactly what Dr. Al-Fadi would say.

"These orders come from the top, Dr. Lord. The Conglomerate will stop at nothing until these perpetrators are found and captured. Dr. Al-Fadi has his own problems to deal with before he can return to surgery. In the meantime, this station requires some significant downtime for repairs."

"I will not be a participant in genocide," Grace said, crossing her arms.

"That is not the Conglomerate's goal."

"What is the Conglomerate's goal exactly?"

"To find the source of the biological weapons and shut the facility down. To arrest the creators of the viruses and bring them back to the USS to face trial for the deaths of billions of innocent people on several now dead planets."

"When are we supposed to leave?"

"A specific date has not yet been decided. The Conglomerate wishes to study the EMP weapon from the *Inferno* first. They need to devise a shield against this devastating new weapon or the entire mission will suffer the same incapacitation as the *Nelson Mandela* did. There is also the time required for the *Destiny* to make all of its repairs before it can transport the *Inferno*. I will notify you when the time approaches, Dr. Lord. Be ready to leave on a moment's notice."

Grace jerked and looked up at the surveillance eye. "I will be coming back here, won't I?"

"That is to be hoped, Dr. Lord."

"Is there a reason I should think otherwise?"

"The planet you are going to has tried to extinguish most of the human race . . . twice. The people are religious extremists, denouncing any type of modification to human beings as sinful and worthy of extermination. Therefore, anyone augmented, adapted, boosted, or altered, may be a target for their enmity. They may not look kindly on androids at all. It might be best that Bud be passed off as a human being. You may want the existence of your aug to be concealed or have it removed. The people of *Glory* will not welcome you on their planet, Dr. Lord.

"The Expeditionary Force will most likely be under threat of violence the entire time you are there. If you are unable to find the facility and the people responsible for the production of these viruses, it does not bode well for the planet. I believe you are well aware of the record the Conglomerate has in regards to the handling of these types of situations. Their policy is one of planetary sterilization, if the governing body does not cooperate with their investigation. You must find the facilities or the people of *Glory* will all die."

"I said I will not be party to genocide."

"Then you had better find their labs, Dr. Lord."

"Or die in the attempt," Grace muttered.

"Your life is precious to us, Dr. Lord. We do not want to lose you."

"Thank you, *Nelson Mandela*."

"We need you back here, too, Bud."

"Thank you, *Nelson Mandela*."

"I wish you both success in this endeavour."

"We'll need it," Grace whispered.

Octavia was sorting through all of the debris in her lab. Everything was covered in crumbled foamcrete rubble. Monitors, recording equipment, computers, amplifiers, helmets, recording chairs, desks—so many of her memprint recording setups—were destroyed. She had only one complete, undamaged memprint recording system still intact, the one situated furthest from the bomb blast. She tried not to cry as she looked around at the devastation.

"Well," she said to everyone around her, "we'll have to rebuild from scratch. There was so much equipment sabotaged and tampered with that nothing was reliable anyway. Rather than spend hours trying to determine what's intact versus what's compromised, let's just reprint everything new and know that it is unscathed."

"I'll help with the cost, Octavia," Jude said from an anti-grav chair. "I'm happy to fund your research."

"You don't have to do that, Jude."

"I want to. If I'd died in that bomb blast, I would've wanted you to bring me back. If you'd died and I was left on my own, I would've insisted we bring you back. Your research provides that. It's invaluable."

"Is it?" Octavia's voice sounded bitter. "Should we be able to rewrite tragedy and just keep bringing people back? What about future generations? I'm beginning to think my research should never be shared. Perhaps the universe would be better off if tyrants, despots, and psychopaths like Nestor were never given the opportunity to live forever."

"Not everyone is evil, Octavia."

"Maybe not, Jude, but I need to carefully rethink why I'm doing this research before I rebuild." Octavia rubbed a cloth across the back of her neck, streaking it with grey mud.

"Hiro would not have been able to come back without your research," Jude said.

"And look what happened!" Octavia waved her arms around.

"Hiro did not plant that bomb, Octavia. He wouldn't know how."

"If Hiro had not been brought back, perhaps José, David, and Amber would still be alive. Perhaps you would not have gotten injured and almost died. So many terrible things have happened. How much of them were due to the existence of my memprint technology?"

"I don't know, Octavia," Jude sighed. "I do agree, however, that your technology in the wrong hands could be disastrous."

Octavia sat down on a segment of desk that had survived the bomb blast and rubbed her face. Grey smears now streaked her forehead, cheeks, and nose. Jude bit his lower lip.

"I really thought I would be helping mankind. Now, I'm not so sure."

Dejan shambled into the lab. He walked as if he'd aged twenty years since the last time Octavia had seen him. His eyes fell on Octavia's face and he stopped dead. He glanced at Jude's face, a question in his eyes. Jude shrugged and Dejan's eyebrows rose. The anesthetist blinked a few times, surveying the damage.

"Octavia, let me offer my condolences for the people you have lost and for the setback your research has taken." Dejan opened his arms.

"Thank you, Dejan." Octavia stood up to accept her friend's hug.

"I'm glad to see you looking so well, Jude." Dejan's face looked miserable.

"Thanks to you, Grace, and Hiro," Jude said, smiling. His jaw fell when Dejan burst into tears.

" . . . Octavia, Jude, I have terrible news." Dejan's complexion was waxy and his hands trembled. He looked as if he would topple over.

"What is it, Dejan?" Octavia grabbed Dejan's hands. "Here, please, sit down." She placed him in the one intact chair.

Dejan stared at his quivering hands and clasped them together. He shook his head, fighting to get the words out.

"Hiro has killed himself." It came out in a sob.

"What?" Octavia and Jude shouted.

Dejan took a deep breath. "Hiro was being guarded constantly by a Security droid. It never left him alone, but somehow Hiro managed to get his hands on a very sharp piece of metal. After Hanako visited him and he told her he was divorcing her, he sliced his carotid artery open. He left a note on his compad outlining why he was committing suicide."

"What did it say?" Jude asked, clutching onto the edge of a desk.

"That he didn't want to commit one more heinous act under the control of Jeffrey Nestor. He'd rather be dead than have that psychopath in his mind. The only way Hiro knew he could be totally free of Nestor was to kill himself. His biggest fear was that some harm might come to Hanako. He said everyone is now safe from him."

"The Security droid didn't stop him?" Jude rasped.

"Hiro had tied and wedged himself under the bed and sliced open his neck while he fought off the droid that was attempting to get him out from under there."

"Well, didn't they put him in a cryopod?" Jude demanded.

"Yes, they did."

"You must save him," Jude shouted.

"Well . . . that is why I have come to speak to you."

Dejan looked at Octavia and Jude with such sadness, it made Jude wince. "We can try to revive a Hiro who no longer wants to live. He will most certainly attempt to kill himself again. His body is dead at this moment. That is irrefutable. Or we could resurrect a Hiro that was never exposed to the tortures of Jeffrey Nestor, never had his mind raped or his will controlled. We could resurrect the Hiro Al-Fadi that was memprinted before the first Al-Fadi virus was brought to the station. Is that not right, Octavia?" Dejan asked.

"Did Hiro say he wanted to be resurrected, Dejan?" Octavia asked. "Hiro never gave me consent to resurrect him. Bud resurrected Hiro technically without permission."

"There was nothing in his final note that mentioned it," Dejan said.

"Hiro would want to be resurrected free of Nestor's influence," Jude said. "I'm sure of that."

"It's all a moot point," Octavia said. "Hiro did not consent to resurrection. I do not have a record of him agreeing to it."

"After this bomb explosion, do you have a record of anyone's consent?" Dejan asked, looking around the shattered lab.

Octavia stood up, looking stunned. There were no consoles still intact in the lab. She had all of the memprint cubes with the memories and DNA templates stored because she'd taken them with her on the *Au Clair.* The computer and equipment with all of the consents and instructions from station personnel were all destroyed in the blast.

"I no longer have any records of what people chose regarding resurrection," Octavia gasped.

"Oh, that is a shame," Dejan said, in an ironic tone. "I guess we'll have to err on the side of caution and resurrect everyone who was killed since we cannot be sure that any of those people had said 'No'."

"I agree," Jude said.

"We must bring Hiro back, Octavia," Dejan pleaded. "This station needs the little tyrant."

"Please." Jude took Octavia's hands within his.

"It will take time to repair everything but we can resurrect everyone who was killed, if we have an intact memprint of them."

"Inspector Rivera also needs to be resurrected and a Security officer, a tiger-adapt, named Juan Rasmussen. Do you have memprints on them?" Dejan asked.

"Yes, I believe so," Octavia said. "Juan has a partner who is a polar bear-adapt. Correct?"

"That's him."

"I'll speak to *Nelson Mandela* about beginning to clone their bodies as well as Amber's, José's, and David's."

"And your graduate student, Ice's body, as well."

"I can look into whether we have an early memprint of her, free of Nestor's influence."

"As soon as you give me all the DNA data, Dr. Weisman, we can begin the accelerated vat cloning."

"I'll transfer the DNA data to you, *Nelson Mandela*."

"It will be my pleasure, Dr. Weisman. The accelerated cloning will begin as soon as I have the data. I must admit, I miss the little tyrant, too."

24. Acceptance

Octavia waved her wristcomp before the access pad and stepped back, wringing her hands. Jude wrapped his arm around her shoulder as they stood, silently waiting. The door slid open and Bud smiled at the two of them.

"Dr. Weisman, Mr. Stefansson, please come in." Bud bowed and backed up to let the neurosurgeon and vid director enter. Octavia gave Bud a big hug and whispered, "I'm so sorry."

"I am sorry, too, Dr. Weisman," Bud said quietly.

Jude shook Bud's hand. "You've lost a father and I've lost a brother."

"I am sorry for your loss, Mr. Stefansson. Dr. Al-Fadi was a great man."

"How is Hanako doing?" Octavia asked.

"My mother is distraught," Bud said.

Octavia and Jude nodded, as they followed Bud into the main room of the Al-Fadi quarters. Hanako was seated between Grace and Sierra on a couch. She stood up to greet Octavia and Jude. The two of them gave Hanako enveloping hugs. Her face was pale, her eyes puffy.

"I'm so sorry about Hiro, Hanako," Octavia said.

"Thank you, Octavia."

Jude took Hanako's hand in both of his. "Thank you for making Hiro so happy. He said he was the luckiest man alive. You made his life a joy, every day."

Tears trickled down Hanako's cheeks but she smiled. "Thank you for those kind words." She bowed deeply. "Hiro always called you his brother; he loved you deeply."

It was Jude's turn to fight back tears.

"I've come with terrible news, Hanako." Octavia glanced at Jude and he wrapped his arm around her, to help hold her up, to give her strength.

Hanako looked afraid. "More terrible news?" she whispered.

"Hiro's memprint was tampered with. It's been wiped clean. So were Dejan's, Grace's, and my memprint cube. I've not gone through all of them yet. I suspect Ice did it. Do you still have Hiro's own memprint cube? He was given a copy of his own to keep."

Hanako covered her face with both hands and shook her head. She could not get her words out. Grace caught her and helped her sit.

"Hiro's memprint cube was damaged during one of his attempts to kill himself. We'd been struggling with a knife and somehow, it got shattered." Hanako dropped her face into her palms.

Octavia reached out and squeezed Hanako's arm. "I'm so sorry."

Jude sighed, his shoulders sagging. Grace held Hanako even tighter.

"It wasn't your fault, Hanako," Grace said.

"I should have put it in a safe place."

Sierra hugged Hanako. They were all softly weeping now.

Bud stood to one side, his eyes enormous.

Grace looked over at Bud's expression and she went to him, her arms outstretched. "Oh Bud, it's normal to feel sad about Dr. Al-Fadi's death. We'll all miss him. There's nothing to be done about it."

Bud's eyes grew wider.

" . . . But there is, Grace," Bud said quietly.

"What, Bud?"

Bud hesitated before reaching up to open his coverall. He exposed his chest and lifted a skin flap overlying where his heart would be if he were human. Bud touched pressure points in a specific pattern and a square slid open. Within a small chamber were three, glistening memprint cubes. He gently extracted the cube inserted within the left square of the small enclosure. He placed it on his palm and showed it to Grace.

The cube sparkled and shimmered in the light of the room. The interior of the memprint cube swirled and flashed its iridescent rainbow glow. Everyone in the room gasped. They all stared at the exquisite beauty of the tiny cube, captivated by hope and possibility . . .

"This is Dr. Al-Fadi's memprint cube, pristine and intact," Bud said, offering it to Octavia.

Hugo McFrenzy screamed at the top of his lungs, "What the fu? Have you seen these bills? What are we paying for? This has to be the cost of the entire medical station! Can't be for resurrecting two Security officers. What are they putting in these guys? Gold testicles?"

"It is the cost of the accelerated vat cloning and upgrades for Inspector Eden Rivera and Corporal Juan Rasmussen."

"Why, this . . . this is highway robbery. Why's it so expensive?"

"The bioprostheses the two are receiving, the expertise involved, the chemicals and hormones administered at precise and specific intervals, the around-the-clock monitoring, the continuous manipulation of the chemical soup, the meticulous timing required at certain times in their growth cycle . . . "

" . . . All right. I get it. But why does Security have to foot this bill? Isn't it part of the station budget? Our department does not have the funds to pay for one of these resurrections, never mind two."

"It doesn't."

"What? Well, why am I being sent all of these bills?"

"To let you know the cost."

"Why?"

"So that in the future, when you complain to me that you do not have enough manpower or funding or equipment or resources, I can explain to you why that is."

"You know, I really hate a smug AI."

"I dislike dealing with whiney humans."

"Who you calling whiney?"

"If the shoe fits . . . "

"So now you're making comments about my feet?"

"Asteroids could fit in those boots."

"Asteroids, my ass."

"No, *that* would have to be an enormous gas giant."

"Oh, yeah? Fat ass comments, now, too eh? Two can play this game, you old dishwasher. Your mother was a rusty old spittoon."

"I did not have a mother."

"That's because she didn't want you."

"You are being illogical."

"Getting really nasty, now, eh? Well, how's this? Your crystal matrix is cheap bottle glass."

"Now that is really uncalled for."

"Hey, Mandolin, you going to throw me a party if I manage to stay alive a whole month on this death trap?"

"I most certainly am not."

"Good. I hate parties."

"I will hold a nice celebration if you do *not* make it to one month, however . . ."

"Make sure there are balloons. I like balloons."

Little Bud was terrified to leave Plant Thing's side. Since returning to the *Nelson Mandela,* it panicked when a human came near. When the alien was destroyed, the possessed humans had all fallen where they stood. Little Bud had been high in their hands, held over their heads at the time, and Little Bud had fallen on them. They'd all lain on the floor as if dead. Little Bud had thought their death was due to Little Bud. When the cargo ship had finally docked, Little Bud had trundled out the door the instant it had opened, fleeing for his life.

Little Bud did not want to spend any more time with humans except perhaps Grace Lord. The rest of the human race was frightening, unpredictable, and violent. Little Bud wanted nothing more to do with them and had decided to spend the rest of its life devoted to worshiping the Biomind and recording its teachings.

Plant Thing could only sigh.

There was a chime announcing someone at the door. Grace was busy packing things she would need on her mission to the planet Glory. She knew she would not be allowed to take much and she was weeding things out. She had her blaster and stunner in their chargers and she had a set of medical instruments and a diagnostic scanner that would all fit inside a field pack that she would carry on her person. She had her lieutenant's uniform and space suit and helmet to take. She was looking at her body armour and wondering what her weight allowance would be.

"Who is it?" Grace asked.

"Captain Alexander Lord," the access pad announced.

Grace stopped what she was doing and sighed. Did she really want to get into this? Had her father learned that she and Bud were both going on a military assignment together? Was he here to express his objections?

Grace didn't want to have an argument. She didn't want to part with her father on bad terms. She might never see him again. She'd basically avoided Alex since Bud had returned to the station. There'd been the tasks of readmitting and examining all of the patients returning to the surgical wards. There had been the tragedy of Dr. Al-Fadi's death and supporting Hanako in her grief. There'd been consultations over the redesign of the new surgical operating rooms and wards being rebuilt. She'd been asked to participate in the discussions and debriefings with the Conglomerate scientists regarding the new variant Al-Fadi virus and the new vaccine. Bud had asked Grace to attend those meetings with him.

Grace felt guilty about how little time she'd spent with Alex but she couldn't face his disapproval, nor accept it.

She sighed. "Open."

The door slid open and Grace looked into her father's blue eyes.

"Hello, Alex."

"Hello, Grace. May I come in?"

"I'm rather busy at the moment," Grace said, spreading her arms to show the disarray.

"It will only take a moment," Alex said. His eyes pleaded with her.

Grace nodded.

Alex gazed around her suite with enormous eyes. "Wow. How do you rate such fine quarters, Grace? I didn't know surgeons got treated so well."

Grace grimaced. "It's a long story. I never asked for these quarters. They were forced upon me."

"I wouldn't complain. You should see my little cubby hole."

Grace's face flared. She should've gone to see her father's quarters by now. Shame flowed through her veins and she wrapped her arms around herself.

"Why have you come, Alex?"

Alex looked down at his feet. She watched him take a big breath.

"Grace, I want to say that no father could be more proud of his daughter than I am of you. I've been doing a lot of soul searching and I'm sorry for what I said to you about Bud. I'm okay with your relationship with Bud, no matter what it is.

"Bud has been a better partner to you than I ever was to your mother. Bud is a better being than I can ever hope to be. He's braver, smarter, stronger, but more importantly, more unselfish than I am. I can't think of anyone who would keep you safer or who would love you more than

Bud. I'm sure you've thought about all of the drawbacks and problems of a relationship such as yours. In truth, it's none of my business. I wanted to tell you that I'm very sorry for any pain I've caused you. I hope one day you'll forgive me. I just wanted you to know." Alex glanced up at Grace's face briefly and turned towards the door.

"Wait."

Alex stopped but did not turn back around to face her.

She walked around and planted herself in front of her father. She stared directly into his eyes.

"Do you really mean what you've said?"

"Yes, I do."

"Thank you." Grace grinned and tried to look apologetic at the same time. "I'm sorry for being so angry with you. I've missed you." She wrapped her arms around him.

Alex's face crumpled. "I'm so ashamed, Grace. You're my daughter and you've all I have left in this world. I'm so proud of you and I don't want to lose you." He squeezed Grace tightly.

"I don't know what will become of Bud and myself or what the future has in store for us. We are both leaving on a mission for the Conglomerate and I hope we make it back. There's not a finer individual I know than Bud, and I do love him, but you are important to me too. It means so much to me that you accept him. Thank you."

"No. *Thank you* for forgiving me," Alex said.

25. What Had He Missed?

Hiro strutted down the corridor. He sniffed the air. For some reason, the air in the *Nelson Mandela* smelled different. There was a scent of fields and flowers and fresh air that he'd never noticed before. It was really quite pleasant and he would compliment the station AI on the improvement later. Now, he simply wanted to enjoy it.

He'd been resurrected, even though he could not remember telling Octavia Weisman that he desired such a thing. He did not believe anyone should be 'immortal'; one lifetime should be good enough for anyone. They'd resurrected him anyway. That was highly unprofessional and he'd told the Chief of Neurosurgery so. She had insisted that the station could not function without him.

Well, he was not surprised about that.

What did surprised him was how much tragedy had befallen the people of the *Nelson Mandela* since the time he'd been memprinted. All the terrible events that had occurred and all of the people that were gone—people Hiro had known and cared about. He'd not been able to take it all in at once.

He viewed the wreckage of entire Levels of the medical station. One alien within one human had managed to almost destroy the *Nelson Mandela*. He'd watched Bud battle the alien on the surveillance recordings with astonishment and pride. In truth, his chest had puffed to near-bursting watching his protégé.

Hanako had been so ecstatic to see him. The weeping and the carrying on had been embarrassing—understandable, of course—but embarrassing all the same. Apparently, he'd committed suicide. Hiro did not believe that. Why would he destroy perfection?

Hiro was an indomitable force. Never one to give up.

Suicide?

Pah!

Ridiculous!

Hiro pushed that nonsense from his mind. He had other things more important to worry about. He'd been astonished at the sight of his surgical fellow, Dr. Grace, and his SAMM-E 777, who now called himself 'Bud'. Dr. Grace was so confident and self-assured. SAMM-E 777 looked so human. Hiro had examined Bud closely and checked his battery pack to confirm it was indeed his android. He'd had to give Dr. Grace a lecture on not distracting his SAMM-E. It was bad enough that the android now operated entirely on his own and much faster than Hiro did, using techniques created by himself, but to have Dr. Grace also surpass him was shocking and difficult to accept.

Hiro was the mentor, the master, the maestro. He knew that one day he would have to accept that his students would surpass him. But to him, it felt like it had happened overnight.

Now the Conglomerate was taking both of them away; the nerve of those bastards. What right did they have to take his surgical fellow *and* his SAMM-E away? Who was going to help him with all of the work? He'd have to get a new surgical fellow and fast.

Since *Nelson Mandela* was not yet open for business, Hiro hoped he'd have time to find some young, eager victim . . . uh, surgeon to work for him. Most would kill to train with him.

Hiro shook his head. Look what happened when he was not around to keep things in order. The *Nelson Mandela* was lucky he was back. He'd put everything right again.

There was a light tap on his shoulder. Funny, he'd not heard anyone coming up behind him. He turned around and stared straight into a cluster of large, light green eyeballs dangling right before his eyes. He looked to the right and there were several more clusters. He looked to the left and there were even more. Hundreds—if not thousands—of eyes all blinking at him rapidly and bounced up and down. All at once, blossoms of every colour in the rainbow opened before him. Hiro was assaulted by a barrage of bouquets, fragrances and colours. In the next instant, clusters of green and purple grapes, apples, peaches, pears, and other exotic fruits were incoming.

A scream tore from his throat. He spun on his heel and started running for his life. He was being attacked by eyeballs, flowers, and produce. Was this the destructive alien?

Hiro sprinted down the corridor as fast as his short legs would carry him, flinging his arms left and right to fend off the assault of bounty and blooms. As he glanced back over his shoulder, he saw the fruits, flowers, and eyeballs chasing him on a tidal wave of slithering green vines.

This was monstrous!

Hiro shrieked for help from everyone he raced past. They only laughed and pointed.

Had everyone on the station gone mad?

The branches with the eyeballs and fruit did not stop to attack anyone else. No one seemed troubled at all by the flurry of flowers, the advance of vegetables, the onslaught of oculars.

What, in space, had he missed?

THE END

S.E. Sasaki is a family physician who works as a surgical assistant in the operating rooms of a local hospital. She lives in a small town in Southern Ontario, Canada, with her chiropractor husband and two mischievous Maine Coon cats. 

S.E. Sasaki is a hidden treasure, a powerhouse artistic talent who in Madhouse brings us medical science fiction on a personal engaging level that is addictive to read, sometimes scary, and always FUN. Recommended!

— Ed Greenwood
Internationally bestselling creator of The Forgotten Realms©

A layered debut that sings odes to the grandmasters of sci-fi.
Kirkus Review of Welcome To The Madhouse, July 2015

Throughout, Sasaki displays a propulsive inventiveness as she weaves grand ideas with humor and soul.
Kirkus Review of Bud by the Grace of God, July 2016

www.ingramcontent.com/pod-product-compliance
Lightning Source LLC
Chambersburg PA
CBHW031939110726
47902CB00001B/227